The Key to Justice

By

Dennis L. Carstens

Additional Marc Kadella Legal Mysteries

Also available on Amazon:

Desperate Justice

Media Justice

Certain Justice

Personal Justice

Delayed Justice

Political Justice

Insider Justice

Exquisite Justice

Copyright 2012 by Dennis L Carstens

email me at: dcarstens514@gmail.com

The Key To Justice Amazon Customer Reviews
4.5 out of 5 stars

5.0 out of 5 stars <u>Compelling, gripping and riveting</u>

From the first chapter, to the last, I was caught up in this novel. Gruesome serial killer, one misguided police officer, who ruins his career for absolutely no reason. The governor's daughter is among the victims, the governor calling for justice. All combined to make this a gripping thriller that had me cheering for the defense. I love the surprising, twisted ending in this novel. This book was a bit scary too, because it was so written that any reader could feel how it could possibly be a real. Bravo, Mr. Carstens on your first novel, and I wish to read many more.

5.0 out of 5 stars <u>Absolutely loved this book!</u>

Wow! I thought this was a fantastic book. I really liked everything about it. The courtroom drama and legal maneuvering were realistic and fun to read. The main character feels about the legal profession, just like the author (a real lawyer) does: less than enthusiastic. After an arrest is finally made in a high-profile case, the main character finds himself in the unenviable position of defending the prime suspect in the murder of 6 women. He is also going through a divorce while simultaneously suing the Federal Government, for unnecessarily making his life hell, for the past ten years. The author assures us that this work of fiction is not actually fiction, where the lawsuit is concerned. I loved that about the book. The cases, one fictional, and the other real, work well together, because most lawyers have more than one case, and most lives are just plain complicated. The lawyer pulls a couple Perry Mason type tricks in the courtroom, royally upsetting the pompous (and biased) judge. The story is told from multiple viewpoints, and interesting enough that you won't want to put it down. It's a very fun book to read, with good character development and plenty of interesting. interactions as the prosecution and the defence prepare for battle and finally go to trial.

5.0 out of 5 stars <u>Move over Grisham, there's a better author in town!!</u>

I have worked in the justice system with lawyers, cops, judges & prosecutors for most of my career & I have a fondness for reading courtroom drama. Having said that, I can unequivocally state that this author has nailed it completely when it comes to telling it like it is concerning investigations, trial conferences, witnesses & everything else connected with being a lawyer. I was amazed at how accurate this story was & how the awesome the writing flowed smoothly, building up excitement to the unexpected twist of an ending that you will never see coming...I'm still in awe. This would make one heck of a movie. The hero, Marc Kadella, was so genuinely real that I felt like I had known him a long time...the plot grabbed you from the first page & I lost a lot of sleep because I couldn't put this book down...My sincere compliments to the author for a GREAT courtroom novel, the best I've read in years. GET THIS BOOK...YOU WILL NOT BE SORRY...I intend to read everything this talented author has written. Thanks, Mr. Carsten for knowing how to write accurate courtroom drama!

5.0 out of 5 stars <u>Sometimes people aren't what they seem to be</u>

I had not read this author before but love legal thrillers. I took a chance on the 5 book bundle deal and hit the jackpot! Key to Justice was an excellent start to the series. The police in Minneapolis/St Paul have a serial killer on their hands and he seems to stay a step in front of them. When the Governor's daughter becomes the next victim, the police are sent scrambling to find the killer quickly. When the lead detective discovers who it is, he makes a decision that will change several lives. The plot takes several twists and turns and doesn't end how you think it will. Excellent read. Highly recommend.

Author's Note

I practiced law for almost twenty years, and like most lawyers, I learned it is a very difficult way to make a living—especially for those in small firms or those practicing on their own. It's a constant grind to procure clients and then convince them to pay you. It's a tough life, even for those lawyers in large, well-established firms where the pay is regular and good. Basically, you become a slave to the firm. Little wonder polls consistently show that 50% of all lawyers would rather do something else.

I have read many novels about lawyers, courtrooms, and legal dramas. With the exception of a very few, almost all of them left me wondering if the author had ever been in a courtroom. Ever actually represented a live, human client with a real legal problem. And most importantly, ever tried to make a living at it. I doubt many have.

When I set out to write this book, my main purpose was to write a novel about a lawyer and the struggles of the practice of law *as it really is*. I wanted to convey how unglamorous it actually is—to exhibit the simple truth that few lawyers get rich from it. And while it is a tough way to make a living, being a lawyer can also be very interesting, challenging, and quite rewarding.

The main case in the book—the prosecution of a serial killer—is totally fictional. However, the case Marc Kadella handles on behalf of his wife against the IRS, the Justice Department, and the U.S. government is not. It is, in fact, a case I personally handled. And every word is absolutely accurate. The names have been changed to protect the truly stupid and incompetent, but all else is factually correct.

Before the book was published, I asked friends and acquaintances if the IRS case was a distraction and should be removed from the book. The consensus was unanimous that it be left in because of the interest it generated. Everyone was fascinated—but not surprised—by the way the government conducted themselves, and they were as caught up in that case as they were the serial killer case. They all wanted to know how it turned out.

At any rate, I believe this is a more realistic look at the practice of law and hope that most lawyers who read the book will agree with me. Thank you and enjoy.

Dennis Carstens

Thank You

A special thanks to my dear friends who helped me with the writing and encouraged me to keep going and not get too discouraged. They are, Beth, Laura and Kathy. And a big thanks to my son, Eric, for getting me to, after several years of sitting in a box, take out the manuscript, polish the story, edit it and get it published. Thank you all.

ONE

"Come on, Shelly, it'll be fun. We'll have a great time. You'll love our lake place. Everybody does," said Thomas Allen Drayton III to the pretty, dark-haired girl he was sitting beside in a moderately-crowded bar.

"Your daddy's lake place," the girl reminded him.

"Mine soon enough," said Tommy.

T. Allen Drayton Jr., Tommy's father, was the new senior partner in the law firm Tommy's grandfather had founded—Drayton, Babcock & Moore—with, as Tommy liked to remind people, offices in Minneapolis, Atlanta, and Washington, D.C. Upon the retirement of Thomas Allen Drayton Sr., T. Allen was not only senior partner but head of the firm's corporate department, which meant T. Allen had to be very good at letting corporate executives beat him at golf. And little else. With eighty-four lawyers in the firm, senior partners and department heads knew what their function was.

Thomas Allen Drayton III fancied himself the preeminent babe hound of his class at the local law school in St. Paul. The girl he was presently using his most practiced charms on was a notch he had wanted on his bedpost since the first day of school, and he was determined to get it. Unfortunately for Tommy, she was just as determined that he would not.

The girl took a long, deep drag on her cigarette, blew the smoke out with an exaggerated sigh, turned her head to Tommy, and mischievously smiled at him. She turned her chair to face him, leaned forward so that her nose was no more than an inch from his and said, "Tommy, you've been trying since last fall to get in my pants, and I keep telling you *it's not going to happen*. Take the hint."

He put on his best disarming smile, the one that almost invariably snared his quarry—along with the thought of his family's money—and said, "You're wrong about me, Shelly. I really like you. Respect you. You're smart and pretty. I admire that a lot."

"Bullshit," she laughed. "Does this actually work on women, or is it just your daddy's firm and money?" She then leaned forward slightly, kissed him lightly on the tip of his nose and said, "I hope you enjoyed that because it's all you'll get." She leaned back in her chair, took her cigarette from the ashtray, and continued to smoke it with a bored look on her face.

Tommy sat up straight, the smile replaced with pursed lips and narrowed eyes, and petulantly said, "Fine. Screw you, bitch. I've been shot down by better women than you."

"I'm sure you have," she said.

"Shit. I can score in this place in ten minutes. You're probably a lousy lay anyway," he said.

"Tommy, please. Just go away. I didn't ask for this. I'm sure you can be very nice and all, but I'm not interested," she said, trying to soften the exchange.

The man seated at the other end of the bar smiled to himself as he watched the blonde young man stand obviously annoyed, turn from the table and walk away from Michelle Dahlstrom. He had a fairly good idea of what had just happened during the little scene he had been observing. In fact, he thought, *welcome to the club of rejected victims of the cool Ms. Dahlstrom*. He continued to sip his beer, alternating his attention between the table where Shelly now sat alone, and the Twins game displayed on several of the many TV sets scattered throughout the bar.

Charlie's was a popular spot among the young and single set, the Grand and Summit Avenues' crowd, especially the students at the local law school. *Charlie's* was a pick-up joint that also served a variety of good food. A place to relax and eat, not dine. Fortunately, thought the man at the bar, this attracted an older clientele as well, which he hoped would keep him from standing out in the crowd. He did not want Michelle, or anyone else, to take notice of him.

He ordered another beer and slightly shook his head at the TV screen as another Seattle batter began circling the bases. *Looks to be another long baseball season for Minnesota*, he thought. Just then, he noticed two young women take chairs at Michelle's table.

"Shelly, my God!" exclaimed Shareena Miller, a classmate of Michelle's. "What did you do?"

"Got a haircut," said Shelly.

"I'll say you did, girl," said Shareena with a laugh, "How come?"

"Got tired of it. It was just too much trouble, so I got a bit cut off," she said.

"A bit?" Asked the third young woman, another friend and classmate, Allison Montgomery. "That's an understatement! It was down to the middle of your back, and now it's just below your ears," she said as all three laughed at Shelly's casual explanation.

"Was that Tommy Drayton I just saw walking away with flames coming out of his ass?" asked Shareena.

"Yes it was," said Shelly with a smile.

"You shot him down, again?" asked Allison. "I'd just like the chance. Just once."

Of the three, only Michelle could be called attractive. Even with her short brown hair, she was, by anyone's standards, a beauty. The other two women were not, but neither was unattractive either. Just somewhat plain and undistinguished.

6

Both were in the top ten percent of their class, however, which Michelle envied because she definitely was not. She didn't care. Beautiful daughters of governors, even someday ex-governors, would do just fine in the legal profession, grades and class rank notwithstanding. Doors would definitely open wide for Michelle Dahlstrom.

"He's a gorgeous devil," said Shareena.

"A fluff-headed little boy," Michelle replied.

"They all are, honey," said Shareena. "Get used to it. At least until they're too old to be useful."

They all laughed. As she rose from her chair, Shelley said, "I gotta pee. Order me another beer, will you?"

The man at the bar watched as Michelle walked away from the table. She had left her coat and purse, so he assumed she was going to the restroom out in the hallway. As she headed in that direction, he followed her with his eyes without turning his head until she passed behind a wall that obscured his vision. Knowing she could not see him, he turned slightly in his chair to try to pick her up as she passed the end of the wall, but he did not see her again. For a Wednesday night, the bar was fairly crowded, especially the area she had to pass through by the pool tables, so he wasn't concerned about not seeing her return.

He turned back to his beer and the ballgame—the Twins were mounting a comeback that would ultimately fall short—and resumed his posture like any other thirty-something guy out for a few beers by himself. He again shifted his attention from the screen to the table where he could see the two remaining girls talking and laughing.

A few minutes passed, and he anxiously looked at his watch as he quickly glanced over toward the doorway leading to the restrooms. He told himself to relax. She wasn't going anywhere without her coat. It was a typical early spring Minnesota evening. A little cool even for late April.

Just then, he heard a voice from directly behind him say, "Hi, Bob. How're you doing?"

He looked down from the TV that he had not really been watching, pinched the bridge of his nose with the thumb and index finger of his left hand, and without turning around, replied with an audible expulsion of breath, knowing he had been caught, "Fine, Michelle. Fancy meeting you here."

She slid onto the barstool to his right, placed her right elbow on the bar, her chin in her right palm, and stared at him without saying anything. Still without turning to look at her, he casually sipped his beer while she watched him. There they sat without speaking for what seemed to him at least, a very long minute.

Finally, without moving his head, he looked at her out of the corner of his eye. The caught-little-boy guilty look on his face caused them both to burst out laughing. After a moment, when they both

7

stopped, she said as he swiveled his stool to face her, "I thought I made it clear to my father that you guys were going to leave me alone. And I thought he made it clear to your boss."

"Hey," he said holding up his hands in protest, "I'm off duty and just having a beer and watching the game."

She narrowed her eyes and responded with a drawn out, "Uh huh."

He lowered his arms and leaned on the bar. "Look, I'm not following you. Honestly. I just had to get out for awhile tonight. I admit, I know you come here, but I would not have bothered you. Even if you hadn't shot that guy down. That was amusing, by the way."

She placed her hand on his arm. "Getting involved, even briefly, was a mistake for both of us. It could've cost you your job. I like you. A lot. But I still think you will end up back with your wife."

"No chance," he said. "That's definite. She's moved in with her boyfriend."

"I'm sorry for you. Really. I'm sure that hurts you—and I'm sorry if I hurt you. You're a terrific guy. I simply don't want state troopers following me, okay? I don't want to go to my father with this, but I will if I have to. Please don't make me. I need my own life, which is why I don't live in the mansion anymore, okay?"

"Okay, okay," he said, again raising his hands in protest. "I'll go now, okay?"

She got up from her chair to return to her table, and as she did, he gently took her right arm and said, "I care about you, you know. And there's a nut out there raping and murdering women."

She placed her left hand over the hand on her arm and said, "I know you do, and I appreciate it. Don't worry, I'm being careful. I still have the whistle and pepper spray you gave me. Besides, the wacko is in Minneapolis." She kissed him lightly on the lips, touching his face as she did so.

"Minneapolis is ten minutes from here and there are plenty of crazies in St. Paul," he said. "Just be careful, okay? Tell your friends, too."

"I know. I will, okay? I promise," she said. "I'll see you, Bob. Take care." With that, she walked around the bar, back to her friends.

Bob watched her walk away and return to her seat at the table. He sat at the bar for a few more minutes, thinking about Michelle and their brief affair when he was assigned to the governor's protective detail as a driver and bodyguard. Separated from his wife, he had been lonely, vulnerable. He thought she was a doll.

The affair had not amounted to much and Michelle quickly ended it. She was after bigger game than a career highway patrolman, even a handsome one, and he was now desperate to get off the governor's staff and back on the streets. The luster of being around the state's heavyweight politicians had quickly worn off. He hated to admit it, but it was painful to see Michelle, even though he was sitting where he was for that precise reason.

He watched the three young women for a few more minutes while he finished his Sam Adams. He thought about giving Michelle a ride home just to be on the safe side. He should insist, he thought, or at least he should make the offer, even if he knew she would turn him down.

Not insisting was a decision that would haunt him for a long, long time.

TWO

A half hour after Bob left, shortly after 11:00, Michelle got up to leave too. As she was slipping into her coat, Allison asked, "Leaving already?"

"Yeah," Michelle replied. "Early class tomorrow and I'm kind of tired."

"We should walk her home," Allison said to Shareena.

"Forget it," said Michelle. "I'm a big girl. I'll be fine."

"Are you sure?" asked Shareena.

"It's only a few blocks. No big deal," Michelle answered her friend.

"We don't mind," Allison said.

"No," said Michelle with finality and a touch of annoyance. "I'll see you tomorrow, okay? Bye guys," she added as she slipped her arm through the shoulder strap of her purse and headed for the door.

While Michelle Dahlstrom was getting ready to leave Charlie's, the most hunted man in Minnesota was in his car heading east on Summit Avenue. While she walked toward Charlie's exit, he was passing directly in front of her father's temporary home—the governor's mansion—on Summit just east of Lexington.

Both hands gripped the steering wheel, his knuckles white and wrists taut from the exertion. His breathing had quickened and was coming in short, deep gulps. His eyes, rarely blinking, stared straight ahead, focused solely on the road in front of the car, almost in a trance. He was beginning to feel the lightness in his head and the slight pressure in his chest and groin as the semaphore he approached at Victoria for eastbound Summit turned from green to yellow and caused his right foot to reflexively push down on the brake pedal, which snapped him back to reality.

Since shortly after nine, he had been cruising around, mostly in Minneapolis, allowing the evening's anticipation to build. In the past few months he had come to know this sensation well: the excitement, pressure, and yes, he admitted to himself, the sexual tension he had come to crave almost as much as an opiate to an addict. Maybe that was it, he thought. Maybe he was simply addicted to it, as sick as he knew he was. At times he convinced himself he had no more control over his urges than someone falling in love. He smiled at the thought as he slowed to a stop at the light.

"Bullshit," he said, laughing out loud to himself. "You're just one sick sonofabitch … Hey! Grand Avenue; plenty there. Why bother with downtown? Head over to Grand."

He flipped on his right turn signal and cruised through the red light as he made his turn. He had started out in Minneapolis, his normal hunting ground, but now decided to try his luck in St. Paul. He figured

10

people in Minneapolis would be too much on edge, too leery and alert. St. Paul would likely be more relaxed. All the worst of the shit, he thought, happens in Minneapolis. Besides, maybe it would throw the cops off. Give them something to worry about. Something else to think about.

More relaxed now, his breathing having returned to normal and with just his left hand lightly holding the steering wheel, he headed south one block to Grand. The light at the intersection turned red for him while he was about halfway there, and then, he saw her. She was walking with the light across Victoria. She was too far away for him to see what she looked like, but the light from the corner and his headlights showed him enough. From a distance she looked to be fairly tall and slender, with short, dark brown hair. He let his imagination fill in the rest and he imagined her as being very pretty. Maybe even striking, he thought, not really knowing what it meant. Even though he had not yet seen her face, his imagination never failed him in this situation—even if it was wrong. She would be exactly what his mind told him she was.

He sat in the car at the red light and stared at the back of her tan, suede coat while she waited at the corner to his right to cross Grand. Without realizing it, both hands had returned to the wheel whitening his knuckles. His breathing had gone back to the short, deep gulps, and the pressure—the delicious anticipation—had returned to his abdomen. His eyes were locked on her as she waited for the light to change. There was just enough traffic moving along Grand to force her to wait for the walk sign, giving him the chance to stare.

He continued to watch as she stepped off the curb to cross Grand. She was almost half way across before he snapped to enough to realize he had a green light. Glancing quickly in his mirror, to his relief, he saw no headlights behind him. Easing off the brake, the car rolled into the intersection. *Calmly now*, he told himself. *Anonymity. Don't do anything to attract her attention or anyone else's.* He passed her before she reached the opposite curb, and for the first time, he noticed the parking lot on the southwest corner to his right. He pushed the gas down slightly and went by her without turning his head, drove the fifty or so feet to the parking lot entrance, and took the sharp right turn into the lot. There were no other cars entering so he eased up directly to the ticket dispenser.

Punching the button for the ticket and pulling it from the machine he glanced quickly to his right and located the girl. He pulled into the lot past the upraised automatic gate after spotting her exactly where he hoped she would be, southbound on Victoria. She had walked straight ahead after crossing the street toward the dimly-lit residential area south of Grand.

He pulled the car around to the dark back of the lot and found an empty space that separated the parking facility from the alley and backyards of the houses behind it. Parking in the space between a van and another car, he was impressed with himself at how calm he was and how clearly he was thinking. He had passed two laughing, hand-holding couples as he had driven through the lot and waited a few seconds to make sure they didn't see him before exiting the car.

While waiting for the couples to pass he laughed softly at how funny fate could be. But for stopping for the light on Grand and Victoria, if he had hit the gas and not the brake, this young girl would make it home and never know how lucky she was. Instead, her luck was about to run out.

He reached over to the passenger seat to gather up his hunting paraphernalia. He pulled a latex surgical glove onto each hand, stuffed the thin cotton ski mask into the pocket of his black nylon wind breaker, and picked up the plastic handled bread knife with the seven-inch serrated blade. The windbreaker wasn't much warmth for a cool night like tonight. The light cotton sweater he wore under it, coupled with his pounding heart, should make up for the chill. The windbreaker's main assets were its disposability, and it was difficult to hold during a struggle.

The chase and the struggle, he smiled to himself; that was the fun. The game.

THREE

Quietly getting out of his car and using the van as a screen, he stepped up to the six-foot wooden fence with the horizontal cedar slats. Two quick steps up the fence and he was over and into the unlit alley.

Crouching, leaning his back against the fence, knife in his right hand and searching the darkness to his left toward the alleyway entrance, the stalker caught a glimpse of what he assumed was the girl less than a hundred feet from where he knelt. *Have to get ahead of her*, he thought, just as her journey put a house between them, blocking his view. *Find a good place, like an alley entrance, to wait for her. Let her come to him. Stealth, speed and surprise*. Those were the keys.

Staying low in a half crouch, he quickly crossed the alley into the back yard of the house directly in front of him. Moving fast but noiselessly, the stalker passed through the backyard and onto the sidewalk that ran along the side of the house to the front. Moving next to the hedge that ran along the property, he silently cursed his luck. The girl was just then coming into view at the street corner forcing him to remain frozen where he was.

From a crouch, motionless, he watched her, still about one hundred feet from him, and listened for anyone or anything stirring in the houses. Hearing nothing except the dim sounds coming from Grand, he focused his attention on the girl. Only a few more steps and she would be across the street and behind the house on the opposite corner.

Having no idea how far she would go to her destination, he had to move faster to get ahead of her. It could be any of the houses—and if she got behind a locked door, the game was over.

Running across the street, his rubber-soled sneakers making barely a sound, he crossed the sidewalk and into the yard of the house facing where he had been hiding. Without slowing down, he ran between the houses, praying he would not run into a fence hidden by the darkness. The moon that night was almost full, but the sky was quite dark from the cloud cover over the city, the only light from the scattered street lamps and the occasional window with a light still on.

Coming to another darkened alley, her pursuer silently hurried through it and looked for the girl toward the light at the alley's entrance. Keeping up the pace, believing he had gotten ahead of her, the stalker ran across the grass through the fresh dirt of what would be a garden later in the spring. He made a mental note to get rid of the shoes, knowing he had just left perfect imprints in the fresh dirt he had traversed.

He crossed the next street, now two blocks from the crowds along Grand and decided the next alley would be it. If she was still coming, he would wait for her and take her there.

He ran to the mouth of the alley and found a perfect place to wait. In the shadows of a garage crouching behind a row of half-bloomed lilac bushes, he put his ski mask in place and looked back down Victoria, hoping he would see her. There she was, coming right at him.

The closest street light was across the street and, even luckier, burnt out, which made him all but invisible between the side of the garage and the bushes. As dark as the place where he waited was, the alley behind him was even darker. With no moonlight and the rows of garages blocking the streetlights, ten feet into the alley was virtually a black void.

Breathing normally again, he watched his quarry through the sparse bushes as she crossed the corner about eighty feet away. He reached between his legs with his gloved left hand and felt his erection. *My God*, he thought, *that's the biggest, hardest one ever*. He squatted waiting and watching, eyes wide and unblinking, his hand unconsciously stroking his penis through the cloth of his dark slacks as she continued to casually stroll along the sidewalk, seemingly without a care in the world.

As she reached the end of the row of lilacs just before the alley entrance, he sprang. She was slightly ahead of him with her back to him but no more than three feet away. With one quick, almost silent motion, he stepped to her, grabbed the back of her hair in his left hand, jerked her head back, and brought the knife up to her throat. She violently gasped, all of the air leaving her body in one huge forced expulsion.

"Don't make a sound bitch. Understand? Be quiet and you won't get hurt." With his mouth up against her right ear, she could feel and smell his breath on her face.

"Please, please don't hurt me," she croaked in a hoarse whisper.

Holding her hair in his hand, he propelled her into the darkness of the alley, repeating several times in his guttural whisper, his admonishment to be quiet and no harm would come to her. Pushing her along, her psycho nightmare held her head back by a fistful of her hair, neck stretched and eyes wide with terror, until they reached the opposite corner of the garage he had crouched alongside while waiting for her.

He jerked her around to face him, and as he did so, her left knee came up aiming for his groin, catching him just to the right of his genitals. At that same instant, he saw her left hand come up and the vaporized spray explode toward his face.

Reflexively, he ducked his head to his left, closed his eyes, stepped forward and threw a fist straight into the girl's jaw. The force of the blow loosened several of her lower teeth, lifted her off the ground and onto her back on the surface of the alley, banging her head and almost knocking her out. For a moment he stood over her, fully as terrified as she was, eyes wide open and nostrils flaring, allowing his conscious mind to comprehend what had just happened. After a second or two, the scent of the pepper spray penetrated his nose and snapped his brain like a slap across the face. No longer afraid, he became enraged.

He leapt, spread eagle, on top of the girl, landed on her hard, wanting to punish her, hurt her, for not obeying him. It excited him though, too. It added excitement to his hunt. As he landed, her right shoulder snapped, loudly dislocating it, and knocked most of the wind out of her, leaving her stunned and helpless, gasping for air.

Straddling the now-disabled girl, he placed the knife on the ground and began to pull at her clothes. None of the others had aroused him this much and he felt as if a fire was consuming him with a rage and desire. No other thoughts or feelings penetrated except the thought of having her, hurting her, taking her.

He unzipped her coat and pushed both halves to the side as he pushed up her sweater, bunching it up around her shoulders exposing her bra-covered breasts. He began working on the button and zipper of her jeans with both hands.

Michelle's breathing returned, her mind and eyes cleared enough even through the excruciating pain in her shoulder. "No. No, please," she pleaded through the pain. "Please wait, no. Please. I'll help you, just don't hurt me, please."

He leaned down and put his mask-covered face almost on hers, their noses
touching, and said, "Shut up, bitch. Whore. I know you'll help and love it."

It was then she realized he was using both hands to disrobe her—he must have put the knife down or dropped it during the attack. Just as he was rising back up, lifting his head away from her, she balled up her left hand in a fist as tightly as she could, and with all of the strength she could summon, punched him on the side of his face. The blow staggered him, causing him to lean to his left and almost knocked him off her. It hurt him, but not enough.

Shaken but still in control, with one quick move, he struck her across the face with the back of his right hand and began to grope on the floor of the dark alley, trying to locate the knife. She tried to raise her right hand to hit him again, the slap she had taken serving only to anger her more. Not knowing what was wrong, why she could not raise her right arm, the pain in her shoulder like a fire, she swung at him again with her left. Except this time, she went for his face and eyes, clawing and scratching in a desperate attempt to blind him or at least hurt him enough to drive him away.

He let out a short, sharp cry as one of her fingers raked him under his left eye. She did not catch the skin enough to scratch him but did snag the mask. She jerked on the eye hole bringing his head down and the mask off as his right hand came up with the knife. As the mask came away in her hand a break appeared in the cloud cover blocking the night sky. Behind the hole in the overcast sky, the moon suddenly flooded the alley with light, as if someone had turned on a light switch.

They froze, predator and prey, suspending their death struggle for no more than one very long second as the sudden light illuminated both their faces so that each could see the other for the first time. Their eyes locked. For the briefest moment, time seemed frozen, a snapshot of the only two people in the universe. For her, it surely was because this was the last moment of her existence.

"You..." she started to say as he thrust the knife under her chin, through her tongue, her mouth, and into her brain. He jammed the blade with such force it went in all the way to the hilt, bending the tip on the underside of the top of her skull. With the same quick motion, he jerked it free just as the blood started to pour from the wound and fill her now-dead mouth. The light of life in her eyes was gone, even though her heart continued to pump, and her lungs continued to expand and contract with breath. They would continue to do so for another minute or so, until the organs realized the brain was no longer able to instruct them.

It was over for her. The fear, panic and pain. Michelle Dahlstrom, the beautiful daughter of the state's number one citizen, was no more. Her life ended with a last second gurgling as her final breaths came to an end.

It was over for him too. This hunt. This game. The moonlight replacing the darkness would make him easy to see, and in his panic, it left him no choice but to bring it to a premature conclusion. *It would have ended this way anyway*, he thought. But he was sorely disappointed. He had wanted more. Not necessarily the rape itself. No, it was the struggle and the fear that he craved. The power over another human being.

Spent now, exhausted but unsatisfied, he stood and grabbed the girl's corpse by a wrist, dragged her out of the alley and left her lying alongside the garage. He knew she would be found soon enough but probably not before morning.

After wiping the knife on her coat, he retrieved her purse and tossed it alongside the body. He then shoved the ski mask into his pocket and stood over her—the moonlight still bright enough to see her face—to take a last look at her.

As the clouds moved their curtain back into place, he turned and trotted off into the night.

FOUR

Jacob Waschke stood at his kitchen counter trying to decide if he should have a third cup of coffee which, he told himself, he should not. It was only 6:45 A.M. and he already had a cup and a cigarette before his morning shower and a second of each afterward. His day just beginning, there would plenty more of each before it was over. "I gotta cut down on the caffeine and quit these damn cigarettes," he said out loud to himself. As he started to reach for the coffee pot, the phone rang, temporarily saving him from himself.

"Yeah, Waschke," he gruffly said as he put the phone to his ear.

"Is this Lieutenant Jake Waschke?" asked the voice.

"Yeah, you got him," he said.

"Jake, this is Gary Linaman with St. Paul. "

"Hey, Gary. What can I do for you?" Waschke replied. Jake knew who the St. Paul detective was but had never actually met him, let alone worked a case with him.

"Well, we got a homicide over here I'd like you to take a look at," Linaman answered.

"Why's that?" asked Waschke without much enthusiasm.

"It may be your stalker," he answered.

"Oh shit. What makes you think so? Describe it for me, Gary," said Waschke, his attention now riveted.

"Okay, let's see. Young woman, early twenties. Very attractive, pretty. Signs of attempted rape."

"Attempted?"

"Yeah, she's still pretty well clothed so I don't think he got the job done. Signs of a struggle. What looks like a knife wound under the jaw line. Won't know for sure until the autopsy, of course."

"It may be our boy," Waschke agreed. "Where are you?"

The detective gave him the location and the Minneapolis police lieutenant was out the door and on his way to St. Paul in just over two minutes.

Waschke found the crime scene off Grand and Victoria easily. He had grown up in St. Paul's Midway area, had lived in the Twin Cities area all his life and knew it as if a map had been photocopied into his memory.

Unable to get any closer because of the St. Paul police, he left his car about a block away. Linaman had put out the word to watch for him and with all of the publicity from the serial killer terrorizing Minneapolis, his face on the evening news made Jake Waschke a well-known personality to all of the local police departments. He made his way past the numerous emergency vehicles and the yellow taped crime scene. By following the activity, Jake easily found the detective who was obviously in charge, and headed for him.

"Detective Linaman?" he said to the man's back.

Linaman turned to face the direction of the inquiry and for a brief moment, his eyes betrayed his slight shock. Jake had that effect on people when they first met him. At six feet it wasn't his height but rather his shoulders and bulk that gave him the initial impression of towering over people. It was usually unsettling when first encountered, especially to a suspect. It was an advantage Jake enjoyed and had learned to use well.

"Jake Waschke," he said as he held out his hand to the officer. The detective took his hand for a perfunctory, businesslike greeting and said, "Gary Linaman, Lieutenant. Thanks for coming. Sorry about bothering you at home but your chief said you'd probably want to see this."

"No problem," said Waschke. "Where's the body? Can I look at it?"

"Over there, by the side of that garage," he answered as they headed in that direction. "Woman driving down the alley, a neighbor, saw her this morning around six. One of our guys, John Lucas, spotted the knife wound and thought of you guys right away."

"I know John," said Waschke. "Good cop. Where is he?"

"Knocking on doors around the neighborhood, checking for possible witnesses," Linaman answered. "Probably won't find much. She's been dead a few hours already. Doubt that anyone saw anything. You got gloves? I don't think our lab people are done yet."

"Yeah, I do," he answered as he took a pair of latex surgical gloves from the exterior pocket of his gray wool sport coat and pulled them onto his hands. Waschke squatted next to the body and gently pushed up on the chin to look at the wound. There was a great deal of blood that had coagulated around the wound and neck. It was a familiar sight Jake had seen four other times over the past three months. He tilted the head slightly to the left to look at the bruising on her right cheek.

"He punched her," he said in a matter of fact voice.

"Yeah," answered Linaman. "And with the way the clothes are, he must've had rape in mind. What do you think, Lieutenant? Same guy?"

"Call me Jake, please. Could be. Yeah, maybe, we'll see. I think so. Odd way for a nut case to kill. Single stab wound under the jaw into the brain. Very distinctive and it's the same as the others we've had across the river," said Waschke as he rose and turned to Linaman. "Something's odd though," said Waschke.

"What's that?"

"I don't get it. Why didn't he finish the rape? He always had before. This one, though, looks like he didn't. Why?" said Jake.

"Maybe she hurt him. Gave him a good shot to the balls or got him with the pepper spray. We found a canister on the ground."

"Maybe. I hope so but I'm not too sure. Not enough signs of a fight. He gave her a good shot and I'll bet that about put her out.

Anyway, you wanted to know if it's the same guy and I'd say yes. It's the wound. Very distinctive"

"Great. Now he's over here. We got a bigger problem."

"What's that?" asked Jake,

"Her," said Linaman, nodding toward the body. "Recognize her?"

"No," said Jake. "Should I? Who is she?"

"Come on," he answered. He led Jake over to the police lab unit, reached into the vehicle's back door and brought out a brown purse with a long leather shoulder strap. "Hers," he said as he pulled a billfold from the purse, folded it open and handed it to Waschke with the driver's license showing through the clear plastic.

"Michelle Marie Dahlstrom," said Waschke as he read the information from the license. "Brown and brown. Age 24. Lives about a block from here. Probably on her way home from a place on Grand last night."

"We're checking," Linaman replied. "Does the name mean anything?"

"Not Ted Dahlstrom?" asked Waschke. "Please don't tell me this is the governor's daughter."

"Afraid so," replied Linaman. "At least, I think so."

"Oh, shit. You have to be kidding. Please say you are," said Waschke as he passed his hand over his face and stood staring vacantly at the back of the lab vehicle.

"I wish I was. Believe me. I'm the one that gets to go tell him," said Linaman.

"Oh, Christ," said Jake. "This is just wonderful. When are you going to see him?"

"Pretty soon. I was gonna make a call and try to track him down."

"Maybe I can help," Jake offered, taking out his cell phone. He punched in a pre-set number, put it to his ear and listened to the ringing.

"You know someone?" Linaman asked, with obvious hope.

"Yeah. My brother," Jake said as he waited for the call to be answered.

19

FIVE

Thirty minutes later, Jake was introducing his younger brother, Daniel, to the St Paul detective in the reception room of the governor's chief of staff's office in the Capitol building.

"What's up, Jake?" asked Danny, as Jake still called him even though he was the top aide to Governor Theodore Dahlstrom.

Jake put his left index finger to his lips and pointed to Daniel's office with his other hand. Daniel gave him a puzzled look, shrugged his shoulders, turned and headed toward the door followed by the two policemen. Jake glanced around at the normally bustling crowd and answered the inquisitive looks with as warm a smile as he could force. *No need for rumors and gossip at this point*, he thought. *They'll all know soon enough.*

After Linaman had quietly closed the door behind them, Jake said to his brother, "Sit down, Danny. We're here with bad news."

"What?" asked Danny as he took his chair behind the large, oak desk. "What is it? Why do you need a private meeting with him?"

"It's Michelle, Danny. She was murdered last night," said Jake, as calmly as he could.

Immediately, Daniel put his hand over his mouth as his back stiffened in the chair. His eyes wide open, unblinking for several seconds, he sat looking back and forth at the two police officers. After a long moment, he brought his hand away from his mouth but remained otherwise frozen in place and said, "Are you sure? No, there must be some mistake," he continued, shaking his head. "This can't be. No. No. I just saw her the other day."

"Show him the billfold," Jake said to the other policeman.

Linaman was standing in front of the large oak door with the translucent frosted window guarding against possible intruders. He reached inside his suit coat as he walked the half dozen steps to the front of Daniel's desk and pulled out a plastic evidence bag containing a brown leather woman's billfold from his inside pocket. As he reached the desk, he held the bag up so the driver's license in the billfold could be seen and placed it into Daniel's proffered hand. Daniel grabbed it, almost jerking it out of Linaman's hand grasping at this last second hope that there had been a mistake, knowing that there wasn't. He held it up and looked at the picture on the driver's license, his heart rising into his throat with the thought of telling a man he greatly admired that the most precious thing in the world to that man was gone forever.

"Yes, that's Michelle," he said as he stared at the plastic image. His arm collapsed as if the muscles had been severed and his hand and the evidence bag hit the desk with a dull thud. He stared vacantly at the wall opposite his desk for three or four seconds, silence among the three men. "Now what?" he asked. "How do we tell him this?"

"We'll do it, Danny," his brother replied. "Just get us in to see him right away. The media was at the crime scene. This is going to get out, and real soon."

"You told the news people?" asked Daniel, a trace of anger and incredulity in his voice.

"Of course not," responded Linaman defensively. "We kept them back and they saw nothing, but they'll get it. This is too big to keep quiet."

"Who else knows it was Michelle?" asked Daniel more calmly.

"Just the three of us, so far," said Jake. "She's on her way to the morgue but someone will recognize her. It's going to get out, Danny. We need to see him now."

"You're right. Okay. Wait here and I'll set it up," said Daniel as he rose from the chair and headed to the office door.

Six minutes later, the two men were ushered into the large, ornately furnished office of the governor of Minnesota. Seated behind the huge rosewood desk was the room's current occupant, Theodore Dahlstrom. He rose to greet them as the secretary quietly closed the door leaving the four men in privacy. Like all good secretaries, even though she did not know what the unscheduled meeting was about, with two cops involved, she instinctively knew it must be serious and prepared to stand guard at the gate.

"Well, Jake, it's good to see you again," he said as he came around the desk, right hand extended, to greet his unexpected visitors. It was immediately clear from his guests' expressions and his aide's silence that, whatever their purpose, it was extremely serious.

Before he had finished moving from behind the desk, Jake stepped up to him, took the governor's hand in both of his and quickly, with forced control, said, "Governor, I think you'd better sit down, sir. We have terrible news for you, I'm afraid."

With a puzzled expression and without removing his hand from the policeman's gentle grasp, he looked back and forth between the three men. Jake gently took him by the elbow and guided him back to his seat.

"It's Michelle," he heard Daniel say as he looked up into the sympathetic eyes of the big lieutenant.

"I'm afraid she's dead," said Jake. "I am terribly sorry for your loss, sir."

"What? No, wait, this can't be. How? No, this can't be. There's a mistake here," said the governor as he searched the faces of the three men, his face pleading for a reprieve from the thunder that crashed in his head. None was forthcoming. Daniel and Detective Linaman, unable to look at the governor, stood silently staring at the floor, their hands held in front of themselves as if they were already attending the funeral. Only Jake was able to keep a grasp on the situation. Move it forward to its inevitable conclusion when the father would break down, sobbing, his head between his knees.

The two policemen stood at the bottom of the granite steps leading down from the Capitol entry to the parking area on the street below. Neither spoke for several long seconds as they both stared at the buildings of downtown St. Paul. Jake twirled an unlit cigarette in his fingers, looked up at the graying sky and rotated his head to loosen the muscles in his neck and relieve the tension he felt in his shoulders.

"No matter how long I do this job, I'll never get used to that," said Linaman.

"Yeah, I know what you mean," Waschke quietly agreed. "It's just so sad and difficult. No matter who it is."

"Trying to quit?" asked Linaman, nodding his head slightly toward Jake's hands, anxious to change the subject.

"Yeah." Jake sighed. "Trying. Not too successfully."

"I know what you mean. Quit myself eight years ago and I still want one sometimes," said Linaman.

"Like now?"

"Yeah, like now."

Waschke handed the smoke to the detective, took out another for himself and as he held out his plastic lighter to Linaman, said, "Who will handle this thing for your department?"

"I was thinking about John Lucas," he replied as he inhaled deeply. "He's passed the test for detective second."

"He'll do fine. We'll want to work with you people on this guy. I've worked with John a couple times before. If it's okay with him, it's sure okay with me."

"I'm sure it will be okay with him," Linaman said. "He's a good cop. Good detective."

"We have to get this asshole," said Jake. "After this," he continued pointing back toward the Capitol building, "the political heat is gonna be unbearable."

"No bullshit there," said Linaman. "Your chief and mine will be all over everyone until we get this guy. "

"I have to get to the office. Have John call me as soon as he can. Here, give him my card," Jake said as he pulled out his wallet.

"Sure thing," came the reply. "Anything anybody needs on this one, we have to do."

22

SIX

Three days later, at Lakewood Cemetery, Jake Waschke and John Lucas stood on a small knoll about a hundred yards away from the huge crowd gathered in a semi-circle around the minister. The casket and grave were protected from the mist that had been descending all day by a yellow and white striped awning. Jake was too far away to hear the graveside service and his attention drifted back and forth from the mourners to the media horde being restrained a respectful distance from the governor, his wife and the brother and sister of Michelle.

Daniel had called the day before to tell him the Governor wanted him and John Lucas to attend. He didn't elaborate but simply asked them to be there. *A gloomy enough business without the rain* thought Jake, as he shifted his feet, hands thrust in the pockets of his raincoat.

"The trees and grass are gonna explode when this rain lets up and we get some sunshine," said Lucas trying to make a little small talk.

"Yeah, looks like spring is finally here," Jake replied. "Here comes Danny," he continued as he noticed his brother break out of the crowd and start walking toward them.

"That's your brother?" asked Lucas, slightly disbelieving.

"Different fathers," explained Jake as if he had said it a thousand times, which he probably had. The physical difference between the two men was striking. Jake was a large, bulky man and Daniel was shorter and had a more normal build. "Mine died working for the railroad shortly after I was born. Mom remarried a couple years later. He fathered Danny."

They waited a few more seconds as Daniel walked toward them. As he approached he held out his hand to Jake who brushed it aside after seeing the look in his brother's eyes and instead, the two men embraced.

"How's the family holding up?" asked Jake as the two of them separated.

"Not too good," Daniel answered. "He'll be all right but Marie and the other two kids," he paused and shrugged, "well, they'll probably need a lot of counseling to get through this."

"Danny, this is John Lucas of the St. Paul Police," said Jake as the two men shook hands. "John's in charge of the St. Paul investigation. We'll be working together on this thing."

"Are you sure this is the same guy? The same guy that killed those women in Minneapolis killed Michelle?" asked Daniel.

"Well, obviously, we can't be positive until we catch him. And we will get him, don't worry about that. But yeah, we're sure it's the same guy," said Jake.

"Okay, good," said Daniel. "Anyway, he wants a word with you. Just a minute or two, okay? As soon as the service is over," said Daniel.

"How much longer?" asked Jake, immediately regretting the insensitive question.

"Pretty soon, I think," said Daniel with a half smile. "I'll get him and bring him here."

He turned and headed back toward the crowd just as it was starting to break up. Jake and John Lucas stood silently watching Daniel make his way through the dissolving crowd and walk to the two figures holding each other near the gravesite, the woman obviously sobbing into the man's chest. Jake watched as Daniel approached the grieving parents and stood a respectful distance away, waiting for the governor to notice him.

After a brief moment, he saw the Governor and his wife separate, the remaining two children moving quickly to their mother. As Daniel and the governor approached, Jake couldn't help but notice the redness in Dahlstrom's eyes and the firmness of his facial muscles. *The guy is really pissed. That's both good and bad*, Jake thought to himself.

"Lieutenant," said Dahlstrom as he and Jake exchanged a brief handshake.

"Governor, this is John Lucas out of St. Paul," Jake replied as the two men shook hands.

"Lieutenant, I want to be kept informed of your investigation. I want you to know, whatever you need, FBI, BCA, anything at all, you let me know and you got it. Understand?" said Dahlstrom being very clear this was not a request.

"Ah, Governor, excuse me …" Lucas began to protest.

"No problem, sir," said Jake, cutting Lucas off before he could go any further. "I'll see to it personally."

"Is there a problem, Lucas?" asked Dahlstrom, glaring at the detective, leaving no doubt about who was in charge.

"No, sir. None at all," Lucas replied.

"Good. Then we understand each other," said Dahlstrom firmly, returning his gaze to Jake.

"Let's be clear, here, okay, Lieutenant? This isn't just because of Michelle. You've seen the news and the papers. Look at that," he continued moving his head toward the roped off media. "It's about all of these victims and their families. This shit doesn't happen in Minnesota. This isn't New York or L.A. For everyone's sake, you have to nail this sonofabitch, now, okay?"

"Yes, sir," both policemen responded, in unison.

"Then we're clear here. Get it done," he said as he turned and walked off.

SEVEN

The early morning traffic moved slowly along Lake Street. In fact, not much faster than a brisk walking speed because of the thorough washing the street was getting from the cloud bank that covered the upper floors of the IDS Center and other concrete monsters that had grown out of the prairie soil of downtown Minneapolis. Marc Kadella liked the rain. Liked the way it washed away the grit and grime that the winter left deposited on the city like an enormous bathtub ring when the snow finally melted away. Today was the fourth day in a row of the rain but the TV news fluffs were predicting high pressure, sunshine and real spring starting tomorrow.

"The rainy days will have washed clean the Twin Cities of Minneapolis and St. Paul and the multiple rings of shiny suburbs with their shiny homes, their shiny new cars and their shiny couples with two point three shiny children," he said out loud to himself as he stared at the MTC bus going westbound along Lake Street. As he continued watching, the bus splashed through a puddle and sprayed the two women standing on the corner. That, at least, brought a brief flicker of a smile to his face.

"Jesus Christ," he softly said aloud to himself, "you're getting to be a cynical asshole."

It was not quite 8:00 A.M. and he had already been in the office over an hour. A few minutes earlier he heard Carolyn come in, one of the three secretaries he shared with the three other lawyers in the office. His door was partially open and he could hear her rustling about preparing to start her day.

Staring at the rain, the traffic and the few pedestrians scurrying along the sidewalks, he once again found himself wondering when he would snap out of his funk, why he ever decided to go to law school and then compound that stupidity with actually attempting to make a living at the practice of law.

He looked up from the street scene below and then north toward downtown Minneapolis. He reached up and pushed the window open as far as it would go to let in the fresh, wet air. A little of the downpour would occasionally splash in after hitting the outside ledge. He didn't mind. In fact, he kind of liked the wetness and freshness of it. It felt cool and invigorating. The ledges on the upper floors kept most of the rain at bay so it was no problem to have the window open, even on the rainiest of days, like today.

The ability to open the windows was one of the best features of the Reardon Building located on the southeast corner of Lake Street and Charles. An older building built in the twenties when the Calhoun area of the city was expensive, trendy and fashionable. Now it was mostly just trendy, the artsy kind of young people drifting in and out.

But he still liked the building with the creaky wooden stairs coming up from the street, the slightly musty odor and of course, the windows you could still open.

He even liked the neighborhood which was still relatively crime free and the inhabitants were certainly interesting. Colorful was a good way to describe them. And they usually made for more interesting clients. Certainly more interesting than the insurance and corporate clients the boys and girls in the downtown towers had to put up with.

He smiled a sly smile as he remembered what a law school classmate, a modern-day slave in one of the big, downtown firms, recently told him about big firm clients.

"Every time you turn around," he had said, "you've got another ass to kiss. I'd rather suck their dicks. At least that's finite. There's an end to it at some point. The ass kissing never ends. When you win a case for these bastards it's because you had an easy case and when you lose it's because you screwed up. They're never satisfied, and they always want their ass kissed. And don't get me started on the senior partners in the firm. They're even worse. Smart, good lawyers but in many ways the dumbest sonsabitches God ever put on the planet. Most of them don't have the sense to open an umbrella in the rain."

"Good morning sunshine," he heard Carolyn say as she came into the office through the door behind him.

He leaned back in his chair, tilted his head back and staring straight up at the ceiling calmly replied, "One of these days you're going to say that to me and I'm going to kill you. And I don't care if your old man is a St. Paul cop. I'm going to get up and beat you to death with your own computer. Now, that would feel good."

"Bullshit," she said. "Want some coffee? You love me and you know it."

"Yes, please," he answered as he leaned forward to retrieve the cup he had left on the windowsill. He held it up for her as she filled it.

"How are you today, Marc?" she asked with sincere concern.

"I'm okay," he replied without much conviction.

"Are you sure?" she asked, "I worry about you, you know. We all do."

"I know you do, love," he said. "And I appreciate it but I'm really doing okay. I need time and patience right now, but I know I'll be all right."

He took her hand and kissed it lightly on the knuckles. She patted him on the shoulder in a motherly kind of way, turned and walked out, leaving him to gaze out the window while he sipped his coffee and gathered his thoughts for the day ahead.

A few minutes later, one of the other three lawyers that shared office space with Marc, Chris Grafton, lightly rapped on Marc's door and walked in.

"How you doing?" Grafton asked as Marc spun his chair around to face his visitor. He had been expecting Chris. Chris was a bit older, but they were good friends going back to their law school days at William Mitchell in St. Paul. They had attended Mitchell because of the evening class program the school offered. Most Mitchell students that attended the evening sessions were a little older and had jobs and families and parents that couldn't afford to put them through law school. Chris still had his family while Marc's was coming apart because of the divorce between himself and Karen, the problem Marc was trying to cope with and that his friends and colleagues were so concerned about. At times he handled it well. Other times, not as well since he found out that Karen was seeing someone long before they separated.

"I'm doing okay," he answered with much more conviction than he had when he responded to Carolyn.

He pulled his chair up to the desk, set his coffee cup on the coaster and began to put the papers on the desk into a file folder. Grafton sat down in one of the two inexpensive client chairs in front of the desk and asked, "Where you off to this morning?"

"Criminal assignment court with Judge Eason and then go see the assigned judge about scheduling for our old friend, Raymont Fuller," Marc answered.

"Raymont Fuller. Which old friend would that one be?" Grafton asked. "One of your public defender assignments?"

"Yeah, he is," said Marc. "You remember, I told you about this guy. Goes into a convenience store with a gun and a driver waiting outside. Holds the place up for seventy-three dollars. Then takes a shot at the clerk - thank God he missed - and the cops catch him half a mile away in a drug bust when he tries to buy crack from an undercover cop. Precisely seventy-three dollars worth. "An amazing coincidence," he added, sarcastically. "The Public Defender's office took the driver to represent so, I got the real stupid one"

"Oh, yeah," said Grafton with a laugh. "Now I remember him. God I'm glad I don't do criminal work. Why do you? I don't get it."

"There are worse things," said Marc.

"Yeah?" asked Grafton. "Name one."

"Eating someone else's vomit," Marc answered as he rose to go.

"How are your kids doing? Have you seen them lately?" asked Grafton as he too got out of his chair and stood facing Marc.

"I see, or at least call them, everyday. They're both doing pretty good, all things considered. I'm trying not to drag them into this but it's not always that easy," Marc said with a resigned shrug and sigh. "At seventeen and sixteen they're both a little too old not to be concerned about their parents. Especially me. I know Jessica's worried about me and how lonely I am. I try to assure her I'm fine, but she knows me too well."

"At least you have a good relationship with them. That's more than most of us have," said Grafton, with a shrug.

"I know. That's what's keeping me sane right now," Marc replied.

"How's Karen?" asked Grafton. "Do you talk to her?"

"Not much," answered Marc. "I blew off some steam at her over the boyfriend. Said some things I shouldn't have and now she doesn't want me around when she's there."

"The boyfriend?" asked Grafton.

"Didn't I tell you?" said Marc. "Guess she's been seeing someone. I'm really not surprised. In fact, I knew it all along even though she lied about it. No one could be as stupid as she thinks I am. Anyway, seems she's doing just fine."

"Hang in there, Marc," said Grafton. "If there's anything I can do, let me know."

"Thanks," said Marc. "Gotta go. Get there early and get out early. See you in a while."

EIGHT

Marc sat in the twelfth-floor courtroom of Hennepin County District Court Judge Martin Eason, waiting for the judge to come out onto the bench to hand out the felony case assignments. He arrived at 8:45 hoping he would be early enough to check in with the clerk and maybe get his case assignment as soon as Eason came out. There were already seven or eight lawyers there when he checked in and another seven or eight came in shortly after. None were from the county attorney's office. Only defense lawyers had to be on time. The prosecutors were never on time. Usually too busy having their morning coffee and doughnuts with the judges, Marc believed. They never failed to whine about how overworked, understaffed and budget-poor they were, but try calling one before 8:30 A.M. after 4:00 P.M. or between noon and 1:30. Good luck. It was now 9:15 and no judge or prosecutor in sight.

He looked around the totally sterile, characterless courtroom. Hearing, but not listening to the buzzing of the conversation between the fifteen or so defense lawyers waiting, just like him, for the prosecutors and judge. He was sitting in the jury box, along with four other lawyers, when a female lawyer broke away from a small group talking by the rail that separates the spectators from the court area and walked toward him.

Veronica McMartin was a woman he had been working on a divorce case with for about six months. Veronica represented the wife and Marc's client was getting absolutely screwed by the Hennepin County Family Court. The case was proceeding and looked like it was going to settle soon. Pretty much exactly the way Marc had warned his client it would. Since Marc had enough experience with divorce cases to prepare the husband his client was not too upset.

He smiled a genuine smile at Veronica as she approached. She had been decent to deal with and the whole case could have been a lot worse, he knew, remembering the first time he had spoken to her over the phone. She had a soft, sultry telephone voice and the name Veronica conjured up, in Marc's imagination, the image of a five-foot, ten-inch slinky redhead. When they finally met at the temporary hearing, the image crashed on the rocks of reality. She was about five feet tall and weighed almost as much as Marc. But she was pleasant, reasonable to work with, a good lawyer and he liked her.

"Hi, Marc," she said as she arrived at the jury box rail and offered her right hand to him. He took it in his and they exchanged a brief handshake.

"Hi, Veronica," he replied. "I didn't know you did criminal work."

"I don't," Veronica said. "I'm doing someone a favor. Just getting the judicial assignment for someone in my office. He had a conflict and I have to be on the fifth floor at ten anyway," she continued referring to the Family Court seven floors below.

"Make sure you make that clear when Eason calls the case, or your ass may be on it for good. Some of these judges can be jerks about that stuff," advised Marc.

"What do you mean?" she asked.

"Once your name is attached to a criminal case," he explained patiently, "you're on it until the court allows you to withdraw. Most judges are good about it, but some can be assholes. It's not like a divorce case. If your client doesn't pay you for a divorce, you send a couple letters and you're out. Not so with criminal defense. You have to ask permission to withdraw and not all judges let you."

"Great," she said. "Now I find this out."

"Welcome to the glamorous world of criminal defense," he replied. "Don't worry, it should be okay. Just be sure to note on the record the name of the lawyer you are appearing for and be clear that you are not the attorney of record."

At that moment the courtroom doors opened and the attorneys from the prosecutor's office came in; five women, two men.

"Are there enough of them?" Veronica whispered to Marc.

"This is Hennepin County," he replied. "They travel in herds."

"What now?" she asked him.

"Now the clerk tells Judge Eason court can begin. He'll be out in a couple minutes," he answered.

"You mean we hang out till they decide to show," she asked referring to the prosecutors, "and then court begins?"

"Again, welcome to the glamorous world of criminal defense," he laughed.

About five minutes later he heard the bailiff intone the traditional "All rise" as his Honor, Judge Martin Eason, came into the courtroom through the door behind his chair, took his seat and pleasantly told all to be seated and started to call cases for assignment.

Judge Eason was an affable, older judge. Appointed to the bench in the early nineties by, for Minnesota, a rare Republican governor. He was a couple years short of retirement and basically treading water. *A middle-of-the-road kind of judge,* Marc thought. Not too tough but not too lenient either. But he also did not take himself too seriously, which Marc liked about him. He took his job seriously enough, but unlike a lot of judges, he seemed to know full well that if he dropped dead right this minute, the world would keep right on turning without missing a beat.

30

Marc stayed seated in the jury box waiting for his client's name to be called. *Eason must be in a hurry for some reason today*, thought Marc. He wasn't chatting with the lawyers the way he normally did.

After ten minutes or so, he heard the clerk call the case of the State of Minnesota versus Raymont Fuller. He got up from his seat, stepped out of the jury box and started walking toward the bench when he heard Eason greet him by saying, "Good morning, Mr. Kadella, how are you today?"

"Good morning, your Honor," Marc replied. "I'm fine, sir."

"Nice to see you again. It's been a while," said Eason as he reached over to take the court's file from the clerk who was seated just to his right and was handing him the case files as they were called. "Let's see now," he continued, reading the case name. "You're here for Raymont Fuller, I guess. Is that right?"

"Yes, your honor," Marc answered.

"Note that for the record," Eason said to Marc.

"Marc Kadella, K-a-d-e-l-l-a, for the defendant Raymont Fuller who is presently in custody, your Honor," Marc replied, spelling his last name for the benefit of the court reporter.

"And for the prosecution?" asked Eason looking at the young woman who had approached the bench from the prosecutor's table when the case was called.

"Jennifer Moore, for the state, your Honor," she replied.

"Mr. Fuller is in custody, you say?" Eason asked Marc.

"Yes, your honor," he answered.

"Has bail been set?" asked Eason.

"Yes, your honor," Marc answered. "One fifty."

"One hundred and fifty thousand?" asked Eason

"He took a shot at someone," answered Moore.

"Allegedly," Marc responded.

"Yeah, right, allegedly," Moore said rolling her eyes toward the ceiling. "And he has very little to keep him here. He's a flight risk."

"Okay," said Eason. "We'll give this one to Judge Tennant."

"Where is she?" Marc asked the clerk.

"1745," answered Moore.

"Okay," said Marc as he stepped forward to take the court's file from the extended hand of Eason. He turned to Moore and said, "I'll take the file up, check in with her and talk to you when you come up and we'll see the judge then."

"I'll be up in just a few minutes," she answered.

Looking back up at Eason, Marc said, "Thank you, your Honor," as he turned to leave.

Eason replied with a polite nod of his head as Marc turned to walk out of the courtroom while the next case was being called. He had waited forty-five minutes for a court appearance that had lasted, at most, a minute and a half, he thought as he headed for the gate in the bar. He made a slight, brief gesture of a wave to Veronica McMartin as he went through the gate with his and the court's file tucked securely under his arm. He walked out of the courtroom doors and headed for the elevators.

NINE

Marc stood in the hall by the bank of elevators on the court side of the government center thinking about what a waste of everyone's time the assignment session was. He only had a five-minute wait for an up elevator. *Shorter than usual,* he thought. Marc got on the already crowded car, punched the button for seventeen and quietly stood facing the doors as it made its way up.

He got off at his floor and headed for the courtroom of Margaret Tennant. She was appointed to the bench three years ago by the previous state administration. At the time, she had been out of law school only five years when the liberal Democrat had appointed her. A push to get more women on the bench. What the hell, thought Marc, she was turning into a pretty decent judge, as were most of the women appointed during that time.

Marc went through the unlocked door of 1745 and into an almost empty courtroom. Empty except for Margaret Tennant chatting at the bench with her clerk. Forty-one years old, Tennant was a very attractive woman. *No longer beautiful in the sense of a fashion model but still, quite pleasing to the eye,* he thought.

Marc had first met her at a continuing legal education seminar about two years before. She was seated directly across from him during lunch that day. They made a little small talk then and at the other breaks and became casual acquaintances. He had seen her a few times since, mostly around the courthouse and two or three times at social functions. He genuinely liked her personally, as much as he knew her, at any rate. This would be his first time in her courtroom and he had looked forward to it ever since Eason had told him of the assignment.

"Well, hello Marc," said Tennant with a warm, wide smile when she saw Marc come through her courtroom doors. "To what do I owe this pleasure?" Marc found himself feeling a slight, pleasing warmth from what seemed to him, a much more personal, genuinely affectionate greeting than what protocol normally calls for from a judge. *Maybe,* he thought, *he was reading a little more into it then what was there*

"The pleasure is mine, judge," he said. "What we have here is a criminal case assigned to you," he continued as he walked through the bar gate into the courtroom well and continued toward the judge. As he reached her he took the court's file from under his arm and offered it to Tennant who accepted it without taking her eyes off Marc's face or relaxing her smile, which her eyes clearly showed was unmistakably genuine.

She read the case name from the file cover from Marc. "And what is our Mr. Fuller charged with?" she asked as she returned her eyes to his and the smile returned.

Marc playfully rolled his eyes up toward the ceiling and flippantly replied, "Oh, no big deal really. Something about attempted murder, robbery and a couple of other minor kinds of things."

The judge and the clerk, who had watched the exchange between Marc and her boss with a curious, amused expression, both laughed at Marc's reference to the charges being minor little things.

"Do you want to talk to me now or wait for the prosecutor?" Tennant asked Marc, turning more serious.

"I suppose I better wait for the prosecutor," Marc answered, noticing that the smile had all but vanished as the judge got down to business. It was then that he noticed that the ring finger on her left hand was empty and he recalled hearing courthouse gossip that Tennant was divorcing.

"Who's the prosecutor?" asked Tennant.

"Oh, jeez," said Marc, pausing to try to remember the young woman's name. "Not one that I know," he continued. "Jennifer something," he said, remembering her first name.

"Jennifer Moore?" interjected the clerk.

"Yeah, that's it," said Marc in reply.

"She's kind of new," said the clerk with a slight shrug to Tennant when Tennant looked at her with an inquiring expression.

Tennant turned back to Marc and said, "How've you been? I haven't seen you for a while."

Marc, noting the return of the smile and the sparkle in the eyes, replied "I've been fine. And you?"

"Good," she said, "Especially since I decided to get rid of a couple hundred pounds of dead weight."

The clerk and the judge laughed heartily at this as Marc stood there, feeling foolish and left out, not getting the joke.

"Did I miss something?" he asked.

"I'm getting divorced," she said

"Oh yeah, okay I get it," he said. "Yeah, I'd heard that somewhere. Me too." It was the first time Marc had said it to someone outside of his office and he felt strangely relieved, as if finally admitting it out loud for the first time.

"Are you really?" she asked seriously. "I'm sorry to hear that."

"Why?" asked Marc, immediately regretting it. "Sorry. It'll be all right. How are you doing with yours?"

"I'm good," she said. "In fact, best decision I ever made. The marriage was going from bad to worse and it needed to be done."

"Yeah, I know what you mean. Mine too," he said.

"Have you talked about a plea?" asked Tennant as she held up the file to indicate Marc's client.

"No, judge," he said. "Not yet."

"Okay. I'll be in my chambers. Let me know when the Ms. Moore gets here and you want to talk to me." With that, the judge and her clerk left through the door behind the bench.

Marc took a seat at one of the lawyer's tables in the now deserted courtroom to wait for his opponent from the Hennepin County Attorney's Office. To help kill the time he opened his file on Raymont Fuller, took out the complaint and started to read through it again. Looking for what, he wasn't sure. After fifteen minutes he heard the door behind him open and he turned to see Jennifer Moore come through it.

"Have you talked to the judge?" she asked as she came through the bar gate.

"Not about the case, no," Marc replied. "But I checked in with her. She'll see us whenever we want."

Moore took the seat next to Marc at the same table putting several case files on the laminated table top. She quickly searched through the short stack of manila folders and removed the one for Marc's client. "What do you want to do with Mr. Fuller?" she asked.

"How about reducing bail, for starters?"

"Let's see," she said, opening the file. "Oh yeah, I remember this guy now. Forget reducing bail. No way. As far as we're concerned, he's exactly where he should be."

"What does your office want for a plea?" Marc asked, not at all surprised with her response to the reduced bail request.

"Got a note here says, if he pleads to the attempted murder and armed robbery, we'll dismiss the rest."

"You'll drop the drug bust. Big deal. Give me something to take to my client."

"What are you looking for?" she asked.

"Plead to the robbery," he answered.

"No way, he's lucky no one was hurt."

"Bullshit. He was supposedly four feet from the store clerk and missed him by five. No one's that bad a shot."

"Forget it. Look, I have to go to another courtroom. Let's go see the judge about scheduling. You can make your pitch for bail and we'll talk on the phone about the plea. All right?"

"You'll check about the plea to robbery?"

"Sure, but I know what I'll be told."

They waited in the back hallway separating the courtrooms from the judge's chamber and clerk's offices. Tennant was on the phone forcing the two lawyers to wait.

"How long have you been a prosecutor?" Marc asked the young woman.

"About a year," she responded.

"How do you like it?"

"It's all right. It's not what I want to do forever, but it's a job for now," she replied pleasantly. "Good litigation experience, but mostly it's a pain in the ass. It is nice to put scumbags away."

"Wow," Marc said, feigning surprise, "and I'll bet you were a liberal before you got this job. Went to law school to study environmental law to save the planet and then found out trees don't pay?"

Before she could respond, Tennant's clerk signaled them through the window in front of her desk that she was off the phone and they could go in.

On the way back to the chamber's area, Moore whispered to Marc, "Fuck you," which elicited a laugh from him.

"Margaret Tennant," said the judge shaking hands with Moore while remaining seated. "Have a seat."

"Jennifer Moore, your Honor. I'm pleased to meet you. You know Mr. Kadella?"

"Yes, we've met," she replied. "Now, I assume Marc wants a bail reduction. I've looked at the file," she continued as she put on the glasses that she had sitting on the desk and held up the court's file, "and I won't reduce bail. If you want it on the record we'll get my reporter in here, but I won't do it," she said looking at Marc.

Marc glanced briefly at Jennifer Moore and noticed her mouth curve into a slight smile with the news of her minor victory.

"No, your Honor, that won't be necessary," he said as flatly as he could. "If you'll just note the court's file that I made the request and you denied it, that should be sufficient to preserve it."

"Sure, no problem," said the judge. "Any plea discussions?"

"Yes, your honor," Moore said. "We want a plea to the attempted murder and the robbery. We'll dismiss the drug charges."

"Mr. Kadella?" Tennant asked, turning to Marc.

"I can probably get him to go with the robbery, judge, but he really didn't try to kill anyone," Marc said. "Maybe an attempted ag assault…"

Tennant leaned back in her chair, removed her glasses, and said, "Of course, I can't tell either of you what to do, but how about this: he pleads to the attempted murder, second degree, and I sentence according to guidelines without deviation?"

"We'd insist on an upward sentencing departure, your Honor. Probably double," replied Moore.

"Mr. Kadella's right, Ms. Moore. He really didn't try to kill anyone, and you may have trouble getting a conviction on it. On the other hand," she continued turning from Moore back to Marc, "he fired a gun during a robbery. He got lucky no one was hurt."

"I understand that, your Honor," said Marc. "I'll run it by my client and see what he says. Does anyone have his history score?"

"Not yet," said Moore. "We're still waiting from probation. I'm not sure I can agree to this."

"I'm confident your boss will see it my way, Ms. Moore," said the judge with a smile. "They're pretty sensible people up there."

With that comment, Marc clamped his teeth tightly together not wanting to comment on how sensible he believed the county attorney's office was.

"Well," Moore said pausing, "I'll check but it would help if you could throw in a sentencing departure. Say, fifty percent over guidelines."

"No way can I sell that to my guy. He's already making waves about any jail time," Marc said.

"No departure," said the judge. "If we want to make a deal it has to be acceptable to everyone, including me. You get your conviction and Mr. Kadella will politely explain to his client that I'll nail his ass but good if he turns the deal down. Okay?" she said to Marc with a charming smile.

"I'll see if I can make him appreciate your Honor's advice," Marc answered. He looked at Jennifer Moore who had turned to stare out of the chamber's window, obviously not pleased.

"Give me a call next week, Monday or Tuesday, and let me know. If it's no deal by then, we'll set up a conference call for scheduling. My calendar's pretty light right now and I see no point in putting this off too long. Mid-June at the latest. If we have a deal we can schedule a time for the plea next week. All right?" said the judge adding, "anything else? Good. Call me next week then."

"That's fine, your Honor," said Marc. "In fact, I'll stop over at the jail and see him now."

"Good," Tennant said. "Ms. Moore?"

"I don't like it much, but it's not up to me," she replied, clearly annoyed.

"Well, you two talk and let me know," the judge said as a way of dismissal. As the lawyers rose to leave, she added to Marc, "Marc, it was nice seeing you again. I'll look forward to hearing from you."

"My pleasure, your Honor," he responded.

"Goodbye, Ms. Moore. Marc," she said.

"Thank you, your Honor," they both replied.

As they exited the courtroom into the outer hallway, Jennifer Moore turned to Marc and said, "What're you, sleeping with her?" an obviously annoyed look on her face.

"What? What are you talking about? It's not a bad deal. Not great but it could be worse," said Marc.

"That's not what I'm talking about," said Moore. "At the end there I thought she was going to ask you to stay. I oughta file on the bitch," she continued as they headed toward the bank of elevators on the deserted floor. "But it wouldn't do any good," she sighed.

"Gimme a break," said Marc as he pushed the down button. "You heard her, if you go to trial you don't get the conviction you want and . . ."

"How does she know that?" Moore interrupted sharply.

"Because she's the judge and she decides what the jury does," said Marc. "And she'll know it was you guys that turned it down. Go ahead and file on her. Get her removed. You have to practice here more than I do and she'll put her notes in the file, so the next judge knows what happened anyway."

With that Marc's elevator arrived and he left her standing in the hall, her face grimly set. But she was now a wiser, more experienced lawyer than she had been a half hour before.

TEN

The enormous, ex-Viking deputy sheriff unlocked the door to the conference room in the jail of the basement of the Old City Hall. Located directly across the street from the government center, Marc had walked the tunnel under Fifth Street to meet with his client, for whom Deputy Carl 'Big Train' Johnson was just now unlocking the door.

Raymont Fuller entered the eight by ten conference room with the one-way mirror and flashed a big shiny smile when he saw Marc already seated at the small table.

Raymont took the chair opposite Marc and said, "Hey man, you get bail reduced?"

"I tried Raymont," Marc said with a shrug. "I really did but the judge is a bit of a hard ass. Said no way."

"Shit, man," Raymont said, rolling his eyes at the ceiling. Looking at Marc, he said, "How the hell am I s'posta come up with a hundred fifty thousand dollars, man?"

"Fifteen, Raymont. The bondsman only needs ten percent."

"Fifteen, one fifty, fifteen million. I ain't got it anyway. I needs to get the hell out of here, you know."

Marc sighed heavily, placed his elbow on the table and his chin in the palm of his upturned hand. He sat this way, staring at the county's involuntary guest, silence between them as Marc stared and Raymont nervously looked about the small room.

"What?" Fuller finally asked, clearly annoyed.

"Raymont," said Marc without moving. "I'm not your mother. I'm a lawyer, you know what I mean?"

"Yeah, I know. You my lawyer. So, what you doin' to get me out of here?" he angrily asked.

"When you're ready to listen to me," Marc said as he began to pick up the case file from the table, "give me a call." And he rose to leave.

"Okay, man, okay," said Raymont calmly. "I just hates it in here. There are really bad people in here."

"I know you do Raymont," Marc said as he sat down again. "I didn't put you here. Try to remember that."

"Did you talk deal with the other lawyer?" Fuller asked.

"Yeah, I did."

"Well?"

"The judge suggested a plea to the attempted murder and she'd go as easy as she could on the sentence."

"Oh, bullshit, man. I didn't try to kill nobody. I was just, you know, kinda warning that clerk dude. You know that."

"Yeah, I believe that. But the judge also indicated if you turn it down and go to trial, she'll nail your ass for everything."

"That's bullshit, man. You s'pose to be my lawyer. Fight for me, you know."

"I am Raymont. I got just about the best sentence you're going to get," said Marc, annoyance now creeping into his voice.

"Yeah, right. Man, I wants what you s'pose to do. You know, jealous representin'. I wants the O.J. defense, man."

"Zealous representation, Raymont," Marc said laughing. Sitting back in his chair he continued in mock surprise, "You should've said you had two or three million dollars to spend. Well shit, I'll call Johnny Cochrane when I get back to the office for you and turn your case over to him. Oh wait, that's right, he's dead. But for three million we can find his replacement."

With that, Raymont busted out in a hearty laugh which Marc joined. Both men laughed for almost half a minute at the exchange until, finally calming down, Fuller said, "Okay man. I get it. Okay, okay. What do you think? How much jail time?"

"Not sure," said Marc, wiping his eyes from the laughter. "We haven't gotten your criminal history score from probation yet."

"Not much there," said Raymont, slyly. "Just a couple. . ."

Marc held up his hands to interrupt and stop him. "Don't go there, Raymont. It won't do you any good to try to bullshit me. We'll find out in a couple days. Besides, the county attorney's office didn't say yes to the deal yet. I think they will though. You don't have to decide anything right now. As soon as I hear something, I'll come back, and we'll talk. All right?"

"All right, my man. I'm sorry I got mad, okay? I did what I did, and I guess I'll take the best deal you can make," Raymont said.

"Raymont, how many times do I have to tell you to stop admitting things to me? I don't want to know what you did or didn't do. It's not important. It's only important what they can prove. Please remember that," said Marc.

"Right, man. I get it. Anyway," Fuller said as he rose, shook Marc's hand and walked to the door. "Let me know right away okay? Stillwater's better than this place and if I gots to go I might as well get on with it."

"Sure thing, Raymont," said Marc with a trace of sympathy. "Probably by Friday."

Fuller banged on the door, yelled loudly for Big Train and gave a slight wave to Marc when the big guard opened the door to take him back inside to the general population area. Marc remained seated on the hard, metal folding chair surveying his surroundings for almost another minute.

Finally, looking directly into the mirror wondering if he was being observed said, "Ah the glamour of criminal defense work. Just like on

40

TV. Nothing but innocent clients, and the guilty party always breaks down on the witness stand in a last-minute tear-filled confession. And the lawyers go away rich and happy knowing justice has prevailed."

ELEVEN

"Oh wait, hang on a second. He just walked through the door," Marc heard his receptionist say into the phone as he closed the office's outer door. He looked at Sandy and silently mouthed the word "Who?" to her as she punched the hold button on her phone.

"It's that lawyer from Washington, what's-her-name, on Karen's case," Sandy replied.

"Oh good. I'll get it. I'll get it," Marc said as he hurried into his office without slowing down to close the door.

He grabbed the phone from its cradle as he rounded the corner of his desk, punched the button on the console and as he dropped into his chair, said, "Deirdre, what did you find out?"

"No deal. My boss wouldn't go for anything barred by statute. She approved the rest but nothing for fees," came the response.

Marc slumped in his chair and leaned on the desk, his left elbow supporting his head with the phone in his left hand. He sat like this and didn't respond to the obviously disappointing news.

"Marc? Are you still there?" he heard the lawyer with the United States Justice Department finally ask, breaking the silence after about half a minute.

"Yeah, I'm here," he softly said. "So, where does that leave us? What have we settled?" he asked as he looked up to see almost everyone in the office crowding into his doorway, each with an inquisitive look on his or her face. While he listened to the response to his question, he frowned at his friends in the doorway and shook his head to let them know he had received negative news.

"We'll drop Karen's liability, credit the refund against your taxes and lift the lien on your house. That's giving you everything except fees."

"If I go forward on the twenty fifth with my motion, can we limit it to attorney fees? Will you still settle the other things?" Marc asked.

"Yes, we will. In fact, I'll send a letter out today confirming this conversation and I'll copy the court. If you're willing to leave it at that, we'll be done."

"Deirdre, why shouldn't I go to court on the twenty-fifth and ask for fees? What have I got to lose?"

"Well, um, uh nothing I guess."

"Send the letter confirming that we settled everything else and I'll see you in about three weeks."

"Okay Marc. Sorry, it wasn't my idea and I know it doesn't make much sense."

"Bye, Deirdre," he said and hung up without waiting for her.

He leaned back in his chair, looked at Chris Grafton who had sat down opposite him, took a deep breath, rolled his eyes back in his head and looked up at the ceiling.

"What'd she say?" asked Grafton.

Marc stared at him for a few seconds, sighed heavily and finally said, "You're not going to believe this. Her boss squelched the deal. At least the part about some fees. Everything else we settled."

"They'll lift Karen's liability?" asked Grafton. "Congratulations. That's great. It's finally over," he said as he leaned across the desk to shake Marc's hand.

"What's this?" Marc heard Barry Cline ask from the doorway. "What are you guys talking about?"

"That's right," Marc said to him. "You're new around here. You don't know about this little farce do you? Well, have a seat and I'll tell you about your government in action.

"A few years ago, almost ten now," Marc began as Cline settled into the chair next to Grafton, "my soon-to-be ex-wife, Karen, worked for a restaurant in Northeast Minneapolis. She did some bookkeeping and she was on the signature card for the checking account."

"Oh, shit," said Cline. "I know what's coming. Payroll taxes weren't sent in and she was found liable. Hell, that's common knowledge. If you sign checks and taxes don't get paid, you're responsible."

"Well," Marc said with a laugh, "you're sorta right."

"What do you mean?" asked Cline.

"It's common knowledge that if you sign checks and taxes don't get paid, you'll be held liable by the IRS. What's not common knowledge is that the law says that's pure, unadulterated bullshit," said Marc.

"Are you sure about this?" asked Cline. "I know accountants and tax lawyers who will swear to this."

"Yeah, so do I," said Marc. "We talked to enough of them about this. Interesting how few of them actually know what they are talking about. Trust me, I know the law on this one. It ain't so. Anyway, the IRS basically forced me to bring suit, which, I did. The lawyer at Justice handling the case just caved in except for attorney fees."

"How much?" asked Grafton.

"Well," Marc continued, still looking at Cline, "over the years they had collected a little over forty-four hundred bucks from us on these taxes."

"What's the total?" asked Cline.

"With interest and penalties, it's up to over thirty-five grand. Anyway, the reason for the suit is I'm asking for a refund of the forty-four hundred. That's what gets you into District Court and not Tax Court. You pay the IRS some of the money you're contesting then bring suit to get it back."

"Yeah, okay," said Cline.

"Because I waited too long to bring the suit, part of the forty-four hundred,

about seventeen fifty, is barred by statute of limitations. So, she agreed to drop Karen's liability and refund all but the seventeen fifty. I tell her that's not good enough. She's only offering me the minimum I can get in court. I tell her I want it all including the seventeen fifty. She won't agree to that, so we dicker around a bit and settle for half the seventeen fifty to go toward attorney fees. About eight seventy-five. Okay? So, she agrees but her boss says no."

"You mean, for an extra eight hundred seventy-five dollars they could've made this thing go away?" asked Grafton.

"Yep," said Marc, turning again to Cline he continued. "Now, imagine telling this to a live client. Explain to a sensible human being what they just did. Tell your client that his choice is to pay an extra eight seventy-five to be done. Or, pay you a lot more than that to go to court for the sole purpose of risking losing even more money. You can't do better, but if you go to court, you could do a lot worse. What do you think your client would say?"

"Yeah, but they don't have to pay their own lawyer more fees. She's salaried anyway," said Cline.

"True, but they're going to pay to fly her out here, put her up in a hotel plus all the extra work she'll do for it. Plus, my time and the court's. It'll be a lot more of the taxpayer's money than eight seventy-five," said Marc.

"How much are you asking for?" asked Grafton.

"It'll be over nine grand by the time we go to court," Marc replied.

"Let me see if I got this straight," said Cline. "They're going to spend, easily, more than you would take to settle for the chance to lose over nine thousand dollars? Who thinks up this stuff?"

"Little wonder people get a little fed up with the government," said Grafton.

"Could you end up paying them?" Cline asked Marc.

"No. That's not possible. The only question is: Do they have to pay me?" said Marc.

"What do you think?" asked Cline. "You think you'll get it."

"Who knows?" said Marc. "I think I should but it's up to the judge and I don't know him at all. The case law says he can pretty much do whatever he wants. I got nothing to lose so, I guess we'll see."

"Amazing," said Cline, shaking his head as he and Grafton rose to leave. "Keep me posted. This could get interesting."

"Actually," said Marc, "I'm disappointed she turned me down. I wanted it over with."

"Hey," said Grafton as he and Cline turned back at the door, "how'd you make out this morning?"

"Fine. We kicked it around a bit, the judge, prosecutor and me, and decided Mr. Fuller should go to prison for a few years. Probably settled it."

"What'd your client say?"

"He wasn't overly enthused about the idea."

"Well, good luck on the twenty-fifth. That's just incredible. It's hard to believe anyone could do something that stupid."

"Who, the government or Ray Fuller'?" asked Marc.

"Are you kidding? What the government's doing makes Ray Fuller look like a sensible individual. He at least knows when to cut his losses."

"I have a question," said Cline stepping back toward Marc's chair, "Why does the IRS pull this shit? Don't they know the law?"

"Of course they know the law," answered Marc. "They do it because they're the IRS and most people can't fight them, and they simply get away with it. With the IRS, you're guilty until you prove different and most people can't fight so, they settle up."

"That sucks," said Cline.

"For sure," said Marc.

"Well," Grafton chimed in, "I hope you make the bastards pay for it once. It'd be nice to know someone who stuck it to them."

"I'm sure gonna try," said Marc.

TWELVE

"You want coffee, Lieutenant?" asked the bartender while staring at the big cop who had come in the bar and taken his usual seat in a booth along the wall opposite the long bar.

"Lieutenant," he said again, louder this time to get the cop's attention, his friend obviously distracted.

"What?" said Waschke suddenly as his head snapped up, his mind returning to the present. "Coffee? Yeah, Louie. Decaf. Sorry."

The man behind the bar grabbed one of the pots off of the warmer on the ledge next to the liquor bottles and taking a cup from below the bar, headed out to serve his customer. "Lot on your mind tonight, huh Jake, what with this stalker and everything," the bartender said, a statement not a question, as he set the cup on the table and poured the man his coffee.

"Yeah," Washcke agreed, passing his hand over his face. "Thanks Louie," he said as he put the cup to his lips.

"It might be a little strong, Jake. I put it on a couple hours ago figuring you'd stop tonight. Haven't seen you for a few days and you're later than usual."

"Almost 10:30 P.M. already," agreed Waschke as he looked up at the clock behind the bar. "You're right, I am kinda late tonight. Out cruising for our boy."

"Any luck?" asked Louie. He had known the police lieutenant for almost fifteen years. He knew better than to ask any specific questions about an ongoing investigation. But his bar, he was the owner of the Lakeview Tavern as well as the head bartender, was one Jake stopped at frequently. In fact, almost every night. Sometimes looking for information, street talk, gossip, whatever. Usually though, Waschke liked to come in, sit quietly in one of the booths, sip a little decaf and relax or, like tonight, gather his thoughts.

Jake responded to the question with a short, wry laugh. More of a quick expulsion of breath than a laugh. A snort, really. "Don't worry, Louie. You'll know as soon as something breaks. Probably before me," he said, looking up at the television above the bar.

"Yeah, no shit," said Louie, shaking his head. "It's been all over the news for weeks, especially since the governor's daughter. Even if they don't have anything to talk about, they talk about it. That must be a helluva pain in the ass for you to put up with, the press, I mean."

"Yeah, it sure is," Waschke replied with a resigned sigh. "It's not so dumb, though. Keep it on the air, keep people, especially women, conscious of it. Hopefully, it will remind them to be careful. Maybe even save someone's life," he said as he held up his cup for a refill.

"Good point. There's more than one loony out there. Pays to be careful, these days. You look tired, Jake. Get some rest."

"Easy for you to say," replied Waschke to Louie's back as Louie walked back toward the bar to continue serving the few regulars seated on the barstools.

Sipping his coffee, oblivious to the sights and sounds of the sparsely crowded bar, he tried to relax and unwind after yet another long, stressful day. There was no let up on the pressure and there would not be until someone was behind bars for at least one of these murders. *With the political heat, it would be best if it was for the Dahlstrom girl's,* he thought. The heat coming from the Capitol was showing no signs of a let up. And why not? If the governor's daughter was not safe, whose was? The problem was, they were no closer to getting this guy than they had been from the beginning. Jake knew why, too.

Homicide, he knew from more than twenty years experience as a police officer, is a relatively easy crime to get away with. Do the deed, get rid of the weapon and other physical evidence such as your clothing, walk away and keep your mouth shut. Most killings were solved not by brilliant police work, although some were, but because in more than seventy percent of all homicides the victim and the perpetrator know each other. A spouse, friend, lover, neighbor. An angry exchange, an emotional burst, a gun goes off. Everyone is sorry afterwards but it's too late now. Jake had to clean up the mess more times than he cared to remember after just such an occurrence.

He leaned back in the booth, put his feet up on the bench seat under the table opposite him and let his mind drift back over the events of this hectic day. A technique he had discovered years ago to help him relax and at the same time, organize his thoughts about the case he was working. He went back to the day's beginning, 8:00 A.M. at the downtown police headquarters, and the meeting with Jake's boss, Deputy Chief Roger Holby, the man overseeing the investigation for the mayor and chief of police.

THIRTEEN

"Can we get started? Let's go people. Find a seat and we'll get going," said the deputy chief. Holby was standing in the front of the conference room, at the head of a long table with more than twenty chairs along its sides. He patiently waited for the dozen detectives, eight from Minneapolis the rest from St. Paul, to finish filling their cups and take a seat so the briefing could begin. "Okay folks, come on, let's get going," he said, less patiently.

Jake took the first chair at the end of the table, just to the left of his boss, and looked over the short, middle-aged woman sitting in a metal folding chair in the corner behind Holby. *She must be the shrink*, he thought. *The one he had been told about. The one who was supposedly some kind of expert flown in to lend a hand. Well,* he thought glumly, *whatever help you can give us lady, will certainly be welcome. We're getting nowhere on our own.* He finished his chocolate-covered doughnut just as the meeting began.

"I'd like to introduce, Dr. Helen Paltrow," Holby began after all the detectives had found their seats around the table. "Dr. Paltrow is a forensic psychiatrist at UCLA and an expert on serial killers. Being from LA, she probably has a lot more experience dealing with this than we do. We've brought her in on this to give us whatever help she can in nailing this guy. Anyway, I'll turn it over to Dr. Paltrow now. Doctor."

The small woman rose from her chair and walked to the head of the table holding a legal-size manila file folder, stuffed with papers and notes to refer to during her presentation. She placed the folder on the table and put the half-moon reading glasses chained around her neck on the bridge of her nose. As she began to open the folder, the deputy chief said, "Would you like to use a podium, doctor?" referring to the small, wooden, portable platform that was sitting on the floor along the wall.

"Yes, please. That would be good," she answered as Holby stepped over to pick it up. "As your chief said, my name is Helen Paltrow," she began after the podium had been placed on the table for her use, "and I'm a professor at the UCLA Medical School. I don't know how much of an expert I am on these matters, but I have spent most of my life, going back to college forty some years ago, studying and profiling what we have come to call serial killers. I have participated in a number of investigations during that time. and have studied, sometimes in person, virtually every serial killer that we have identified. I've spent a lot of time personally interviewing as many as I could. Some whose names you'd recognize such as Ted Bundy, John Wayne Gacy and Jeffrey Dahmer."

"You were in the same room with Jeffrey Dahmer?" interrupted Joyce Rollins, one of the three women sitting at the table. "Not without a weapon, I wouldn't be," she added, invoking laughter from the assembled group.

"Well, he was quite secure. Believe me, I made sure before I saw him," said the psychiatrist with a laugh. "Besides, he didn't like girls, remember? The boys here would've been in bigger trouble with him than me," a comment that elicited more laughter, which helped to relax everyone.

As a rule, Jake did not like shrinks. He didn't believe that they were very helpful. He had been involved with them in the past, both personally and professionally. He had put himself into counseling when his first marriage broke up and grudgingly believed it might have helped him get through it. Two other times he had been ordered to see a police psychologist following the two times he had shot someone. Both good shootings when the suspect had drawn down on him first. Neither event had bothered him in the least bit, especially the one where the man died. Jake believed that was a suicide by cop and he had no regrets about it. For the most part, he believed shrinks were a waste of time and taxpayer's money.

"Anyway," the doctor continued, "I was sent the material on your victims and flown here to tell you what I can about the killer. Frankly, there's not much here, which also tells me something about your man."

"First off," she said as she removed the glasses and looked over the faces peering intently at her, "let me run through some of the general things we've learned studying these guys. Odds are, your guy is white, between the ages of twenty-five and forty. Probably married or at least was at some time in his past. More than likely, something wrong in his childhood. Dysfunctional family or some trauma that's coming to the surface now and he's acting on impulse. These attacks, by the fact that they appear to be random, by that I mean there's no real apparent pattern, seem to be almost spontaneous. There doesn't seem to be a lot of preparation or planning. At least, that's my best guess right now."

"You mean, he's not able to control himself. Can't control his urges or whatever. You think he's insane?" asked Jake. "He's driving along, sees a tall, slender, attractive brunette girl and can't stop himself?"

"Probably not that spontaneous," she said looking directly at Jake as she brushed back a strand of her slightly graying black hair, "As I'm sure you know, there's legally insane and then there's medically psychotic. Do I think he's legally insane in that he doesn't know what he's doing is wrong? No, I don't. Obviously, I think they are all medically insane, which, as you probably know, isn't a medical term at all. But do I think he's crazy? He's crazy as a shit house rat. Does that answer your question?

"Otherwise, he wouldn't be doing this. Legally insane though, not at all. He knows what he's doing, and he knows it's wrong. They all do, which is why they try to get away with it. If he didn't know right from wrong, why hide? Why try to avoid detection?"

"Would you testify to that in court?" asked Waschke while thinking, he may not like shrinks too much, but he was beginning to like this one.

"Obviously not without at least meeting your guy and spending some time with him. Look," she continued, returning her gaze to the room as a whole, "what I'm saying here is; this guy will look and act as normal as anybody. He could be sitting in this room."

"If he's sitting in this room, he's anything but normal," joked one of the women.

After the laughter died down, Paltrow continued. "On the surface, he'll appear to be your average Joe Citizen. Middle class, white male probably in his late twenties to mid-thirties. Job, maybe even a professional. Could have a family at home. Likely, but not necessarily, some type of mental or emotional trauma in his background.

"He's not some out-of-control nut. In fact, just the opposite. That's what this whole thing is about. What he's after. To control his victim and feed off of her fear. These attacks have nothing to do with sex. In fact, the reason you're not finding physical evidence from this guy could be, just possibly, because he's not penetrating her with his penis. He may be using some type of phallus. It's the fear and control.

"You're not going to find him by picking up mental cases, derelicts or homeless street guys. You probably won't have him on file somewhere. Possible, but that's not typical. He might be but probably isn't a felon or ex-con with a history. He'll be of above-average intelligence and I think for your guy, is likely very intelligent."

"Why do you say that?" asked Holby.

"Look at your case," the doctor answered. "Very little physical evidence. Maybe one semen sample even though all but the last show signs of sexual trauma, rape. No hair samples, fibers, skin under finger nails. He has thought all of this through very thoroughly except one other thing. I believe he wants to be caught. Wants to be stopped.

"The reason I say that is twofold: First, I believe they all do. It's kind of a common thread we've seen with these guys. Even if they don't admit it, which they usually don't, they're looking for the attention to make up for something missing in their lives. Second, specifically about your guy, he's very public in his acts. Right out in the open in the middle of a large metropolitan area. Normally, these guys get access to their victims behind closed doors. Either their own place or the victim's. And those that are outdoors types, Bundy did a lot of that, it's usually in some secluded rural setting. Not the middle of a city.

"Also, I think he's very intelligent and having a good time laughing at you people. Thinking he's smarter than you. And the way he's going about this he is going to keep at it until he runs out of victims or you get him. If he runs out of victims, meaning the population becomes so scared he can't find any, he'll very likely move on. Go somewhere else.

"I'm sorry I can't be more specific at this point. I just received your material yesterday," she said as she briefly held up the folder. "I only had time to look it over on the plane and last night in the hotel. I'm going to spend the next few days here, studying the case, so I'll be around for a while. If you have any questions, I'll do my best to answer them."

What followed was a half hour question and answer session, mostly general terms about the characteristics of a serial killer and what makes him tick or, depending upon your viewpoint, explode. Jake sat back in his chair, listened and watched as the questions and discussion went around the table. The shrink obviously knew her business, but it wasn't too helpful. He had not expected it to be, having pulled a book about serial killers from the public library a couple weeks before. The discussion taking place and the doctors brief lecture had pretty much coincided with what Jake had learned on his own. It didn't hurt either though, he thought. Getting inside this guy's head and figure him out could only help.

It had been almost three weeks since the Dahlstrom girl's death and that trail had grown mighty cold. Jake had come to the sad conclusion that it was likely there was only one way they were going to catch this guy. He was going to have to make a mistake which, Jake was certain, sooner or later he would. The problem with that reality was, to make that mistake, he was going to have to attack someone again. Maybe kill again. Hopefully, they would get a witness or something concrete to tie to this guy.

The discussion died out and Holby rose and said, "Thank you, doctor. It's been very informative and I'm sure we'll have more questions come up."

Looking over the table of detectives the psychiatrist replied, "I'll be around. Please feel free to call or stop by anytime. You never know what might be useful. What might be significant. Don't hesitate to ask. I'm just sorry I can't be more specific."

"Lieutenant," said Holby turning his attention to Waschke. "You wanted to go over what we have on each victim?"

"Yeah, right Chief," Jake answered.

"Why don't you and the doctor trade places and we'll do that now, then," said Holby.

Jake stood and walked around the small woman as she gathered her materials and moved to take the chair vacated by the imposing detective. Jake took her place at the podium, respectfully waited a moment for her to get seated, gather herself and prepare to take notes.

"Like the Chief said," Jake began as he looked over the faces in the room. "I'd like to take some time now to go over the victims one-by-one to refresh everyone and bring everyone up to date with what we have.

"Victim number one or, as far as we know, we believe is his first victim," he said as the doctor stretched her neck to see the podium surface, impressed that the detective doing the speaking was not using a single note, "Mary Margaret Briggs. Age thirty-eight. Divorced. Two kids. Boy and a girl. Both now living with their dad."

"How long ago was the divorce?" asked Mitch Klein, one of the detectives brought over from St. Paul with John Lucas.

"Four years. Forget it, Mitch. We checked thoroughly. Amicable split. They got along well. Nothing there. Anyway," Jake continued, "she worked as a broker in one of the downtown firms, Hollings and Jenkins. Killed Thursday, January twenty-fifth around 9:30 or 10:00 P.M. in a parking ramp over on Second and Eleventh. Found naked next to her car. Yes, in a parking ramp, in Minneapolis, in freeze-your-ass-off January. She had been out with a friend, a woman, for a couple of drinks. That's how we established the time of death. Hands bound with her own bra. Sexually assaulted. Single knife wound under the chin into the brain. Death almost instantaneous. Physical characteristics; tall, five ten, one hundred thirty pounds. Brunette. Very attractive woman. No physical evidence found except fibers from ordinary blue jeans. Levi's. Fairly new ones according to the lab boys and obviously very common. Everyone in this room probably owns a pair."

"Victim number two," he said without taking his hands from the podium and still without notes. He continued this way for another twenty minutes running through the names, backgrounds, physical characteristics and evidence, or lack of it, for each of the first three victims.

"What about the semen found on number three, Kimberly Mason?" asked the doctor.

"Boyfriend," Jake replied. "We matched it up. His alibi is solid. He was working as a bartender from five until almost two in the morning when it happened. Plenty of witnesses."

"Okay," said Helen Paltrow.

"Anybody notice anything so far?" asked Jake looking over the group as a whole. "All tall, five eight to five ten. All attractive. All brunettes," came the response from one of Jake's officers, a woman named Denise Anderson.

"Very good, Detective Anderson, you win a cookie. Anything else?" asked Jake.

"All killed on a Wednesday or Thursday between roughly, 9:30 and 11:00," replied another of the Minneapolis officers, Mike Santell.

"Very good, Detective Santell. You too win a cookie," said Jake. "What does that tell us?" Jake asked rhetorically. "Not much except he likes tall, attractive brunettes."

"Who doesn't?" said Santell, eliciting a hearty laugh from all in the room and a playful punch from the blonde-haired Denise Anderson seated next to him.

"Good point, Mike," Waschke said after the room had calmed down. "John, give us the rundown on Michelle Dahlstrom will you please. Victim number five."

"Sure Jake," said John Lucas, the lead detective from the St. Paul Police as he rose to address the group. "Michelle Marie Dahlstrom. Age 24," he began looking at his notes standing at his chair. "Five foot eight, one hundred twenty-seven pounds. Brunette. You've all seen her picture so, you know how pretty she was. Killed Wednesday, April twenty-fourth between 11:15 and 11:30. Times verified by coroner and witnesses who were with her in a bar on Grand Charlie's, just before the attack. Witnesses included a state trooper who knew her from the governor's detail, Bob Murphy. Murphy says he saw her but left before she did. Says around 10:30 or 10:45."

"You check this Murphy out?" asked the deputy chief.

"Yes, sir," replied Lucas. "Looks pretty straight. No alibi for the time of death but solidly alibied through his work records for the other victims."

"Which brings us back to who we believe is victim number four," said Waschke. "Constance Ann Gavin. Age thirty-four. Sandy blonde hair. Five foot four. One hundred forty pounds. Pretty average all around. Nice enough looking but more average than really attractive. By comparison, the others could all be called stunning, except this one. Plus, she was attacked on a Sunday evening between 9:00 and 9:30.

"Semen sample found that does not belong to her husband. He says she was at church that evening. Witnesses verify it. She left around 8:45. Her car, with her naked in the back seat, hands bound with her bra just like the others, was found behind a closed gas station four blocks from the church."

"Does the husband know about the semen sample," asked one of the St. Paul detectives.

"He does now. We had to take a blood sample for a DNA comparison from him and he had a right to know why. No doubt, it's not his. He says they weren't getting along, but he was still pretty shook up. Has no idea who it might be from. We have questioned everyone that knew her about a possible boyfriend but came up empty."

"Why do you think she's one of his victims?" asked Doctor Paltrow "His pattern, such as it is, and victim profile, seem well established and this one is seriously out of the norm."

"The cause of death, Doctor," Jake answered. "Single stab wound under the jaw and through the brain. Very distinctive. And it matches exactly. In twenty-three years on the force, I've never seen anything quite like it and as far as I know, no one else has, either. Plus, using the bra to tie her up like the others."

"That's not unusual," said the doctor.

"Yeah, I know. But it is common to all of the other victims. Except Michelle Dahlstrom. He didn't get that far with her and we don't know why," said Jake. "Could be any number of reasons," he added.

"What about the semen sample?" asked the deputy chief, even though he knew the answer.

"No luck, so far. The BCA ran it but no match," replied Waschke.

"BCA?" asked the doctor.

"Bureau of Criminal Apprehension. That's the state agency over in St. Paul. Their lab and computers tried to come up with a match, but the data base hasn't come up with anything. Our guy may not be on file for any number of reasons. When we get him, we'll match it then," said Jake. "Anything else?"

"The footprints," he heard John Lucas say. "We found a set of footprints about a block away from where the Dahlstrom girl was found. Reeboks, size ten. By the placement of each print, whoever made them was running. They were over four feet apart. We're working on tracking down make, model and where they may have been sold, but don't hold your breath that it will lead anywhere."

"Forget it," said Paltrow. "Your guy's too smart for that. Even if he is the one that made the prints, those shoes are long gone, and he won't buy Reeboks again."

"Jeff, what about the computers?" Waschke said, looking down the table at the quiet, balding, bespectacled man seated on the far end. Jeffrey Miller looked to be the furthest thing possible from a police officer with his glasses, bow tie and ever-present stack of computer printouts. Typically, the butt of good natured teasing, he was one of the most popular members of the department because of his genius with computers. He had solved more cases than anyone in the room with his gift, grit and determination.

"Easily a couple hundred possible based on the sex crime aspect of the case. I've run into a brick wall with the method of killing. The single stab wound. Crazies seem to go for the multiple stabs when they use a knife so, the computer hasn't turned up anything," Miller replied.

"What about the possibles?" asked the deputy chief.

"We're running them down, but no luck so far," replied Jake.

"What are you looking for?" asked the doctor.

"Violent sex offenders. Rapists that used a knife, especially. We may have to expand the search which is where you come in doctor. If you could get together with Jeff and go over what we've looked for so far, maybe you could come up with some suggestions," said Jake.

Bringing the meeting to a conclusion, he looked around the room and added, "One more thing, folks. The knife wound. The method of killing. As a reminder, that is absolutely confidential. No one, I mean no one, outside of this room is to know it. The coroner's office is being damn good about this and let's be sure we are, too. If I read about it in the papers or hear it on TV I will have someone's ass. Any questions? Anything else? Good. Well, let's get back to work."

FOURTEEN

Deputy Chief Holby caught up with Waschke in the hall, gently grabbed him by the arm and said, "Jake, the mayor wants to see you, me and the Chief in her office at 10:00 this morning and then there's a press conference at 10:30."

"Are these things really necessary? Do I have to be there, again?" asked Jake, obviously annoyed. "I'm not running for office."

"Yes. The chief was quite explicit about it. Besides," he continued poking a finger in Jake's ribcage, "the press loves you, remember?" he said with a laugh.

"Yeah, right. Kiss my ass," Jake said as he leaned his head to the deputy chief so only the two of them could hear the last remark. Holby let out a hearty laugh and slapped Jake on the shoulder taking the gloomy look off Jake's face.

The two men took the elevator in the Old City Hall Building, an oddly shaped architectural eyesore from another era, up to the floor that housed the offices and staff of the Mayor of Minneapolis.

Jake dreaded these weekly press briefings that he was forced to attend at the mayor's insistence. The briefings started with victim number three, Kimberly Mason, when the police were forced to admit there was a serial killer on the loose. At first, the briefings were heavily attended. Attendance had started to decline as the daily papers and local radio and TV stations moved on to other things. Jake had begun to wonder if the lack of publicity might be the trigger that caused the stalker to strike. Then came Michelle Dahlstrom and all hell broke loose. The story went national at that point and now the networks were camped in town.

They arrived on the third floor and went through the double glass doors leading into the mayor's offices. Without breaking stride, the two men walked past the mayor's receptionist and straight into her Honor's office where the mayor, her press secretary and the police chief awaited their arrival.

"Good morning, gentlemen," said Mayor Gillette as Jake quietly closed the door behind him. "Come in and please, give me some good news. It would be nice to have some around here for a change."

"Your honor, I'm shocked to see you smoking in a nonsmoking building," Jake said in mock admonishment.

"Screw you, Waschke," she replied as the other three men laughed at the exchange. "So, arrest me for smoking."

"Might not be a bad idea," broke in Chief Frederick Romey. "It would get us out of this press conference and give them something to write about."

"Hey Fred," said the mayor, "you may have something there. Let's do it."

"Too much paperwork," said Jake. "Not worth the bother."

Jake sat in the booth at the Lakeview Tavern sipping his coffee recalling the scene in the mayor's office, trying to suppress a smile the memory brought on. He genuinely liked Susan Gillette, a self-described 'tough old broad' who had won the mayor's office the year before on a get-tough-with-the-gangs platform. A sixty-two-year-old white grandmother who could appeal to a broad cross-section of the voters by reminding the minority community who the crime victims were. Jake was beginning to take it a little too personally that, right after she got the job, this mess with the stalker had fallen in her lap and Jake was not doing much about it.

The press conference itself had gone fairly well. The mayor's press secretary, Ron Goldman, had started it off with a brief statement that basically said nothing. This came as a surprise to no one, especially Jake, since there was nothing new to report and even if there was, it likely would not have been reported anyway. *A total waste of time*, thought Waschke. *These people know perfectly well that as soon as something breaks, they will be told.* For the next half hour Jake sat behind the mayor as she stood at the podium taking the heat. He had to give her credit for it. She could have sent any number of people up there to take it, but it was her city and she would not let anyone do it for her.

"Tough old broad," he heard himself say.

"Who's a tough old broad, Jake?" he heard Louie ask as he snapped out of his reverie to find Louie hovering over him with the coffee pot in one hand. "More?" he asked.

"Uh, no thanks, Louie. Gotta get going," Jake answered as he placed his right hand over the cup.

"So, who's a tough old broad?" Louie repeated.

"Oh, that," Jake laughed. "The mayor. She really is a tough old broad, just like she claimed last fall, remember? Hey Louie," he continued, "why do they call this place the Lakeview Tavern? You can't see a lake from here."

"Screw you, Waschke. You've asked me that dumb question a hundred times. How the hell do I know why? I didn't name it for chrissakes."

"Always a pleasure to see you, Louie. Such a pleasant atmosphere. What do I owe you?"

"Same as always, flatfoot. Get yer ass out there and catch the nut job and I'll take care of the coffee."

Louie headed back to the bar with the coffee pot in one hand and Jake's empty cup in the other. Jake pulled his feet from the opposite bench, stood and reached across the table to retrieve the raincoat he had tossed on the booth's other bench. Heading toward the front door leading to Lyndale, he waved a goodbye to his friend and put on the coat as he stepped through the door onto the wet sidewalk. Standing on the sidewalk stretching his back, he looked up and down the almost empty avenue. "We're going to have to get lucky to get this guy," he grumbled. "And it better be pretty damn soon."

FIFTEEN

Marvin Henderson relaxed in his Lay-Z-Boy watching the ten o'clock news on local channel 8 as was his normal custom. Seventy-two years old and retired after over forty years with Honeywell, he had lived alone for the past three years, since the death of his wife. The kids were grown with families of their own. They all kept an eye on their dad, seeing him more often than most children did in this day and age. He lived alone now except for the collie whose muzzle he now felt nudging his right arm as it rested on the chair. A reminder that it was beyond the normal time for their nightly walk. She needed a respite outdoors and it was time to go.

"Okay, old girl," Marvin said as he pushed down the chair's footrest, patted his companion on the head and rose from his seat. "Let me check the weather first." He walked toward the front door, the collie at his heels, and peered through the small window in the solid wooden door that led to the front of the house on 35th Street in south Minneapolis.

"Looks like it stopped raining. Well, Keesha, guess I'll go with after all. Let me grab an umbrella and your leash and I'll be right with you," he said to the dog as he bent to retrieve the leash lying in a corner by the door. He went into a closet, took a coat from a hanger, an umbrella from the shelf, snapped the leash to his old friend's collar and followed her through the door into the night.

"Let's go down by the lake for a bit," he said to the dog as he patiently waited for her on the front lawn of their home. "As long as it's not raining we might as well get a little exercise."

He walked out into the street and headed west the two blocks to Lake Calhoun and the walking path around it. It was a familiar route her master had taken literally hundreds of times over the years. The dog knew where they were headed and she patiently walked alongside the old man, the leash hanging loose between them.

They reached the path, deserted in this evening's rainy weather and late-evening darkness. She automatically headed north along the east side of Calhoun, as they always did, and began their stroll along the asphalt trail. They had gone less than one hundred yards when Keesha began a growl, deep in her throat, obviously sensing something out of the ordinary. She began pulling the old man along, straining the leash, toward a small copse of trees by the water's edge, a dozen or so steps from the path.

Suddenly, a figure came bursting out from the trees, a dark form sprinting across the rain-soaked grass, running away from the elderly man and his four-legged companion. Keesha barked loudly three times at the figure but then slinked between Marvin's legs to lie down on her haunches behind him, as if seeking his protection from the danger she sensed.

"What the hell was he doing there?" asked Marvin out loud to himself. He quickened his pace, almost to a run toward the place where they had first seen the escaping form. He reached the spot in a few strides, pushed aside a few bare, wet branches of the undergrowth bushes and gasped at the sight, the bile coming up in his throat. The light from the city was fairly bright here and he could clearly see the remains of who would come to be known as victim number six, Donna Sharon Senser. Her wet, muddy, blood covered corpse, its white naked skin in stark contrast to the dark bushes and ground around it. Her clothes, muddy and wet, crumpled in a ball lying next to her.

"Hey, you, come back here," he yelled as he turned in the direction of the escapee. He looked down the path and saw the figure a hundred or so yards away now, walking on the path almost casually. He began to run after what he believed was a man but after a dozen or so strides realized that he was not likely to catch him and if he did, he would probably be the next victim.

He knelt beside the dog urging her to give chase but the dog, obviously realizing the danger before her master had, could not be budged. For her too, her best days were behind her and she could sense the evil that strolled away from the scent of death behind them. Her master was here and in no immediate danger himself, so she would not leave his side. It was then that he heard it; laughter, loud and cold coming from the sinister figure now standing under one of the lights that illuminated the pathway circumventing the lake. For the next ten or twelve seconds the laughter continued, not the kind of hearty laugh from a good joke, but an evil, dark, cold laugh from the recesses of a sick mind and soul.

"Tell them from me: Go to hell!" the figure yelled. "And you and your dog, too, old man," he yelled and laughed again.

Marvin and his friend rose from the wet grass, began to trot toward the street, his only thought to call to get help and wishing he carried the cell phone his daughter had given him.

When Marvin reached the street, he glanced to his left and saw the dark, sinister figure casually strolling across the same street, parallel to the man and the dog, and start to climb the short hill to the dead-end barrier that halted 34th Street. The old man turned to his right, as much to move away from the evil as to seek assistance, just as a car came around the corner from 36th and began to slowly head toward them as the old man began to move toward it.

Doug Foley had been on the force for almost fourteen years and he never grew tired of cruising the streets. A sergeant for the past two years working out of the third precinct in South Minneapolis, he enjoyed the evening shift the best even though it meant less time with

Cindy and his two young boys. In a way, he reminded himself, it worked out for the best. Because Cindy worked days and he worked evenings the day care cost was minimal and the kids spent most of their time with at least one parent. Well worth the minor sacrifice, he knew.

As he pulled through the intersection on Hennepin and 36th a flash of lightning lit up the dark sky, illuminating the large cemetery to his left, the one where the governor's daughter had recently been buried. The rain would be coming down again soon, he realized as he headed west on 36th toward the lakes.

Probably not much point in cruising the lakes on a night like this. With the rain that had fallen earlier in the evening and what would be coming down soon, he realized, there won't be many people out. It was then that he thought of Michelle Dahlstrom and decided he had just enough time before his shift ended to make one more cruise around the lakes, Calhoun, Lake of the Isles, Harriet and Cedar.

He reached the corner of 36th and the Parkway as the drops began to splatter on his windshield. Foley turned on the wipers and made the right turn to head north on the east side of Calhoun and immediately saw a man with a dog in the middle of the street about a block ahead of him. The man began waving his arm, slowly at first and then, almost frantically. Foley pushed down the accelerator to quickly close the distance as the rain began to come down harder and a huge roll of thunder rumbled across the city.

He pulled up to the old man, now clearly illuminated in his headlights, rolled down his window as he slowed to a stop and said, "Is there a problem, sir?"

"Down. . . down there. . ." Marvin breathlessly stammered, more frightened than winded.

"Slow down, sir. Catch your breath."

"No, dammit. Over there," he continued, pointing toward the trees and bushes along the shoreline. "A body. A woman . . ."

"What? Where?" said the policeman, alarmed now.

"No, no. Down there," Marvin continued, now pointing down the street. "A man. He did it. I saw him. He went up the hill to those houses."

"When?" asked the now charged up policeman.

"A minute ago. No more than that. He should be real close," Marvin answered, calmed now by the presence of the policeman.

"Put your umbrella up and wait right here. I'll be back," said Foley as he punched down on the gas and sped off down the street toward the place where the old man had been pointing.

He slowed the squad car at the spot where he believed the old man had indicated, reached for his radio and peered up the hill in the darkness. Pressing the send button on the microphone, he raised the dispatcher, gave his location and a brief description of the incident including the location of Marvin and Keesha. Once again he pressed hard on the accelerator and raced to the stop sign where 33rd met the Parkway. Barely slowing, his tires squealing and sliding on the wet pavement, he made the sharp right turn on to 33rd and headed into the residential area fronting the lake as a voice crackled over his radio.

After leaving the bar, Waschke got into his car, started the engine and sat while the engine idled, waiting for traffic to clear. He made a U-turn from his parking space along the curb and headed north on Lyndale, intending to cruise east on Lake Street to get to 35W. He had decided that wasting the city's gas cruising around town hoping for what, he did not know, was a fruitless effort again this evening. He had done it every Wednesday and Thursday, as had all of the members of his squad, for the past two weeks. Hoping somehow, someone would see or hear something, report it in and give the police the break they so desperately needed.

As he began to turn right onto Lake, he heard the dispatcher's voice come out of the speaker to inform all patrols of the call received from Doug Foley. Waschke quickly pulled the car to the curb and listened as the dispatcher described the situation not far from where he was. He listened for about ten seconds as the monotone voice calmly relayed the details, and then turned on the car's emergency flashers on the dash and in the grill. He picked up the car's radio microphone, pressed the send button and as he pulled away from the curb and made a u-turn in the middle of the busy street said into the mic, "This is Waschke. I'm on Lake and Lyndale, westbound on Lake. Patch me through to the reporting officer."

After taunting the old man and the dog who had abruptly startled him while he admired his night's work in the bushes, the stalker calmly crossed the Parkway and climbed the short, steep hill heading away from the lake. He passed through the yard of a darkened house on top of the hill, removed the ski mask and calmly stepped out onto 34th. It took tremendous effort to control his almost overwhelming urge to run, but he managed it and quickly began walking, turning left at the first corner. He quickened his pace to move away from the scene to get to the safety of his car. It was probably only a matter of minutes before the area would be crawling with cops.

"This is Lieutenant Jake Waschke," Foley heard from his radio speaker as he straightened the car to go up 33rd. "Pick-up Foley, I need to speak with you."

"This is Foley," he answered. "Go ahead, Lieutenant."

"Listen carefully Doug. This could be our stalker. Be careful. No lights, no sirens. Dispatch keep me patched through directly to Sergeant Foley and I want every cop in the city in that neighborhood in two minutes. We have to get it sealed off now!"

Foley had reached the corner of Irving and 33rd when he heard Waschke make the last demand. Slowing, Foley began to go through the intersection, looking first to his left, then turning to his right to look up Irving. When he did, he saw him. A dark form half-way down the block walking through the rain across the street parallel to the direction Foley was headed. Foley hit his brakes, reversed the car and said into his radio, "I see him. He's crossing Irving heading into the yards."

Jake was flying down Lake, red light flashing, windshield wipers thumping, bobbing in and out of the sparse traffic, heading as fast as he dared in the general direction of Foley and his suspect. His heart was racing as fast as the car was in anticipation of maybe getting the lucky break he had literally prayed for. After going about a mile down Lake, all the while speaking on his radio, he made a sharp left turn onto Holmes Ave. and began his run through the residential area as he turned off the lights on the dashboard and in the grill.

The stalker looked down Irving to see a car's brake lights come suddenly on as it passed the corner on 33rd. He quickened his pace and headed toward the yard directly in front of him as the car began to come up Irving toward him. All caution aside now, he broke into a run as he reached the yard and headed past the lighted porch to the dark side between the houses, uncertain if he had been seen but taking no chances.

"Go after him. Take your radio and give chase on foot. Keep me posted where you are," Foley heard Waschke's voice instruct as he headed up Irving toward the dark figure crossing the street in the rain. At that moment, from the light above the porch of the house the figure was headed toward, Foley saw the man begin to run onto the lawn of the same house.

Foley screeched to a stop in front of the house, slammed the car into park and was out the door before the car stopped rocking, engine still running. Holding his .40 caliber in one hand he tried to follow the beam of his flashlight in the rain as he ran through the yard, the alley in back and into the yard directly behind the one he saw the suspect enter.

The rain was coming down hard now, so hard the light reflected back in his eyes. Just as he was entering the yard of the second house he saw him. Or, at least, caught a glimpse of the dark figure as it broke into the opening between the two houses and dashed to his left, in front of the house next-door.

"Hold it, police," he yelled through the rain. "Stop right there." Foley raced up the side of the house and just as he was about to reach the front, his left foot hit a small hole in the ground twisted his ankle sharply causing him to lose his footing and go down hard. He landed hard on his hip, dropped the flashlight and just managed to get his hands down before he hit the ground.

Seated on the grass, holding the pistol in front of him, waving it back and forth in the darkness, the injured cop pulled a handheld radio from his pocket. Clenching his teeth from the pain in his ankle and hip, he pressed the button on the radio to let Waschke know what just happened.

"I'm down," Waschke heard the radio squawk "He's on Humboldt headed toward 33rd. Pick him up there."

"What happened? Are you all right?" Waschke said into the mike.

"I fell. I'll be okay but I'm out of it. I lost him," came the reply just as Waschke reached 33rd Street heading south. He made the right-hand turn onto 33rd to head in the direction he was certain the suspect would be coming from. He had gone almost the full length of the short block, doing almost forty through the hard rain on the quiet residential street, when he saw him. There, right up ahead to his left on the sidewalk was a dark clothed man running along the street. Instinctively, without a moment's hesitation or thought, Waschke jerked the steering wheel hard to his left. The heart pounding and adrenaline rushing to his brain made him react too quickly. Without thinking, he failed to realize how fast he was going. There was no way to could make the turn.

The stalker reached the corner and without slowing, he quickly glanced back over his shoulder in the direction of the voice he had heard commanding him to stop. To his relief, he saw no one and heard no footsteps pounding down the street except his own. When he reached the corner, he turned right and still running as fast as he could, headed east, still moving quickly down the sidewalk away from the lake. After he had taken a dozen or so strides, he saw the headlights speeding up the street toward him. *Too late to slow down now*, he thought as he sped past a large elm tree and approached the streetlight at the entrance to the alley. It was at that precise moment that the speeding car came even with him and suddenly, tires squealing and one side of the car virtually off the pavement, made a half-circle to head right toward him.

As Waschke's right foot jammed down hard on the brake pedal, he furiously began to spin the steering wheel back to his right to correct the squealing tires on the wet pavement. At the last moment he realized it was too late. He had been going far too fast for the attempted maneuver so all he could do was tighten his grip on the wheel and hope for the best as the huge tree anchored to the boulevard came looming up to fill his view through the windshield.

As the front wheels hit the curb, both wheels exploded causing most of the underside of the car's front end to be torn, twisted and smashed and delayed the deployment of the air bag long enough for Jake's forehead to hit the steering wheel. Just as his head hit the steering wheel, the air bag deployed and smashed him in the face with the force of a heavyweight's punch. The car then bounced over the ten inches of concrete curb, which absorbed most of the shock. As the car hit the tree, it was hardly moving at all which, fortunately for Jake, meant the tree caused little additional damage. Jake would later be told had it not been for the bounce from the curb, the tree would have ended up in his back seat and his own mother would not have recognized him.

After hearing the shrieking tires, the stalker inexplicably stopped dead in his tracks. Like the proverbial deer in the headlights, frozen for a brief moment as if glued to the sidewalk. As the big car screamed toward him, just as it reached the curb, his reflexes took over and he dove to his right, away from the two tons of oncoming metal. He covered his head with his arms, rolled three or four times away from the enormous explosion of grinding, crashing steel and came to a stop, lying flat on his stomach, directly under the streetlight.

Jake's head bounced backward after striking the steering wheel, his entire body convulsed by the sudden crashing stop. He sat staring, eyes barely open obviously stunned, looking through the cracked but still intact windshield, as the steam rose up from the smashed radiator. Slowly, he turned his head to his left, blinking his eyes to clear the fuzziness he was seeing, trying to comprehend what had just happened. Squinting through the unscathed driver's window, he reached up to his forehead with his right hand and felt the wet, warm blood that began flowing from the three-inch gash. He saw a dark, fuzzy form on the sidewalk slowly began to rise under the light. Just as the fog of unconsciousness began to envelop his brain, unsure of what he was looking at, Jake's and the stalker's eyes met, no more than ten feet between them, locked together through the haze they both felt.

Almost unconscious, Jake looked through the driver's side window at the man he had been chasing. Shaking his head to focus his foggy mind, he tried staring intently at what he saw. He squinted his eyes together just before his bloody forehead thumped against the glass, his mind going blank as his quarry trotted off.

SIXTEEN

Marc Kadella stepped through the elevator doors and walked down the hallway toward courtroom 1745 of the Hennepin County Government Center. He reached the double doors of the courtroom entrance and looked through one of the small glass windows set in the doors. Seeing no one in the room and looking at his watch to note he was fifteen minutes early, Marc turned and walked over to the glass paneled wall along the hallway. He stood staring out at the offices on the building's west side about one hundred feet away, across the empty space between the buildings two sides, watching, but not really seeing, the county employees going about their daily routines. Turning his head to his right, he saw the tower clock in the Old City Hall building across the street. Shifting the small leather briefcase - a birthday gift from his wife during better days - from his left hand to his right, he again glanced at his watch as he began to pace back and forth over ten feet of the carpeted floor. After several short trips on his pointless journey, he checked his watch again, turned and headed through the door of the men's room.

After using the urinal, he stood bent over the sink thoroughly scrubbing his hands, staring at his image no more than six inches away in the mirror above the sinks. He dried his hands from the paper towel dispenser and again faced himself in the mirror. Straightened the knot in his meticulously tied tie, ran his hands over the lapels of his suitcoat, touched up a few loose strands of his sandy blonde hair and said out loud to the image in the glass. "Well, pal, sorry but that's about as good as it's going to get. Not too bad," he continued as he leaned closer to study his face, "but you are starting to show your age a bit."

He reached in his pants' pocket to retrieve a breath mint, popped it into his mouth, picked up the briefcase, took one last look in the mirror and headed out of the restroom and into the court.

"Good morning," he heard Margaret Tennant's clerk, Lois, pleasantly say as he stepped through the gate."

"Good morning," he replied as he walked up to her perch next to the judge's chair.

"You're Marc Kadella and here for Raymont Fuller," she said, a statement not a question, as she marked her copy of the court's calendar to note that Marc had checked in. "The judge wants to see you. She said you could go back as soon as you got here."

"Oh, really. Okay. Um, is my client here?"

"Not yet. They're bringing him up now. I'll let you know as soon as he gets here."

"Okay. Good. I guess I'll go see what the judge wants."

He turned and walked to the back corner of the courtroom toward the door leading to the chambers' area. When he reached the door, he turned and saw the clerk watching him with a big grin on her face.

"Hi, there," Margaret Tennant said as he entered her chambers. "How are you?"

"I'm good, judge," he replied.

"It's nice to see you, again," she said softly as she rose from her chair and held out her hand to him. He took the hand in his, their eyes locked, and they warmly shook hands.

"Have a seat, Marc."

"Thanks."

"Is your client here yet?"

"No, they're bringing him up now."

"How about a prosecutor'?"

"Not yet."

"Are you busy Saturday night? What do you say we go out to dinner?" he heard her say.

He involuntarily sat up in the chair and stared at her for a long moment, the silence hanging in the air between them. "Sure," he finally managed to croak. "That'd be good."

"A little forward?" she said with a laugh that broke the brief tension between them.

"Well, ah, a little unexpected," he answered with a smile. He relaxed and leaned forward, placed his forearms on the desk, lightly entwined his fingers together and said, "Now that I'm over the shock, I'd be delighted to go out with you. In fact, I was trying to work up the nerve to ask."

"You mean I could've waited?" she said rolling her eyes upward and laughing again.

"It's okay. I don't mind. In fact, it's kinda nice for the ego to be asked once," he said as he sat back in the chair.

"Really? See, we're taught that men don't like pushy, aggressive women. But I figured, to hell with it, it's the 21st century, right?"

"I'm not sure that's so true anymore. I mean, that men don't like to be asked. Some probably don't but I think it's okay. Besides, it sure let's us know you're interested. Anyway, I'll call you, what, Friday, and we'll set something up."

"Good," she said smiling. "Another murder last night. What's that, six now?"

"Yeah, six. The cops had a shot at him, I guess. At least according to the news I heard on the radio. I haven't seen a paper yet today."

"It's getting damned frightening. I hope they nail this guy soon," she said as the intercom on her phone buzzed. "Yes," she said as she brushed back her auburn hair and put the phone to her ear. "Okay, I'll tell him. Your client's here," she said to Marc as she replaced the phone in its cradle.

"I better go see him. Get him ready for the plea," Marc said as he rose to go.

"Let me know when you're ready. Tell the clerk and as soon as a prosecutor graces us with his or her presence, we'll do this."

"Right," Marc replied, smiling at the judge's subtle shot at the punctuality habits of the county attorney's office.

"Hey, Ray, how are you holding up?" he asked as he stepped through the door of the small conference room adjoining the courtroom.

"Hey, man," his client replied looking up at Marc. Raymont sat in one of the chairs surrounding the small, round wooden topped conference room table. Wearing his one-piece county orange jumpsuit, Raymont had pushed the chair back against the wall and sat hunched over, his legs spread, his elbows on his knees, manacled hands clasped together with his shoulders hunched over and head down as if in prayer or deep thought. He rose to shake hands with Marc as Marc turned to the deputy leaning against the wall opposite from Raymont.

"Can we take these off?" Marc asked, referring to the handcuffs.

"Nope. Not unless the judge okays it," the guard answered as he pushed himself away from the wall and began leaving. "I'll be right outside the door. "

"He's not going anywhere," Marc continued. "Take these things off."

"Sorry, counselor. We have our rules too."

"You think I'd risk my license to bust him out?" asked Marc, obviously irritated, to the guard's back as the door swung closed. "Asshole."

"It's all right, dude. They ain't that tight. I'll be cool."

Marc took the chair directly opposite his client, no more than three feet from him. The two men sat silently for almost two minutes, Marc sitting back in the chair with his legs crossed, his head still light from the startling revelation from Margaret Tennant. Raymont continued staring at the floor, obviously reflecting on his immediate future and its bleak prospects. Finally, Marc came back to the present reality and quietly asked, "So, you okay with this? You ready for this?"

"Yeah, man. I'm okay," Raymont responded, sighing audibly as he sat up in his chair, rubbed the stubble on his face and looked directly at Marc. "You know what's bullshit about this? I'm gotta say I did the one thing I didn't do; try to kill someone. You know it, I know it, everybody knows I didn't try to kill nobody."

"Yeah, you're right, Ray. It's ironic."

"Yeah, right. Ironic, man, whatever the hell that means," he laughed.

"Look, Ray. They have the bullet, they have the gun, they have witnesses," Marc began to explain, once again.

"I know, I know," said Raymont, cutting him off. "I'm cool, okay. Like I said, man, I did what I did, and I'll take it like a man. Besides, man, I can do six years."

"Four with good time."

"Yeah, okay. Four with good time assumin' I behave," Raymont said. "But what the hell, the brothers'll think I'm a bad ass."

Just then, there was a light knock on the conference room door. Marc looked over at it just as the deputy opened it slightly and said, "The prosecutor's here. Just wanted to let you know."

"We'll be out in a minute," Marc replied.

"Okay, counselor. I'll let the judge know," the deputy said as he quietly closed the door.

"You ready?" Marc asked after he turned back to his client.

"Yeah, man. Let's do it."

SEVENTEEN

Jake Waschke, dressed in a flimsy hospital gown, sat on the edge of the hospital bed in which he had spent the night. He stared at his reflection in the mirror through the open door of the bathroom. The pounding he had felt in his head when he first awoke had been replaced by a dull, steady pain. More of an irritant than anything debilitating.

As he looked at the image in the mirror, he gingerly reached up to his forehead and lightly ran his fingers over the white patch covering the egg-shaped purple knot and the gash with the dozen or so stitches holding it closed. He ran his fingers back through his graying head of dirty hair, over the stubble on his face and thought about how good a shave and shower would feel. Jake continued to stare at the image of the middle age man in the mirror. The eyes looked old and tired, as hazy and unfocused as his memory of the night before. He had been awake almost two hours now and had spent the entire time trying to get his mind and memory of the past evening's events to come into focus.

Gradually, over the last two hours, the haze in his head had begun to dissipate and his memory began to return, recalling the chase, the sighting of the suspect and a vague recollection of an accident. It was only now that the details were coming back but only in bits and pieces. Like out of focus pictures flashing on a screen.

Just then, the door to his room slowly opened and a doctor who, to Jake at least, looked to be all of twenty-five, came through the door and into the room with Deputy Chief Holby hard on his heels.

"How's the head?" the young doctor asked.

"Still there, I guess," Jake replied with a weak smile while remaining seated, his bare, white legs dangling above the floor.

"I meant the headache."

"Not as bad."

"I'll give you a prescription for Tylenol with codeine."

"Great, I know where I can sell those on the street."

"Very funny, Jacob," the deputy chief said.

"I'll just get some regular ibuprofen and I'll be all right. Just get me my clothes so I can get out of here," he growled in reply.

"You should stay another day, at least, so we can keep an eye on you," the doctor said as he stepped in front of his uncooperative patient. He removed a small pen light from the pocket of his white hospital smock, bent slightly at the waist and gently held open Waschke's eyelids and examined the pupils with his light. "You have a concussion; Lieutenant and we can't be responsible if you leave too soon. I recommend that you spend another day here."

"I'll be all right," said Jake as he slid off the edge of the bed, his feet lightly slapping the cold, tiled floor.

"Did anything significant leak out of that hole in his head?" the deputy chief asked, obviously pleased at the chance to make a joke at Waschke's expense.

"We did a very thorough examination of his head," said the young doctor in mock seriousness, "and found absolutely nothing."

"Very funny, you two. You should go on stage with that act."

"Seriously, Lieutenant," the doctor continued, "you should stay."

"I got things to do, Doc. I'll be fine. Is this thing gonna scar?" Jake asked, lightly touching his forehead.

"Oh, yeah," said the deputy chief sarcastically. "A scar would really detract from that face."

"How's my car?" Jake asked Holby, knowing the damage he had done to his police vehicle would be a sore spot to his superior.

"Not funny, Waschke," Holby replied. "The whole front end, including the engine and undercarriage, is totaled."

"Oh, sorry," Jake replied meekly, a smile on his face, knowing this attitude would annoy Holby even more.

"Not yet you're not. You will be, though," said Holby.

"Yeah, right. Why do I doubt that? Anyway, I need to get out of here, Doctor. I have things to do."

"That's your choice," the doctor wearily replied. "We have plenty of other patients. The neurologist is on the way up. Stick around a bit longer and let her check you over first. Okay?"

"How long?" Jake asked.

"Not long. I spoke to her a few minutes ago and she said she'd be right up."

"Okay. I'll wait."

"I'll give you this prescription anyway," the younger man continued as he tore a page from the prescription pad he had been writing on and handed the slip of paper to the big cop. "If you feel like you need it, get it filled."

"If you're done, Doctor," said Holby, "I'd like to talk to him alone."

Holby patiently waited for the physician to leave then turned to Jake and said, "So, tell me what happened last night."

"Well, let's see," Jake began as he massaged the back of his neck with his left hand attempting to relieve the stiffness and pain in his head and neck.

"You probably have some whiplash," said Holby.

"I'll be okay," Waschke said, irritated. "What happened last night?" he continued. "I remember getting the call from dispatch, that reminds me, how's the other cop? What's-his-name?"

"Foley. He's fine. Sprained ankle and bruised hip. He'll be okay in a couple days."

"What happened to him, anyway?"

"Slipped and fell in the rain chasing our guy through one of the yards. What can I tell you, shit happens."

"Yeah, tough break. We might've had him if he hadn't gone down. Anyway, I'm following over the radio. I come wheeling around a corner, go down this street and see a guy running down the sidewalk right at me. I jerk the wheel around to cut him off and the next thing I know, I wake up here."

"Did you get a look at him? Did you see him?"

"I don't know. Yeah, maybe. It happened pretty fast and it was raining and dark. I remember he was in dark clothes." He closed his eyes trying to concentrate and after a moment said, "A white guy. I got enough of a look to know that. About average size and height. Nothing unusual. Nothing to distinguish him. That's about all. It's all pretty hazy."

"Shit," said Holby, obviously disappointed. "Well, maybe it'll come back to you. In the meantime, we found number six," he continued as he reached in his inside coat pocket and pulled out a small notebook. "Donna Anderson, twenty-six. Brown and brown. Five eight, one hundred twenty pounds, according to her driver's license. We're running her down now. Should know more later today."

"It all sounds too familiar," Jake said. "What happened after I crashed."

"That's the bitch about the whole damn thing," said Holby, his voice rising in anger as he began to pace about the small room. "We had ten cars in the neighborhood within five minutes and the whole square mile completely sealed in fifteen. Spent the whole damn night and a lot of overtime searching every house, yard, you name it and found nothing. Knocked on every door. He just slipped by us."

"Run down an alley and you're on Lake Street in two minutes. From there," Waschke continued, "a car, a bus, whatever and he's gone."

"Yeah and now the media's really howling. Calling for the chief to resign, all kinds of crap."

"They're idiots. They're just using this to sell newspapers and TV time. Who cares what those assholes think," said Jake, obviously annoyed.

"Yeah, easy for you to say. Unfortunately, the mayor can't take that attitude with them. She'd like to but it don't work that way."

"I guess," Jake replied with a resigned shrug.

"You look like shit," said Holby.

"Thanks."

"What're friends for. Look, when you get out of here, go home for a while. Clean up, get something to eat, maybe take a nap. Come downtown around 4:30. Everybody's out on the streets trying to track down the victim's whereabouts last night or maybe see if we can locate another witness."

"Another witness?" Jake asked, surprised.

"We have one, sort of. Some old guy out walking his dog found the body and saw the freak. Scared the shit out of him and the dog."

"Did he see anything? Give a description?" Jake asked, as calmly as he could.

"Nah. Nothing useful. Pretty vague. When the old man saw him, he was wearing a hoodie or a mask on his head. He must've taken it off cause Doug Foley caught a glimpse of a white guy, like you. The old guy couldn't even give us that much."

"Too bad," Jake replied, doing his best to keep the relief he felt out of his voice.

The door opened and a woman in a doctor's coat with a stethoscope draped around her neck walked into the room, looked over the two men and said, "I'm Dr. Canby and you must be Lieutenant Waschke," she said as she stepped over to Jake as he sat back down on the bed. She removed the same style penlight that the first doctor had, turned it on and looked into Jake's eyes, pointing the light into his pupils.

"Don't they have any real doctors around here? You know, gray haired old guys," Waschke asked.

"Great. Just what I need this morning. A dinosaur," answered the thirty- something blonde woman.

"Aww, come on Doctor. I'm just kidding," he said with a weak laugh.

"Oh, that was a joke. I'll remember to laugh later."

She spent the next two minutes poking and prodding, trying to annoy him as much as she could without being too obvious. Finally, satisfied with her inspection, she pronounced him likely to survive if she didn't kill him herself.

"You're a class act, Jake," said Holby as the door clicked closed after the neurologist had left.

"I was trying to flirt with her," he said, defensively. "How was I to know she couldn't take a joke?"

"I'll get the word out to everybody to be back by 4:30. We'll have a briefing then to see what, if anything, anyone's turned up. Meantime, you go home for a while and that's an order."

"Yeah, I suppose you're right. I don't feel much like pounding the pavement today, anyway. I'll need a ride."

"After what you cost the city last night, call a cab."

EIGHTEEN

"Thanks, Mac," said Waschke to the uniformed officer as the squad slowed to a stop in front of Jake's apartment building in South Minneapolis. "Now get yer ass out there and catch this guy for me, will you?"

"He's your problem, dickhead," replied Sergeant Steven McDonough. "I'm just here to eat doughnuts, write a ticket once in a while and wait for my pension."

"Yeah, I can see that about the doughnuts," Jake answered, poking his friend in the spare tire encircling his waist.

"Ask me for a ride again sometime, Jake. See what it gets you."

"It'll get me a ride."

"Go on, get out of here. I gotta go protect and serve for a while."

"That'll make me sleep better," Jake said as he wearily pulled himself out of the door of the car. "Thanks again," he continued as he slammed the door.

He closed and locked the door to his apartment, walked into the living room tossed his raincoat on the only chair in the almost empty room, flipped open his cell and punched in the private number he knew by heart, impatiently waiting for an answering voice. After the fourth ring, he heard a click then a female voice finally responded.

"Daniel Waschke, please," Jake said to the receptionist at his brother's office.

"I'm sorry, sir," the voice replied, "but Mr. Waschke is in a meeting. May I take a message?"

"How long will he be?" Jake asked.

"I'm not sure, sir," she said. "Probably not much longer. Would you like to leave a message?"

"Yeah, I guess. Tell him to call his brother, and it's urgent," Jake said. He gave her the number just to be sure his brother had it, hung up the phone and headed toward the bathroom.

Twenty minutes later, feeling a little better after washing away the grime leftover from the previous night, he stood at the small living room window staring out at the alley that ran behind his building. He was dressed in his terry cloth bathrobe, his hair still wet from the shower, thinking about the difficult phone call he awaited, impatiently wondering why the phone would not ring yet tremendously dreading it at the same time. Hoping for a reprieve from somewhere, anywhere.

He finished his cigarette, smashing it out in the ashtray he had been holding, and went into the bedroom to get dressed. As he was buttoning the jeans that were becoming a little too tight around the middle, the silence was finally broken by the ringing of his cell. He hurried back into the living room, zipping up his pants as he rushed to the small table where he had left the phone.

"Yeah, Waschke," he answered as he put the phone to his ear.

"Jake," he heard his brother say. "How are you? Are you all right? I called the hospital as soon as I heard, and they told me you'd been in an accident and had a mild concussion."

"I'm all right. Listen, we have to meet. Today. Right now," Jake said trying to sound controlled.

"We need to meet? Right away? Why?" Daniel asked, confusion and uncertainty in his voice.

"Why!" Jake roared. "What do you mean, why? You know damn well why."

"I do? What? Calm down. Why are you yelling? If you want to meet I guess we can, but I don't know what you're talking about. You want to come here, to my office?"

"What? Huh? No, Danny. Not at your office. Look, one hour. You know where we used to hang out when we were kids? Above the river at the end of Summit? I'll meet you there, alone, in one hour. Okay?" Jake said, confused with his brother's attitude.

"I'll have to check my appointments first ..."

"Bullshit. Cancel them. Be there in one hour, Danny. No excuses."

"All right Jake. I'll be there. See you then," Daniel said as Jake hung up the phone.

Jake crossed the Mississippi over the Lake Street bridge and took the first right at the bridge's east end to head south on East River Road Parkway. The previous night's storm had moved on into Wisconsin leaving in its wake a bright, beautiful, warm spring day. The kind of day that invariably uplifted the spirits of all who experienced it. It put a smile on the faces of all Minnesotans, a bounce in their steps and oddly, added ten miles per hour to the freeway traffic. Everyone feeling just a little more alive, a little bit better at having survived another Minnesota winter and the knowledge that summer was finally approaching.

All, that is, except for Jacob Waschke. The last thing Waschke felt as he swung around the corner to head down the tree lined avenue running parallel to the Father of Waters was springtime elation. He was in his prized, pet car, his one real indulgence, a vintage 1982 cream-colored T-top Corvette. He had bought the car used about ten years before and drove it only when necessary or, on a day like this one, when the weather and his mood both matched. Today, however, was a necessity since last night's attempt at trick driving down the side streets of Minneapolis had, literally, blown up in his face and cost him his department car.

He pushed down on the accelerator to send the sleek sports car quickly up to fifty for the one mile run to his rendezvous. A meeting he would have given anything to make go away, his life included, were it not so necessary. He had stayed off the freeway and taken surface streets instead, to give himself a little extra time alone to think. To attempt to work out in his mind what he would say and how he could handle the situation in which he now found himself.

Nothing had come to mind, still a bit hazy from the welt on his forehead, to prepare him for this confrontation with the brother he had loved, pushed, prodded, protected and ultimately, come to be so proud of as the governor's top man.

He parked the car along the cul-de-sac at the place where Summit meets the bluff overlooking the river, walked down the grassy incline to the edge of the cliff and stood on the lip of the limestone ledge. Jake looked out over the river valley, watching the river flow past. After a few minutes, he turned his back to the cliff and walked up the grassy knoll to the park bench placed forty or so feet from his perch.

At almost precisely the time he had told Daniel, he heard a car pull up and park in the circle. A moment later he heard a car door close and footsteps on the asphalt driveway. He remained seated on one end of the long bench, bent at the waist, forearms resting on his thighs while he continued to smoke waiting for the other half of the bench to be occupied.

"So, what's so urgent?" Daniel still standing as he looked over the parking area. Jake leaned forward as he sat on the opposite end of the bench. Daniel sat down, made a half turn in his seat to face his older brother, crossed his legs, smoothed his tie, draped one arm over the back of the bench and waited for Jake to respond.

Finally, after an almost full-minute's silence between them, Jake took one last hit on his cigarette, dropped it on the wet dirt at his feet, blew out the smoke and without turning to look at Daniel, said, "Remember when we were kids, how we used to come down here, along the river and the hills? We could spend the whole day down along here. From the Ford dam all the way down to the Franklin bridge. Hell, we knew every rock and tree along here. Just roaming around. I just realized a bit ago how much I miss that."

"Is that what you wanted? To come down here to reminisce about what we did when we were kids? I have things to do, Jake."

"And we used to come down here sometimes to escape, too," Jake continued, ignoring Daniel as if he had not spoken.

"I remember how pissed off Mom would be when she'd find out where we'd been."

"Yeah, Louise didn't like us coming down here. Remember the time you fell, down off that big sewer below the bridge on Lake? And you fractured your leg and I had to carry you home. Took almost two hours."

"Yeah, I do remember that," said Daniel, warming to the subject. "Mom wanted to kill us both," he continued, laughing at the memory.

"I was happy to do it, too," Jake said as he sat up and placed a brotherly hand on Daniel's shoulder. "I was always there for you and I'm there for you now, too."

"I know you were, Jake. I always appreciated everything you did for me."

"And I was always proud of you, happy to be there for you. Help you and protect you. You know that don't you?"

"Jake, just, uh, what's the problem? What do you think is wrong?" Daniel softly asked, looking straight into his brother's reddening eyes.

Jake sat silently staring at Daniel for thirty or so seconds, Daniel staring back. Finally, Jake said, "What's wrong? Where were you last night, Danny? Between ten and midnight."

"Why? What do you mean, where was I? Um, uh, where do you think I was?" he answered as his eyes darted furtively around the cul-de-sac. "I was uh, home, of course."

"Can Lori verify that?"

"What? Why? I mean, yeah, of course she can."

"Can Lori verify that you were home last night between ten and midnight?"

"Well, um, no, she can't. She was out. A bridge game or something."

"Can anyone else verify it? The kids? Anyone?"

"Well, no, I guess not. They're in bed by nine on school nights. Just uh, what are you getting at here, Jake?" Daniel asked suspiciously. "Am I a suspect of some kind? That woman that was murdered. You think I did it?"

Jake looked his younger brother directly in the eyes and quietly asked, "Why would you ask that? I didn't say anything about that. What would make you ask me something like that?"

Daniel took another quick look around the area, leaned toward his older brother and said, "Well, I, uh, don't know. What else could you be asking about?"

"Are you still in therapy?" Jake asked ignoring his brother's remark.

"That's none of your business."

"Who are you talking to, Danny? Remember me?" Jake said, firmly, calmly and back in control.

"Okay, you're right. Sorry," Daniel answered, admonished. "No, I'm not in therapy anymore. I thought you knew that. I haven't been for a while now."

"I want you to go back to that shrink. What's his name? Dr. Lester. Call him today and make an appointment."

"Why? I don't need to. I'm fine. I had some issues, sure. But I'm fine."

"Danny," Jake continued as he slid across the bench, placed an arm around his shoulders, leaned over and whispered directly into his ear, "I saw you last night. That was me who crashed the car while you were running down the street away from the other cop. I know it was you."

"Whoa!" Daniel almost yelled. He threw up his hands as if to ward off his older brother, stood up from the bench and took several backward steps away from his accuser. Still holding his hands up, palms out, again looking quickly about, he said, "No way, you couldn't have seen me. No, no, you ah, must've, ah, thought you saw me when you took that shot to the head. But," he continued, "I swear, it wasn't me."

"Danny, Danny, Danny. Calm down. This conversation stays right here. Just between us. You know I'll protect you. I just want you to get some help. Please. For your sake," Jake said as he rose from his seat and stepped closer to Daniel.

Daniel dropped his arms, a mistrustful look on his face as the larger man gently took his left arm to lead him back to the bench.

"Jake, wait, wait a minute," Daniel tried to protest.

"Just sit down and listen to me a minute will you? I just want to talk."

"Jake, no, look," Daniel said as he tried to pull his arm from his brother's grasp, "It wasn't me, I swear. "

Jake stepped forward right up to the smaller, younger man, the burly intimidating cop taking over, taking control. He grabbed both of Daniel's arms, pinning them to his sides, put his face so close to his younger brother their noses almost touched, the foul odor of the cigarettes penetrating Daniel's sudden fear, and said, "Listen to me, goddamnit, remember me? Remember who I am? This is not bullshit. We have to deal with this. I know what I saw. I told my boss I can't remember, but I saw you lying on the sidewalk, under that light. You looked right at me so don't tell me it wasn't you?"

"No, no, no," Daniel protested as he again pulled away from Jake's hold and tried to push the bigger man away.

"Keep your voice down," Jake snarled.

"No, damnit," Daniel said, lowering his voice. "I'm telling you, it wasn't me. I'm not your little brother anymore," he continued. "You can't push me around and you can't prove anything. You hit your head and suffered a concussion.

"I'm telling you, I don't know what you think you saw but it wasn't me. I was home last night, by myself and I don't need to prove shit. I'm a lawyer, remember? You need to get that head looked at. I'm out of here," he continued as he took several more steps backward, turned and walked across the parking area up the short incline in the direction of his car.

Jake stood frozen by his brother's outburst. So out of character for the relationship the two of them had ever since they were small boys. Stunned by Daniel's assertiveness, for several seconds all he could do was stand in place, his mouth slightly open, a disbelieving look in his eyes, staring at the sight of his brother's back as it moved away from him.

His mind snapped back and his feet began to move, tentatively for the first few steps then quickly breaking into a run, an exercise he religiously avoided. He caught up with Daniel just as Daniel began to open the minivan's door and breathlessly said, "Danny, come on, wait a second. . ."

Daniel turned to face him, his lips pressed firmly together, his eyes narrowed, his body stiffened and said, "No. You wait a second. I'm fine, Jake. I've been fine for many years now. I don't need therapy and I don't care what you think you saw." He paused as Jake caught his breath, softened his tone and added,

"Look, you took a good shot to the head. You have a concussion for chrissake. When that happens, the mind can do some funny things. When you're ready to admit your mistake, give me a call. I still love you. You're my brother and I always will, but you've got to get a grip. You're obviously stressed out over this thing. Give me a call when you've settled down." He got into the van, closed the door and started the engine. Jake could only stand and watch as the van made the circle to head east on Summit.

As it drove off, Jake quietly said to himself, "I know what I saw, little brother."

NINETEEN

Jake sat impatiently waiting for the westbound light on Lake Street at Forty Second to turn green. He was drumming the fingers of his left hand on the steering wheel, staring straight ahead at the grinning face of a personal injury lawyer staring back at him from the billboard on the rear-end of a bus he sat behind. "Asshole," he said to himself. "Behind every ambulance you'll find one of our mobile units," he chuckled thinking that should be the guy's advertising slogan.

His eyes shifted slightly to his left as he noticed a man crossing the intersection almost in front of the bus. The man had short brown hair and was wearing a green army fatigue jacket and faded blue jeans. He walked quickly toward the opposite corner, his hands thrust into his pockets which Jake found odd on such a warm day.

The man's head moved back and forth in quick jerky motions apparently surveying his immediate surroundings. Just a couple steps from the front of the bus his head turned toward Jake, giving him an excellent view of the man's face through the windshield. For a moment, the two of them stared directly at each other. Instead of turning his head to continue the surveillance of his surroundings, the man continued to look straight at Jake as he made the final two steps to put the bus between them. A look that lasted less than two seconds but caused Jake to refocus his attention.

The light turned green and the bus pulled away, but Jake remained motionless, wanting another look at the pedestrian. As the bus moved out of his line of sight, he saw the man again, now crossing Forty Second heading in the same direction as Jake. He remained stopped, staring at the man's back for another two or three seconds until the car behind him impatiently beeped, causing his foot to reflexively move from the brake to the accelerator. The Vette's powerful engine quietly rumbled as he slowly moved forward to pass through the intersection.

He pulled alongside the man, almost to the opposite corner, and turned his head to get a last look at the face his memory told him he knew but could not identify. As he pulled alongside the man, he slowed the car, not much faster than the walking figure and the man, once again, looked directly at Jake, no more than ten feet away. They stayed this way for another one or two seconds and just as the walker reached the curb, he turned to look straight ahead and continue down the sidewalk.

Jake pushed down on the gas and the sleek car sped off down the street while he tried to shake the cobwebs from his memory to determine the man's name. "I know him from somewhere," Jake said quietly to himself. "A dirtbag, that's for sure. But who and from when and where?"

Jake continued west on Lake, intending to get on 35W for the trip home, still trying to put a name to the face. As he passed Minnehaha, the light in his head came on as the name came suddenly to him. His thoughts racing now and suddenly the throbbing in his head gone, he flipped the turn signal on to move to his right, punched down on the gas sending the car surging forward, cut in front of a car to his right and made the sharp right turn on Hiawatha, his tires loudly squealing as he went through the turn. The thought of going home replaced by a new sense of urgency to get downtown, back to his office and a certain closed case file.

TWENTY

Marc sat in the hallway on one of the padded benches, his legs crossed resting his back against the wall by the doors of courtroom 1250. He was waiting for his divorce client to arrive, so they could do the brief, formal hearing to finalize the case. He was a few minutes earlier than he would normally be for a court appearance like this one and his client was probably unfamiliar with downtown Minneapolis so, he assumed, she was trying to find parking and would be along shortly. He had done, literally, hundreds of these types of hearings over the years and only needed about one minute to brief his client to prepare her for it.

He glanced at his watch for the third time since he had taken his seat. He heard the soft bell of the elevators announce the arrival of one of the cars and hoped it meant his client had arrived. Relieved to see her come around the corner from the bank of elevators and into the hallway he held up a hand and waved it slightly, so she would notice him on the semi-crowded floor. Her face lit up with recognition and she wiggled the fingers of her right hand at him as she quickly walked toward him.

"Hi," she began as she dropped onto the seat next to Marc. "I had a helluva time finding a place to park."

"It's okay. You're on time."

"Christ I'm nervous, Marc. Can I smoke? I sure could use a cigarette," she said

"No," he laughed. "No smoking in Minnesota. You know the rules. Anyone caught smoking in Minnesota will be shot on sight, for his own good," Marc said in mock seriousness.

"Really," she agreed with a laugh.

"Calm down," he said, becoming serious. "This is no big deal, Kathy."

"Really?"

"Really. Look, when we go in, you go up by the witness stand the clerk will swear you in and you sit down in the witness chair. I'll ask you a series of questions, mostly yes and no type stuff, and that'll be that. It's no big deal. Nothing to it. Takes ten minutes."

"Are you sure? Okay I mean, it's just, I've never been in court before and I'm a little nervous."

"I understand. Trust me. There's nothing to it. Just don't start laughing. Tears are alright but no laughing. I had a client do that once."

"Are you serious?"

"Yeah. She was having a great time divorcing the jackass she was married to. I had all I could do to keep her calmed down. By the time I got her out of there, she was practically rolling on the floor," he said telling her a true story he liked to tell nervous clients to help ease the anxiety and relax them.

"I won't laugh, I promise. I can't believe anyone could. Is that true or are you just telling me that?"

"True story. I swear. It was pretty funny actually. Um, Kathy, about your bill," he continued.

"Oh, yeah, that's right. How much is it?" she asked reaching into her purse and retrieving her checkbook.

"With today's deal and the little bit left to finish it up, eleven hundred dollars," Marc said.

"That much? Okay. Listen, I'll give you half today and half next month, Okay?"

"Kathy, you promised me you'd pay it all today and clear it up. Remember? I know you have the money."

"Oh, all right I will. You're right. I just don't like writing a check for that much."

"I didn't earn it?"

"Every penny, and more. Thanks again for making that cheating asshole pay."

"More? Well, let's see. . ."

"Forget it," she laughed as she began to write the check.

Marc breathed an inaudible sigh of relief as he watched her make out the check. *Well, I can pay my apartment and office rent for another month*, he thought. *Now I can work on next month's child support for Karen and my other bills.* She tore the check from her checkbook and handed it to him. He took it from her hand and handed her the receipt he had already prepared in anticipation.

"Thanks," he said.

"No, really Marc," she said placing a hand on his arm. "Thank you. You've been a big help."

"My pleasure," he said, "Listen, Kathy, there's something else I need to tell you. Warn you about."

"What?" she asked, her apprehension rising again.

"Relax. I just need to, kind of, warn you about something. It's possible, just a little, that the judge might not accept the deal. He may kick us out and not grant the divorce."

"Why? "

"Take it easy. I said it's only slightly possible. Because the agreement that we shoved down your husband's throat is so grossly one-sided."

"Listen," she hissed, "that asshole deserves everything he gets. Cheating on me for three years with that bimbo. He's lucky I didn't cut off his. . ."

"I'm not arguing," Marc said holding up his hands in protest and laughing. "Playing on his guilt is how we did this. Let me explain. Just listen for a minute, okay?

"Divorces are supposed to be fair to both parties. The judge is supposed to be neutral, look it over and make sure that, as best as possible without taking into account any marital misconduct, the divorce is fair and reasonable for both people."

"It is," she interrupted, emphatically.

"It is not," Marc said, "and you know it. You're getting the kids and over fifty percent of his income, plus the house, all of the furniture and personal property, half of his pension plus the business property. This stuff is supposed to be divided up, as close as possible, fifty-fifty," he said as he ticked off the items on his fingers. "He's basically getting his car, his clothes, half his pension and after you get your cut, about a thousand bucks a month to live on."

"Screw him," she said.

"Not my job," Marc said, which made her smile.

"Not mine anymore, either," she chuckled. "He wasn't worth a damn at that either."

"Let me put this away," he continued. "If I was sitting here with your husband and we had the same deal with him getting everything you're getting, and you getting his share, no way would the judge accept it."

"Really?"

"Not a chance. He shouldn't accept it. Hell, I wouldn't have even submitted this deal on behalf of a man. Wouldn't even try it."

"So, you think he'll throw us out?" she asked, now becoming very concerned.

"No, not at all. This is Hennepin County. I think he'll sign it without batting an eye."

"Why do you say that?" she asked, obviously relieved.

"Because this is Hennepin County and I'm sitting here with the wife, not the husband," Marc said sarcastically.

"Yeah, but everything you see on TV and in the papers, the woman always gets screwed in the divorce," she said again with emphasis. "So, it's only fair that it goes the other way once in a while."

Marc laughed heartily at this last statement and said, "Well, don't you believe everything you see in the papers. It ain't so. Look," he continued, "it might be true of wealthy people, in fact, it probably is, and for the poor. But for them, divorce is always a lousy deal simply because they're poor and don't have enough money to go around. But for the vast majority of people in the middle, if anyone gets screwed, it's going to be the husband every time."

"Do you really believe that?" she asked.

"That's certainly been my experience. And I've talked to a lot of women lawyers about this and every single one of them agrees. That crap in the papers is basically feminist nonsense. Usually, no one makes out in the divorce. Both parties suffer. But financially, at least in the short term, the husband is going to get it worse. As far as the courts are concerned, the husband's role in divorce is to pay. Write the checks."

"You think we'll be okay today?"

"Yeah, I think it'll go through, but I figured I better warn you there's a very slim chance it won't. In fact, if the courts were really fair, it wouldn't. But like I said this is Hennepin County, so, I think it will," he said with a resigned shrug. "You look nice today. You wouldn't believe the way some people come dressed to court. Dirty jeans, t-shirts. It's like they're children and you have to tell them to wash their hands before dinner. Unbelievable sometimes."

"Well, thanks," she said laughing. "I figured I could at least put on a dress. Do we have to tell him how old I am? I mean, in front of everybody."

"Kathy, come on. Relax. You're a lovely woman. Besides, he already knows and knowing this judge, he may take a shot at you."

"Hey, that might not be so bad. Judges make pretty good dough, don't they?"

"He's an old geezer. In fact, I don't know how this got assigned to him. Normally, we'd be in front of one of the Family Court Referees. I don't know why it got sent to a judge."

"Is that bad?"

"Kathy relax. It's not anything. It'll be okay, trust me," he said as the court deputy stepped into the hall and called her name.

They followed the deputy into the almost empty courtroom. Marc stopped at the table, placed his file on it and pointed to the place where his client was to go. She was placed under oath, took her seat on the witness stand and after a few preliminary remarks by the judge, calmly answered Marc's questions to build a factual record for the divorce. After seven or eight minutes of questions about the parties, their children and property, Marc walked up to his client with the court's copy of their agreement and had her testify to its fairness for both parties, during which he somehow managed to keep a straight face.

He finished up, returned to his seat at the table and patiently waited for any possible remarks from the bench.

The judge, a gray headed man with many years experience, looked down at Marc's client from his soft, high-backed, leather chair. He leaned toward her as close as he could, smiled brightly at her as she looked back and watching the exchange, Marc began to wonder if the old boy was going to hit on her right there in open court, on the record.

Instead, Marc listened for the next two minutes as the man glowingly praised Marc to his client for what a wonderful job he had done. What a good lawyer she had and what a great settlement he had gotten for her. The whole time Marc quietly sat, his hands folded on the table, his best poker-face expression in place, patiently waiting for the judge to finish.

Finally, the judge looked directly at Marc and said, "Mr. Kadella, you've done an excellent job for your client and I'll gladly accept the agreement and grant the divorce. Ms. Sanders," he continued turning back to the witness, "you may step down and good luck to you."

"Thank you, your Honor," Marc and Kathy said, in unison.

When they got out in the hall, they turned to head for the elevators and she said to Marc, "I thought you said there could be a problem. He thought it was a great deal."

"Hennepin County. What can I tell you?" he answered as he pressed both the up and the down buttons for the elevators. "I have to go upstairs to see someone. I'll let you know when I get the final papers," he said as a down elevator arrived and opened its doors.

"Thanks for everything, Marc. I'll talk to you later," she said as she entered the empty car.

TWENTY-ONE

As he walked into the office entryway he saw Chris Grafton leaving the big office of Connie Mickelson, heartily laughing. Connie was Marc's landlord, the woman who inherited the building from her parents and from whom the others rented space.

"What's so funny?" Marc asked.

"Marc, come on in here," he heard Connie call through the open door. Connie was in her sixties, did divorce and personal injury work and made a good living at both. Divorced four times herself, she clearly knew family law and had a good reputation in the Cities, especially for helping women through difficult divorces. She had been in practice for over thirty years, beginning long before women lawyers became fashionable, and it was the rare case she could not get a judge to nail a husband for a big chunk of her fees.

"You have to hear this," Chris said as he jerked a thumb at the open door. "This could be one for the top ten list."

Marc went into Connie's office, took one of the client's seats at her desk, Carolyn and Sandy following him through the door.

"You won't fucking believe this," said Connie. It always amused Marc to listen to Connie because the woman could out cuss any sailor in the fleet.

"What a dumb broad this one is."

"What?" Marc asked, knowing this would be good.

"Woman calls with a personal injury question, right? So, I take it and she says she wants to sue the cable company that services her apartment building. Says it's their fault she tore up her knee. I ask her to tell me how it happened, and she says they didn't install the cable right.

"She says when they put in the cable for the TV they put the cable outlet on the wall on the opposite side of her living room from her TV set. So, she gets a friend of hers to run a cable from the outlet box to her TV. A couple days ago she trips over the cable and screws up her knee and now she wants to sue."

"How is this the cable company's fault?"

"Well, of course, that was my first question. She says they're to blame because they shoulda put the outlet on the wall by her TV, so she wouldn't have to have the cable on the floor. I said, ma'am, why didn't you just move the TV closer to the outlet? Now get this, she says, 'Oh, you mean I could've done that?'"

"Good god," Marc said amid the laughter from Carolyn and Sandy. "I'm amazed some of these people can even feed themselves."

"Yeah, and she wanted to sue for a hundred grand. Believe that? I, politely, explained to her that it really wasn't the cable company's fault that she tripped over the cable that her friend put in. I wished her luck."

"There's one for the list," said Marc.

"What list?" asked Sandy.

"The top ten dumbest clients list," Carolyn answered.

"Trouble is, that list keeps growing. Ten isn't nearly enough," said Connie.

"She'll call around 'til she finds a lawyer hungry enough to take a shot at it," Marc said.

"No one's that hungry," answered Connie. "Even if she does find someone, he'll learn. Sooner or later the cable company's lawyers will stick it right up his ass anyway, as they should."

"As they should," agreed Marc.

"How'd your default go?" Connie asked, referring to Marc's divorce case. "Old horny Barney Curran let it right through, didn't he?"

"Went fine," Marc answered. "In fact, he spent two full minutes praising me, on the record in front of my client. I couldn't believe it."

"I'm not surprised," she said as she motioned to Marc to close the door after the secretaries had gone back to their work stations. Marc closed the door and took his seat again in front of Connie's desk.

She leaned forward on her desk as a breeze came through the window behind her, rattling the venetian blinds slightly, and whispered to Marc, "Did I ever tell you, I banged his old ass a couple of times?"

"I don't want to hear this, Connie," Marc said, laughing. "This is an image I don't want to have."

"Oh, it's no big deal," she continued, waving her hand at him. "It was a few years back and I was between husbands. Thought it might not hurt me in court. The old fools been on the family bench, off and on, forever. I'll tell you, I think it has done me some good, too. I get some pretty good results in front of him."

"What are you saying, I should sleep with him?" Marc asked, sarcastically.

"Might not hurt," she said, laughing.

"I beg to differ. I think it would hurt."

"Hey! That's not a bad idea. Get on down to his club and do a pick-up-the-soap routine in the shower. Knowing old Barney, he'd take the shot."

"Will you stop."

"What about Tennant? You get in her pants yet?"

"That's none of your business."

"You haven't, huh? Too bad. She's a good looking broad."

"You're a piece of work, Connie. You know that?"

"Yeah, but I have my fun. Life's too short to take it too seriously. Anything new on Karen's tax case?"

"No. We go see the judge on the twenty-fifth. I'll find out then, I guess."

"Well, good luck. I hope you stick one right up the IRS's ass."

"Me too. Besides, I can always use the money."

"Did you tell Karen? About her liability being lifted."

"Yeah, she was pretty pleased."

"Did she at least thank you?"

"Yes, Connie. She did."

"Hey, don't get defensive. She should thank you. You worked hard for her and did a helluva job. She should appreciate it."

"Well, I'm not sure she appreciates it, but she did thank me. No, wait a minute," he continued waving his hands as if in protest. "She appreciates it, I'm sure. It's a helluva weight off her shoulders. It's been quite a nightmare for her. For both of us, really."

"What do you mean?" asked Connie as she leaned back in her leather covered swivel chair and placed both feet up on the desk. "How did this happen, anyway?"

"Many years ago, almost ten now, Karen worked for a restaurant up Northeast. She managed the dining room, did some bookkeeping that kinda stuff. She was put on the signature card at the bank for the owners' convenience because the guy who was running the place had to take a job."

"How many owners were there?"

"Four total. One of them was in the restaurant as a sort of General Manager. He's the one that took the job. Anyway, he'd come in in the morning to open up and tell Karen what deliveries and bills to pay. She signed the checks but what's important here is, she had no independent decision-making authority. Time goes by and these knotheads aren't paying the taxes."

"That's not as unusual as you might think. People do that just trying to keep the business going. They're not trying to screw the government. Just trying to stay afloat. Did Karen know they weren't paying the taxes? "

"Sure, she knew. She filled out the quarterly returns. Even signed them. She'd tell the owners that taxes were owing and they'd tell her it would be taken care of."

"She signed tax returns? No wonder they found her liable."

"Actually, it wasn't that that got her into the soup. It was signing checks. The IRS told her: Because you signed checks, you decided to pay other creditors before the IRS and therefore, you're responsible," he said in a bureaucratic, officious sounding voice which provoked a laugh from Connie.

"It's bullshit and they know it. What really happened was the General Manager died, left no estate for them to grab so, the guy doing the investigation got lazy and just laid it on Karen. It wasn't a real big case for him so, he took the easy way out and nailed the bookkeeper."

"What about the other owners?" she asked.

"He hit a couple of them for a little of it. I found out they settled out for five grand. Karen got hit for the rest," Marc answered.

"Asshole," she said.

"He's just a lazy bureaucrat. Small potatoes to him. You know the type. Lay it on someone, anyone will do, get the file off your desk and get on to other things. Lazy and careless."

"Must've made your lives hell," Connie said sympathetically.

"You don't know the half of it," he replied.

"Didn't you appeal the guy's decision?" she asked.

"Oh yeah, we did. What a joke that was. We go downtown St. Paul, to the IRS office in the federal building. We go into this pissant size office with this kid behind a desk. He couldn't have been more than twenty-five. Tells us he's a lawyer with the IRS. This is no bullshit. The guy looks at Karen and says: 'You know, I didn't know you could be liable for taxes just by signing checks. My wife signs checks where she works and when I get home tonight, I'm going to tell her to get off that signature card. But for your case, sorry it's right here in our rules and there's nothing I can do.' I swear, that's exactly what happened. The whole thing took two, maybe three minutes. That was our appeal. Fool that I was, I assumed this pipsqueak knew the law since he claimed he was a lawyer with the IRS."

"You think he lied?"

"No, not at all. At least I don't think he lied. I think he was just stupid. Didn't know what the hell he was talking about. We were lied to though. I'm sure of that. By a lot of those people down there," Marc said, anger creeping into his voice.

"I'll bet they were fun to deal with, huh?"

"Especially the time they threatened to take our house from us."

"Are you serious?"

"Oh yeah. I had to put us into a Chapter 13 bankruptcy to get them to back off. Between that and this tax thing, our credit is thoroughly shot. Well," he continued with a resigned shrug, "at least the worst is over. It just kind of pisses me off that they pull this shit and nobody has to pay. No one's ever responsible or accountable for it. They just do this to people and go about their merry business. 'Too bad you got shafted but it's not my job to fix it.' You have no idea how many times we heard that line."

"I think this judge will stick it right up their ass for this," she said.

"I hope so. We'll see. I guess I should get some work done today. See you later," he said as he gathered up his coat and file and headed toward the door. He went through Connie's office door and as he headed across the reception area he heard Sandy say into the telephone, "He just came out. Can you hold for a minute, please?"

"Who is it?" Marc asked.

"Linda Martin," Sandy answered, reluctance in her voice.

Marc stopped dead in his tracks, his shoulders slumped, head down and said, "Do I have to talk to her? Tell her I'm dead. Tell her you found me dead in my office."

"No," Sandy said, laughing. "I'm not going to tell her you're dead. Yes, you have to talk to her. Now, get in there and pick up line two."

"Go on, you big baby," Carolyn added.

"You want to talk to her?" he asked, looking at Carolyn.

"She's your client," Carolyn said, both women laughing now.

"That was a mistake," he answered as he walked toward his office door. He quietly closed the door behind him, hung his coat on the coat rack in the corner, took his seat at the desk and stared at the small, green light on his telephone blinking up at him. He sat like this for another thirty seconds or so until he heard Sandy yell at him through the door. He took a deep breath, exhaled loudly, removed the phone from its cradle, punched the blinking button and said, "Hello, Linda. What's up?"

"Do I have to let him see my kids?" he heard his client say without so much as a 'hello' first.

"What now?" he asked wearily while trying to remain pleasant.

"The child support is late. Can I keep him from taking my kids for the weekend?"

"First of all, Linda," Marc began patiently, "they're not your kids. You don't own them. He's their father and he has a right to spend time with them. And they need to spend time with him. We've been through this, remember? Secondly, it's not his fault if the check is late. You wanted the county to withhold the money from his paycheck and send it to you. Call them if you haven't gotten it."

"I can never get through to them," she said.

"That doesn't surprise me. To answer your question, no you cannot withhold visitation from him."

"What if the girlfriend is there? That's immoral and I don't want my kids exposed to it."

"Linda be reasonable. Do you expect the guy to be celibate? He's their father and you'll just have to trust that he's careful around them. We talked to him and his lawyer and he said he would. Okay?"

"It's bullshit. He can do whatever he wants, and I don't get my money and he can still have my kids for the weekend. It sucks."

"They're not your kids only. They're his too. Call the county about your money. They should have it. Anything else?" he asked, his patience now obviously gone.

"No, I guess not," she said.

"I have to go, Linda," he said, calmly.

"All right, sorry Marc," she said chastened. "I just needed to vent a bit, I guess."

"It's all right, Linda. I do have to go now, though. I'll talk to you later."

"Bye, Marc," he heard her say as he began to hang up the phone.

91

He heard a soft knock on his door and before he could answer, Sandy opened it and said, "How was she?"

"Much better than usual," Marc answered.

"She needs a boyfriend. Someone to help her get over the anger and get on with her life," Sandy said.

"That's the nice way of putting it," Marc replied. "Leave the door open, Sandy," he said as he swiveled in his chair and raised the window behind his desk to air the stuffy office.

Marc spent the remainder of the day working at his desk. He went through several files of ongoing cases to make sure everything was up to date. Prepared some final paperwork for court appearances he would make in the near future, dictated several letters to go out the following week and in general, used the time to catch up on the mundane, routine details of his practice and his cases. All the while listening to, and sometimes participating in, the office interplay and casual banter occurring in the office among its inhabitants.

Finally, just before four o'clock, Connie stuck her mostly gray head into the open doorway and said, "You got one more week to score with Tennant or find a new girlfriend. You got it?"

Marc laughed heartily with her and said, "Yes, Mom. I'll do my best."

"Have a good weekend, Marc. I'm out of here," Connie said. "Did I tell you? I may have husband number five lined up. And he has more money than any of the others"

"Keep trying and good luck, Connie" Marc replied giving her a thumbs up sign.

"Luck's got nothing to do with it," she said. "It's how good a blow-"

"I don't want to know," Marc hastily interrupted, laughing.

"You don't know what you're missing. See you Monday," she said as she turned to leave.

TWENTY-TWO

Marc rang the doorbell at Margaret's upscale suburban home and stood patiently waiting for her to answer. He shifted the dozen long-stemmed red roses from hand to hand as he looked over the front of the house. *Has to be six hundred grand if it's a penny,* he thought. *And I live in a six-hundred-dollar a month one-bedroom apartment. She's done all right for herself.*

Just then, he heard the doorknob click and a moment later she stood in the open entryway wearing a black cocktail dress that came just below the knees and black high heeled shoes. He stood staring at her, literally holding his breath without realizing it, for about ten seconds. Finally, she broke the silence by saying, "Well, what do you think?"

"I think you look incredible," he managed to mutter.

"Got the effect I wanted," she said. "For me?" she added referring to the flowers.

"Oh, yeah," he said as he handed them to her.

She took the roses from him and said, "They're beautiful. You're sweet and you shouldn't have. Come in," she added as she backed into the house. "Let me put these in some water and we'll go. I made reservations for 7:30. My treat tonight okay?"

"I remember," he said. "Where we going?" He followed her into the kitchen and waited while she put water and the flowers in a vase. "I like your hair. Looks great."

"Really? Thank God. I spent two hours at the hair salon today so, you better like it," she said as she playfully poked a finger into his chest.

He took the hand she had poked him with and they exchanged a light kiss. "It's always a risk to compliment a woman on her hair," he said. "Because, if she doesn't like it, you look like an idiot. If she does like it, you're okay. You never know. It's just risky. Where are we going?" he asked, again.

"The Riverview Room. Ever been there?" she answered as she turned to the table to get her shawl and a small purse.

"No, I haven't," he said. "I hear it's a nice place."

"Let's go," she said as she took his arm and they headed to the door. "Nice suit. You look good."

Thirty minutes later, they followed the snooty maitre'd through the crowded dining room, along the edge of the empty dance floor in front of the unoccupied bandstand with the idle quartet instruments leaning in their stands. He reached their table and held the chair for Margaret. Marc could not help noticing the admiring glances of several male patrons as they made their way to the table. It made him feel good that other men noticed the woman he was with and it reminded him of the early years of his marriage to Karen. She too could be an attractive lady when she took the time to fix herself up a bit. Unlike a lot of men, it made him proud to know that his taste was shared by others.

She ordered wine and an appetizer and the two of them made awkward small talk for a while even though it was not their first date and they were becoming quite comfortable with each other. *It's a strange ritual*, he thought, *this dating business. It's a wonder people manage to get together at all.*

They ordered dinner and between the wine and the music that had started up, they both began to relax, laugh and enjoy each other's company. The restaurant was a popular place with the downtown legal world. A world in which Marc had had little opportunity, or inclination, to frequent. Margaret was quite at home in the setting as she occasionally nodded or briefly waved an acknowledgement to people, mostly lawyers and other judges, she recognized.

The evening wore on as they ate their meal and he took her onto the dance floor. They laughed at their own clumsiness, their lack of dancing polish. They made several trips back and forth from the table and the wine to the dance floor, becoming more and more oblivious to the other patrons in the restaurant. Caught up in their own laughter and the sight and scent of each other. This went on for the entire evening and after the third bottle of wine had been emptied, were sitting at their table, fingers locked together, sipping coffee and looking at each other like teenagers, when a tall, handsome man with a full head of mostly brown hair, graying at the temples, suddenly appeared at their table.

"Hello, Margaret," the man said. "Nice to see you here."

"Oh, hello, Gordon," Margaret responded as she released Marc's hand obviously slightly startled at the sudden intrusion.

"I'm sorry to interrupt. . .," the man began to say.

"No, it's all right Gordon," Margaret said, back in control.

"I saw you when I came in and I just wanted to say hello," the man continued with, what Marc thought, a slightly arrogant, condescending air. "Marc, this is Judge Gordon Prentiss," Margaret said introducing the man as Marc rose from his chair and exchanged a brief handshake.

"Marc Kadella, Judge," Marc said. "It's a pleasure to meet you,' he added politely.

"Pleased," Prentiss said as he released his grip.

"When did you get here, Gordon? I didn't see you come in," said Margaret.

"Just a few minutes ago," the tall judge replied. "I'm having a late supper with a law school classmate," he added nodding toward a man seated in a booth across the room. He put up his left hand and gestured with it to his dinner companion, indicating that the man should join them. The three of them waited silently the few seconds it took for the average sized man in the obviously expensive double-breasted suit to make his way to their table. When he was within hearing distance, Prentiss turned to Margaret and said, "Perhaps you know him. Margaret, this is Governor Dahlstrom's Chief-of-Staff, Daniel Waschke. Daniel, Judge Margaret Tennant."

"It's a pleasure," Daniel said flashing his politician's smile as he reached down to shake her hand.

Prentiss turned to Marc, who had remained standing, and said, "And this is Margaret's friend. . ., I'm sorry, your name is. . ."

"Kadella, Marc Kadella," Marc said as he shook hands with Daniel. "Pleased to meet you, Mr. Waschke."

"My pleasure, entirely," Daniel said far more sincerely than Prentiss.

"Waschke. I know that name from somewhere," Marc said with a puzzled look. "Do you have a brother or cousin?"

"Jacob," Daniel answered. "Jake Waschke. He's a lieutenant with the Minneapolis police."

"Oh sure," Marc said. "Now I remember. Big guy, right? I defended a case he was involved with. I remember him, now. Decent guy. Straight cop."

"You're a criminal defense lawyer?" Prentiss asked with that same slight condescension that was beginning to annoy Marc. "Well, I suppose someone must."

"It was nice to see you, Gordon," said Margaret almost in dismissal. "And it was nice to meet you, Mr. Waschke,"

"Me too," Daniel said, bowing slightly to Margaret.

"Have a nice evening, Margaret, Mr. Kadella," said Prentiss as he nodded his head slightly at both of them and headed toward his table.

Marc took his seat and Margaret reached across the table, took his hand and said, "You okay?"

"Fine," Marc said with genuine sincerity. "We should probably go, though."

They made the ride back to her home in silence, Margaret worried that the intrusion had done some damage to their evening. Marc, lost in his own thoughts, pulled into her driveway, put the car in park and shut off the engine. He turned in his seat to face her, she looked at him and asked, "A penny for your thoughts?"

Marc leaned on the armrest between them, reached over with his left hand and took her right hand in it, silently wrapping their fingers together. He paused like this for a moment then, finally smiled and said, "J. Gordon Prentiss the third. Or is it the fourth, fifth or eleventh. I can never keep it straight with these guys."

"Is that what's bothering you? That pompous ass?"

He leaned over toward her and she moved slightly to meet him, exchanging a solid, open-mouthed kiss. When they stopped he continued saying, "No. He's not bothering me. I don't let people like that bother me. In fact, I find him and his attitude amusing. I better not tell Connie I ran into him. She'll blow a gasket."

"Connie? Who's Connie?" Margaret asked in a feigned jealous voice.

"Connie Mickelson. She's in my office. A few years back she had a personal injury case. Five-year-old little girl badly mauled by a dog. A mean damn thing. A Doberman as I recall. Anyway, Prentiss was the insurance company's lawyer and he was an absolute asshole to deal with. Convinced the judge it was the kid's fault and found some obscure way to screw the kid out of any money. The judge caved into him and Connie didn't get a dime for the kid."

"She should've appealed. I can't believe she wouldn't have won on appeal," said Margaret.

"Probably. The judge screwed up. But the parents were so intimidated by Prentiss that they didn't want to put the little girl through any more of it so, they dropped it. Connie's still mad about it. She offered to cut her fee for the whole thing to ten percent, but Prentiss had done it to the parents, but good."

"That's a shame."

"Yeah, it is. Well, it happens. What're you going to do? Move on," Marc said. "How well do you know him?"

"Not very. He's been on the bench for a couple years. Was appointed shortly after Dahlstrom's election. He and his firm have heavy political connections," she answered.

"Obviously," Marc said with a laugh, referring to Prentiss' dinner companion.

"From what little I've seen of him, he thinks he should be on the Supreme Court. Not the Minnesota Supreme Court. The United States."

"Well, he's got his eye on you."

"Stop it."

"I'm serious. I know the look."

"Like the one you have now," she said as he continued to lean on the armrest staring straight into her eyes.

He straightened up, removed the keys from the ignition and as he opened his door to get out, said, "That's the one."

They stood at the doorway, their arms wrapped around each other, their mouths locked together. She broke the grip and still in his arms, leaned back and looked up at him. They exchanged several more light, affectionate kisses while he held her, and she held the lapels of his suit coat. Finally, she stepped back breaking his hold, smoothed his coat and said, "Hmmm. Ah, what is this, our third date?"

"Yeah, I guess. Our third official date, I suppose," he agreed.

"Well, I guess that's enough, isn't it?" she asked as she grabbed his tie below his chin and gently began to pull him toward the door. "Come with me, mister. I have use for you."

TWENTY-THREE

As the calendar crept closer to the summer solstice, the sun continued to rise higher in the sky and the days became increasingly longer. Jake had some time to kill, another half hour, maybe a little less, before he took up his Wednesday and Thursday night vigil. This would be the third week in a row he would spend these evenings on his unauthorized stakeout, keeping watch on a house that was not even located in his city. So far, his efforts had yielded no results and it was becoming more difficult to convince his superiors that he was on the streets of Minneapolis with the rest of task force. He was supposed to be cruising the streets, checking informants, hoping for a break that would lead to an arrest.

Maybe that's why everyone's interest was heightened by a case like this one. A serial killer and rapist on the loose was different; a break from the monotony and routine. Jake Waschke, for one would like nothing better than a return to the routine of life. If what he did for a living could ever be called routine. At least an arrest would give the media something else to focus their macabre voyeurism on besides the lack of progress.

Jake pulled his new department issued dark blue Chevy sedan onto 35W at 46th Street and headed south to pick up the Crosstown freeway. He checked the watch on his left wrist and mentally calculated the distance and time to his destination. Satisfied that his timing would have him arrive just as dusk gave way to dark, he settled back in his seat as he headed east on the Crosstown for the drive past Ft. Snelling and the bridge into St. Paul.

A few minutes later he made the left off West Seventh to take the winding ascent up Snelling Avenue and into the Highland Park neighborhood where his younger brother and family lived their comfortable, quiet upper-middle class life.

He arrived at Daniel's street shortly after 9:00 P.M., still light enough to see but it would be totally dark within fifteen minutes. Jake believed that if anything happened it would not be until after dark, but he wanted to be on station before that, just in case Daniel left early. He cruised past Daniel's four bedroom, two story home with the immaculate lawn and shrubbery and to his relief, saw both the van and Lori's Volvo parked in the driveway in front of the garage. He sped up a bit and made a U-turn at the corner and parked his car three houses down from his brother's on the same side of the street. He pulled up behind another car and between the car in his front and the neighbor's trees and bushes blocking the sightlines to the house, he believed he would not be detected by anyone looking out a window.

Settling in for the wait, he slightly turned up the volume on the car's police radio and poured a cup of coffee from the thermos he had brought along. Jake hoped with a great deal of ambivalence that something would happen soon. Hopefully, tonight. The members of the task force were still out cruising the streets where he should be too except he believed he was in the right place now. Sipping the hot coffee, allowing his mind to replay the scene on the bluff above the river when he had confronted Daniel. Since then, instead of the memory from the accident fading with the passage of time as might be expected, the image of his brother lying in the rain under the streetlight had become clearer to him. More focused and real.

Jake had left the scene on the river bluff after confronting Daniel and seeing the familiar man walking down the street. Instead of going home to get some rest, he had hurried straight downtown to police headquarters. During the drive downtown, he searched his memory for the name of the man and it finally came to him just as he pulled into a parking space.

He went straight to the records section to search for a closed case file, hoping no one would notice him and ask any awkward questions. Going into the room with its rows of file cabinets he quickly found the alphabetized drawer he was seeking. Jake pulled the file he was after, looked around to see if any of the other officers in the room were watching him, and then carried the folder to a small table in a remote corner of the room.

Jake sat down at the table and opened the folder to go through its contents, the beginnings of a plan starting to formulate. He read over the basics, the biographical data on the subject to first be sure that this man would fit the profile. Carl Milton Fornich, he read. Age, now, thirty-four. Five feet, ten inches tall, weight one seventy, hair and eye color; light brown and brown.

So far, thought Jake, *just fine*. Pleaded guilty five years ago to one count of second degree criminal sexual conduct. Disappointed, he noticed there was no mention in the file of any use of a weapon during the assault to which he had pled. The investigator's notes in the file indicated Fornich was suspected of at least three or four other rapes, all occurring in public places.

From the records in the file Fornich's criminal history showed two prior misdemeanor assault convictions, one at age twenty-two for beating up a girlfriend, the other a simple bar fight. The history of violence against the girlfriend brought a brief flicker of a smile, but still no weapons used in either case. A weapon would be nice. A knife would be icing on the cake. The file contained a small manila envelope and Jake emptied the contents onto the table. A half dozen photos of Fornich, obviously taken after his arrest, fell out of the envelope. Jake picked them up and looked them over noting that time and prison had not appreciably changed the short haired, plain looking man. He picked up the file's inventory sheet and ran his finger down the column until he came to the line marking the photographs. To his mild surprise, the sheet recorded five photographs, not the six he held in his hand. Looking over the pictures he selected the one that best resembled the Carl Fornich he had just seen on the street, then placed the other photos on top of the folder. Jake sat back in the chair, raised his arms above his head as if stretching, and moved his head back and forth to check the others in the room. Satisfied that no one was watching, he quickly slipped the picture he wanted into his shirt pocket, straightened out the folder and replaced it in the file cabinet before leaving the room.

TWENTY-FOUR

While he waited in the car on Daniel's street, Jake set the half-empty styrofoam cup on the dashboard, rolled the window down and lit his twenty-fifth cigarette of the day. As he reached for the white cup, he noticed a car's taillights come on in Daniel's driveway, visible through the blooming bushes that ran along the neighbor's property line. Jake started the engine as the minivan backed out onto the street and began moving away from him. Waiting until the van reached the next corner, without turning on his lights, he slowly pulled away from the curb to follow. Expecting the van to turn north to travel the short distance to Ford Parkway, the closest main avenue in the area, he was surprised to see the van go straight through the intersection at the corner.

As he passed Daniel's house, he noticed the lights of the Volvo in the driveway come on, momentarily startling him and making him wonder which vehicle Daniel was in. Instinctively, he quickly pulled the car to the curb of the now dark street, parked and watched in his mirror. A few moments later he saw the Volvo back onto the street and head in the same direction as the van. Slumped down and watching as the car went past, Jake saw the clear silhouette of a woman's head and recognized it as his sister-in-law, Lori, driving the car. Waiting until he saw its left turn rear blinker come on at the corner to turn toward Ford Parkway, he quickly pulled away to follow, hoping he had not lost the van.

Jake slowed at the corner to go through the intersection, hoping he could still catch the van, and glanced to his left. Seeing the lights of the Volvo almost two blocks away, he started through the intersection in time to see the minivan pull out of a side street the next block over and speed off in the direction of Lori. He jerked the wheel hard to his left, turned on the lights and pressed down on the accelerator to close the gap between himself and Daniel. As he approached the light at Ford Parkway, he saw the Volvo turn left toward Minneapolis and the van follow it as the amber light came on the corner's semaphore. Again, he punched down on the gas and entered the intersection a second after the light turned red, tires squealing, making the turn onto the Parkway, muttering to himself about his conspicuous driving.

All three cars, Lori, in the lead, went west on Ford. As they did, Jake noticed Daniel do something he thought odd. Instead of closing the distance between himself and his wife, it seemed as if he intentionally allowed several cars to get in between them. They continued this way for another half mile when, abruptly, Lori pulled the Volvo to the curb, stopped the car, quickly exited the vehicle and waved the van over.

Jake pulled into the lot of a Burger King on the corner and slipped into a space that afforded him an unobstructed view of his brother and sister-in-law. They were directly in front of him, across the side street, parked under a bright overhanging streetlight. He was unable to hear their conversation, but it was quite obvious, from her gestures and the look on her face, that Lori was very agitated about something. Jake watched as Daniel left the van and stood passively in the street while Lori, with animated motions and gestures, clearly ripped into him. After more than a minute of this byplay, Lori turned on her heel to head back to the car as Daniel reached for her arm. As he grabbed her, the evening breeze picked up and blew her long brown hair around her face. With one quick motion, she jerked her left arm free of Daniel's grip and brushed the hair from her face so that Jake could clearly see her angrily mouth the words, "Don't follow me." She quickly went to the Volvo's door, Daniel on her heels all the way, got in and slammed the door in his face as he stood helplessly in the street. She backed up the car and sped around him as she raced off down the street to continue her journey, leaving her bewildered husband to sullenly plod back to the van.

So as not to be noticed, Jake had turned off his headlights but kept the engine idling while he watched the almost comic scene on the street. He saw Daniel get back in the van and waited another three minutes while Daniel sat still at the curb. Finally seeing the van's brake lights come on, knowing Daniel was getting ready to drive off, Jake pulled out of his parking space to continue following west on Ford Parkway. They continued this way across the bridge over the Mississippi into Minneapolis. Alarmed now, knowing for sure that Daniel was not reversing course to go home, Jake pressed down on the gas to close the gap between them.

After crossing the bridge, they continued west on Minnehaha Parkway, past the golf course and through the park, to Hiawatha. Daniel stopped for the red light at Hiawatha then made the right turn to head north toward the heart of the city. Jake, who had almost been forced to come up right behind Daniel at the light, rolled through the corner so Daniel would not get too far ahead.

Daniel moved into the left lane and Jake stayed in the right as Daniel moved up alongside a commercial truck. They stayed like this for several blocks, Daniel to the left of the truck, Jake a couple of car lengths behind it, as they cruised down Hiawatha. As they approached 35th Street, a pick-up truck suddenly appeared to Jake's left as the light at 35th turned from green to amber. All at once, the pick-up's driver turned on its right turn signal as the brake lights for the truck came on. The pick-up swerved into the space between Jake and the truck and realizing too late that the truck was stopping, slammed on his brakes. Jake in the split second that these events took place, jammed down on the brake pedal, tightened his grip on the steering wheel, bracing for the impact as Daniel, oblivious to it all, rolled right through the intersection and continued down the street.

The screaming tires of both Jake's sedan and the pick-up shattered the quiet street as the side of the pick-up began to fill Jake's windshield. It kept coming on, closer and closer but also, slower and slower until Jake hit him with a slight thud that lightly shook the car and only managed to push it over a foot or two toward the curb. He came to a complete stop still tightly gripping the wheel, loudly exhaled and slowly allowed his eyes to move about surveying the scene. Realizing the damage was minimal, he shifted into reverse, turned in his seat and saw headlights blazing through the rear windshield, trapping him. He shoved the shift lever into park, unbuckled the seatbelt, jumped from the car and ran around the back of the pick-up in time to see a car, about a block away, change lanes to move behind Daniel.

"Sonofabitch," Jake bellowed as he slammed his palm down on top of the truck's tailgate. He stood in the street alongside the pick-up, fists clenched, the knuckles on his hips and stared down the wide avenue.

"Oh shit, man," he heard the pick-up's driver say as the door thumped closed. "I didn't think the truck would stop, dude. I thought it would go through and I could make the turn."

"Are you all right?" Jake calmly asked the young man with the baggy shorts and baseball cap turned backwards.

"Yeah, dude. I'm okay. How about you?"

"I'm all right. Let's look at the damage," Jake answered as he turned to go back to his car. Jake walked past the dent in the pick-up's passenger door, bent down to look at the police car's front end and ran his hand over the car's bumper.

"Look what you did to my door, dude." he heard the teenager say as he rose from his inspection.

"What I did? You cut in front of me, kid," Jake said as he reached in his coat pocket to retrieve his wallet.

"What do you mean, man. I signaled and everything," the young man began to protest as Jake opened the wallet and stuck the police badge in his face. "Shit. Not good, huh dude?" the young man said as the truck pulled away with a roar that enveloped them in a cloud of smelly diesel fumes.

"Look, kid. There's no damage to my car. I'm too busy for this shit. Get this thing out of my way and we'll call it even. Okay, dude?" Jake added sarcastically.

TWENTY-FIVE

Back in the police sedan, Jake continued up Hiawatha toward downtown, several times considering using the flashing light to clear the minimal traffic. With the three to four-minute lead Daniel gained while Jake dealt with the minor accident, he knew it was futile, with or without the lights. Three times he ran through red lights hoping to close the gap and spot the maroon minivan. Twice his heart jumped and his breathing stopped when he spotted small vans like Daniel's only to discover, when they passed under a streetlight, they were a different color.

He did the fifteen-minute run downtown in under ten, knowing with each block he passed, and red light he ran, his chances of finding his younger brother became less and less. He found himself trying to think like Daniel. Where would he go? What would he do? Would Lori's curbside outburst trigger the monster that Jake believed lurked somewhere deep in Daniel's dark side. A dark side that Jake, from his years as a cop, knew lurked within everyone waiting for someone or something to unlock the door and let the demons loose.

Trying to suppress those thoughts and think like a cop and not a brother, he continued his search for the van. Try to find Daniel and protect him, save him and any potential victim from Daniel's demon. This was the chance he had waited for parked on the street by Daniel's house. The chance he hoped for but prayed would not happen.

He entered the fringe of downtown Minneapolis on the east end by the site where the new stadium was being built and saw another van exactly like Daniel's. This time though, his reaction was calm and controlled. After watching the van for a few moments, he quickly realized it was not the right one. Jake spent the next half hour cruising the almost empty streets of downtown, once waving at Denise Anderson when he saw her waiting for the light at a cross street. He made the short loop down Hennepin and around the bars in the neighborhood of the Target Center. All pretty quiet on this midweek evening. Jake then decided to try Uptown, hoping maybe Daniel went back to his hunting ground off Lake Street. He went quickly down Eighth, weaving through the traffic, and decided he would head for Chicago Avenue, take that south to Lake Street then go west on Lake back toward the last murder scene.

He made the right onto Chicago and as he sped down the street passing under an overhanging light, glanced at his watch, noting that it was almost 10:30. A few blocks before the intersection at Lake, he heard the call numbers for his car and then the dispatcher crackle his name over the speaker as he reached for the microphone.

"This is Waschke," he heard himself say into the small mike in his hand. "Go ahead dispatch."

"Lieutenant, we have a report from a woman in the eleven hundred block of Thirty Fifth Street of a suspicious looking man with a woman entering Powderhorn Park. What is your present location, over?" the female dispatcher explained in her concise monotone.

"I'm northbound on Chicago almost to Lake Street. I can be there in two minutes. What's the status, over?"

"We've dispatched a blue and white to the scene who should be there by the time you arrive. Over."

"Tell him I'm on my way," Jake said as he turned on the the cars flashers in the grill and the dashboard and pressed down on the accelerator.

"Shall we notify the other members of the task force, over?" the voice asked. Thinking faster than he drove, Jake pressed the send button on the mike and replied, "Negative. Hold off on that. Probably just a couple of kids sneaking into the park to fool around. Let me check on it. Over and out." The last thing he wanted, if it was Daniel, was that park crawling with cops. One cop in one squad he could handle. He had to be first on the scene to keep control of things, if at all possible.

TWENTY-SIX

Making the left onto Thirty-Fifth a little too fast caused his tires to squeal and his rear end to slide in the street on the sand left over from the winter. Red light still flashing, speeding down Thirty-Fifth until he saw the squad car, facing in his direction, parked on the wrong side of the street. He came to a stop a few feet in front of the blue and white and put the transmission in park and shut off his flashing lights. Jake left the engine idling, got out of the car and approached the uniformed policeman, illuminated by the lights of the two cars, speaking to a salt and pepper haired elderly woman.

"Lieutenant Waschke," he said as he flashed his badge to the officer. "What do you have?"

"Yes sir, I know. Well, Lieutenant, I just got here myself," replied the young officer. Turning to the woman, he continued, "Ma'am, why don't you tell the Lieutenant what you started telling me?"

"Are you a policeman, too?" she politely asked Jake. She was standing on the boulevard grass, looking frail and frightened, her arms folded together against her small breasts, shivering slightly in the thin cotton dress in the cool of the dark night.

"Yes, ma'am. Now, please tell us why you called," Jake said patiently. He stood in the street at the curb, six inches below the woman who just came up to his chin and knew his presence, a large white cop, would be both unsettling and reassuring to her.

"Well, like I started to tell this young man," she slowly began, nodding toward the uniform. Jake looked at the other cop noting the name on the shirt tag as Lund as the woman continued. "I seen 'em a little bit ago. You know, a white man with a woman going into the park. Well, I thought it looked, strange. What with them killings and all going on. Well anyway, they was walking kinda strange. So, I figured I'd better call the police."

"How do you mean, ma'am," Jake said, "walking strange?"

"Well, you know, he had his arm around her shoulders. It didn't look like they was, you know, walking together. More like, he was forcing her. Almost pushing her along, like. She didn't seem like she was willing to go along, you know what I mean?"

"Yes ma'am. I think I do," Jake said. "Could you see their faces? Could you tell what they looked like?"

"No, not from where I was. I live over there," she said, pointing to the house next to where they were standing. "I was on the porch, just getting some air and I noticed them going past that light across the street there, in the park by the trail. There's a walk down there by the lake and I seen them heading that way," she continued, pointing now across the street, into the park to her left. "They was going down by that bunch of pine trees over there, last I seen them."

"Could you see what color clothes they were wearing?" Jake asked.

"No. I'm getting a little along and my eyes aren't that good. Looked like dark clothes. But I could see they was both white when they went by the light."

"You got her name and address?" Jake asked Patrolman Lund.

"Yes, sir. Mildred. . ." the policeman started to respond but was cut off by a sharp, piercing scream. A scream from an obvious female throat that shattered the quiet south Minneapolis neighborhood and sent both men scrambling.

"Go back inside your house, lock the door and wait for us," Jake shouted at the now terrified woman as she turned to hurry toward her home. "Get up to the north side of the park. Call for back up. I'll try to flush them to you. Hurry goddammit," he said to the startled patrolman as Jake ran back to his car. Just as he reached the door and began to fling it open, the stillness of the night was again shattered by the same ear-splitting scream. Only this one was abruptly cut off after less than three seconds, just long enough for Jake to locate its origin.

Jumping into the driver's seat, Jake jerked the shift lever into reverse and backed up a few feet to clear the squad car. He spun the wheel to his left to head the car into the park and slowly went over the curb, his sore, very stiff neck a reminder of his last encounter with a concrete curb. Jake eased the car up onto the park grass and as soon as the back wheels cleared the curb, angled the car toward the direction of the scream. He went down a short hill, the car's headlights reflecting off the surface of the small lake for which the park is named, made a sharp left turn when he reached the asphalt path. As the car straightened from the turn, he caught a glimpse of movement in the wash of its headlights. A shadow flitting between the trunks of a stand of tall fir trees about a hundred feet straight in front of him.

Following the walkway, he pressed hard on the gas to get to the opposite side of the pines. Passing the edge of the trees, the walkway came a little too close to the lake's edge for a car and the rear wheels went over the edge and into the soft wet sand along the shoreline. Anxious now, he pressed the accelerator too hard with the predictable result of burying the rear wheels up to the hubs. Muttering curses at himself for his stupidity, Jake quickly reached in the glove compartment for the large silver flashlight, grabbed a hand-held radio and went out the door to give chase on foot.

Jake ran toward the trees and when he reached them, began walking along the edge of the stand of tall firs slowly moving the light back and forth as he went. He began climbing the hill that would lead him out of the park to the houses on the west side when his eye caught sight of another shadow of movement up the hill to his right. Playing the light over the area where he saw the movement, working the flashlight back and forth, he trotted slowly up the hill toward the spot.

As he placed the radio in a pocket of his sport coat, the light's beam flashed over a dark object wiggling in the grass. Had they not been moving he would not have noticed the man's legs working to regain their footing on this steep part of the hill. Jerking the light back he was just in time to see the figure reach the hill's crest and begin sprinting away.

Jake began to give chase, huffing and puffing his way up the hill knowing there was no way he would catch his quarry even if he wanted to. He slowed to a walk where his flashlight had caught his quick glimpse of the man, the hill at this point rising almost straight up the final fifteen feet to the top. As he was about to begin the ascent, he felt his left foot kick a solid object on the ground. Instead of continuing his futile pursuit, he stopped and pointed the light down at the spot where he had kicked the object. Playing the light over the thick grass, just as he was about to give up and finish his climb, the light flashed off a bright metal object lying a few feet to his left.

He stepped over to the spot encircled by the beam, squatted in the grass and softly said, "Well, well, what have we here?"

Waschke removed a handkerchief from the hip pocket of his slacks, held it by one corner and unfolded it with a flick of his wrist. Carefully, he used the handkerchief to pick up the shiny object and held it up in the light. He turned the serrated seven-inch knife over in his fingers as one or two drops of fresh blood dripped from the blade onto the grassy hill. Taking a quick look around to be sure he was unobserved, Jake quickly wrapped the handkerchief around the long blade which left part of the white plastic handle exposed and carefully placed the knife in the inside pocket of his coat.

Rising from his squat, he started back down the hill toward the stand of pine trees. As he walked, he removed the radio from his pocket, turned it on, pressed the transmit button and said, "This is Waschke. I think I saw him heading to the east side of the park to Twelfth Avenue. Anybody copy? Over."

"This is Lund, Lieutenant. I read you and I'll be on Twelfth in a minute. Over."

"Did you call for back-up? Over," Waschke said into the radio as he reached the edge of the trees.

"Roger that, Lieutenant. They'll be here any second."

"Here's one now. You continue searching east of the park. I'll send help to you. My car's stuck in the lake. Over," Jake said as he passed through the trees toward the headlights coming at him from the same hill he had driven down. Waving the squad car to a stop, Jake went to the driver and instructed her to go back on the street to the east side of the park to help Lund in the search. Before finishing his misdirected instruction, two more cars, both with their lights flashing, came careening over the crest of the short hill. He waved them both to a stop as the first car began to circle around to go back up the hill to the street.

A short while later, after instructing other arriving cops to search the streets and the park; Jake heard one of the police officers searching the park grounds yell, "Over here. Lieutenant! Hey. Over here," the man continued to yell in an agitated, excited voice. Jake hurried toward the sound of the voice and the flashlight beaming back and forth, as did the other eight officers searching the park. He was the second one to arrive at the source of the yelling and as he hurried up to the man, he heard him say, "There, Lieutenant. Right over there. Behind those bushes," pointing his light at a small bush on the edge of the pines.

"Okay. Take it easy. I'll take a look," Jake said. He turned to the other officer, the first to arrive and said to her, "Keep everyone back. We don't need a bunch of people stomping around in there."

"Sure thing, Lieutenant," she said.

"It's just awful. I think I'm going to be sick," said the one that discovered the body.

"Take it easy, son. You'll be all right," Jake replied as he gingerly began following his flashlight to the other side of the bush.

A half hour later, after his car had been pushed from the edge of the water, he stood in the street leaning on the door watching Roger Holby walk out of the park toward him. Jake casually puffing on a cigarette, waiting for his boss.

"He slipped us again," Holby said as he stepped up to Jake, disappointment obvious in his voice. "We picked up a couple of guys, but they don't sound right."

"Yeah, I heard," Waschke said.

"You sure he went out that way," Holby said, pointing east down the street.

"No Roger, I told you, I'm not sure," Jake replied obviously irritated. "I went up the far edge of those trees," he continued as he pointed, "and I thought I might've seen some movement through the trees on the other side. It was pretty dark where I was standing. I'm not sure at all. I didn't see him go out the other way so, I figured that was our best shot. Okay? He could've gone anywhere but I didn't see him."

"We'll seal off the whole park tonight and get the lab guys out here at first light. We'll go over this place with a fine-tooth comb."

Jake dropped the cigarette on the ground, crushed it underfoot and said, "Well, I'm bushed. I'll be in first thing in the morning. I'll talk to you then."

"All right, Jake. See you then," Holby said. Then added, "Jesus Christ, Jake. This has to stop. We have to get this guy."

Jake paused before he got into the car and standing with the open car door between himself and the deputy chief, wearily sighed and said,

"Yeah, Roger. I know. We'll get him eventually, but we need something. A witness would be good. Too bad the old lady didn't get a better look. Who knows, maybe somebody saw him running down the street."

"I know," said Holby. "I'm going to pull everyone in and do a house-to-house, see if anyone might've seen him. Maybe see if we can get something in the media. You know, put out the word for anyone who might've seen somebody running or acting suspicious."

"Great. Every nut in town will call. You better get more detectives on this. But you never know. It might get us something. I'll see you in the morning," Waschke said as he got in the car, shut the door and started the engine.

TWENTY-SEVEN

Jake quickly drove out of the area in the general direction of his home. After he had gone about two miles, not wanting to use his cell phone, he found an all-night gas station with a pay phone in the lot. He pulled into the lot and over to the phone to place his call. He listened to it ring almost twenty times and just as he was about to hang up, he heard a familiar voice answer.

"Do you recognize my voice?" Jake asked.

"Yeah, dude. What time is it, anyway," the man said.

"A little after midnight," Jake replied. "Where were you?"

"I was in bed, man. Sleeping."

"I need to see you. Tonight, now," Waschke growled. "Get your ass out of bed and meet me at Tooey's in twenty minutes."

"Now? You gotta be shittin' me, dude," came the irritated response.

"Twenty minutes," Jake said and hung up the phone.

Twenty-three minutes later, as Jake finished a small glass of beer, he saw a scruffy looking man come through the front door of the quiet neighborhood tavern two blocks from the informant's home. The small man looked around the dimly lit bar and after spotting Jake in the corner booth, made his way past the mostly empty tables and took the seat opposite Jake.

"You didn't have to get all dressed up," Jake said, sarcastically referring to the dirty flannel shirt and ripped up blue jeans. "You could've at least run a comb through that mop," he added looking at the man's disheveled curly brown hair.

"I was sleeping, dude. Ya know?"

Just then, a waitress appeared at the booth and said, "Can I get you guys anything?"

"Yeah," Jake replied. "Another couple glasses of Miller."

The bored, middle-aged woman turned to get their drinks and when she was out of hearing range, Jake turned to his companion and said, "Listen, Marty. You want to square things with me, once and for all?"

"I don't mind helping you out, Jake. You know that. Besides, you've always been fair with me. I got no complaints."

"Yeah, I know," Jake said, nodding somberly. "But this time, we're going to have to clean you up because you'll have to testify."

"Hold it," the man whispered as he leaned over the table, an anxious look in his eyes as they darted back and forth. "That wasn't the deal, dude, remember? No testifying. You promised."

Jake started to respond then checked himself as the waitress approached with their drinks. Jake gave her a ten for the six-dollar charge which brought a friendly smile when he told her to keep the change. He turned his attention back to Marty Hobbs and said, "I promised nothing you little cockroach. You'll do as I say, or I'll have your ass. You got it? Now, relax. It's no big deal to testify. You're a bright guy. You can handle it. I'll help you through it, no problem."

"I don't know, Jake," Marty said shaking his curly head. "What am I testifying to, anyway? I don't even know what the hell you're talking about."

Waschke pulled out of his shirt pocket the picture he had pilfered from the closed case file and slid it across the table to his co-conspirator. Marty picked it up, held it up in the poor light and said, "Yeah. So, who is it?"

"Where were you tonight, around 10:30?" Jake asked, ignoring the question.

"Home. I got home about 9:00. Why? Who is this guy?"

"Relax. We'll get to it. Were you alone?"

"Yeah, I was. I watched a little TV, did a little smoke and went to bed around 11:30. I got a job. Have to be at work at 7:00."

"Not tomorrow. Call in sick. You're staying home," Jake said pulling two fifty-dollar bills from his wallet and handing them across the table.

"Okay, why am I staying home?"

"Tomorrow morning, at 9:20 precisely, I want you to call the number on the back of that picture and ask for me, personally. Tell whoever answers that you want to talk to the cop you've seen on TV. The one looking for the serial killer. Don't ask for me by name. You got it?"

"Yeah, I got it. Then what?"

"I'll take the call, but just in case there's some reason I can't, you tell whoever you're talking to you might've seen someone we want last night. That means tonight. We had another killing tonight at Powderhorn. I know who it is and I need your help. I need a witness to stop this guy."

"No shit," Hobbs said, his eyes wide with amazement. "How do you know, dude?"

"That's not important. That guy in the picture, that's him and I need you to identify him. You'll say you were walking down the east side of Chicago, going south, when you saw this guy come tearing ass around the corner of Thirty Fourth and Chicago. You got a good look at him and you can identify him."

"Why am I calling?" Marty asked, becoming serious, now.

"Good question. Because you heard on the news about the killing at Powderhorn and you saw this guy a little after 10:30 just a couple blocks from the park. You'll look through mug books, I'll help you, and maybe talk to a sketch artist. Probably not because you're going to pick this guy out of the second book. Understand?"

"Yeah, no problem."

"You have to make it look good though, okay? Take your time. Be cool about it. You spot him in the second book and I'll do everything else. Okay?"

"What was I doing on Chicago and Thirty-Fourth at 10:30 tonight? That's three miles from my place. What if somebody asks?"

"I don't know," Jake said, annoyed. "Think of something. You went for a walk. Were out looking for a hooker. It doesn't matter. No one will ask. You'll be dealing only with me, remember?"

"This is gonna be big shit, Jake. Hell man, you'll make captain for sure."

"I just want to get this guy off the street," Waschke grunted. "I'll worry about making captain later. Keep the picture for now but be careful with it. It's the only one I have and I'll want it back. Don't worry about testifying. For now, just help me get a warrant. All right?"

TWENTY-EIGHT

Jake stood at his kitchen sink, lukewarm water slowly trickling from the faucet. He wore long, rubber cleaning gloves as he carefully examined the knife, turning it over under the magnifying glass he intently peered through. After rinsing the blood from the knife's blade, he was looking for the traces he knew he had left where the blade came out of the handle. Invisible to the naked eye, the magnifying glass revealed minute traces from the bloody naked corpse found in the park. Just enough for the police lab to link this knife, and whoever possessed it, with victim number seven. And he thought, if he was real lucky, there might be other traces of blood from one or more of the other victims as well. Probably too much to hope for, but he would find out soon enough.

The next morning Waschke strolled briskly through the empty squad room of the stalker task force just before 8:00 A.M. He headed straight for the glass paneled office at the back of the room, his office, to check for reports of the previous night's events. There was no one else in the room yet and he wondered where everyone was then realized they had been late at the park. As he turned the knob to go into his office, he heard the exterior door open. He turned to see who it was and heard Owen Jefferson, a sergeant and his senior detective, call out to him.

"What do you have, Owen?" Jake asked."

"I got the dope on the girl. You want to hear it?"

"Christ, Jefferson. You look like shit," Jake observed as Jefferson walked up to him.

"I been up all night. What do you expect?"

"Is there any coffee made?" Jake asked when he saw Carol Johnson come around the corner leading from the break room.

"It'll be ready in a minute," the pretty young college student/police intern answered. "I'll bring some in for you when it's done."

"Good Carol, thanks," Jake replied. "Come on in Owen and tell me what you've got," Jefferson followed him into the cluttered office and as Jake was taking his seat behind the old, beat up desk he used, noticed the outer door open and Roger Holby and Helen Paltrow, the serial killer expert, come into the squad room. Jefferson opened his small notebook and was about to speak when Jake held up a hand to stop him and said, "Here comes Holby and the shrink. They might as well hear this, too."

The two newcomers took seats in the office and Jefferson began, "Girl's name is Alice Faye Darwin, age eighteen. Works as a waitress at Marone's Deli on Lake. Got off work ten o'clock last night. Hung out for a bit and left by herself."

"How'd you get that already?" Holby asked.

"The parents. Their names were in her purse. I gave them the bad news last night. That was fun," he added sarcastically. "Anyway, they told us where she worked and we got someone over there before the manager left. Now comes the interesting part. According to her license, she was five foot eight, a hundred thirty pounds. Brown hair with a weird kinda haircut, you know, kinda spiked like. Pretty attractive, like the others."

"Anything from the lab guys at the scene?" Jake asked Holby.

"Not yet. We'll know more later. I figured I'd go out there after I met with you," Holby replied.

The conversation in the office continued for almost an hour and as it did so, the squad room began to fill up with members of the task force, most of whom had little or no sleep. Jake noticed several new faces, mostly women, who stood around looking a bit lost and confused as to why they were where they were.

"What's with the new people?" Jake asked Holby.

"They're to answer phones. Try to weed out the cranks. We've got this all over the news asking for anyone with information to call. We've got a hotline set up."

With that, the discussion ended and all four rose to leave. Jefferson to head home. Holby to the crime scene and Jake to talk to the other detectives.

At exactly 9:20, one of the female phone operators interrupted Jake with a call. "He insists on talking to you, Lieutenant. Says he saw someone near the scene last night."

"I'll take it in my office," Jake said. "Yeah, Waschke," he growled into the phone.

"It's me," the voice replied. "What now?"

"Where are you?" Jake asked.

"In a phone booth about six blocks from my place. You know how hard it is to find one of these things? It's by a drugstore."

"Okay. Now, go home and wait out front. I'll send someone for you to bring you in. Got it?"

A half hour later, Marty Hobbs was seated in a chair in front of one of the squad room's desks while several of the detectives, including Jake, listened to his story. "I was walking down Chicago," he began for the fourth time. "At about Thirty-Fourth, when I seen this guy come tearing around the corner. He saw me and almost stopped, right under a light," he continued looking around at the group of faces intently staring at him. "Then, he walks past me and as soon as he gets by me, he starts running again."

"What was he wearing?" one of the detectives asked.

"I told you, I don't know, dude. Dark clothes. Jeans maybe. I didn't notice what he was wearing. I just noticed his face. He was sweaty and breathing hard. Like he'd been running or was excited or something."

"You got a good look at his face?" another officer asked.

"Yeah, dude. I got a good look at him. Look, I heard on the news this morning about what happened last night. So, I figured I'd call and tell you what I saw. I'm trying to help you guys and you're acting like this is some bullshit or something. I don't need this shit."

"Take it easy, Mr. Hobbs," Jake said in a soft, reassuring voice. "We're just trying to be careful. Do you think you'd recognize this guy, again?"

"Yeah, I think I could," Hobbs said, obviously more relaxed.

"Okay, good. Santell," Jake said to one of the detectives, "see if you can round up a sketch artist for Mr. Hobbs here. In the meantime, I'll have him go over some mug shots. The rest of you, keep a lid on this and get back to work."

Forty-five minutes later Marty Hobbs, trying his best not to look as bored as he was, turned the tenth page of the second big book of photographs and spotted the face he was seeking in the upper right-hand corner. Jake, stealing glances at his snitch through the glass front of his office, was at his desk pretending to work but anxiously waiting for Hobbs to make his identification. *Any second now*, he thought as he noticed Hobbs pause when he saw the picture. Hobbs turned in his chair, waved at Waschke and Jake was out of his office as quickly as he could.

TWENTY-NINE

"Anybody see anything, yet?" Jake said into the radio. He received negative replies from the dozen detectives scattered at various locations around the southeast Minneapolis neighborhood. Jake had asked the question about every ten minutes since two o'clock that afternoon. He looked at his watch for at least the fifteenth time since taking up their surveillance posts, watching the suspect's small apartment building, waiting for him to appear. It was now past eight and still no sign of the man Marty Hobbs had picked out of the book that morning.

The rest had been as easy as Jake had planned. A quick affidavit for a judge to casually look over before the formality of a search and arrest warrant. A call to the suspect's parole officer for an address and here they were, impatiently waiting for Fornich to return. They knew he was not in the apartment, a phone call every thirty minutes confirmed it. Sooner or later, he would show up and they would take him, hopefully on the street.

"Dispatch, this is Waschke," Jake said into the car's radio.

"Go ahead, Lieutenant," came the response.

"Have someone get a hold of John Lucas over in St. Paul. I forgot to call him. Tell him to come downtown to my office, over."

"Roger that, Lieutenant. We'll find him," the dispatcher said.

As Jake was replacing the microphone in its cradle, he heard a voice from the portable radio the stakeout team was using, lying on the seat beside him.

"Heads up everybody. Our guy's coming up the street toward home," he heard Denise Anderson say. She was in a car a block behind Jake and as he crouched in his seat, he turned backwards to look down the street to see an older, run-down Ford coming toward him.

"He's in the dark blue Ford," Anderson said over the radio.

The car came to a stop in the street directly in front of the building. All eyes watched as Fornich got out of the car, walked around the front of the car turning to go toward the building. Just as he stepped onto the grass of the boulevard, three men and a woman materialized as if from thin air, guns drawn and in a matter of seconds the suspect was down on the ground, handcuffed then hurtled into a car that screeched to a halt while he was dragged from the grass.

Jake was out of his car and crossing the street as the suspect was being tossed in the back of the police sedan. Walking up to the four arresting detectives he said, "Good job everyone. Nicely done. Beth," he said turning to the lone female, "you take charge down here. Read him his rights, show him the warrants and keep the civilians away. I'm going inside."

"Right, Lieutenant," the woman said to Jake's back as he hurried up the sidewalk to enter the building.

Jake was the first one into the small apartment, casually strolling around, instructing the others conducting the search. He went into the bedroom and while another detective went through the contents of the cheap dresser, Jake went into the small closet. At first, he rummaged around in the almost empty closet, making as much noise as possible. After a few moments he came out into the bedroom holding the knife carefully with two fingers and a handkerchief.

"Well, well. Look what we have here. Carlson," he said to the other officer in the small room. "Get me an evidence bag."

"Right away, Lieutenant,"

After placing the knife in the clear plastic bag, sealing and marking it, Jake hung around in the apartment for another fifteen minutes while the detectives tore the place to shreds. Satisfied they were being thorough, he said to Owen Jefferson, "Owen, make sure you get every stitch of clothing, bagged and marked. Plus, any silverware and knives. Anything that might be a weapon."

"You got it, Lieutenant," Jefferson said.

"I'm going out to talk to our suspect. With what we have now, we can at least take him in," said Waschke. "I'll see you downtown. Be thorough."

"Count on it. I'll hang out here 'till the lab guys are done. Too bad they didn't turn up anything at the park this morning."

"Yeah, too bad. I have to tell you though, this one feels right. I think we may have him," Jake said as he held up the plastic enclosed bread knife.

He approached the car in which the suspect was seated, the seat belt pulled tight around his waist and his hands cuffed in his lap.

Jake walked past the small crowd in front of the building, held at bay by a group of uniformed officers. When he reached the side of his car, he said to the woman he had left in charge of the street scene, "You read him his rights?"

"Twice, Lieutenant. With witnesses and he definitely responded that he understood," Beth answered.

"Has he said anything? "

"What the hell is this all about and I ain't done nothing is about all."

Jake stepped over to the car, opened the door next to his suspect, and leaned in to look at him just as Fornich yelled, "What the hell is goin' on? What's this bullshit? This is about those women, isn't it?"

"Why do you think that?" asked Jake calmly.

Fornich paused, uncertainty in his eyes and on his face, then said, "I recognize you. The cop on TV. I watch the news and read the papers. I ain't no dummy."

With that, Jake thumped the door closed, turned back to Beth Johnson and said, "Let's get him downtown. Try to do this quick and quiet. I want no one talking to him until we get downtown. You drive this car. Get one of the uniforms to go with you. I'll lead."

At the Old City Hall Building, in the basement hallway in front of the task force squad room, a mob of reporters and defense lawyers was already waiting for them. From any one of a dozen places, the news of the arrest had leaked out. A small group of people bringing in the suspect, Waschke in the lead and Fornich surrounded by three plainclothes detectives all followed by two uniformed cops, came round a hallway corner and ran straight into bedlam. The group closed up and Jake used his size to plow through the crush of people with their recorders, lights and minicams while Waschke repeated a "no comment" to the pointlessly shouted questions.

They somehow managed to bull their way to the squad room door and as Waschke was about to turn the knob a sudden calm and silence came over the crowd. Opening the door to lead Fornich inside, a reporter with Channel 8, standing right next to Jake with her cameraman's light directly in his face, got off the question they all wanted answered, "Is this the killer, Lieutenant Waschke?" she said as she thrust her microphone toward Jake.

Before Jake could get out the "no comment", the fear, anger and anxiety overcame the suspect and he jerked his arms free of the detectives. He stepped right up to the woman, his face a contorted mask of rage, raised his manacled hands extending the middle finger of both, pointed them at the crowd, and screamed, "Yeah! Fuck you! Yer damn right. I did it. . ." as a dozen strobe lights flashed and minicams whirred. Jake and two of the other detectives grabbed him, flinging him through the door and into the first available chair then slammed and locked the door behind them.

Jake knelt down in front of him, his nose inches from the suspect's and yelled, "You sit right there and keep your mouth shut. Not another word. You got it? "

"Assholes," responded Fornich.

"You could've called me sooner, Jake," Jake heard John Lucas say as Lucas got up from his perch on top of one of the desks.

"John, I'm really sorry," Jake calmly replied. "It all came up kind of fast and to be totally honest, no bullshit, no excuses, I forgot about you. I'm sorry."

"What do we have?" Lucas asked nodding at the surly suspect with the defiant look on his face.

"Not sure yet, John," Jake whispered so the suspect would not overhear. "May have a witness who can place him at the scene last night. Plus, we found a knife that could be our weapon at his apartment." He turned to the other officers and said, "Beth, you and Bob come here a second. Listen," he continued quietly to the two detectives, Lucas listening over his shoulder. "Set up a lineup right away. Do it right. Get guys who're close to him in appearance. I want a lawyer down here for him to cover the lineup. Call the Public Defenders office and have them send someone over."

"Why not just get one of the vultures in the hall? Must be a dozen of them out there. I thought they were gonna start throwing business cards at the guy," Bob Sherman said.

"Lock him in the room until we get it set up. No one talks to him," Waschke commanded.

After Fornich was locked away, still handcuffed, in the small interrogation room, Jake said, "Where's our witness? What's-his-name?"

"Hobbs, Lieutenant. Marty Hobbs. He's upstairs. We've been taking real good care of him," answered one of the uniforms that had squeezed through the mob in the hall.

"Get him down here. I want to talk to him before the lineup," Jake said.

"Sure thing, Lieutenant. Be right back," the same man said.

"Oh, Jake," said Lucas after he returned to his seat on the desktop, "I just remembered. Your brother called just before you came in. Asked me to have you call. Said it was important. Said to call him at home."

"You going to stick around, John?" Jake asked.

"Are you kidding? You couldn't drag me away," Lucas replied.

"Good. Well, I'll call my brother. He'll tell the governor what's going on. Let me know when Hobbs gets here," Jake said to Lucas as he headed for his office.

"Danny, it's Jake. What's up?" he said into the phone.

"Oh, Jake. Look, um, I can't really talk right now," Daniel began. "I just wanted to let you know I saw Dr. Lester today and he put me on my meds. Pretty heavy dose, he said. Anyway, I wanted you to know I feel better already. More in control. More relaxed. I can't go into it now. Don't worry, I'll be okay."

"That's great, Danny. Now, listen. We made an arrest today on the killings. You understand? We arrested someone and everything will work out. Just keep seeing Lester and promise me you'll do what he says and take the medication. Promise me that, Danny."

"Yeah, Jake, I promise. I swear I will," Danny whispered. "You made an arrest? Who? What's the guy's name?"

"Don't worry about that now. Watch the news. There's a howling herd of them out in the hall already," Jake said. "You can tell your boss but no one else. Okay? I'll be in touch. I have to go now," Jake said when he saw Marty Hobbs being led through the door. "Bye, Danny. Be cool," he finished as he hung up the phone.

He stood behind his desk for a moment, looking first at Hobbs and then, his gaze focused on the detective from St. Paul, John Lucas. Lucas had sat back down on the edge of the desk, his legs dangling and crossed at the ankles, his arms at his side with the palms of his hands pressed against the desktop. He was staring directly at Hobbs. His brow furrowed, eyes narrowed. A puzzled expression on his face.

THIRTY

"What time is it?" Margaret sleepily asked Marc as she rolled over and pulled the bedclothes above her naked shoulders.

"A little after six," Marc answered. "Sorry," he continued as he sat down on the edge of the bed and bent over to lightly kiss her. "I didn't mean to wake you."

"It's okay," she said, smiling up at him. "Why are you up so early?"

"I have to be downtown St. Paul by 8:30, remember? Federal court. We're first up and I don't want to be late."

"Oh, yeah. That's right," she purred. "Come back to bed," she continued as she held out her arms to him.

"No way. Besides, you need to brush your teeth," he answered with a laugh as he stood up.

"What are we going to do this weekend?" she asked, now fully awake.

"I need to spend some time at my place. I've been here so much the last couple weeks the laundry is starting to spill out into the living room," Marc said. Margaret got out of bed, still naked, grabbed her bathrobe and headed for the bathroom as she slipped it over her shoulders.

A few minutes later, as Marc was gulping down the last of his coffee, she came down the stairs and said, "You know, I've yet to see this alleged apartment of yours. For all I know, you're just another married man having a little fling on the side."

"Yeah, right," he laughed. "And she hasn't noticed how much I've been gone lately. Look," he continued as he glanced at his watch, walked over to her and put both arms around her. "I have to go. I'll call you later and we'll make plans. You can come over and help me clean and wash clothes."

"Sweet talker," she said as they kissed. "You sure know how to show a girl a good time. Good luck in court. Let me know how it goes."

Marc walked quickly down the sidewalk from the lot where he left his car, hurrying the short block to the federal court even though he knew he had plenty of time. Approaching the building's entrance, he passed the blue and green newspaper boxes of the Twin Cities' two daily papers in front of the building. Passing both, he looked through the plastic window of the dispensary machines. On the front page of each was the angry, twisted face of Carl Fornich making the obscene gesture. Marc stopped and read the headline of each, both with the same basic message informing the reader about the arrest. He went through the glass entryway door, stopped at the security desk to pass through the metal detector and headed directly to the bank of elevators.

He got off the elevator on the seventh floor at precisely 8:15 A.M., walked quickly down the hall to the wide, wooden double doors of the appropriate courtroom. When he stepped through the doors to the interior, he inhaled deeply, gulped a swallow and looked around the cavernous, oak-paneled room. It had been many years since he had been in one of the federal courtrooms in St. Paul. Being used to the newer, more modern but characterless and sterile state courts of the various counties around the area, the sight literally left him a bit breathless.

"Nice aren't they?" he heard a female voice to his right say in the almost empty courtroom.

"Hi, Deirdre," Marc whispered to the young woman sitting alone on one of the hard, wooden benches. "Yeah, it is something. I'd forgotten how nice these places are. It's been a while," Marc continued as they exchanged a quick handshake.

"They sure are," Deirdre McConnell, the lawyer the United States Justice Department had flown in for the hearing said. "I travel all over, for my job," she continued, "and these in St. Paul are my favorites. Really nice."

"Excuse me, sir, you are...?" Marc heard the court clerk ask. He gave her his name as both lawyers passed through the gate in the bar. They each took one of the long, dark, highly polished tables in front of the bench and spent the next several minutes arranging their files on the tabletop. Marc was seated with his back to his opponent and when he finished with his file, he turned the cushioned, leather chair to face the bench and made a little small talk with Deirdre while they waited for the judge.

"I see they made an arrest on the big serial killer case," Deirdre said.

"Yeah, guess so," Marc answered. "I just noticed it from the newspaper outside. You know about this?"

"Yeah, we heard about it in Washington. Besides, I'm from here originally. In fact, I'm working on getting transferred back. So, I kind of watch the news from here. I hope they nail this sicko."

"I just hope it's the right guy," Marc said as the door behind the bench opened precisely at 8:30. Marc, not being used to punctual judges, was a bit startled and he practically jumped out of his chair as the bailiff said "All rise" as the judge swept through the door and took his seat on the bench.

"I understand there's been a settlement of some of the issues. Is that correct counselor?" the distinguished looking silver-haired man in the black robe said while looking down at Marc.

"That's correct, your Honor," they both answered.

"Well, good," the judge said genially. "Why don't we put the terms of the settlement on the record before we get down to business. Ms. McConnell, go ahead and put the settlement on the record, please."

"Certainly, your Honor," she answered. They both stood while she told the judge that the Internal Revenue Service and the federal government had finally decided to drop Karen's liability for the unpaid payroll taxes and refund that portion of the money the IRS had collected that was not barred by statute of limitations.

"Is that correct, Mr. Kadella?" the judge asked Marc when Deirdre had finished.

"Yes, your Honor," Marc answered.

"So, as I understand it," the judge continued, "all we have left is the matter of attorney fees. Correct?"

"Yes, your Honor," Marc again replied, a little surprised that the judge must have read the pleadings and knew what was being done today.

"Exactly how much are you asking for?" he said to Marc.

Before answering, Marc turned to the table, selected a document from his file, read the last line and said, "$9,190.00 in total, your Honor. "

"Okay. Fine. Let's get going then. Mr. Kadella, it's your motion so you're first. We're starting to run a little late so, try to make it brief, okay?" the judge politely told Marc.

Marc picked up the legal pad with his notes, stepped up to the lectern directly in front of the judge, introduced himself formally for the record and began his presentation. A little nervous in the beginning he concentrated on what the IRS had done and why the court should award attorney fees. Marc spoke for seven or eight minutes, totally without interruption from the judge, which struck him as a bit unusual since they are never shy about asking questions or interjecting statements. This one, though, did not say a word the entire time Marc spoke, merely solemnly nodded when Marc pounded a bit on the surface of the podium to emphasize the callous indifference of the IRS, the cavalier manner in which Karen had been assessed the unpaid taxes and the constant, official harassment by the federal government.

"One final point, your honor," he said to sum up, "this entire fiasco should have never happened. There was a memo in the IRS file, a copy was submitted to the court with my pleadings for this morning's hearing, written by an IRS supervisor. The supervisor wrote to the investigator who handled the case, clearly stating Karen was not liable for the taxes and her assessment should be re-evaluated. A memo that the investigator simply ignored because it was the easy way out. He just decided to lay it all on the bookkeeper. Take the easy way out and get the file off his desk.

"The standard for awarding attorney fees, as I am sure you are well aware, is: Did the government act reasonably? I submit, your Honor, that the federal government not only did not act reasonably but handled this matter up to, and including this hearing, with a shocking display of indifference to and a callous disregard for the rights of one of its citizens. For that, your Honor, at the very least, they should have to pay my fees. None of this would have happened if they had conducted themselves with a minimal amount of decency, competence and integrity. Thank you, your Honor."

With that, still without a word from the bench, Marc gathered up his notes and returned to his seat as Deirdre McConnell took his place in front of the bench. She began to present the government's defense, attempting to persuade the judge that the IRS and the Justice Department acted reasonably, and attorney fees should not be assessed even though they had caved in and dropped the entire case. She spoke for, at most, one minute and then it hit the fan.

"You wouldn't settle this case for seventeen hundred dollars?" the judge literally thundered down at her, a look of dismay clearly apparent on his face. "You're down here wasting the court's time and more money than that because you wouldn't settle for seventeen hundred dollars?"

"Well, um, uh," she stammered, "that amount of the refund is barred by statute of limitations, your Honor, and . . ."

"I know that," the judge growled. "But that doesn't mean you couldn't settle for it and be done with this thing. It has nothing to do with attorney fees. I'll tell you right now, I'm going to give him every dime he's asking for."

When the judge first let loose with his initial blast at the government's lawyer, Marc stopped making notes for his rebuttal. With Deirdre directly in front of him blocking his view of the judge, he leaned in his seat to see around her, so he could get a better view. With the last remark from the bench that the judge would award all he asked for, his back momentarily stiffened as he inhaled a large gulp of air and joyfully thought: *Damn, he's going to give me all of it. I should've asked for more.* With that, he relaxed in his seat to enjoy the show.

"I just don't know what those people in Washington think about," the judge continued. "You put these people through ten years of hell, and he's right, it should never have happened in the first place, and then you waste more of my time and the taxpayer's money than he was willing to settle for. What do those people in Washington think about?"

For the next seven- or eight-minutes Marc gleefully sat back in his chair and listened to the judge rip the federal government, through its representative, up one side and down the other. Deirdre did her best to justify her client's actions, obviously with no effect. At one-point Marc was tempted to whisper to her to shut up and sit down. Finally, the judge calmed down and offered a slight personal apology to Deirdre, looked at Marc and said, "Do you have anything more to offer, Mr. Kadella?"

Marc rose from his chair, as Deirdre slumped into hers, and began walking toward the bench. "Be careful, now," the judge said with a smile, "you're on a winning roll here."

"Oh no, no, your Honor," Marc said returning the judge's smile, wondering if he should mention that it was not seventeen hundred they refused to settle for but half that amount. Deciding to give Deirdre a break he did not bring it up and continued with. "You obviously don't need any help from me. I just want to submit to the court an affidavit from me itemizing my time on this case, if I may."

"Certainly," the judge said as he took the document from Marc's outstretched hand. "Did you put some time on here for this morning?" he asked Marc.

"Yes, your Honor, I did."

"Good. We don't want to miss anything. Ms. McConnell, do you have a copy of this?"

"Yes, your Honor," Deirdre meekly replied. "I got it this morning."

"Okay. I'll give the government two weeks to object to the affidavit before my order becomes final. Any objections?" the judge asked both lawyers.

"No, your Honor," they responded.

"Good. Well, good luck, Mr. Kadella," the judge said to Marc, obviously ending the hearing. Little did Marc know how much he would need that last remark.

THIRTY-ONE

"Well, how'd it go?" Carolyn asked as Marc stepped into the office and closed the door. He turned to face the secretaries' work stations, saw Chris Grafton and Barry Cline came out of their offices and slowly said, "That's the most fun I've ever had in a courtroom. The judge was absolutely livid with the government."

"What about fees?" he heard Grafton ask.

"He's giving me all of it. Every dime. I just had the pleasure of witnessing the best ass chewing I've ever seen in a courtroom. You should've seen the guy. I've never seen a judge so pissed off."

"Damn," said Grafton, "now I wish I'd gone. I thought about it too. I almost went down there."

With that, the small room exploded as all four of them offered hearty congratulations amid a great deal of laughter, handshaking and backslapping while Marc told them the details. After several minutes the celebration for one of their own whipping the IRS and federal government, Carolyn said, "Marc, someone's here to see you." She nodded her head slightly at the man quietly, patiently waiting unnoticed in one of the reception area chairs,

Marc turned and said, "Hey, Joe, what's up? I didn't know you were coming in."

"I need to see you," the man said as he rose from the chair and shook Marc's hand. "I need to see you right away. Big problem."

"Sure, Joe, no problem. Do I have time now?" he said as he turned to Sandra, the secretary with the office's appointment book.

"You don't have anything until this afternoon," she answered.

"Okay, Joe. Come on in," he said as he headed toward his office door. "What can I do for you?" Marc continued after both men took their seats.

"What was that all about?" his client asked.

"An ass whipping I just handed to the IRS," Marc said. "Now, what're you up to. This looks serious."

"Well, uh, let's see," he began. "It's not me. It's my brother, Carl. Have you seen the paper today?"

"Not yet, no," Marc answered warily, figuring it must be some kind of serious criminal matter if it was in the newspaper. "What's he done?"

Without answering, Joe stood up and left the room, returned a few seconds later with the A section of the morning Star Tribune from the reception area. He closed the door and silently placed the paper in front of Marc, then slumped back into the chair in front of the desk. Joe leaned forward, placed his elbows on his knees and covered his face with his open palms as Marc stared down at the face he had seen in the machines in front of the federal court earlier that morning. Marc picked

126

up the paper and held it closer to read the caption that went with the picture. When he read the name of the accused killer, his jaw dropped open, he lowered the paper and said to his client, "This guy here. The guy accused of murdering all these women. This is your brother? Carl Fornich? Holy shit," Marc said incredulously while Joe, with his face still in his hands, nodded his assent. "Jesus Christ, Joe. I mean, I didn't know. I hadn't heard the guys name till just now. How, I mean. . ., what the hell? How are you holding up?"

"I'm a bit shocked. I don't know what to think," Joe said while Marc continued to stare. "I got a call from him around midnight last night. Told me he'd been arrested and needed a lawyer. I went down to the jail and they let me talk to him for a few minutes. I been up all night. Marc," he continued, leaning forward on the desk, pleading, "he swears he's innocent. Swears they got the wrong guy, this time."

"What do you mean, this time?" Marc asked.

"Okay, I better tell you up front," Joe continued, as he sat back in the chair. "I'll be honest with you. . ."

"That would be good," Marc said, trying not to be sarcastic.

Marc's client sighed heavily before he continued, "He just got out of prison a few months ago. Got out in December. Did almost four years for rape."

"Okay," Marc said trying not to sound judgmental.

"He said he was innocent then, too. But the witnesses had him cold and . . ."

"Witnesses? More than one witness to a rape?" Marc asked.

"More than one rape. They only convicted him of one. But there were at least two others and all three identified Carl as the guy," he shrugged.

"So, he copped a plea to one. Made a deal, right?"

"Yeah, I think that's right. His lawyer talked him into it."

"Don't blame it on the lawyer. He probably made a damn good deal for him."

"I'm not even sure he had a lawyer. I think it might've been a public defender guy."

"Public Defenders are lawyers and most of them are damn good ones," Marc said.

"Well, anyway, I figured you'd better hear that from me because you'll probably find out about the prison thing sooner or later," Joe said.

"What do you want with me, Joe?"

"I want you to represent him, of course," he answered staring at Marc with a puzzled look on his face.

"I don't think so, Joe," Marc said leaning back in his chair. "I don't think this is a case I want to get involved with. You're going to want one of the local heavyweight criminal lawyers here in town.

Someone like Klingenbach or Bruce Dolan, over in St. Paul. Those guys drool over cases like this. They love the attention and publicity."

"I don't want one of those assholes. I want you," he began as Marc leaned forward and held his hands up to stop Joe. "No, wait. Hear me out. Okay? Just listen a minute, Marc. Please," he continued as Marc sat back again, with a slight, resigned shrug.

"Okay. I'm listening," Marc said.

"Look," Joe began, "I'm thirty-eight years old and I've been around the block a couple times. I mean, you know, two divorces and a few scrapes with the law. Nothing serious. You know that. But I've dealt with a lotta lawyers in my time and you're the first one that I feel didn't screw me over. The first one I think was straight with me and really tried to help me and not just take my money."

"Well," Marc said, "that's nice to hear. Nice of you to say especially since the divorce I did could've gone better."

"Hey, that wasn't your fault. I know that. Besides, it went better than the first one. Anyway, I trust you and I know Carl trusts me. Okay?"

"Did he see a lawyer last night?" Marc asked. "Or, this morning?"

"He saw a guy from the public defender's office before he called me. He don't want no damn public defender again, Marc. Please. Will you just go down there with me and see him?"

"What'd the public defender tell him?"

"Just to keep his mouth shut."

"Good advice," Marc agreed. "A little late, maybe," he said as he pointed at the newspaper on his desk.

"Will you see him? Please?" Joe again pleaded, looking directly into Marc's eyes.

Marc folded his arms across his chest, wrinkling his shirt and tie, leaned back in his chair, rolled his eyes up at the ceiling and said, "Oh shit. Why not? I've just had one of the best days I've had for a long time. Might as well see if I can ruin it."

"All right," Joe said as he jumped from his chair. "I really appreciate this. And I'll see to it you get paid. Money's no problem. Don't worry about it."

"Money's no problem?" Marc asked as he rose and began to slip into his suit coat. "I know how much you have, remember? Besides, I didn't say I'd take the case, yet. Only that I'd go meet with him."

"I know. You'll take it once you see how bad Carl's getting hosed," Joe said. "Hey, that reminds me. Have you ever done a murder case?"

"Now's a fine time to ask that. After you practically begged me to take the case. Yes, I have done or been involved in four of them," Marc answered.

"Good enough. Let's go," Joe said as he held open the door for Marc.

THIRTY-TWO

While Marc was driving to his office from the federal court in St. Paul, thoroughly enjoying the beautiful spring morning and his victory over the dark forces of the IRS, a meeting was being held across the river in downtown Minneapolis. In attendance, in the office of Lieutenant Jacob Waschke, were Deputy Chief Roger Holby, County Attorney Craig T. Slocum and his top prosecutor, Steven Gondeck, and of course, Jake Waschke. Holby was seated behind Jake's desk and the two lawyers who would ultimately be responsible for prosecuting the case of The State of Minnesota vs. Carl Milton Fornich, had the two chairs in front of the desk. Jake was leaning against the windowsill, his arms casually folded across his chest, behind and to the left of his boss, the deputy chief of police.

The two lawyers had taken their seats and Slocum started the discussion by asking, "So, what do we have so far?"

"A witness who places him at the scene, running away from it actually, at the time of the last murder," Jake answered.

"And a knife," added Holby.

"And a knife," Jake agreed.

"What about the knife?" asked Gondeck.

"Preliminary dusting showed no fingerprints," Jake said with a shrug. "The lab boys have it. We should know more later."

"That's not much, Jake," said Gondeck. "Unless they can positively tie that knife to the murder, we don't have much of a case, yet."

"I know," Jake said quietly, nodding his head in agreement. "We'll see what they come up with. It's enough to hold this guy for now."

"What about him? Has he said anything? Made any statements?" asked Slocum.

"Except for the outburst in front of the cameras when we were bringing him in, no, he hasn't talked at all. We got a lawyer for him right away, a guy from the public defender's office. That's him now," Jake said as he looked through the office window at the tall black man who was just then coming through the squad room's door. "Saw his brother last night, too."

"This Fornich guy saw his brother last night?" asked Gondeck as he and Slocum turned in their seats to see the man Jake had indicated. Gondeck held up a hand and waved slightly to the lawyer and then held up his index finger to indicate he would be with him in a minute or two. The public defender nodded his recognition and took a seat at one of the desks.

"You know him?" Slocum asked his assistant as both men turned back to face Jake and Holby.

"Yeah. Franklin Morrison. Been around a couple years. Pretty good guy. Knows his business," Gondeck answered.

"Yeah, he saw his brother. Called him around midnight so, I think he's going to try to get a private attorney," Jake said in response to Gondeck's question.

"Try. Hell, there's a dozen of them floating around this place. Circling like vultures. Just waiting to get their hands on this," said Slocum.

"What about your witness, Jake? What do you know about him?" Gondeck asked.

"Not much," Jake answered. "He called in after he saw it on the news. The Powderhorn Park thing. Said he was by there and saw this guy running from the scene at the right time. Came in and found Fornich in the mug book. Was sure of the ID. So, we got an arrest and search warrant, picked up Fornich and found the knife. It's in the report."

"Yeah, I know. I read it," said Gondeck. "What I want to know is, what's your witness' background? What kind of a witness will he make?"

"Denise Anderson is running all that down. She should have more this afternoon or tomorrow," Jake said. "I know it's pretty thin right now, but we're still working it, okay?" Jake said, a trace of annoyance creeping into his voice.

"What now?" asked Slocum.

"We're going to do a photo array, here in the office with the witness," said Holby. "That's why the Public Defender is here. Then we'll set up a lineup with him."

"I thought you'd do the lineup last night," Holby continued looking at Jake.

"Yeah, I almost did, but thought better of it. Figured we'd wait 'til today with everybody here," Jake replied.

"There's the witness," Jake continued. "The guy there with Sherman," indicating the two men, one Detective Bob Sherman, the other a shorter, younger man wearing jeans and a Gopher's Basketball sweatshirt, coming through the same door as the accused's public defender had shortly before. The two men walked toward the office, but the witness took a seat that Sherman had pointed to. Sherman rapped lightly on the door's window, opened it, stuck his head in and said, "Whenever you're ready, Lieutenant."

"Okay, Bob. In a minute. Keep an eye on the witness," said Jake. Sherman knew exactly what his superior meant; sit on the guy and don't let anyone near him, especially the lawyer from the PD's office.

"How do you want to handle this?" asked Holby as he swiveled in the chair to face Jake.

"I figured I'd lay the photos out on the desk, bring in this guy Hobbs, and Fornich's PD, let Hobbs look them over and see if he picks out Fornich. Nobody says a word to him. Okay?" Jake asked the other three men. "Let's do it."

Jake reached onto his desk and picked up a stack of eight Polaroid pictures. All eight were of men of approximately the same age, color and size of Carl Fornich. Jake spread them out on the front of the desk as Holby and Slocum left through the office door. When Jake had finished lining up the pictures, he looked at Gondeck and asked, "Well, what do you think?"

"Should be fine," he answered.

As Jake was leaving his office to get Hobbs, he saw John Lucas come into the squad room. Jake walked over to Hobbs now encircled by the men in the office, except for Gondeck, who was conferring with the public defender. Jake held out his hand to Hobbs and Hobbs rose and took it as Jake said, "Mr. Hobbs. I don't know if you remember me but I'm Lieutenant Jake Waschke."

"Sure, I remember," Hobbs answered with a trace of nervousness and uncertainty in his voice.

Jake then introduced Hobbs to the other men, including Gondeck and Franklin Morrison as they walked up to the small group. "Can I call you Marty?" Jake asked pleasantly.

"Sure, Lieutenant," Hobbs answered.

"Okay, Marty. First of all," Jake began as he sat on a corner of the desk, maintaining his friendly, relaxed attitude. "Thanks for coming down today. We appreciate your cooperation. Now, what we're going to do here is, in a couple minutes, we're all going to go into the office there. On the desk, I've set out some photos, eight of them. I want you to take a seat in front of the desk, look over the pictures and tell us if you recognize anyone. Okay?"

"Sure. Sounds easy enough," Hobbs said.

"We okay so far, counselor?" Jake said, looking at Morrison.

"Sounds fine," he answered.

Jake led the way into the now crowded office and pointed to a chair for Hobbs. The government's star witness took the seat and began looking over the two rows of four photos. In less than ten seconds, knowing ahead of time exactly where he would find the correct one, picked it up and said, "This is the guy. No doubt about it. Saw him running down Chicago night before last. Just like I told you."

"You're sure?" Jake asked. "You can take more time if you want. We're in no hurry."

"No, this is the guy. I got a real good look at him," he said positively.

All the while this scene with the photos was taking place, John Lucas leaned against the door with an impassive look on his face. Silently surveying the scene while something in the back of his mind kept telling him, almost like a slight itch, that something was wrong here. Something not quite right. He dismissed it as the crowd began to break up, but Lucas had been a cop too long to know that the uneasy feeling would be back.

THIRTY-THREE

"Look, Joe," Marc said while the two men waited in the small jailhouse conference room for the sheriff's deputy to bring Carl down. "After they bring him in, when introductions are done, I'll probably ask you to leave. I'll want to talk to him alone."

"No problem. Whatever you say."

"Just so you understand," Marc continued. "Anything he says to me is privileged. I can't be forced to testify. But you can. If he says something I don't want you to hear, you could be put on a witness stand and forced to tell it to a jury."

"I understand. No problem. How long do you think it'll take them to get him down here?" Joe said as he began to pace around the small room.

"Few minutes. Relax."

"Yeah, right. Easy for you to say," Joe said as he continued to pace. They waited in silence for several more minutes. Joe pacing about the room while Marc sat at the table, lightly drumming the fingers of his right hand on the table top. Finally, the two men heard a key turning in the door and a moment later a shackled Carl stepped into the room, his forlorn look brightening when he saw his brother. The two brothers exchanged a brief embrace then Joe introduced Carl to Marc. "Carl," Marc began after all three had taken a chair, "I want you to listen to me. Okay? Don't say anything until I tell you to."

"You want me to leave?" Joe asked.

"No, not yet. You're okay. I'll let you know," Marc answered. Turning back to Carl, Marc continued: "It's very important for you to understand some things here, Carl. First of all, I don't want to know whether you did anything or not. At this point, I don't even know what you're charged with. More importantly, it doesn't matter whether or not you did anything and to be honest, I really don't care. From now until this whole thing is over, the only thing that's important is what they can prove. You understand?"

"Yeah, I get it," Carl answered cautiously.

"I just want be clear about that. Just so you understand. Okay?'

"You don't care whether or not I did it? You think I'm guilty. Great. You find me a lawyer that thinks I'm guilty."

"Listen to him, Carl," Joe said, gently placing a hand on his brother's arm.

"I didn't say that," Marc said, leaning forward on the table. "I just want you to understand exactly what's going on here, is all. It doesn't make any difference what I believe. If I take your case, I'll fight like hell for you."

"What do you mean, if you take my case?"

"I wanted to meet you first before I decide. Besides, it's up to you who you hire to represent you. Joe asked me but it's your call, not his."

"Well, I trust Joe," Carl said slumping in his chair.

"And I trust Marc. So listen to him, Carl."

"Okay, that's cool." Carl continued as he sat up and leaned forward to look directly into Marc's eyes, "I want you to know something right now. I'm innocent. I didn't do this. It's all bullshit!"

"Okay. That's fine," Marc said softly, wondering why these idiots can't listen and keep their mouths shut. "It still doesn't matter. The only thing that matters is the evidence they come up with. And right now, I don't know what that is. Have they said anything to you?"

"No, not really," Carl said as he slumped back in the chair.

"First things first," Marc said. "Do you want me to represent you?"

"Do you believe me?" Carl asked.

"It doesn't matter," Marc answered.

"It matters to me goddammit. Do you believe that I'm innocent, yes or no?"

Marc placed his left elbow on the table and ran his hand over his mouth and chin while he and Carl stared at each other. There was an uncomfortable silence in the room while Marc contemplated the question. Finally, after almost a full minute, Marc nodded his head and said, "Yeah. Yes, I do. But. . ." he shrugged.

"Yeah, I know," Carl said. "It doesn't matter. I want a lawyer that believes in me. Believes I'm innocent. Can you understand that?"

"Of course, I do. Now, we have to talk about the hard part. What about money?" Marc said. "Do you have any?"

"We can talk about money later," Joe said.

"No, Joe," Marc patiently said. "We need to talk about it now. I still haven't decided if I want to take the case. Do you have any money or assets of any kind?" he continued turning back to Carl.

"Where'd you find this guy?" Carl said to his brother.

Before Joe could respond, Marc held up a hand to him to cut him off and softly said, "Look Carl, I'm not the kind of lawyer who will feed you a bunch of bullshit just so I can get your case and run up a big bill. I'll be up front and honest with you every step of the way and that includes me getting paid. I don't do this because it's so much fun. I do this to earn a living to feed my children and pay my bills just like everybody else. Okay?

"I have news for you," Marc continued. "Despite what you might see on TV, damn few lawyers get rich. Most of them are lucky if they make a decent living. Your case is going to take up almost all of my life for the next few months and I need to know I'm going to get paid for it. I don't mean to be an asshole about it, but that's the reality."

"Yeah, okay," Carl said relaxing. "I understand. You're right."

"How much you gonna need?" Joe asked.

"That's a good question," Marc said looking at Joe. "I mean, there's no set amount for something like this. There's going to be expenses and I'll have to devote almost all of my time to it. I should get fifty grand up front, but I'll settle for thirty."

"Thirty thousand dollars," Joe said whistling softly. "I was figuring ten or fifteen which I can get, no problem. Thirty's gonna be tough."

"That's the beginning," Marc said. "I'll keep track of my time and bill against that at a two fifty per hour. When it's gone I'll need more."

"More?" Joe asked. "You think you'll need more?"

"Look, Joe," Marc said placing a hand on his arm. "If this goes to trial, and it probably will, it will be a lot more. I'm basically just warning you. Okay? Hit up every relative you know. Hock your homes and anything else you can. These things are expensive. Right now, I don't know anything about this case. We'll see. Okay? If it goes to trial, you can probably figure I'm going to need triple that. Now, if you guys can't handle that. . ."

"No, no," Joe said. "I'll get it. I believe Carl. I believe he's innocent and we'll do whatever's necessary."

"There ain't gonna be no plea bargain on this thing," Carl said rapping on the table and rattling his chains for emphasis. "You have to know that up front. I won't plead. Not again. They either drop it or we go to trial."

"Whatever," Marc said with a shrug thinking at the same time, "Yeah, we'll see. I wish I had a hundred bucks for every time a client said that to me." He reached down to the small leather, satchel briefcase he had resting at his feet and removed a single sheet of paper. He handed the document to Carl and said, "Read this Carl, it's a retainer agreement. Joe, I'm going to want some kind of contract with you guaranteeing the fees. Okay?"

"Sure, Marc. No problem," Joe said.

After Carl finished reading the retainer, he signed it and handed it back to Marc who filled in some blank spaces on the document setting out the agreed upon amounts, and then Marc, too, signed it. He turned to Joe and said, "Joe I want you to leave now so I can talk to Carl alone."

"He can stay," Carl said.

"No he can't," Marc said while Joe rose from his chair. "That's first on the list Carl. If you want me to help you, you have to listen to me. Understood?"

"It's okay, buddy. I don't mind. And he's right. You have to listen to him," Joe said placing a tender hand on his younger brother's shoulder. "I'll be back, don't worry."

"Yeah, drop in anytime. I'll be here," Carl said.

"What about that?" Joe asked looking down at Marc. "What about bail?"

"If they charge him with those killings, forget it. No way will a judge grant bail. We'll ask but it won't happen. At least not for less than a couple million. We'll see," Marc continued with a shrug, "but I doubt it."

After Joe left Marc spent the next half hour with Carl. Going over the previous night's events including the arrest and everything that happened or was said to him on the street by his apartment, the trip downtown and his night in custody. Marc went over every detail several times, especially the scene in the hallway when Carl raged at the cameras.

Finally, Marc was satisfied that no detail, no matter how minor had been thoroughly covered and recorded on his legal pad. He then went over the court process with his client. Explaining to him the multiple steps in the proceeding, the reason for each to let his new client know exactly what to expect. Essentially letting him know that, even though Carl had been through it before on more than one occasion, a real criminal proceeding was not like television. There would not be an arrest and trial all in one hour. It would take weeks, if not months all the while Carl would be a guest of Hennepin County. Carl sat quietly nodding his head in understanding, relaxing and warming to Marc.

"Any questions?" Marc asked as he gathered up his notes, placed them in the briefcase and prepared to leave.

"No, I guess not," Carl answered. "Thanks for explaining it all to me, though. No one ever did that before."

"Yeah, I know. Most lawyers can't be bothered. I like my clients to know exactly what's going on. Besides, it's your ass on the line. I think you have the right to know." Marc said. "Look," he continued sliding a business card to Carl, "call me anytime. My cell number's on there, too. If you want to call me, they have to let you, so, feel free."

"I have to call collect," Carl said.

"Yeah, I know," Marc said wryly. "Cheap assholes won't even let you make a local phone call. Anyway," he continued rising to leave, "I'm going upstairs now and talk to the cops and maybe a prosecutor. I'll try to find out what's going on. Soon as I know something, I'll be back. Probably this afternoon. In the meantime, just hang in there. And talk to absolutely no one. Especially the other inmates. The cops will try to put someone in with you to get you to talk. Try to get you to say things they can use against you. No matter what, you keep your mouth shut to everybody. Until this thing is over, I'm the only one you get to talk to. Understand?"

"I got nothing to say to anybody anyway," Carl answered.

"Well, just be careful."

THIRTY-FOUR

Jake stared vacantly through the small window above his kitchen sink, watching the rain and wondering why it always rained on weekends in Minnesota. Especially Saturdays. Or maybe it just seemed like it. He finished the cigarette he was smoking, crushed it out in the ashtray on the counter and tossed the last remnants of the coffee he had been drinking into the sink. Reaching across the sink he opened the window and was immediately hit by the cool, moist air that came pouring into the small kitchen. He leaned on the sink breathing in the fresh air for another minute or so while continuing to watch the rain and gave his mind a moment of rest. Wondering, after twenty-three years of being as straight as any cop on the force, how he had gotten himself tangled in the web he found himself?

Jake walked back to the small kitchen table, the one he had picked up with four slightly beat up chairs at a garage sale, sat back down in the chair he had used for the past three hours and for at least the tenth time, went over the list he had made. In the early morning quiet, he had taken paper and pencil to chronicle the events of the previous few months, a case review technique he had developed over the years. Placing special emphasis on the time since he crashed his car and saw his brother lying on the sidewalk under the streetlight, he again reviewed his notes and what was still needed.

Satisfied that he had not overlooked anything or left any loose ends to tie up, he carried the pages into the bathroom, tore them into small pieces and flushed them down the toilet. As he watched the last of the pages swirl away, his thoughts turned to Carl Fornich, a twinge of guilt creeping into his consciousness. "Too bad pal," he thought. "Someone had to take the fall and it made no sense to sacrifice Danny and everything he has accomplished. What good would it do those women or anyone else?" "Besides scumbag," he said aloud to himself, "you'd end up back in the slam sooner or later anyway." At that moment, the telephone rang snapping him out of his reverie and he hurried from the bathroom to take the call.

"Yeah, Waschke," he said into the mouthpiece.

"Jake, it's me, Danny," he heard his brother say.

"Hey guy. What's up?"

"Are you busy now?" Daniel asked.

"I have some things to do but nothing that can't wait. Why? How're you doing, anyway?"

"I'm fine. Or, at least okay. Dr. Lester thinks the meds will level me out. It's just the stress and everything. I'll be fine now, Jake," Daniel said, his voice just above a whisper.

"Good, Danny. Just stay cool and it'll all work out. Trust me. Okay?"

"Sure Jake. Anyway, the reason I called, the governor would like to see you this morning. Say in half an hour, at ten?"

"Yeah, I guess I can," Jake said looking at his watch. "Why, what's he want?"

"He wants an update on the case. The arrest and everything."

"I shouldn't do that Danny. You know it's not kosher."

"Jake . . ." Daniel began to protest.

"I know," Jake said cutting him off. "It'll be okay. I'll do it. Where?"

"The mansion. Come around the back. I'll look for you and bring you in myself."

THIRTY-FIVE

A few minutes before 10:00 on this wet Saturday morning, Jake pulled into the driveway of the Governor's Mansion on Summit Avenue in St. Paul. He drove through the overhanging, granite carriage entrance and parked his department issued car in the back of the old house. The rain had almost stopped during the trip over the river from Minneapolis, but just as he stepped from the car the skies began to open up. He ran the short distance to the back door and looked up to see his brother opening it for him as he jumped up the stairs.

"How's things? Everything good?" Jake said to the smaller man as he placed a gentle hand on Daniel's cheek.

"Better now, Jake," Daniel softly said looking up into Jake's eyes.

"How's he doing?" Jake whispered.

"About as good as can be expected," Daniel answered with a shrug. "I think it helped that an arrest was made," he continued as he began leading Jake down the hallway. He led the way up a couple of flights of stairs into the family living quarters and took him into a nicely furnished den. Standing at the window, his back to the door, was Daniel's boss, casually dressed in a shirt, slacks and a light maroon and gold sweater with the University of Minnesota logo above the left breast.

The governor turned from the window as Daniel closed the door and the corners of his mouth went up into a slight smile as he walked over to Jake with his hand outstretched. Jake was immediately struck by how much the familiar face had aged in the past two months. Still tall, fit and handsome, the full head of hair was noticeably grayer and the face more lined and sagging, especially around the eyes. Obviously, the man was still not sleeping well.

"Thanks for coming, Lieutenant," Dahlstrom said while the two men shook hands. "You mind if I call you Jake?"

"Not at all sir," Jake replied as Dahlstrom led him to a sofa and took the opposite chair.

"Now, I know this is irregular," Dahlstrom began. "Frankly, I don't give a damn. I asked you here, of course, to give me an off-the-record rundown, or update if you will, on your case."

"I know, Governor," Jake said somberly as Daniel took the seat on the sofa next to his brother. "I thought about it on the way over and I guess I won't tell you anything you're not going to find out anyway."

For the next fifteen minutes Dahlstrom and Daniel sat back and listened while Jake ran over the murder at Powderhorn Park, the tip from Hobbs, the arrest and search of Fornich's apartment.

"What about the evidence?" asked Daniel.

"The witness, this Hobbs, he picked Fornich's picture out and made a positive ID at the lineup. The woman who first called that night, the one that lives along the park, couldn't positively identify him but she did say he fit the general description. He was the same height and build of the man she saw," Jake said.

"What about the knife?" asked the governor.

"We got the results back from the lab yesterday morning. Traces of blood from two of the victims was found. So, we definitely have the murder weapon and can tie it to Fornich," Jake answered.

"Whose blood?" asked Dahlstrom.

"Not your daughter, sir. I'm sorry."

"Anything else. Any other evidence?" Daniel asked quickly when he saw the brief flicker of a pained expression in the governor's eyes.

"We have a semen sample from one of the other victims. We're going to have to go to court to get permission to draw blood for a DNA test. His lawyer's already made that clear."

"Who's his lawyer?" asked Daniel.

"Guy by the name of Marc Kadella," Jake answered looking back and forth between the other two men.

"Do you know him?" Dahlstrom said looking at Daniel.

"No, sir. Never heard of him," Daniel said. "No, wait, I think I met him recently when I was at dinner with Gordon Prentiss. If it's the same man. Don't know anything about him though. I'm surprised one of the local heavies didn't get this case."

"They tried, believe me," said Jake. "They were all over the jail trying to get at this guy. I don't know how Kadella beat them to it. I know him a little bit. Seen him a few times. Seems to know his business."

"What is the status of the case now?" Dahlstrom asked.

"He's been charged with two counts of second-degree intentional murder. That'll hold him for now. The case will go to the Grand Jury on Monday for first degree indictments on all of the Hennepin County victims. Six counts. He was arraigned on the second-degree charges yesterday and bail was set at two million," Jake said.

"Will the Grand Jury indict?" asked the governor.

"The Grand Jury will do whatever the prosecution tells them," Daniel answered. "Indictments are almost meaningless because of that," he added.

"Anything else, Jake?" Dahlstrom asked with a friendly look.

"No, sir. That's about it for now. We're still digging. Going over everything the guy owns with a fine-tooth comb to try to find more physical evidence to tie this guy to these crimes."

"What do you think? Is what you have enough for a conviction?" Dahlstrom asked.

"Who knows, Governor," Jake shrugged. "You never know what a jury will do. "

"What about you, Jake," Dahlstrom said. "Do you think this is the guy who killed all of these women, including Michelle?"

"Yes, sir. Oh yeah, absolutely. The pattern is too distinctive. Yeah," he continued, "we got the right guy, I'm sure of it."

"Well," Dahlstrom said rising from his chair. "Thanks for coming over." As Jake stood up to leave the governor said, "And Jake, I'd appreciate being kept informed. Not just because I'm a father of one of the victims, but because I'm the governor of this state. We need to get this behind us. Well," he continued, "I'll let Daniel show you out. Thanks again, Jake."

A few minutes later, having shown his brother out, Daniel re-entered the room where all three men had conversed. The governor was patiently waiting for Daniel's return. After Daniel had returned to his seat on the sofa, Dahlstrom said, "We need a friendly judge handling this case."

"I was just thinking the same thing," Daniel replied nodding his head in agreement.

"Anybody in mind?"

"Well, sir, how about Gordon Prentiss? You remember him, I'm sure. One of your first appointments."

"Oh, sure, I do remember him. Was a partner at Baker, Finch and Prentiss. Isn't he a friend of yours, Daniel? Kind of an arrogant ass, as I recall."

"Well, sir, he's not really a friend of mine. I went to law school with him and see him socially on occasion. And yes, he's an arrogant ass. But I think he'd know what to do without having to be told. He's not much for criminal rights, I can tell you that."

"Hmmmm, kind of new to the bench" Dahlstrom said lightly tapping an index finger against his lips. "Anybody else?"

"I don't really know many judges in Hennepin County, sir," Daniel answered. "Besides, most of them will run for cover when this case gets assigned. Prentiss, with his ego, will love it. The media attention and everything."

"Okay, Prentiss it is," said Dahlstrom as he sat forward, "Here's what we do. You get a hold of Harold Jennrich, he's the Chief Judge over there. Find him today if possible. He owes me. Anyway, get him over here. Also, call Prentiss and get him over here too. Not at the same time, but he needs to know he's going to take this case."

"What if he refuses?"

"Then we pull the plug on all of the business his former law firm does for the state. Don't worry, he'll play ball. I have to see Jennrich to make sure we get this case assigned to Prentiss. Don't worry. I've known Harold for years. He'll help us out."

"Okay, Governor," Daniel said as he rose from the sofa and headed to the door. "I'll get right on it."

THIRTY-SIX

After leaving the Governor's Mansion, Jake pulled on to Summit and drove west toward the Mississippi to get back to Minneapolis. The quicker route, of course, would be the short run to the freeway and then back to his city but he preferred surface streets. The freeways were a bit faster and at times, more convenient. Also, too impersonal. He had always liked the comfort and familiarity of driving through neighborhoods and business areas. Where people actually worked and lived. Jake had always believed it was important for a cop to know his environment and the people and places in it.

At River Road he headed north past the bluff where he had first confronted Daniel then took the same route back across the river that he had taken after that troublesome meeting. The rain continued to come down in intermittent amounts and the quiet of the car's interior was disrupted only by the thumping of the windshield wipers. Setting a cadence for the thoughts that disturbed him as he drove to his luncheon rendezvous.

After parking behind the single-story strip mall and running through the rain, he entered the rear door of his destination, a mom and pop pizzeria. After allowing his eyes a few seconds to adjust to the darkness, he took a booth across the room from the entryway.

Jake ordered coffee, checked his watch and settled in to wait for his lunch companion. He had selected this particular place because of its privacy and more importantly, because it was not one of the usual haunts for members of the department. The last thing he needed was to be seen with the person he awaited. "Are you ready to order?" he vaguely heard a voice next to him say. After a few seconds he heard the voice repeat the question, which finally brought him back to reality and answered,

"Oh, um, no. Ah, I'm waiting for someone. Sorry."

"That's okay. Just let me know when you're ready," the pretty, blonde, pony-tailed teenager said. Jake watched her as she turned and hurried away to a different table in the semi-crowded restaurant. *They're getting younger all the time,* he thought. *No,* he continued to himself, *that's not the problem. They're not getting any younger, you old goat. You're thinking too much,* he continued changing his thoughts back to the subject that had so distracted him. *You made your decision and it was the right thing to do at the time. Don't start second guessing yourself. Besides, it's a little late at this point.*

Jake looked at the front door as Marty Hobbs came in, looked around for a moment and headed toward Jake's booth as Jake leaned slightly out of the booth flicking his left hand in a brief wave to catch Hobbs' attention.

"Hey, Jake," Hobbs said quietly as he slid into the booth opposite Waschke. "How you doing?"

"I'm good, Marty," Jake replied. "How are you holding up?"

"I'm cool, dude. No problems. How'd I do the other day, anyway?" he said with a broad grin on his face.

"You did just fine," Jake answered nodding somberly. "Especially, the business about the guy's clothes."

"What about the guy's clothes? I don't remember it."

"Somebody asked you what the guy was wearing. Remember? You handled it real well."

"Oh, yeah. Now I remember. Didn't I just say I didn't notice? I thought they were dark or something like that, right?"

"Yeah. You did fine. Listen, that's why I wanted to meet you today," he said, then stopped when the smiley teenager came back to the booth. Jake ordered a pizza for them to share and after the waitress left to place their order, said to Hobbs, "First, we have to be real careful. We can't be seen together at all."

"That's cool. I understand. No problem."

"And," Jake continued, "as far as the clothes go, just stick to the dark clothes. We have another witness, an older woman, who saw him but can't identify him. But she did say he was wearing dark clothes. So, if we can find some clothes that we can tie to the crime, you can always identify them later."

"How?"

"Just say you thought about it and remembered. It's not that big a deal. You're doing fine. Don't worry. Just stick to your story that you got a good look at the guy's face. That's the main thing. Okay?"

"Sure, Jake."

"It's best if we just keep it simple. The more complicated your story gets, the harder it will be to keep it straight."

"Yeah, right. I get it," Hobbs said nodding his head in agreement.

"That reminds me," Jake continued. "I drove by the spot-on Chicago where you saw him, this guy Fornich, on my way here this morning. There's a streetlight on that side of the street located just right for us. Right in front of the third house from the corner. Maybe a hundred, hundred-twenty feet from it."

"Yeah, I figured there probably was one somewhere along there," said Hobbs flashing the toothy grin again.

"Listen," Jake said as he leaned forward on the table, pointing an index finger at Hobbs, "this is serious shit. Don't get cocky. Keep it simple from here on in. Got it?"

"You're right, man," Hobbs agreed. "I'll be cool. No problem."

THIRTY-SEVEN

"What exactly are you trying to tell me, Mr. Kadella?" Judge Eason sternly said looking directly at Marc. It was 9:05 A.M., on the Monday following Carl Fornich's arrest and Marc was standing uncomfortably in front of Eason's bench to receive the judge assignment for the case. Steve Gondeck, whom Marc knew fairly well, stood next to Marc, his hands casually held together in front, silently enjoying Marc's momentary discomfort. "Are you the defendant's lawyer or not?" Eason asked.

"Well, um, I, ah," Marc stammered shifting his weight back and forth between his feet. "I haven't actually been paid yet, your Honor."

"Well, Mr. Kadella, you know the rules, I assume. While I may personally sympathize with your situation, I need to know now. In or out?" Eason said as he continued to look at Marc.

"In, your Honor," Marc said after a long pause.

"You are the attorney of record for the defendant, Carl Milton Fornich, is that correct, Mr. Kadella?" Eason said formally for the court's record.

"Yes, your Honor," Marc reluctantly replied.

"As you know," Eason continued, "if you have grounds you can always bring a motion to withdraw if done properly."

"Yes, your Honor. I understand." Marc said while thinking, "I'm in this thing up to my ass now. I sure hope Joe comes up with some money soon."

"Good. Now, gentlemen," Eason continued as he picked up the court's file of Fornich's case, "this has been assigned to Judge Prentiss. He's in 1440. I believe he's there now waiting for you both."

"We'll go right up, your Honor," said Gondeck as he stepped forward to take the file the judge held toward him.

While the brief exchange between Marc and Eason was taking place, two floors above them J. Gordon Prentiss III was reclining in the big, overstuffed, leather chair behind his desk, contemplating what this case, with a proper verdict, would do for his future. He leaned back and stared at the picture in the antique gold frame sitting on the credenza. It was a photo of himself shaking hands with the man who had appointed him to his present position, Theodore Dahlstrom. A man whom TIME Magazine had labeled a real comer within the Republican Party. At the very least, a shoo-in for reelection next year, especially with the voter sympathy over the murder of his daughter.

My God, Prentiss thought, *the polls must be skyrocketing for the man. And after that, who knows? He's a picture-perfect Republican. Handsome man, lots of sympathy and anti-abortion to boot. At the very least,* Prentiss thought, *nail this little weasel Fornich and a grateful*

Ted Dahlstrom will certainly put me on the Minnesota State Supreme Court. And at forty-four, if Dahlstrom gets to national prominence, who's to say? A seat on the U.S. Supreme Court is not out of the question. All because he had the good fortune to go to law school with Daniel Waschke and have a father who was a founding partner in one of the state's most political firms. He looked at the gold Rolex on his left wrist and realized the lawyers were probably on their way up. Getting this case assignment had been easier than he thought. A call to that fool of a Chief Judge, Jennrich, a call from Jennrich to Eason and the future looked bright indeed, he smiled.

Leaning back in his chair, staring up at the ceiling, he thought about the two lawyers who would be here any minute. *Handle them gently,* he thought. *Be firm with the prosecutor and friendly with the defense lawyer, whoever that scumball is.* Prosecutor's never file motions to remove judges. At least those that know what's good for them. Defense lawyers do it all the time. Looking for a judge who'll go easy on their slimy clients. *Yeah,* he continued thinking to himself, *be a little pleasant, sympathetic even. The last thing I want is to lose this case to another judge. Plenty of time later to see to it that justice gets done.*

He sat up, swiveled the chair around up to the desk at the sound of the soft knock on his open door and looked toward it to see his clerk standing in the opening.

"A couple of lawyers here to see you, judge," she said.

"Fine, Barbara. Show them in, please," he answered, surprising her with this unusual politeness.

"Come in, gentlemen," Prentiss said when Marc and Gondeck appeared at his door. The two lawyers walked toward the desk as Prentiss rose to greet them. After handshakes and introductions, Gondeck and Marc sat in the two chairs in front of the desk. Prentiss looked at Marc, smiled and said, "Have we met? You look familiar."

"We met a couple weeks ago at a restaurant, judge. I was with Margaret Tennant," Marc replied.

"Oh, sure, sure. Now I remember. Are you seeing her? How is she?"

"Fine, judge. Yes, we're dating."

"Well, that's nice. Anyway," Prentiss continued turning to Gondeck, "where are we? Bearing in mind, I don't know anything about this case. I assume you're here on Fornich. I was informed this morning it was being assigned to me."

"Well, your Honor. We're going to need a blood sample for a DNA comparison. Mr. Kadella and I have talked a bit and it's my understanding, he's opposed. So, we'll need a motion for that."

"Is that correct, Mr. Kadella?" Prentiss asked Marc.

"That is correct, your Honor," Marc concurred.

"Okay. I assume the State wants that as soon as possible. What's your schedule like?" he politely asked Marc. "I don't want to push you, but I have to be fair to both of you. Is the first part of next week too soon?"

"No, your Honor," Marc said while Gondeck sat silently listening.

"How about, say, Tuesday morning? Would that be okay?" he said, still looking at Marc. "Any other motions you have can be brought at the same time."

Marc reached into the pocket of his suit coat and brought out his appointment book. The one he used exclusively for court appearances. He quickly found the appropriate page, and seeing nothing scheduled, told Prentiss the following Tuesday would be fine.

"Good. Ten o'clock okay with everybody?" Prentiss said looking back and forth at the two men.

"Fine, your Honor," they both replied.

"I understand bail was set at two million," Prentiss said as he opened the court's file that Gondeck had placed on the desk.

"That's correct, your Honor," Marc said. "I plan on bringing a motion on it."

"That's fine," Prentiss said, again looking at Marc. "Why don't you bring it next Tuesday at the same time. We'll do it first and then the evidentiary hearing on the prosecution's motion for the blood sample."

"You want a full-blown evidentiary hearing for the blood request?" asked Gondeck while thinking, great, now I have to line up witnesses and have testimony and the whole nine yards for what should be a formality.

"Absolutely," the judge replied while looking severely at Gondeck. "Look, Mr. Gondeck. This is an extremely serious matter and we're going to do it by the book. There will be no cutting corners here. Do I make myself clear?"

"Yes, your Honor," Gondeck replied, obviously chastened.

"That goes for you, too, Mr. Kadella," Prentiss said much more mildly. "Any questions? After next week's hearing, we'll get together and discuss scheduling. I assume this is before the Grand Jury now?" he said looking at Gondeck.

"Yes, your Honor," Gondeck answered.

"By next week, we should hear from them. Anything else today?" Prentiss asked, again looking at both of them.

"No, your Honor," the two men again replied in unison. "Okay. Here," Prentiss said as he opened a desk drawer, "let me give each of you one of my cards. If anything comes up, call me right away." Prentiss stood as both lawyers rose from their seats.

THIRTY-EIGHT

Jake leaned back in his chair, feet on the desk, the phone propped between his chin and left shoulder, listening to the excuses coming from the crime lab people. He twirled a pencil with the fingers of his right hand silently rolling his eyes and occasionally shaking his head. Quietly cursing under his breath at what, he believed, was nothing more than bureaucratic bullshit coming from the other end of the line.

Finally, after two to three minutes, he let his size twelve feet drop to the floor with a loud thud, sat up straight in his chair and said "Listen, let's cut to the chase here, okay? Why don't I just have the chief, or the mayor give you guys a call and explain some facts of life? This isn't some bullshit deal. This isn't some dickhead that we busted for peddling a couple ounces of weed. This is a serial killer that's terrorized the city for months. You understand? Are we clear? This case gets your highest priority and I don't want to hear anymore crap about how overworked and understaffed you are or the next voice you hear will be Deputy Chief Holby. Got it?"

"Okay, Jake," he heard the voice say, "We're doing our best."

"Well, your best isn't getting it done! It's Friday. You've had all the stuff in this guy's apartment for a week and I want some results by Monday." Without waiting for a response, he slammed down the phone, muttered a few well-chosen curses and ran a hand wearily across his face while surveying the paperwork on his desk.

He picked up the report Denise Anderson had written about her background check on Marty Hobbs. Hobbs looked good, as Jake had obviously known. But more importantly, Anderson failed to turn up anything that Jake might not have known about. No criminal convictions thanks to Jake years ago wiping his slate clean and having Hobbs in his pocket. *A good report*, he thought, *not the CEO of 3M, but nothing that a defense lawyer could really use either.*

Jake put the copy of the report in his case folder and picked up the inventory sheets for the items found in Fornich's apartment. He read it over for the third time that morning and again, found nothing really useful or out of the ordinary. He placed it back on the desktop and picked up the booking inventory form listing the items Fornich had on his person when arrested.

A brown leather wallet with eleven dollars in it, some change, a comb, a set of keys and the clothing he had been wearing. He ran his eyes down the list and stopped at an item he didn't understand. L. key 119. "What the hell is an L. key 119?" he whispered quietly to himself? It was listed on the form above the amount of money and change Fornich had when booked. Again, he thought, this is odd. What is an L. key 119? After a minute or so of contemplating the question, his curiosity got the better of him and he headed out the door, list in hand.

"Hey, Charlie," Jake yelled through the opening in the wire mesh screen. He leaned against the counter looking into the huge property department holding area while waiting for the police officer to come to the window. Jake watched the man stroll slowly toward him, coming down the aisle between a row of ceiling high shelves piled with evidence of closed and in-progress cases. The man had a slight smile as he came toward Jake and Jake sarcastically said, "Take your time shithead. I got all day."

The officer's smile turned to a broad grin as he stepped up to the screen and said, "Hey, Jake. How you doing? What can I do for you?"

Jake slid the inventory sheet through the opening and said, "I need to see the envelope with these items in it, Charlie. It's that Fornich guy. I want to check something.

"Sure, Jake. Be right back."

Less than a minute later, the same man suddenly materialized at the counter, having come from the side out of Jake's line of sight. He held a large manila envelope with the original of the inventory list stapled to the front.

Charlie handed Jake's paperwork back through the aperture, turned the envelope over, placed it on the counter and as he began to unwind the string that held it closed, said, "Okay, Lieutenant. Let's take a look."

The attendant emptied the few contents onto the counter and as they spilled slowly out, Jake quietly said to himself, "Ah, that must be it." He reached through the opening in the grillwork, picked up the object, turned it over in his fingers examining the heavy, brass key. It had a square handle and was slightly larger and heavier than a normal key. Jake turned it over and read the number 119 stamped into it.

"It's a locker key," Charlie said flatly.

"Very good, Sherlock," Jake drolly replied. "I don't understand why you haven't made detective."

"'Cause I'm having too much fun down here."

"Yeah, and probably getting rich in the process," Jake added, drawing a chuckle from Charlie. "Listen," Jake continued, "I want to check this key out."

"Let me get a slip. You have to sign for it," Charlie said opening a drawer under the counter and removed a small form. Jake continued to silently examine the key while the officer filled out the form. Charlie slid it through the screen and Jake finished filling it out writing his name and badge number on it. He scrawled his signature at the bottom, handed it back to the attendant, thanked him as he turned and walked off, dropping the key into his pants' pocket.

THIRTY-NINE

Jake drove slowly along the crowded residential street in the pleasant, middle class suburban neighborhood looking for a place to park. It was the day after he had found the key in Fornich's property envelope, a beautiful, warm, sunny June Saturday. Earlier, he had scanned through the want ads and had found an ad for a neighborhood garage sale where he figured he could easily find the items he sought. He had driven south on 35W to the advertised location where he now found himself slowly cruising the streets. "My God," he muttered to himself in disbelief, "there must be a good square mile of houses involved in this sale and easily three or four thousand people walking around. Amazing. Garage sale season in Minnesota."

Jake drove around for another five minutes and finally found a parking place a half mile from the center of the neighborhood. He then spent the next forty-five minutes walking around, going from house to house searching for the items on his short list. He made his four purchases from four different sales then found his way back to his car. Jake placed the items in a black plastic garbage bag, tossed it in the trunk, got in the car and headed back to Minneapolis.

That evening he spent several hours at his apartment, watching the Twins drop another game while working on his laundry in the room down the hall. Along with his own clothing, but in a separate machine, he was washing his purchases in a heavy strength lye detergent. In fact, he washed and dried all five items three times using up the entire small box of soap. After completing the third laundering, he carefully placed the five items back in the garbage bag, carried it back to his car and put it in the trunk.

Back in the car, he drove north on 35W to the area of Minneapolis he had cruised the night before. Then, his destination had been uncertain. He had known what he was looking for, but it had taken several stops to find the right place. Now, knowing the exact destination, there was no need for him to take side streets. He wanted to get where he was going and the freeway was the obvious best route.

Jake pulled into the parking lot of the thirty-year-old small shopping mall and quickly drove around to the back. Parking the car by the mall's back door, he opened the trunk and holding a clean rag in his right hand removed the items from the plastic bag. He took out the nylon zippered carryall and carefully placed the other four items inside of it, being careful with how he handled the separate pieces. He zipped up the bag and holding it by the nylon straps, went into the mall through the back door.

Jake entered a hallway with a row of metal lockers lining one side from the floor to just above head height. Finding the one he wanted he reached in his pants' pocket and removed a key, placed it in the lock and opened the door. Turning his head for a quick look to see if he was being observed, satisfied that he wasn't, Jake placed the carryall in the locker removed four quarters from his pocket and used the handkerchief to rub the coins clean of fingerprints. One by one he dropped them in the slot, turned the key to lock the door, removed it and as he headed back toward the exit, turned it over in his fingers to read the number 119 stamped in the side of the square handled metal key.

FORTY

"You wanted to see me, Jake?" Jake heard Owen Jefferson ask as Jefferson stepped through the open doorway of Jake's office.

"Yeah Owen, come on in and sit down a second. I've got a job for you," Waschke said.

"What's up?" Jefferson asked as he slid his six-foot five basketball player frame into a chair in front of his lieutenant's desk. Jefferson and Waschke had known each other for over ten years. Jefferson had been a young patrolman and had been the first cop on the scene of Jake's first case after being promoted to a detective sergeant. They had worked together off and on over the years when their cases overlapped. Jefferson had become a detective in narcotics and with Jake working homicide, overlapping caseloads were a frequent occurrence.

Despite their acquaintance and professional relationship, Jefferson had been mildly, but pleasantly, surprised when Jake had selected the street-wise former Gopher basketball player as a member of the Task Force. He would still smile every time he thought about Waschke's response when Jefferson had thanked him for the selection. Waschke had simply looked at him with an indifferent expression and said, "Don't screw it up," turned and walked away.

Jake reached into the top right-hand drawer of his desk and came out holding a square handled, heavy brass key. He held the key up for Jefferson to see then lightly tossed it across the desk to the detective. Jefferson held it in the palm of his right hand and stared at it for two or three seconds.

Looking at Jake he said, "It's a locker key. So?"

"So," Jake began as he closed the desk drawer, "I want you to find the locker it goes to."

Jefferson continued to silently watch his superior for another moment only now his eyebrows were raised with the corners of his mouth silently downturned.

"I know," Jake said, holding up his hands, palms out toward Jefferson. "It seems kind of trivial but it's not." He let his hands fall quietly to the desk top as he continued. "That key was on Fornich when he was picked up. It may be nothing, it may be something. I don't know. I wanted somebody good to go look for it. I don't want to give this to somebody who might not take it seriously. I want someone who knows his way around this town and will give it his best shot. I'd really like to know what's in that locker."

"Okay, that's cool," Jefferson replied knowing he was not being sent on a fool's errand just to give him something to do. "Where do I find lockers?" he asked, mostly to himself, as he began counting off the number of places on the fingers of his left hand.

"The bus station, although that's probably too obvious."

"Check it anyway, Owen."

"For sure. Then, let's see, there are bowling alleys, the YMCA."

"Health clubs, country clubs, though our boy Fornich didn't likely belong to one."

"City swimming pools and public beaches."

"Shopping centers," Jake added, "Especially the bigger malls. They all have lockers for people to store things."

"Right. I better make a list. Shit man, this is going to be a bigger job than I thought."

"Look, Owen. Let me make a suggestion. Start in Fornich's neighborhood and work your way out from there. The guy owned a car, so it could be anywhere. But he probably stuck pretty close to home. Anyway, it's a place to start. I'm serious about this though, I want that locker found and whatever is in it."

"Will we need a search warrant?"

"I hadn't thought about that. Hang on a second, let's find out," Jake said as he picked up the phone and started punching the buttons.

A woman in the Hennepin County Attorney's Office answered and placed him on hold while she rang through to Steve Gondeck's office. After a long moment, he heard Gondeck answer the phone. "Steve, it's Jake Waschke," he said into the mouthpiece.

"What can I do for you Jake?" came the pleasant reply. Jake quickly explained why he called and what he wanted and Gondeck, not wanting to bother with the paperwork necessary for a warrant, told him to go ahead and look for the locker. "Tell your detective that if he finds the locker don't remove anything until we check with the judge. We may want to get one at that point. If he finds the locker we can get a warrant then. We may want to, so we can grab the coin box from it and check the coins for prints."

"Okay. Good idea."

"We probably don't need one. Fornich would have no expectation of privacy for a public locker. Then again, he might because he paid for it. Whatever evidence we might find could be admitted and let the jury conclude whatever they want from it. It's probably safer to get a warrant. Find the locker first then we'll get a warrant."

"Fine, Steve. Thanks. I'll see you at two to go over my testimony for tomorrow," Jake said and hung up the phone.

"There you have it," he said turning back to Jefferson. "Look but don't touch. If you do find it," he continued pointing a finger at Jefferson's chest and sternly admonishing him, "you stay put. Phone it in. Better still, lock it back up and stand guard over the thing till we get there with a search warrant."

"Sure thing, Lieutenant. I'll get right on it."

"Good, Owen. Good luck. It's a long shot. We'll see if anything turns up."

FORTY-ONE

Marc replaced the telephone in its cradle on the desk and sat staring, unblinking, at the phone. He stayed this way for a full minute after hanging up thinking about the conversation he just finished. A client, or more accurately, now a former client, had called to fire him as her divorce lawyer and demanded a refund of the three-thousand-dollar retainer she had paid. No explanation. No reason given at all. Simply told him she had decided she didn't want him to represent her. Technically, he didn't have to give her back a dime of the money. The retainer agreement she had signed had the standard boilerplate language in it proclaiming that none of the money was refundable. He knew it was probably bullshit, though. If he didn't give her back the money she would raise holy hell with the ethics board and probably sue him for it.

Marc leaned back in his chair and stared up at the ceiling with his arms folded across his chest. He exhaled heavily and softly said to himself, "To hell with it. It's not worth the headache. I'll deduct the amount I have coming for the two or three hours I've done and give her back the rest." What really bothered him was not the fact that a client had fired him. That happens from time-to-time to all lawyers. Clients sometimes changed their minds for any number of reasons. What was worrisome was that she was the third one in just the past few days. All unexpected and all without explanation although Marc was beginning to see the picture pretty clearly. Carl Fornich could get to be a pretty expensive proposition if this keeps up. *Especially if Carl's brother doesn't come up with some money, and soon,* he thought.

Marc sat forward in the chair, pulled up to the desk and resumed the task that the phone call had interrupted. He was working his way through Carl's file, the police reports and other documents given to him by Steve Gondeck, preparing for tomorrow's evidentiary hearing. Though it was not quite nine o'clock, he had been at it for over three hours already this Monday morning. Marc wanted to finish by noon because of the four appointments he had in the afternoon, three with new clients all of whom looked good for a decent retainer for basically straight forward, simple cases.

He continued like this for another half hour, bent over the desk, making notes on one yellow legal pad and writing out questions on another one for his cross examination of the witnesses the prosecution would call. Marc was so absorbed in his work he didn't hear the soft knock on his door or the sound of it being opened. He looked up, startled, when he heard Carolyn's voice say, "Marc, Deirdre McConnell's on the phone from Washington. And Joe Fornich called a few minutes ago. He's on his way in. Says he has money for you."

"Thank God," Marc replied. "I just lost another client."

"Yeah, I figured that. More bad news. All of your appointments for this afternoon called and cancelled."

"All of them? Are you serious?" Marc asked incredulously.

"Afraid so, sorry" she replied

"Shit. Well, let me know when Joe gets here," he said as he picked up the phone and pressed the line one button. "Hello, Deirdre. Thanks for calling back. So, since the government didn't object to the amount of the award, when can I expect a check?"

"Probably about four to six weeks. It's usually sent out in two or thrce, but I always tell people four to six just to be on the safe side. The IRS and I signed off on the appeal. Recommending no appeal of the judge's decision."

"You'd lose anyway and end up paying me for that, too," Marc said with a laugh.

"No doubt," Deirdre agreed. "The judge's decision on these things is entirely up to him and unless he's really out of whack, which he isn't, there's no way an appellate court would overturn him. Anyway, the Solicitor General's office has it now and as soon as they sign off on the appeal, Treasury will issue the check. Should be any day now."

After having dealt with the government for many years with his wife's case, Marc had learned his lesson about writing things down. Not that he believed they were liars. It just seemed that what they said and what they did were usually two very different things. As soon as he began talking to her, he reached for a notepad and as he always did when talking to anyone with the IRS or the Justice Department, began taking notes of the conversation.

"What about the tax lien against our house? Has that been lifted?" Marc asked.

"Should be by now. I know I sent the paperwork to the Service telling them to lift the lien. I sent that three or four weeks ago. I'm sure it's done by now."

"I haven't gotten anything from them to verify that," Marc said pleasantly. "Would you mind checking on it for me? We're still trying to get the house refinanced and the lien was holding that up."

"Sure, I'll check it. I thought you were getting divorced?"

"I am. I still want to try to get the house refinanced. Lower the payment for her. What about the refund? Any luck on that?"

"That'll take a while longer since the payments were collected over time. They'll have to go back and figure out interest you have coming on each payment from the date it was made. So, that will take a lot of work and more time."

"Has the IRS heard about a new invention called a computer? It might speed up the process a bit if they use one," Marc said sarcastically. "That was a joke Deirdre," he added when she made no response.

"Oh, yeah right," she said flatly. "Anyway, since you owe personal taxes they'll just apply the refund to those."

"I know. I'd just like to get it all done and figured so we can get them paid. I don't want to send any money until we're sure what we owe."

"Okay. Well, I'll check on the refund, but it'll be at least a few more weeks.

"That's okay. Let me know as soon as you know anything."

"Sure thing, Marc. Bye now."

Marc spent a few minutes making notes of the phone call just completed. Making special note of the assurance that the federal government's lawyer had given him about the futility of an appeal and when he could expect the check for the award of attorney fees. He tore the page from the notepad, opened a drawer in his desk and placed it in the portion of Karen's case file that he kept in the desk. The full file was almost a foot thick and consisted of several folders. Most of them were kept in a file cabinet, but he kept one for ongoing correspondence and communications in a desk drawer for convenience and access. He was about to resume his work on the Fornich file when he heard a soft rap on his door and looked up to see Carolyn again appear and say, "Joe Fornich is here."

"Have him come in," Marc beamed as he sat up in the chair. "Hey, Joe, how you doing?" Marc asked as Carolyn quietly closed the door while Joe sat down in front of the desk. "What do you have for me?"

"Look, Marc. I got some of it. I cleaned out my 401(K) and I got fifteen grand for you today. I know it's not enough. Me and my sister are both trying to refinance our homes. We'll come up with the rest, but it'll take a little time. Okay?"

Marc leaned forward in his chair, placed his left elbow on the desk and covered his mouth with his left hand. He sat this way for a moment, silently staring at Joe to give him the impression that he was thinking it over. Knowing the effect would be to make Joe extremely uncomfortable, which it obviously did as Joe lowered his eyes and fidgeted in the chair. All the while Marc was thinking about how relieved he was to finally get a chunk of money for this case and what bills he could get paid knowing he had already billed more time than fifteen thousand could cover.

After a long minute, satisfied he had created the impression he wanted, removed his hand from his mouth and said, "Okay, Joe. I guess that'll be okay for now."

With obvious relief, Joe pulled a folded check from his shirt pocket, reached across the desk and handed it to Marc. "I'll get the rest, Marc. Shouldn't take more than a couple weeks or so. Believe me, you'll get it."

"There's a couple things you've got to understand," Marc said as he opened the top left-hand desk drawer and removed a receipt for the check. While filling out the receipt he continued. "Just so we're clear, the first thirty grand is the retainer. I'll bill against it, but when it's gone, and with a case like this it'll go pretty quick, I'll need more."

"I understand," Joe answered quickly as Marc held up a hand to interrupt him.

"More importantly, you have to understand that I work for Carl. Just because you're paying me, doesn't mean that you have any say in how things go or what I do or how I handle things," Marc said as he again held up a hand to Joe to politely stop him as he started to protest. "I know we've been over this and I know you understand. I have to make this absolutely clear, okay? Not everyone gets this."

"I understand. Really, Marc. You won't have any problems with me. I trust your judgment. You're the lawyer, not me. My sister, too. I talked to her and she doesn't want to get too involved at all."

"Look, Joe, I know you do, and I don't expect it to be a problem. At least not from you. Sometimes though, it can be. Mostly in divorces. You get a young woman going through a divorce and mom or dad paying for it and just because they're picking up the tab they think that entitles them to call the shots. Tell the lawyer what to do and how things are supposed to go. Let me tell you that can be one helluva pain-in-the-ass to try to deal with. If I thought you'd be like that on a case like this, I wouldn't dream about taking it."

"No, no problems from me. What about this thing tomorrow? You mind explaining stuff to me as we go along?"

"No, I don't mind. At least as much as I can. This thing tomorrow is kind of a mini-trial. The prosecution wants a blood sample from Carl. We'll have a hearing, so the judge can figure a way to give it to them. They'll have to put some witnesses on to explain why they need it."

"You mean the judge will let them take a blood sample from Carl for some kind of test?"

"Oh, sure. No problem. If there's any reason at all, he'll let them do it. And they have a semen sample from one of the victims so, they'll run a DNA test to see if it matches Carl."

"Then why do the hearing?"

"Discovery. Gives us a chance to look at their case. Hear from some witnesses. See what they have. Even though they're supposed to give it to me, show me everything they have, sometimes they try to hedge on it a bit. So they can pull something at trial I'm not prepared for."

"What about Carl? Does he know what's going on?"

"Yes, I saw him yesterday and reminded him about it. You can come tomorrow but I may not bother to have Carl there. Let me think about it.

"Which brings me back to the money, again," Marc continued as he held up the check Joe had given him. "We're going to have to run our own DNA tests. Hire our own expert witnesses to go over their test results and try to find a way to cast some doubt on any scientific evidence they come up with if it matches Carl. Those tests are not cheap."

"If it matches Carl? Why would it match Carl? "

"I don't know that it will. Don't get ahead of yourself here. We'll see, okay?"

"Yeah, okay. No problem," Joe responded. "Whatever you need to do, do it. Me and Brenda, my sister, we'll get the equity from our homes. I think she can get 25 or 30 grand herself and I can probably get another twenty."

"That won't be enough, Joe," Marc answered.

"Another forty to fifty grand won't be enough?" Joe asked with a look of disbelief.

"I wouldn't count on it," Marc answered. "We'll see but. . . "

"I suppose I can hit my boss up for a loan. The guy's loaded. A millionaire easy. I can always threaten to go to his wife with all the shit I know he's been up to over the years," Joe chuckled. "Jesus Christ, Marc how do most people pay for this?"

"They don't," Marc answered with a casual shrug. "The prisons are full of people who can't afford to pay. You want to fight something like this, it costs. And attorney fees are only a small part of it. There's witness fees, lab tests, investigator fees, you name it and none of this is cheap. I warned you. Besides, in this particular case, I think it will be money well spent. I don't know how or why yet but I believe your brother's getting hosed. Someone's setting him up to take a fall here. Which reminds me, I have to hire an investigator."

"You know one? A good one?"

"Yeah, I know a couple," Marc nodded soberly. "One in particular, an ex-cop, I think they're all ex-cops. Anyway, he's real good. Got great connections around the Cities. In fact," he continued with a puzzled look on his face, "now that I think about it, I'm surprised I haven't heard from him, what with all the publicity this thing's generated."

Marc swiveled in his chair and retrieved the rolodex from the top of the small credenza and heard Joe ask, "How much will he need?"

"For this, he'll probably need a retainer of around five grand. That should be enough to at least get him started. Here he is," Marc said as he pulled a card from the 'C' section of the rolodex. "Anthony Carvelli."

"Sounds like a mob guy."

"No," Marc said laughing. "But he's originally from Chicago so, who knows? I wouldn't be surprised if he knows some down home goodfellas."

157

"Listen, Marc. You need me anymore?" Joe said as he rose from his chair and looked at his wristwatch. "I should get to work. This Caramelli guy, sounds like someone I'd like to meet."

"You may get the chance," Marc laughed. "Tony's a good guy. Very likeable, personable Italian. And it's Carvelli, not Caramelli. Give me a call in a couple of days," he added as he picked up the phone and punched in the number on the card he was holding. Before the second ring finished it was answered by a gruff sounding voice from a throat that had too many cigarettes and too much whiskey pass through it for too many years.

"Carvelli," the voice growled.

"Tony, it's Marc Kadella. How the hell are ya?"

"Well, hello counselor," the growl continued. "I've been expecting you to call."

"Listen," Marc began.

"Not on the phone, Marc," Tony said, the voice having lost its edge.

"What? What are you talking about?" Marc stammered uncertainly.

"Listen. Not on the phone. Tell you what. You can buy me lunch. Remember that last place we went?"

"No. Wait, yeah I do, it was ...."

"Don't say it. Just meet me there in half an hour."

"Man, what're you getting' paranoid?"

"See you about noon and Marc, a word of advice, keep an eye over your shoulder."

"What? What the hell are you talking about?"

"Think about it, counselor," Marc heard the voice say just before the buzz of the dial tone came into his ear.

FORTY-TWO

A half hour later Marc walked through the door of the bar section
of a neighborhood restaurant in Northeast Minneapolis. After removing
his sunglasses, he stood in the entryway for several seconds and
allowed his eyes to adjust to the dimly lit room. Concentrating his
attention on the row of booths that ran along the right-hand wall,
looking over their occupants until he looked at the very last one in line.
There a solitary figure sat staring back at him, an expressionless look
on the face of his luncheon companion.

"Tony, how ya doing?" Marc asked as he slid into the booth
across from Carvelli. The two men exchanged a brief handshake and
Marc continued, "I've half expected you to call, what with the publicity
and everything."

"I've been kinda busy, counselor," Carvelli answered. "So, how
are you doing? How's the big case going?"

"Obviously, Tony, that's what I wanted to talk to you about. I
need an investigator."

"Yeah," the throat growled. "I figured as much. Tell me about it. I
want to hear your story."

For the next half-hour, around ordering and eating their lunch,
Marc gave Tony an outline of the case against Carl Fornich. The
witnesses, the victims and as much as he knew about the evidence
against Carl. Tony sat quietly eating his corned beef sandwich and
intently listening to Marc's story. Nodding occasionally and grunting
an acknowledgement at appropriate times.

"So," Marc said in conclusion, "that's about it up to this point. I
need an investigator. You know the drill. Run down witnesses and I
need someone who can track down my client's life. Hopefully build an
alibi. Maybe someone who can place him somewhere else at the time of
the Powderhorn killing and maybe one or two others."

"Where does he say he was?"

"In a bar over by the U. He thinks. I went there myself the other
night. Talked to the owner and a couple of bartenders. They know him.
It's not far from where he lives but they can't say for sure if he was
there that night."

"Uh huh," Tony grunted as he took a swallow from his whiskey
soda. "What do you think, counselor? Is your boy innocent?"

Marc pushed his half-eaten lunch aside, leaned forward crossing
his arms on the table, looked directly into his companion's eyes and
said, "Yeah, I do think he's innocent. And I'll tell you something else.
Something doesn't feel right about this case. Nothing I can put my
finger on, but I get a weird kinda feeling something's not right here.
Like there's more here than just a simple mistaken identity thing. It's
the knife, I guess. How the hell did that knife turn up in his apartment?

Somebody put it there, but why? Why would the cops want to frame Carl Fornich? He's a nobody."

"That's the question isn't it?" Tony agreed. "Come up with an answer to that and your boy may walk. On the other hand, what're you going to do about this confession that was all over the TV news? You know, when they were bringing him in and he screamed at the cameras."

"Aw, come on, Tony. That's bullshit, and you know it."

"Sure, counselor," Tony said with a shrug. "I know it's bullshit, but you have to pick a jury of twelve people who either haven't seen it or who also believe it's bullshit. Let me tell you, I've seen it probably a half dozen times and it makes a pretty strong impression. Good luck with it. You have to ask for a change of venue."

"Yeah, I know. I'm bringing the motion tomorrow. Actually, I think that's the least of my problems. It's the physical evidence I'm worried about. Especially that damn knife. I'm not sure what to do about it," Marc said with a sigh as he slumped back in his seat. "Can you help me?"

"How's business?" Tony asked, ignoring Marc's question.

"Not too good. I think this case is costing me clients. Hey, that reminds me," Marc continued as he again leaned forward on the table. "What did you mean on the phone before? You know, about watching my back and not talking on the phone. "

"Words of advice, counselor. Just words of advice."

"Bullshit. You know something," Marc said as he stabbed the tabletop with an index finger and continued, almost in a whisper, "Now, what the hell did you mean by that? Will you help me with this case or not?"

Carvelli tugged on the cuffs of his expensive white silk shirt, adjusted the collar and finally leaned forward on the table, his arms crossed like Marc's so that the two men were only inches apart. Finally, after another few seconds of silence had passed between them, the former police detective answered the question.

"No, Marc. I'm sorry but I can't. Couple reasons," he continued as Marc started to protest. "First, I am too busy, but to be honest, that's not the main problem. I've done a little nosing around, just idle chit chat with some cop friends here and there. I figured sooner or later you'd call, and I was naturally curious about this case, what with all the publicity and everything. Anyway, one of my friends, a guy I've known over twenty years, told me flat out it wouldn't be a good idea to get involved too directly. That the cops want this guy convicted and it would be best to steer clear of it."

"When did you start to care about things like that?"

"Let me tell you something, I always cared about things like that. I have to live in this town and my best connections have always been with the Department. Besides, I can help you a little, but it'll have to be subtle. Not too direct okay? I know somebody to recommend. In fact, I'll set it up for you after lunch this afternoon. Somebody new. Hungry and damn good."

"What's his name?"

"Her."

"Her?"

"Yeah, her name. Madeline Elizabeth Rivers. Maddy. You'll like her. She's only been in town a year or so and I've helped her out a bit. Tossed some business to her and stuff. She's sharp as hell. Besides, like I said, I can help out around the fringes a bit this way. And I won't charge you nothing for it."

"Why? You sleeping with her?" Marc asked, mildly irritated.

"Shit," Tony grunted and growled, "I wish. Wait'll you see her. Anyway, this should work out fine for you. Trust me okay?"

"Okay. Have her give me a call."

"One other thing for now, Marc. Something for Maddy to look into. About the knife. Something one of my department friends said to me. He just thought it was kind of strange the way the knife was found like that and nothing else. You know, in the guy's apartment and all. Look into that."

"What do you mean? What'd your guy say?"

"Mmmm, nothing specific, really. Just that, well, he's not sure, but he thinks maybe some other cop might have looked in that closet before the guy who found the knife did."

"Was your guy there? Does he know something?" Marc asked, his voice rising in agitation.

"Keep it down," Carvelli said as he held up his right hand to calm Marc. "Yeah, he was at the scene, but he wasn't in the bedroom with Waschke when Waschke found the knife."

"You know this Waschke guy?"

"Jake? Sure. I've known him a long time. Good guy. Good cop. A straight shooter. That's why I think it's probably bullshit but it's worth looking at. Who knows," he continued with a shrug, "what's really in another person's heart. It's something for you to check out. A place to start."

"Great. Investigate the cop heading up the investigation."

"Hey!" Carvelli said, "I just remembered what I wanted to ask you. How'd you make out with that case you have against the IRS?"

"Kicked their ass," Marc beamed. "Including a decent chunk of attorney fees."

"No shit? That's great, I'm glad somebody stuck it to those assholes once. "

"Yeah, it felt pretty good. As I recall, you've had some problems with them yourself, haven't you?"

"Who hasn't? Cost me a ton of dough but it's all straightened out now. Anyway," he continued as he handed the lunch check to Marc, "I believe this is yours. I'll get a hold of Maddy for you and call you later."

"Thanks, Tony. I appreciate it," Marc answered as they both rose to leave.

FORTY-THREE

At about the same time that Marc and Tony Carvelli were discreetly mentioning his name as a source to investigate, Jake was locking his office door from the inside and closing the blinds covering the windows that overlooked the squad room. The room was empty except for the civilian secretary and Jake. Most of his people had been reassigned as the case wound down and headed toward trial and the few remaining still assigned to Jake were out of the office.

Jake sat down at the desk and dumped the contents of the envelope he had retrieved from the evidence storage room on to the blotter on the desktop. Switching on the desk lamp, he reached in one of the drawers and removed several items placing them carefully next to the envelope's contents.

He replaced all of the items from the envelope except for three coins, which had been in Carl Fornich's pocket on the night of his arrest. Jake spent the next several minutes applying the fine fingerprint dust to each one and holding them with tweezers as he held them under a magnifying glass to examine the results. The first two came up empty, no usable prints on either one. The third one, however, a quarter, appeared to have a full thumbprint and a partial of what was probably an index finger, both clearly readable on the shiny new coin.

He placed a copy of Carl's fingerprints on the desk, a set taken at the time of his booking and compared the thumbprint on the coin to Carl's. Satisfied that the print on the coin was from Carl's right thumb he blew the dust off of the coin with a small can of compressed air. Still holding the coin with the tweezers, he dropped it into a plastic zip lock sandwich bag and closed it tight. Taking a quarter from his pocket, he wiped it clean, blew the dust off of the other two and put all of them into the evidence envelope and resealed it by winding the string around the two button sized clasps.

As he started to get up to return the envelope to the storage room, the phone on the desk shattered his concentration. He stared at it for a moment, small beads of sweat breaking out on his forehead as he held his right hand to his chest to calm his breathing. Realizing that the phone ringing at that moment was merely coincidence and that no one could possibly have seen what he had just done, he reached for the handle just as the fourth ring began.

"Yeah, Waschke," he growled, trying to sound as normal as possible.

"Lieutenant, it's Jefferson," he heard a voice answer. "I've found the locker and we may have something here."

"Where are you Owen?" Jake asked completely composed now as he drew his free hand across his forehead to wipe the small droplets of sweat away.

The detective relayed his precise location and Jake wrote it down in a notebook as he normally would then ordered Jefferson to standby and guard the area and wait for Jake who would be there shortly.

He called Steve Gondeck and told him what Jefferson had found and asked the prosecutor to get a search warrant for him. Gondeck assured him he would have it by the time he came across the street to the county attorney's office.

Before leaving the building, he returned the envelope to the evidence locker then stopped to pick up the warrant before he headed out for his rendezvous with Owen Jefferson.

After arriving at the little mall and parking his car in the exact spot he parked in before, Jake went in through the same door that he previously used and immediately saw Jefferson standing guard in front of the lockers, precisely where Jake knew he would find him.

"What do you have, Owen?" he asked as Jefferson stepped aside while Jake pulled on a pair of surgical gloves and opened the metal locker.

"Don't know, Lieutenant. A bag in here. Haven't opened it yet," the detective answered.

"You got gloves?" Jake asked as he pulled the bag from the locker.

"Sure, Lieutenant," Jefferson answered.

"Let me have them," Jake said as he reached in to remove the bag. "I have a lab team coming over. They'll check for prints around here," he continued as he placed the bag on the floor and unzipped it. "First, go see if you can find the manager. We'll want the contents of the coin box."

As soon as Jefferson rounded the corner in search for a manager of the mall, Jake removed the coin from the plastic bag, carefully held it by the edge and dropped it into the slot on the locker's coin box. He took another one from his pants pocket, rubbed it between his thumb and index finger to be certain of smudging any possible prints and dropped it into the slot as well. Having paid the necessary amount, he turned the key to lock the door and without bothering to remove it, turned it again to unlock it once more.

FORTY-FOUR

When Marc arrived back at his office there were several messages and Connie Mickelson waiting for him. As he quickly read through the pink notes, saving only those from his wife, Margaret Tennant and Tony Carvelli, he heard Connie say, "Marc, we have to talk."

"Sure, Connie. What's up?" he answered.

"Business business. Come on in and see me when you've got a few minutes," his landlord said, not unpleasantly.

"Okay Connie. Let me return a few calls and I'll be right with you."

He spent the next fifteen minutes on the phone. Marc assured his wife that the child support check was in the mail. He then called and made a date with Margaret, whom he had not seen for almost a week, for that evening and confirmed an appointment with Carvelli's investigator friend for later that afternoon.

"What's up, Connie?" Marc said as he walked through Connie's office door.

"Sit down, Marc," Connie answered without her usual good-natured banter. "It's business around here. I don't know if you've noticed, but things are starting to dry up a bit. I hate to say it but it's because of this Fornich business. You've got yourself one very unpopular client and I think that it's starting to hurt the rest of us. Barry's had two people flat out tell him they were going somewhere else because of it and I've lost a couple of long-time clients. They didn't come out and say it but they both strongly hinted that was the reason. Wait, Marc," she said holding up a hand to cut him off as he began to protest. She rose from her chair behind the desk, placed a motherly hand on his arm and continued. "My personal opinion is: fuck 'em if they can't understand why a guy like Carl Fornich needs a lawyer. For chrissakes, any idiot oughta be able to see that. But people are people."

"And business is business," Marc said, repeating a favorite phrase of Connie's.

"One of the first things we're taught in synagogue," she said with a smile and soft chuckle. "Are you sure this case is worth it? I've talked to the girls out front and I know how many clients you've lost lately. Are you sure this case is worth it?" she repeated.

"Hell no I'm not sure," Marc answered softly.

"I'm not telling you what to do. In fact, I'll help you anyway I can but…" she said letting the last word trail off.

"He's innocent, Connie," Marc said turning slightly to face her directly. "In my heart of hearts, I know he's innocent and someone's setting him up. I'm not sure who or why, yet. But I really believe it."

"You have a theory?" she asked.

"The cops."

"Why would the cops set him up?" she asked, taking on the role of devil's advocate.

"Don't know for sure. Get a conviction if for no other reason. I don't know," he shrugged. "High profile case. Lotta heat. Lotta political pressure. Hell, Connie, the governor's daughter. You won't get more heat than that."

"True enough," Connie answered. "Assume for a minute you're right, that the cops got Fornich just to make an arrest, just to convict somebody of these murders. That would mean that the real killer's still out there. And sooner or later, he'll strike again. Then what will the cops look like?"

"I know, I know," Marc said nodding in agreement. "I've thought of all that. But what if they know who it is? What if they're protecting someone or know he's gone? They still need to convict someone to clear the case. Take the heat off. Make the governor happy."

"Okay. Let's say you're right. You know you're going to have to prove that at trial. It won't be good enough just to create reasonable doubt here to get this guy off. In fact, it may be worse if you do. This isn't L.A. You won't become a celebrity if you win this case with legalistic bullshit. You're going to have to convince this community that the cops got the wrong guy, or your career may be in jeopardy. Have you thought about that? Hell, we'd all be better off if you fought a helluva good fight and lost. Not that I'm telling you to do that. I'm telling you maybe it's time you thought about getting out of this. This case could ruin you in the long run."

"He trusts me. The family trusts me. Besides, it could have the opposite effect. If I win it my reputation and business could explode."

"True. It could. Let me give you a little advice. Get this thing to trial ASAP. The sooner it's over the better. If it drags on for months it could be a disaster around here. Right now, we're all okay. If this thing drags on for a year we could be in trouble."

"Carl wants it over too. He wants a quick trial date. Scares the hell out of me though. Sometimes I can't help thinking I'm about five feet over my head with this thing."

"That's good. That'll help make you cautious. Careful."

"Are Barry and Chris complaining?"

"No, not at all," Connie said shaking her head with emphasis. "In fact, I think Barry's a little envious. Like he'd like in on the case with you. If you need anything, any help at all, don't hesitate to ask. I still think you oughta remove that bastard Prentiss. Don't trust him Marc. He's the epitome of why people hate lawyers."

"We'll see. He's been okay so far. Even seems like he's going out of his way to be fair to me. Besides, sometimes better the devil you know. None of the other judges want this case and I'm not sure I want to deal with one that's pissed off because he's been assigned a case because I filed on the original judge. We'll see."

"Prentiss is a political snake. Be careful with him."

Two hours later Marc looked up from his desk when he heard a sharp rap on his door. It opened, and Carolyn poked her head in and with a strange smirk and raised eyebrows, informed him that Madeline Rivers had arrived. He gave Carolyn a quizzical look as he passed through his office doorway she held open for him, all the while wondering what was up with the mischievous look she gave him. Marc took two steps past the doorway and immediately understood Carolyn's amusement. Seated on one of the reception area chairs was a woman in a light summer dress, her long shapely legs crossed as she casually paged through the current edition of TIME magazine. Marc's mouth immediately went cotton dry and he involuntarily wiped the palms of his hands on his pants as he approached her, for Madeline Rivers may have been the most beautiful female he had ever had the good fortune to gaze upon.

She glanced up at Marc, lightly tossed the magazine onto the coffee table from where it came and stood to greet him. As he came up to her, his right hand extended toward hers, he straightened to his full height, threw his shoulders back, contracted his stomach muscles and found himself vainly hoping his hair wasn't too tousled.

"Hello," he heard her say as their hands began to touch. "I'm Maddy Rivers."

"Marc, um, Kadella," he managed to croak as he took in the perfect smile, the sparkling blue eyes and shoulder length brown hair with auburn highlights. "It's a pleasure to meet you," he said as he noticed in her two-inch heeled pumps she was as tall as he was.

"Me too," she said pleasantly. "Tony told me all about you. He really likes you and I didn't know Tony liked anyone."

"Cynical ex-cop," Marc answered as they released each other's grip. "Come on in," he said, regaining his composure as he pointed toward his office door. He followed her into his office, pausing to whisper to Carolyn as Maddy took a seat, "You could've warned me."

"And miss that? Not a chance," she whispered back as she closed the door behind him.

"I don't mean to be offensive," he began as he landed in his chair behind his desk, "but you're not exactly anyone's idea of what a private investigator looks like. I mean, well, Tony. Now he looks like a private investigator. But you, well…"

"I'm not offended," she said laughing. "In fact, I did some modeling when I was younger. Before I joined the Chicago PD."

"You were a cop in Chicago?" Marc asked seriously.

"Yeah, almost six years."

"What happened? Why'd you quit?"

"Who said I quit?" she answered pleasantly. "In fact, I guess I did quit. Or at least was forced to. I posed in PLAYBOY."

"Really?" Marc said, his eyes widening.

"Yeah, really. About three years ago. I thought it'd be fun. You know. Very flattering and all. It was about the dumbest thing I've ever done."

"I can just imagine," Marc said shaking his head. "I can imagine what you had to put up with afterwards from the little boys on the police force."

"Exactly."

"No offense, Ms. Rivers . . . "

"Maddy" she corrected him.

"Okay, Maddy. No offense but what were you thinking?"

"I wasn't, obviously," she said laughing her delightful laugh.

"Say, um," Marc said, shifting his eyes around the room as if someone was watching. "You wouldn't happen to have a copy of that particular magazine would you?"

"Find it yourself you lech," again with her laugh.

"Maybe we better get down to business before it gets any warmer in here," Marc said smiling.

"Good idea," she answered.

"You may have guessed what case I need you for," Marc began.

"I assume the serial murder case. Tony told me a bit about it."

"Right. Anyway," Marc continued, "what I want you to do first is start doing a background on my client. I need somebody to do some leg work on him. Try to track down his whereabouts on the nights of these murders."

"Looking for an alibi," she interjected.

"And I need you to do some of the preliminary work on the other side's witnesses. Especially this one," Marc said as he pulled a single sheet of paper from a file folder on the desk. "Martin Dale Hobbs," he continued as he handed the sheet of paper to her across the desk. "Here's a list of their witnesses, so far. Hobbs is at the top. Name, address what little I have on him."

"You want me to interview him?"

"No, not yet. We'll see about that later. For now, just get me as much background on him as you can. Tony can help you with some of that. Maybe with any arrest records and such. Find out anything and everything you can. This is the guy we've got to discredit at trial so nothing about him is inconsequential. The more we know, the better."

"Which do you want me to do first? This Hobbs guy or your client, Fornich?" She asked.

"Fornich," Marc answered. "He should be easier. We can get all the help we need from him."

"I'll need to see him."

"No problem. We can run down to the jail today and get you started. Now, about your fee..."

"Case like this is going to take a lot of my time," she began. "I'll need a twenty-five-hundred-dollar retainer. I'll bill you at one twenty-five per hour plus expenses."

"Okay," Marc said swallowing hard. "That's about what I expected," he added as he pulled his office checkbook from a desk drawer.

"Let's go meet Mr. Fornich," she said as she slipped the check into her small handbag. "By the way, how long do we have? How long before trial?"

"Probably six weeks or so. We haven't set a trial date yet, but Carl wants to get out of jail. He doesn't want to sit there for months waiting for it so, I'll push for an early trial date. No later than mid-August."

"Not much time," she said.

"No," Marc said with a shrug. "But I'm not sure I want to give the cops more time to come up with more evidence. So we're going as soon as we can."

"The prosecution won't like that either," she said. "A case like this they'll want plenty of time to prepare."

"And play the media for attention. Slocum's up for reelection next year. He'll want to play this one for all he can. You want to ride down to the jail with me or follow me?" he asked as he rose to leave.

"I'll follow you," she answered.

FORTY-FIVE

Saturday evening Marc found himself walking from the driveway to the front door of Margaret's house, guilt gnawing at his conscience for not seeing her for almost two weeks. In fact, he had difficulty finding time to return one or two of her calls. When he received the 'Get Well Soon Card' from her the day after the hearing for the blood test request, Marc took the hint, called her and made the date he was now walking toward, a peace offering of a dozen roses in hand. Plus, she had offered to make dinner and the prospect of spending the night with her had easily overcome a slightly guilty conscience.

"Well, hello stranger," she said when she opened the door after deliberately letting him stand in the early evening July steam bath for a full three minutes.

"I was beginning to wonder if you were home," he answered, not bothering to conceal his annoyance as he handed her the flowers.

"Is it still hot out there? Let me put these in water. Come on in and mix us a drink," she said over her shoulder as Marc stepped through the doorway.

"Boiling. Still in the 90's," he answered as the dry, air-conditioned air surrounded him. "Nice in here, though."

He went to the bar and fixed two highballs, very light. As he turned around, drinks in hand he almost ran into her as she stood staring at him, arms folded across her breasts, head slightly tilted to one side with a stern look on her face. He waited a moment for her to say something, expecting an admonishment for his recent neglect. He looked her up and down, casually dressed in a white light summer blouse and navy-blue shorts and sandals.

"I'd almost forgotten how beautiful you are," he softly said as he held out a glass to her.

"Nice try, buster," she said without changing her stance or expression as she took the proffered drink from him.

"Are we going to fight tonight?" he asked as he stepped forward and slipped his arm around her waist.

"Maybe," she answered doing her best to act indifferent to his attention. "Then again, maybe not," she said as he kissed her softly on the neck and pulled her close.

"It's not like I've been seeing another woman," he whispered softly into her ear.

"Great. He's been ignoring me for a serial killer. Somehow, I'm not sure that's better."

"Accused," he said smiling down at her. "I have missed you and I am sorry," he added.

"Let's eat. I'm starving and you're late," she said as she gently broke away from him and began walking toward the dining room.

"We'll see how good a boy you are before I decide if you get to spend the night."

"And how horny you are," Marc muttered under his breath.

"I heard that," she said laughing.

"So, how's the case going?" she asked as they began to eat.

"Okay, so far. We had an evidentiary hearing the other day on some pretrial motions. The prosecution has a semen sample from one of the victims and they want DNA testing. I asked for bail and a change of venue. Prentiss ruled on all of it from the bench. They get their blood test, bail and venue denied. I expected both so no big surprise."

"You going to get your own blood test?"

"Yeah, I suppose I better. Risky though."

"Why?"

"Because if their's turns up negative, and mine positive that could be interesting. We'll see."

"Where are you having it done?"

"Place in Wisconsin. It'll take a couple weeks. Then I'll have to find an expert to discredit their test if it turns up positive."

"You know any?"

"Not really."

"Let me know. I can get you a list. I know a couple good ones. Expensive though. You seem tired."

"I am a bit," he answered as he gently took her right hand and lightly kissed it. "I am glad to see you. I've missed you," he added.

"I've missed you, too," she said. "You could call once in a while. It would be good for you too. To have someone to talk to. This case is going to eat you up otherwise."

"Yeah, I know," he said as he released her hand and continued eating.

"How's business?" she asked.

"Sucks," came the one-word reply. "Practicing law is a damn tough way to make a living."

"I know," she answered soberly. "Every day I see it in my courtroom. Lawyers who are all struggling. Too many of them out there. Every day I'm thankful I don't have to deal with it anymore. Did you get your money from the IRS case yet?"

"Nope. Not yet. Talked to her yesterday. Same old bull. Should be along any day now. As soon as the solicitor general signs off on the appeal etc. blah, blah, blah."

They spent the rest of the evening laughing, talking and simply enjoying each other's company. The comfort of two people being together without pretense or concern. It was the best night Marc had had in several weeks, especially once they had exhausted the topic of Carl Fornich. Of course, he spent the night and they fell asleep, naked in each other's arms.

At six the next morning the phone on the nightstand next to the bed rang startling them both awake. Margaret answered it and Marc heard her tell the caller that he was there.

"It's Connie Mickelson," she whispered.

"Connie?" Marc asked, surprised, as he took the phone from her. "Yeah,

Connie, Marc here. What's up?"

"Sorry to bother you, Marc. Apologize to her Honor for me. I just got a call from our answering service and thought I'd better find you ASAP. Your boy, Fornich, he's been taken to the hospital. Assaulted and beaten by other inmates."

"Shit," was all Marc said as his head fell back on the pillow.

FORTY-SIX

Marc stepped through the hospital elevator doors the instant they opened wide enough to permit it and was immediately confronted by a crush of media people. He took two steps into the hallway, stopped and held up a hand to quiet the horde before he began the impromptu press conference on this early Sunday morning. Minicam lights began to blaze away and after a few moments the crowd settled, waiting for Marc to speak. Finally, one of the local TV reporters, a woman Marc had been interviewed by before, having elbowed her way to the front of the crowd, shoved a microphone in his face and asked, "What is your reaction to the alleged assault on your client?"

"Alleged assault?" Marc responded staring directly at the woman. "Look," he began, "right now, you probably know more about this than I do. I will say this, my client has been in police custody and presumably under their protection and now, here we are standing in a hospital corridor on a Sunday morning. I don't know exactly what happened but if you'll give me a little time, I'm sure I'll find out and have a statement for you then. Please," he tried to continue as the throng all started firing questions at him, "let me see my client and then I'll talk to you," he concluded as he began to shove his way past the unruly mob.

Marc walked down the hallway in the direction of a small crowd of uniformed and plainclothes police officers milling about in front of one of the rooms. When he got within a couple steps of the door one of the uniforms held up a hand to stiff arm his chest and as Marc hesitated, he heard the voice of Jake Waschke growl at the uniform to let him pass. Without saying a word, he continued on passing through the closed door to find his client lying on a bed with a white coated doctor leaning over him, using a pen light to examine the dilation of his pupils.

"Hey counselor, how you doing?" he heard Carl quietly ask. As he approached the bed the doctor straightened and gave him a quizzical look.

"Marc Kadella, Doctor," Marc said as he held his hand out to the man. "I'm Mr. Fornich's lawyer. How is he?"

"On the whole, pretty lucky I'd say. Most of the injuries look a lot worse than they are. A slight concussion and some bruised ribs. A lot of bruising but he'll be okay," the doctor answered as Marc stared down at the battered and swollen face that stared back at him, weakly trying to smile. "We'll probably keep him here for a couple of days, just for observation. It looks like he'll be all right."

"Good. Thanks, doctor," Marc replied. "Could I have some time alone with him now?"

"Okay but keep it short. He'll need rest. I'll check back in a bit. You rest and relax. Just take it easy," the young man said to Carl as he began to back up toward the door.

"I'm not going anywhere," Carl said as he weakly waved at the barred windows.

Marc waited for the door to close then pulled a chair alongside the bed, wearily sat down and said, "So, what happened?"

"Not much," Carl replied through his swollen lips and still bloody mouth. "Couple guys jumped me in the john last night while one of the guards watched the door."

"What?" Marc asked straightening in the chair.

"Yeah, that's right, counselor. One of the guards watched the door for them while they worked me over."

"Are you serious?"

"Yeah. Why are you so surprised? It happens," Carl said with a shrug.

"Which guard?"

"Guy named Olson. A real asshole. I've seen him around. A real prick."

"This is bullshit," Marc hissed, obviously seething.

"Relax, Marc. I've been through worse. Besides, good luck proving it. There was me, the two guys who kicked my ass and the guard. Who's gonna believe me?"

"Who were the two guys?"

"Don't know them," Carl answered. "Seen 'em around the jail but never talked to either of them. I'll be okay. Besides, like I said it's not too bad. I've been through worse."

Marc silently stared at his client, the blood draining from his face as he calmed down while he did so. "Well, at least I can go out there and play the media a bit. I can make the accusation that a guard was involved. As liberal as this town is that will play pretty well for a few days."

"You think so?"

"No doubt. Listen, I have to take off for a while, but I'll be back. I want to get a good camera and get some pictures of you. Okay?"

"For your scrapbook?" Carl asked, again weakly attempting a smile.

"For the lawsuit," Marc answered grimly.

"Whatever you say, Marc. I'm not going anywhere. Besides, I'm getting a little tired. Think I'll get some sleep. Didn't get much last night."

"Okay, Carl," Marc said patting him on the leg as he rose to go. "You take it easy and I'll be back in a couple of hours."

"Sure thing," Carl said as his eyes closed.

Marc exited the room and stepped into the middle of the crowd of police outside the doorway. He hesitated for a moment looked over the group and then, spotting the one he wanted, put an angry look on his face and. went after him.

"One of your damn guards was in on this," Marc snarled into Waschke's face as he stepped up to the big cop.

Jake took an involuntary step backwards and held up his hands as if to ward off an attack. The next thing Marc knew, three of the other officers had him sprawled across the counter of the nurses' station, two of them pinning his arms while the third one began to pat him down. Marc glanced over at the media crowd who were swinging into action as Waschke quickly regained command stepped forward and pushed his three protectors aside saying, "Let him go, let him go, for chrissakes. We'll be all over the evening news, you idiots."

Waschke got in between Marc and the other police, all of whom were by now gathered around their lieutenant and the lawyer who continued to remain spread out across the counter for the obvious benefit of the now whirring TV cameras.

"Get those people back," Jake whispered to his subordinates jerking a thumb toward the news people. "Everything's under control here folks. Just a little misunderstanding," he said into the cameras as the officers began to gently guide the reporters away from the scene.

Jake turned back to Marc, leaned over and quietly whispered into his ear, "You can get up now, counselor. The show's over. The cameras are off. You want to talk to me," he continued as Marc straightened himself, "come talk to me," he said nodding his head toward a small waiting area and began to walk off in that direction.

Marc followed the big cop and took a chair directly opposite from Waschke who had seated himself in the farthest corner.

"Now, counselor, what did you want to talk to me about?" Jake began.

"One of your jail guards stood by and watched while a couple of the other inmates worked him over."

"First of all, they're not one of my guards. I have nothing to do with what goes on in the jail," Jake answered as he leaned back and calmly crossed his legs. "More importantly, you got any proof of this pretty serious accusation? Other than the word of your client?"

"Not yet. How much do you think it'll take to get one of your jailbirds to start singing? Especially if a guard did put them up to it. I'll find out. Count on it," Marc said, anger creeping into his voice.

Waschke quickly uncrossed his legs, leaned forward and jabbing an index finger toward Marc, menacingly said, "You listen to me, lawyer. This is a police matter and I suggest you steer clear of it. It'll be investigated like any other crime. You got that?"

"That sounds like a threat, Lieutenant," Marc said calmly. "Maybe you'd like to go discuss this in front of your chief or a judge. Or, better yet, how about I walk down the hall and get the police department a little more free publicity? Sunday's a slow news day and I'm not sure they got enough footage a few minutes ago."

With that, both men sat back in their chairs and silently stared directly into each other's eyes. Marc, surprising himself at how calm and unintimidated he was. Waschke calming himself trying to regain some measure of control knowing full well that Marc could do exactly what he threatened.

After almost a full minute of the staring contest, Waschke blinked first by saying, "Okay. You're right. Point taken. But I promise you, I will look into this. What's the name of the guard?"

"Olson," Marc replied. "And I will investigate this myself. I have every right to and I will."

"Do what you have to," Jake said as he opened a small notebook to write down the guard's name. "Who were the inmates?"

"He doesn't know their names but I'm sure he'll be able to identify them."

"Okay, counselor. You okay with me talking to him now?"

"No, he's sleeping. Maybe later, but under no circumstances is he to be questioned unless I'm there. I want to make that absolutely clear, okay?"

"No problem," Jake said.

"I'm going to take off for a while. I'll be back in about an hour or so. You can talk to him then. In the meantime, nobody except hospital personnel goes into that room."

"Absolutely, counselor. I'll send a detective to start checking out this Olson, but don't hold your breath. Seems no one at the jail saw or heard anything," Jake said with a shrug.

With that, both men rose to leave and to Marc's surprise Waschke stuck out his big right hand to Marc, which Marc took, both men with the brief handshake acknowledging that each had a job to do and hard feelings wouldn't interfere. They parted company in front of Carl's room, Waschke to oversee security and assign a detective to discreetly check into Carl's allegations. Marc to finish his press conference and to make the allegations public.

FORTY-SEVEN

Several days after the hospital fracas, Maddy Rivers wore a puzzled expression as she drove toward an appointment with her current employer. She had spent the past week or so checking out their client. Interviewing his few friends, neighbors and co-workers. Attempting to come up with an alibi for Carl. At first, she began by checking into where he was just for the nights of the two murders he was charged for. Coming up empty there, she expanded her search to at least come up with something to cast some doubt that Carl had anything to do with any of them. Not surprisingly, she drew a complete blank. Very few people can positively establish where they were on any given date and time and Carl was no exception.

What puzzled her was Carl himself. Since being released on parole the previous December, he was obviously living a pretty quiet life. The people in his apartment building all said pretty much the same thing. None of them knew him too well except to say he was friendly enough on the occasions when they passed in the hallway or ran into each other by the mailboxes. Kept to himself. Few friends or visitors that anyone had noticed.

Coworkers had basically said the same thing. Carl had obtained a job through his parole officer at a small mail order warehouse in Southeast Minneapolis shortly after his release from prison. It had been the Christmas rush time for them, but Carl had worked hard and been very dependable so, they kept him on after the seasonal rush had died down. His fellow employees all seemed to like him well enough. Dependable and helpful. Always willing to work hard and lend a hand when needed. Even joining them a few times for an after-work beer on a Friday night.

His supervisor had thought so highly of him that he had recommended Carl for a raise just before his arrest. Always on time, never called in sick and did a good job. A rarity for the type of transient workers the business normally employed.

Maddy had interviewed his parole officer and she, too, had nothing but positive things to say. Good reports from his job and always made their meetings on time. No rescheduling with excuses and seemed to be staying out of trouble. All of which added up to Maddy's current bewilderment. Hardly the profile, or so it seemed to her, for some kind of mad dog stalker, rapist and serial killer. *Then again,* she thought, *maybe it was the precise personality.* After all, whenever one of these whackos gets caught, isn't it always the neighbors being interviewed on TV talking about what a quiet, nice man he seemed to be? How surprised they all were?

She parked her car in the small lot behind Marc's building, went in through the back door and up the stairs to his office. She cheerfully greeted Carolyn, Sandy and one of the lawyers, she didn't know his name though she did recognize the stunned look on his face as he looked her over. The same one that she normally elicited from men that rarely flattered her, normally bored her and this time annoyed her.

Maddy took one of the chairs in the reception area as Carolyn lifted the telephone receiver to let Marc know she had arrived. A few minutes later Marc appeared through his office door, greeted her and politely stepped aside as she went past him into this office.

"Who's the leering lech?" she asked as she slumped heavily into one of the chairs.

"You're in a good mood today," Marc replied. "That was Barry Cline," Marc continued as he took his chair. "Why, did he do something?"

"No, he didn't," Maddy sighed. "Forget it. You're right. I'm just in a rotten mood. PMS, maybe. I don't know."

"Oh, good," Marc said smiling. "PMS and you carry a gun. There's a combination."

"And don't forget it," she said as she threw her head back laughing heartily.

"So," Marc said as he got down to business. "What do you have on our boy?"

"Like I said on the phone," she replied shrugging her shoulders and shaking her head. "Not much. Nothing for an alibi, but then, Carl wasn't much help there. As far as what I could find out about him, nothing unusual. Pretty quiet guy living alone. No real close friends but everybody he knows seems to like him well enough. All pretty surprised by the arrest and everything. Nothing to suggest anything like this but nothing to rule it out either. "

"Other than the rape conviction."

"Right. Other than that. Listen," she continued, "what about a shrink? Have you thought about calling one as a witness? Having one examine Carl?"

"Yeah, I've thought about it, but I don't think so. I don't want to open that door for the prosecution. Our defense is going to be the standard SODDI. Some other dude did it. Plain and simple. We just need to come up with some way to prove that. Or, at least, cast reasonable doubt on their case. Which brings me to your next assignment. Their main witness. This Hobbs guy. I want you to start on him."

"You want a written report on what I've found on Carl so far?"

"No, nothing that might be discoverable. Nothing I would have to turn over to the other side."

"I have more coming on Carl anyway. Arrest reports, prison record. Stuff like that."

"How are you getting all that?"

"Don't ask. Let's just say Tony's been helpful."

"Okay, I won't ask. Start in on their witnesses. Hobbs first. Background check. Friends, neighbors. You know the drill. Take a few days. Give me a call and we'll look at what you've found. Then I'll set up an interview with Hobbs."

"You don't want me to talk to him?"

"No, not yet. Let's see what we can come up with on him. How's the money holding out?"

"I'm okay for now. I'll do up an itemized statement today or tomorrow and get it to you. You having problems getting paid?"

"A little. Don't worry about it. I've got more coming. At least, I'm supposed to."

"You looked real good on TV the other night. You know, that business at the hospital."

"You liked that?" Marc asked, grinning broadly.

"Oh yeah," she said, laughing her delightful laugh. "Very convincing stuff."

"There's an editorial in yesterday's paper about it too. Did you see it?"

"No, I didn't."

"Very pious and righteous sounding. You know, 'police zealousness' and all that crap. This, of course, is the same paper that was all over their ass before they made an arrest. Quite humorous actually."

"I'm sure," she agreed. "I have to go," she said looking at her watch as she rose to leave. "I have an appointment with a snitch. Tony tells me he may be able to give us some background on Carl."

"Do the cops know about him?" Marc asked as he came around the desk to get the door for her.

"I don't think so," she said, slightly shaking her head. "Tony knows him. He told Tony he knew Carl and hinted he knows some things about him. I'll check it out and call you later," she answered as they made their way through the reception area to the exterior doorway.

"Okay, Maddy. I'll talk to you later."

After the door had closed behind her, he turned to go back to his office just as Sandy said, "The mail's here Marc. You're not going to like this."

"Now what?" he wearily asked.

"The IRS has filed an appeal."

"What?" he asked disbelievingly as he took the single paged document from Sandy's outstretched hand. He quickly read it over, dropped his hands to his side allowing the Notice of Appeal to drop to the floor, slumped his shoulders, rolled his eyes toward the ceiling and said, "What in God's name is wrong with these people?"

"Can they win?" Carolyn asked.

"No," Marc said emphatically as he stooped to retrieve the document.

"Are you sure?" Sandy asked, obviously relieved.

"Yes, I'm sure. Hell, Deirdre McConnell even admitted it to me after we were in court last time. The judge's decision is entirely within his discretion. No way would an appeals court overturn it. In fact, I'll get more money out of them for this," he said waving the paper in the air.

"What about Karen's liability for the taxes? Can they get that overturned?" Carolyn asked.

"No. They agreed to that. That's not appealable."

"What are they appealing then?" Sandy asked.

"The award of attorney fees," he answered as he walked quickly to his office. He went to his desk, pulled a card from his rolodex, dialed the number and heard the familiar female voice answer it on the second ring.

"Deirdre, it's Marc Kadella," he said tersely trying to keep the anger from showing. "What the hell is this about?"

"I'm sorry, Marc," she replied, knowing exactly what he was referring to. "I had to file it in order to preserve the right to appeal."

"You can't win this thing," he said.

"I know," she answered defensively. "It's just that, well, the solicitor general's office hasn't signed off on it yet so, I had to file the appeal to give them more time."

"Call them up. Tell them to sign the damn thing," he said, still struggling with his control.

"I can't do that Marc. It's not proper procedure," she answered.

"I don't give a damn about their procedure. What's the number? I'll call them,"

"Relax, Marc. I understand why you're mad but calling the SG won't help. Trust me. They'll sign off and you'll get your money."

"Deirdre," he said more calmly. "I can't just ignore this and hope it all works out. I'll be hearing from the Eighth Circuit now and I'll have more work to do that I don't have time for."

"Don't rush into anything. We have time..."

"That's the problem, Deirdre. Those people in Washington have been sitting on this for two months and now they have more time. Little wonder the taxpayers are getting fed up."

"It'll work out, Marc. Trust me," she said defensively.

"Why do I doubt that? G'bye Deirdre," he said as he hung up the phone without waiting for her reply.

Placing an elbow on the desk, his chin in the palm of his hand Marc stared at the wall directly in front of his desk. As he silently pondered the inefficiency of the federal government's bureaucracy, he sensed, more than saw, someone standing in his doorway.

"What did she say?" Carolyn asked.

"Oh, the usual crap you get from those people. Sorry, some kind of mix up. We'll get it straightened out soon. Don't worry."

"Are they going to go through with the appeal?"

"She says no," he continued as he picked up the Notice of Appeal and waved it at Carolyn, "but they have. I can't just ignore it and hope they get their act together. I have to go on the assumption that an appeal is taking place and start to prepare for it."

"Will you get more money from them," Carolyn asked.

"Oh, yeah," he answered as he pulled the manila envelope of Karen's tax case from the desk drawer. "If I have to do any more work on this thing," he continued as he began making notes of his conversation with the government's lawyer, "I will definitely go after them for more fees."

FORTY-EIGHT

Jake rapped lightly on the window of the office door of the head of the crime lab unit and without waiting for a response, turned the knob, opened the door and walked in. He took two short steps, stopped and surveyed the clutter that filled the small room.

"Jesus Christ, Jacobson," Jake said shaking his head as he took the solitary chair in front of the shabby metal desk. "How the hell can you live like this?"

"Did you come down here to critique my interior decorating?" the short bald man seated behind the desk asked. "Believe it or not, Jake," the man continued waving an arm about the room, "I know where everything is and there is a system to all of this."

"What, the bulldozer filing system? What do you have for me?"

"A prelim on the stuff in the locker. Let me see, what did I do with my glasses?" The little man began as he looked over his desktop.

Jake leaned forward and quietly whispered, "They're on your bald-ass head, Paul."

Jacobson leaned back, rolled his eyes up and said, "Oh yeah. I knew I put them somewhere. Anyway," he continued as he slipped the half-moon glasses onto his nose and began reading from a single sheet of handwritten notes. "The contents of the locker: one pair of size ten and a half Reebok tennis shoes. One pair of Levi's blue jeans and a black windbreaker. The shoes and jeans are the same size as your suspect's other clothes and the windbreaker appears to be the same size or, at least, could certainly fit him. There's no tag on it so I can't say for sure what size it is. And one nylon carry-all handbag, slightly used."

"Find anything in your analysis?"

"Sort of. No blood, hair or tissue samples on any of the items ..."

"Damn," Jake muttered.

"They've been washed. Thoroughly. Several times I'd say and with a very strong detergent."

"Strong enough to remove any blood or tissues?"

"Maybe," Jacobson shrugged. "Hard to say for sure. The obvious question would be: why would anyone use a detergent like that on ordinary clothes? A question a jury would obviously want answered."

"Yeah, probably true," Jake replied. "What about prints?"

"Nothing on the clothes or in and around the locker. But on the ten quarters we found in the coin box, we came up with usable matches on three of them."

"How many?" Jake asked somewhat startled.

"Three. Good thumbprints from your boy on two of them. Perfect match. No doubt about it. A thumb and two other prints, right index finger. Enough of a match on these to testify to. No doubt about it,

Jake. Your boy dropped some coins into that locker," Jacobson said laying the sheet of paper on the desk and removing the glasses.

Jake sat back in the chair, crossed his legs and began rubbing his chin with his left hand. He sat this way silently reflecting about the news he had just been given. After about a minute, he dropped his hand to his lap, looked at the crime lab chief and said, "So what does that mean? We have clothing that he washed with a strong detergent and then hid in a locker. But what does it mean?"

"Who knows," Jacobson said as he dropped the glasses on the desk, leaned back and placed his hands behind his head, lacing the fingers together. "You know how this stuff goes, Jake. I get on the witness stand and testify as to the scientific analysis and the finger prints and let the jury decide it means whatever they want. The pretty obvious conclusion is that your boy was hiding something. How'd you come up with the locker anyway?"

"The key was on him when he was booked," Jake quietly replied.

"Well, there you go. That definitely ties him to the locker and the contents."

"Reebok tennis shoes?" Jake asked.

"Yeah, size ten and a half. Same as this Fornich."

"That reminds me," Jake said snapping his fingers. "Over in St. Paul, I think they got a footprint near where the governor's kid got it. And if I'm not mistaken, it was a Reebok size ten and a half. Thanks, Paul," Jake said as he rose to leave. "I think I'd better call John Lucas."

"I'll have a written report for you by tomorrow, Jake. I wouldn't get too excited about the tennis shoes. Pretty common brand name and there are lots of different styles."

"We'll see. Worth checking out. Send the report up as soon as you can, Paul. I'll talk to you later."

Jake hurried back to his office, puzzled over the revelation about the three coins with Fornich's fingerprints. He found John Lucas' business card, picked up the phone and punched in the numbers. While he listened to the ringing, he picked up the pink message slip that had been placed on the desk requesting that he call his brother. Halfway through the fifth ring a female voice came on the line. He asked for Lucas but was told he wasn't available. He left a message for a call back on Lucas' voice mail, hung up and dialed his brother.

"What's up, Danny?" he asked when his brother came on the line.

"Hey, Jake. Thanks for calling," Daniel said pleasantly. "The man would like to see you if you can spare a few minutes."

"Sure, Danny. Whatever you say. When?"

"How's today look for you? Tell me a time and I'll arrange it."

"Slow day?"

"Actually, yeah," Daniel laughed. "It'll only take a few minutes. I can sneak you in and out. No problem."

"Tell you what. How about around noon. I'll swing over and see him and then you and I can grab some lunch. What do you think?"

"Okay, sure. Sounds good. Come up to my office in the Capitol and I'll get you in through a back hallway. Come over just before noon. He'll be here then and in his office."

"Okay, Danny. Everything all right? How's he doing?"

"He tries to keep busy, but it's been tough on him and the family."

"How're you getting along with him? Any problems?"

"Me? No, why do you ask? No, no problems. I kind of keep my distance. You know, just do my job and be there when he needs me. Everything's cool, Jake," the last part said in a whisper.

"Okay, Danny. See you in a little while."

FORTY-NINE

On his way to St. Paul, a call from John Lucas was patched through to him in his car. Jake told Lucas about the locker and the tennis shoes and promised to have a photo sent to him for comparison with the footprint found near the alley where Michelle Dahlstrom was killed. He placed another call to arrange that and made the rest of the journey without interruption.

After arriving at the Capitol, he entered the anteroom of the governor's staff offices and the receptionist, recognizing her superior's brother, smiled sweetly as she picked up the phone to inform Daniel of Jake's arrival. He had momentarily seated himself in one of the reception area chairs when his brother's door opened, and Daniel appeared. They exchanged a brief greeting and handshake, almost as if the two men were only casually acquainted, and Jake followed his younger brother into his office.

"I can't make lunch after all, Jake," Daniel said after Jake closed the door. Some things have come up and I'll have to take a rain check."

"That's okay, Danny. Some other time," Jake said, hiding his disappointment.

"Jake," Daniel said hesitantly, "have you given any thought to Mom, lately? I mean, well, you know, maybe go to see her?"

Before responding, Jake sat down in one of the large leather chairs in front of Daniel's desk while Daniel remained standing, leaning against the edge of the desk to look down at his brother. Jake sighed heavily, rubbed a hand across his face as if pondering the question while Daniel awaited his reply.

"It's not that easy for me, Danny," Jake softly said. "I don't know how you can see her as much as you do. Speaking of which, how're you doing, anyway? That's why I wanted to have lunch. I wanted to talk to you."

"I'm doing good, Jake. Really. Don't change the subject."

"I'm not changing the subject. It's the same topic, remember? How're you doing around here? You know, with your boss and everything?"

"I'm uh, doing okay. I mean, well, you know, with, well um, the governor and all. It's a little strained. I uh, just sorta keep my distance. Do my job. Try to be professional and run things here."

"Still taking your medication? Still seeing the shrink?"

"Yeah, yeah Jake," Daniel said as he moved around the desk keeping his head turned to avoid his brother's gaze.

"You sure?" Jake asked. "You wouldn't bullshit me about that, would you?"

"No, Jake," Daniel said as he sat down in his chair. "That's helped me, a lot. You know, with issues to deal with and all. I'm doing fine, really."

"How're things at home?" Jake asked.

"None of your business," Daniel said a bit testily, immediately regretting his tone. "I'm sorry, I'm sorry, Jake," he quickly added, holding his hands up when he saw the stern look on Jake's face. "It's just, well, things have been better. You know, we're working it out. It'll be okay."

Just then his phone rang and the button lit up for the direct line to his boss saving Daniel from the necessity of further explanation. He picked up the receiver, told the governor they would be right in and as the two men began to walk towards the door in the corner, said to Jake, "What about seeing Mom. She needs us Jake. She's not going to live much longer."

"Yeah, I suppose," Jake replied with obvious reluctance. "I guess I can put up with her again for a couple hours. It's just, well, the drinking and all. The poor me bullshit. It's hard to take."

"Since the accident, the drinking's about all she has. What's the harm?"

"Let's go see your boss, Danny," Jake said.

The two men walked quickly and silently down the back hallway stopping at the first door they came to. Daniel rapped softly and opened the door without waiting for a response. They entered the governor's Capitol office and the man came around the desk to greet them. As they shook hands, Jake noticed the grip was firmer than the last time they met. The eyes a lot less puffy and the facial muscles tighter. Dahlstrom gently took Jake's left elbow and guided him toward the chairs in front of the desk. They each took one of the chairs leaving Daniel to remain standing behind them.

After a very brief exchange of pleasantries Jake went quickly into a monologue explanation of the case and evidence against Carl Fornich.

"So, Jake," the governor began when Jake finished. "There might be some evidence to tie him to Michelle's death?"

"Well, sir," Jake replied, shifting slightly in his seat. "It's a little early to tell for sure. We don't know yet."

"This man, Lucas. He'll check it out?"

"Oh, yes sir. No doubt about that. He'll get his people to do a comparison on the footprint. But sir, even if it's a match, well, that's pretty thin evidence. Certainly not enough for a conviction."

"I see. Yes, I suppose you're right," Dahlstrom said somberly nodding his head in agreement. "But," he continued as he lightly placed his right hand on Jake's left arm, "it may be enough to give her mother and me some peace of mind. Especially if we can put this animal away for a long time, Lieutenant. See what I mean."

"Of course, sir. Of course I understand," Jake said looking directly into Dahlstrom's eyes. "Governor," he continued. "Fornich is the guy. No doubt about it."

"Yes. Yes, I do believe you Jake," Dahlstrom said quietly moving his gaze to stare vacantly at the wall behind the desk. He sat this way for a moment, his hand still resting on Jake's arm, the only sound in the room the soft tapping of the clock on the wall.

After a brief moment of awkward silence, he turned back to Jake, smiled slightly as he stood extending his hand to his guest, "Thanks for coming by, Jake. I mean it. I really appreciate these, ah, informal, off-the-record chats."

"No problem, Governor," Jake said as the two men shook hands.

Dahlstrom walked with them back to the back-hallway door and as Daniel held the door for his brother, Dahlstrom said, "Daniel, after you've shown Jake out, I'd like to see you, please. Thanks again, Lieutenant," he said to Jake who waited in the hall. "See you again, soon. When this is all over, I'll have to have you and your wife to dinner. Just to show my appreciation."

"That would be nice, Governor. I'll look forward to it, sir," Jake replied not bothering to correct the man about his marital status. "Goodbye, sir," Jake said as Daniel closed the door to lead Jake away.

A few minutes later Dahlstrom was seated at his desk, his reading glasses in place as he read over a document he could not concentrate on. He heard a soft rap on his back door just before Daniel reappeared through it. He removed the glasses, placed them and the paper he held on the desktop, gestured to a chair as Daniel approached and said, "Sit down, Daniel. Please. I want to see this cop, Lucas, your brother talked about. Arrange a private meeting in two days."

"Yes, sir," Daniel said after he sat down.

"And Mills. Have you heard anything from him yet?"

"No, sir. But it's only been a few days," Daniel replied.

"Your brother knows nothing about him?"

"No, sir. At least not that I know of. If Jake knew he was poking around, he would've called me, I'm sure of that," Daniel answered.

"Good. Anyway," Dahlstrom continued, "give Mills a call. I want a progress report. Set up a meeting with him for early next week. Have Slocum, the Hennepin County Attorney and Judge Prentiss there, too. I have something to discuss with them."

"Yes, sir. I'll get right on it," Daniel replied.

FIFTY

Marc replaced the telephone receiver in its cradle and stared silently at it, the beginnings of a tension headache making its appearance at the base of his skull. He had just spent ten minutes having his ass chewed off by his wife for neglecting his children and of course, the not so subtle reminder that he was again late with the support check. What made him feel worse was that she was right. He hadn't seen his son and daughter for almost a month and he felt guilty as hell about it. Knowing they missed him and needed him. Even though they weren't little kids anymore, their parents' breakup had been very difficult on both of them. And he missed and needed them, too.

The intercom on the phone went off but he didn't bother to answer it. He knew what it was. Carolyn or Sandy letting him know that Joe Fornich had arrived. *He damn well better have more money*, Marc thought as he opened his door.

"Come on in, Joe," he said trying to keep the annoyance from his voice as he stood aside to let the man enter his office.

"Bad day?"

"I've had better," Marc answered. "What do you have for me Joe? Please give me some good news."

"I have some more money, Marc," he said with obvious hesitation. "And more coming."

"How much?" Marc asked hiding his disappointment.

"I talked to my boss and he'll come up with some and my sister is closing on her loan in a couple weeks. I guess she had some problems to straighten out first. With her credit or something," Joe said to soften the news.

"How much?" Marc asked again.

"Well, um, I got another four grand today. That should hold you for a while, shouldn't it?" Joe asked hopefully.

"Joe," Marc began slowly, leaning forward on the desk. "That won't cover the money I owe the testing labs I've had to hire to go over the evidence. The semen sample found on one of the victims, the knife and clothing they took from Carl's apartment. That kind of stuff. I told you this wouldn't be cheap."

"I'm doing the best I can, Marc. I'll get it for you. I swear," Joe pleaded.

"I know, Joe," Marc said softly. "Let me have it," he continued as he held out his hand.

Fifteen minutes after Joe Fornich left, Marc was seated in his chair staring out the open window behind his desk. Unconsciously looking at the tall buildings extending skyward from the pavement of downtown Minneapolis. Reflecting on what life must be like with the security of steady employment and a regular paycheck when he heard Carolyn's voice behind him from the open doorway.

"Maddy Rivers is here, Marc. She says it's important. She needs to see you."

He swiveled the chair around to face her, lifted his hands with the palms up and grinning, said, "Why not? Must be bad news. Today seems to be the day for it. Hi there," he said to Maddy as she appeared over Carolyn's shoulder. "Come on in and have a seat. Tell me your bad news."

"Well," she began as Carolyn closed the door. "You're not going to like it. I saw that guy that did time with Carl, Leo Shepley. He's a creepy little dude. Anyway, seems our boy didn't always play well with the other children."

"How so?" Marc asked.

"He stabbed a couple of other inmates. Damn near killed one of them."

"What?" Marc asked. "Bullshit. How'd he make parole?"

"No one would testify. He was charged with two of them and according to this jailbird Shepley, he may have done a couple more. In fact, Shepley says it was well known that he did it."

"That's just beautiful," Marc said.

"Isn't it though," Maddy said, a statement not a question. "You suppose the cops have this?"

"Of course they do."

"Why haven't they told you?"

"Because they're trying to hold it until the last possible moment. They'll claim they weren't sure they could use it at trial so, no need to disclose it. It's nonsense, of course, but that's what they'll say."

"Can they use it at trial?"

"Probably not," Marc answered. "Prentiss might want to let it in with a warning to the jury about what it means. Technical crap that will not help us, obviously. But I'll make damn sure he'll know he'll have an appeal because of it if he does. That will probably stop him. Let's go," Marc said as he got up, grabbed his coat and headed for the door. "You can tell me the details in the car."

"Where are we going?" she asked.

"It's time we paid a visit to our client. I want an explanation of this."

They took Marc's car and as he drove toward downtown she went over her notes of her meeting with Shepley. According to Tony Carvelli, Shepley had done time for a sex offense involving a child and Tony knew some cons who claimed Shepley was a bit of a jailhouse snitch. Not exactly the most popular or trustworthy type.

"Also, according to Tony," she told Marc, "Shepley's information was usually pretty reliable."

"Combine this with the girlfriend thing and Carl won't look too pretty to a jury," she said.

"What girlfriend thing?" Marc asked staring straight ahead through the windshield as he pulled into the parking ramp a block from the jail.

"You remember, I told you about it. The assault conviction for beating up a girlfriend," she answered.

"Oh, yeah that's right. I'd forgotten about that one. Hell, he was nineteen at the time. That was thirteen years ago, and I can probably keep that out at trial. Too long ago."

"And then, of course, there's the rape conviction," she added.

Marc parked the car on the fourth floor of the ramp, they took the elevator down to the street level and quickly walked the block to city hall. Even with his thoughts obviously preoccupied on their upcoming meeting with his client, Marc couldn't help noticing the number of male heads turning at the sight of Maddy Rivers. It even caused a mild ego rush thinking they might believe she was with him in a personal way.

They waited silently for Carl in one of the small conference rooms. Marc **was** seated at the table in the cheap plastic chair, his legs casually crossed trying to look calmer than he felt. Maddy alternated between leaning against the wall next to the one-way mirror and pacing behind Marc. After fifteen minutes or so, the door Marc was facing opened and Carl appeared, the bruise on his face fading and the swelling almost gone.

"What's up, Marc?" he asked cautiously, glancing back and forth between his two visitors.

"Sit down, Carl. We have to talk," Marc said pointing to the chair across the table from himself as Maddy took the seat in the chair to Marc's right.

"Why didn't you tell me about the stabbings in prison?" Marc calmly asked staring straight into Carl's eyes.

"What? What're you talking about?" Carl stammered, averting Marc's gaze.

"Cut the bullshit, Carl. If we found out about it, you can bet the cops have it, too!" Marc yelled slapping the tabletop.

The room remained silent as Marc continued to stare at Carl with an angry look on his face. Maddy sat calmly, her legs crossed, and her hands folded in her lap, carefully examining Carl's reaction. Carl fidgeted in his chair nervously flexing his fingers, folding and unfolding his hands as he tried to avoid Marc's eyes.

"Well?" Marc asked quietly. "I'm waiting."

"I, uh, I guess I didn't think it mattered and um, ..."

"You didn't think it mattered?" Marc asked. "Let's get something straight once and for all, Carl," Marc continued as he leaned back in his chair. "There is nothing, and I mean absolutely nothing about you and your life that doesn't matter. I have to know everything about you and your background. Is that clear enough? You don't decide what I'm to know. For chrissake, Carl. They could've clobbered us at trial with this if we hadn't found out. I need to know everything, so I can prepare for it. Do you understand?" Marc said, the last three words spoken very slowly and deliberately.

"Yeah, okay," Carl said softly. "It's just, well, it's kinda embarrassing, ya know," he added, shifting his eyes to Maddy and back to Marc.

"There's nothing you can say that she hasn't heard before," Marc answered.

"Okay, yeah, I guess," Carl said. "Okay, there was these two guys. Couple a damn queers, you know. Anyway, they tried to, well, uh, you know, do me. So, I had to defend myself is all. Stop them. Make them leave me alone."

"So, you stabbed them in self defense because they were trying to sexually assault you. Sodomize you? Is that correct?" Marc asked calmly.

"Yeah, that's what happened. You got a smoke? I could use a cigarette," Carl said.

"I don't smoke anymore," Marc answered as Maddy opened the long-strapped purse that had been dangling at her side. She removed a pack of Marlboro Lights and a book of matches and slid them across the table to Carl.

"Keep them," she said as he began to hand them back.

"Thanks. Anyway, that's all there was to it. There was no charges or nothing. They didn't want to testify cause of what they'd tried to do to me so, the whole thing kinda went away," Carl said. "And nobody messed with me after that so, it kinda helped, ya know?"

"What about the other two?" Marc asked. "We heard there were two others."

"No," Carl said shaking his head as he exhaled cigarette smoke at the floor. "I know what you're talking about and it wasn't me. Couple other guys got shived a month or two later, but I had nothing to do with them. Everybody thought I did, but I didn't."

"No more bullshit here, Carl," Marc said after staring at his client for a moment. "I have to tell you; this stuff doesn't look good for you. Now the prosecution can tie you to the use of a knife in an assault. They already have the rape conviction and an assault against a girlfriend many years ago. If they get all this in before a jury ..."

"What're you saying, Marc? Are you saying they could convict me?" Carl asked, his eyes pleading to his lawyer. "Do you believe me? Do you still believe I'm innocent? I didn't hurt those women, Marc. I swear," he continued as those same eyes began to glisten with tears.

"Relax, Carl. Yes, I still believe you. But no more secrets. Okay?" Marc answered reaching across the table to pat his client reassuringly on the hand.

"There's nothing else, Marc. I swear, there's nothing else," Carl said softly.

"What do you think?" Maddy asked as they stood outside the city hall entryway in the afternoon heat, "Can they bring that in at trial?"

"I don't think so," Marc answered after a long pause. "Unless they can find one of the victims and get him to testify. Something else for you to look into. See if you can find them or, better yet, hope like hell they're gone. Do you have their names?"

"Yeah. Both were released from prison about a year and a half or so ago. I'll see what I can do about finding them."

After parting company in the parking lot behind his office building, Marc entered the office through the hallway door and stood for a moment as Carolyn looked him over. His tie was completely undone and draped around his neck. His shirt was open at the collar and stuck to his back from the afternoon heat and the broken air conditioner in his car. His shoulders were slumped, and he held his crumpled suit coat with his left hand as the sweat on his forehead began to dry in the air-conditioned building.

"Rough day?" she asked sympathetically.

"You could say that," he answered wearily. "Any messages?"

"Yeah, Steve Gondeck called. Says it's important. Left his home number if you can't get him at the office," she said as he took the pink slip from her outstretched hand.

Before calling Gondeck, he dialed the private line of Margaret Tennant, hoping to hear a sympathetic voice. "Hello, your worship," he said when she answered.

"Hello, Marc," she answered without the usual warmth in her tone.

"Can I see you tonight?" he asked.

"Oh, geez, Marc. Um, tonight's not really good," she answered trying not to sound evasive.

"Gotta date?" Marc asked, trying to make it sound like a joke but knowing the answer before it came.

"Well, um, uh, yes, Marc, I do. Sorry. If you had called sooner. Or, at all," the last added because she knew she sounded defensive and didn't want to, did not feel that it was necessary.

"No, it's okay. You're right. You don't owe me an explanation. Listen, I got another call to make and I'm sure you're busy. I have to go," he answered quickly.

"Marc, ..."

"I'll talk to you soon, judge," he said and hung up the phone.

"Well," he said aloud to himself as he again picked up the phone. "I might as well call Gondeck and top this day off with whatever bad news he has."

"Steve Gondeck," he heard the voice say on the other end of the line.

"Steve, Marc Kadella."

"Marc, good. I'm glad you called. I wanted to tell you before you heard it somewhere else. We got the DNA results back this afternoon on the semen sample, the one found on victim number four, Constance Ann Gavin."

"Yeah," Marc said quietly, a knot forming in his stomach as he anticipated the news.

"It's a match, Marc. No doubt about it. It's from your boy."

FIFTY-ONE

Gordon Prentiss backed out of his suburban driveway in an irritable mood. *Another in a never-ending series of squabbles with that alcoholic bitch of a wife,* he thought, *was the last thing I need right now.* Something was going to have to give there, and soon. Either the booze had to go, or she did. Funny thing, he continued thinking as he headed the Lincoln Town Car toward his meeting at the Governor's Mansion, after all these years and all of the problems, he still loved her. Not so much in a sexual way since that was so infrequent as to hardly be worth the bother. He simply still loved her and there was no rational explanation for it.

Prentiss entered the moderately heavy traffic on 494, moved to the inside lane and pushed lightly on the accelerator. The luxury car's big V-8 purred as the speedometer quickly jumped to seventy, Prentiss not the least bit worried about another speeding ticket. A judge could make those go away easily enough. Settling into the plush leather seats he allowed his mind to speculate on his summons by the governor's top aide. It irritated him to be summoned by Daniel Waschke, whom Prentiss considered to be his inferior in every way imaginable. But then, for that matter, J. Gordon Prentiss III pretty much considered everyone to be his inferior. Especially the dolt who currently occupied the state's top office.

Arriving at the mansion intentionally five minutes late, pleased with himself at his precise timing, he exited the car and went to the back door, as instructed, and was greeted by his former classmate.

"Good evening, Judge," Daniel said as he held the door open for Prentiss.

"Hello, Daniel," Prentiss replied as the two men shook hands.

"Daniel," Prentiss continued in a whisper, "this is extremely unusual. I'm not sure how comfortable I am with this."

"I understand Gordon," Daniel said. "Don't worry, the governor is a man who remembers his friends." With that, Daniel turned to lead his guest down the hallway toward the backstairs as Prentiss followed, a sly smile on his lips.

Daniel took him through a door on the mansion's second floor and the two men entered the governor's private study. As they walked in, Prentiss noticed three men already in the room. Dahlstrom was seated on one of the two small sofas to Prentiss's left, the one facing the door. Seated opposite the governor was a man whose back was to Prentiss. That man rose as Prentiss and Daniel entered, turned to face Prentiss and the judge immediately recognized the Hennepin County Attorney, Craig Slocum, another obvious inferior whom Prentiss secretly detested. He shook hands with Slocum then moved to Dahlstrom who remained seated while they exchanged a brief greeting.

"I apologize for my tardiness, Governor," Prentiss said. "Traffic was a little heavier than what I expected." He then glanced at the third man in the room who was standing impassively by a window, a look of indifference on his face. All of the men were dressed casually in light summer shirts and slacks except for him. The only one in the room that Prentiss did not know. This one, Prentiss noticed, was dressed in an obviously cheap, somewhat shabby business suit. *The kind criminal defense lawyers wore into his courtroom,* he thought.

"Have a seat, Judge," Dahlstrom said indicating the space next to Slocum. "So," he continued as Prentiss and Slocum sat down, "we can get started now. First off, I'd like to thank you for taking the time to come here this evening. If you'll bear with me for a bit, I'm sure the point of this meeting will be clear shortly. This gentleman here," Dahlstrom said pointing a hand at the stranger, "is Tom Mills. Mr. Mills is an investigator who has done some, ah, sensitive work for people in the past. Very discreet type investigating. He has a report to make regarding some work he's done for me recently and I'd like you two to hear it and then I'll explain why. Mr. Mills..."

"Thank you, Governor," Mills said interrupting Dahlstrom while reaching into his suit coat and removing several sheets of paper from the inside pocket. "The subject's name is Marc Alan Kadella. A lawyer in private practice with an office in Minneapolis. I'll skip most of the biographical detail to get right to the most pertinent information. There's really nothing out of the ordinary in his background, anyway. Certainly nothing useful.

"The subject is having some pretty obvious money problems. In fact, all of the lawyers in the office seem to be struggling a bit right now. He rents space from a woman, one Constance Mickelson," Mills continued as he occasionally referred to the pages he held, "who seems to be well off financially herself, the result of inheritance from her parents and several successful divorces," he added looking at the three men, ignoring Daniel who had taken a chair near the door.

"The other two lawyers are a Christopher Grafton and Barry Cline."

"Do you know them?" Dahlstrom interjected, directing the question at Prentiss and Slocum.

"I know the Mickelson woman, slightly," Prentiss answered. "The other two don't sound familiar."

"I don't recall any of their names," Slocum said.

"As I said," Mills continued, "Cline and Grafton are both struggling a bit. Business has taken a downturn recently, it seems. It's Kadella himself who seems to be in the biggest trouble. Behind on his rent, child support and maxed out on his credit cards. He has very few clients right now and his main one is having difficulty coming up with the fees. Kadella is hanging on, but just."

"His best year," Dahlstrom said as he leaned forward, folded his hands together and placed his elbows on his knees, "was four years ago. Even then, he grossed eighty thousand. Typically, he makes around fifty to fifty-five. It's cost him his marriage and he's currently living in a somewhat shabby one-bedroom apartment not far from his office over in Uptown. Not exactly the glamorous lifestyle most people envision when they finish law school. Thank you, Mr. Mills," Dahlstrom said turning back to the speaker. "I think that's enough for now. Daniel, take Tom to the other room, please. I'll want to see him when we're finished here."

Daniel held the door open as Mills passed through it wearing the same impassive look on his face that he had maintained throughout his brief report.

Dahlstrom waited for the other two men to leave and the door to close and then continued. "Now, gentleman," he began as he leaned back on the sofa and draped his left arm casually over the back. "I've been doing some thinking about this case against this fella, Fornich. From what I understand it looks pretty solid, would you agree Craig?"

"Oh, yes sir. We're going to convict him all right. In fact, Governor, this hasn't been made public yet," Slocum said as he shifted his eyes around the room, "but the Grand Jury returned indictments against him today on all six victims in Hennepin County. The positive DNA test from one of the women seems to have done the trick. We may not get a conviction on all counts but he's going away for a long time."

"Yes, I see," Dahlstrom said showing no emotion at Slocum's revelation. "It's just, well, I guess, I mean, that's all well and good, but that still leaves Michelle and from what I understand there's virtually no evidence to tie this Fornich to her murder," the last few words trailing off quietly as he again leaned forward, elbows on his knees as he clenched and unclenched his fists several times. "And," he continued looking at his two guests, "I want that. I want her killer to admit it. Or, at least get convicted for it."

During this exchange Prentiss sat quietly, indifferent to Dahlstrom's obvious anguish. Listening to the conversation and mentally calculating how any of this could help him to further ingratiate himself into the governor's good will. "I know exactly what we can do," Prentiss said breaking the momentary silence. "A plea arrangement."

"I don't think so," Slocum said, emphatically shaking his head. "I can't believe he'd plead guilty to first degree murder and rape."

"How about this?" Prentiss said. "You offer him two counts of second-degree murder. All other charges get dropped if one of the charges includes the governor's daughter. We square it with Ramsey County so that I do the sentencing and handle the plea. We offer him an upward departure from the sentencing guidelines to say, thirty years..."

"Why would he be fool enough to take a deal like that?" Slocum asked looking at Prentiss.

"Because, Slocum," Prentiss said patronizingly patting Slocum on the knee, "if he doesn't and he's convicted of more than one count of anything, I'll sentence him to consecutive terms and he won't ever get out of prison. This way, he'll have a chance to get out and still have a life. And I guarantee he will be convicted. I'll see to that. But Governor," he continued looking directly at Dahlstrom, "what does any of this have to do with the information you gathered about his lawyer?"

"Wait a minute," Slocum interrupted. "It's my office that would have to handle the plea agreement. I'm not sure I want to go along with this. Why should I?"

"Because if you don't, I'll sit back and let the jury decide the case. And at this point, I haven't decided if all of your evidence is admissible," Prentiss said.

"Also, Craig, let's just say, politically, it is in your best interest," Dahlstrom interjected. "Besides, we're just kicking the idea around. As I recall, you're up for reelection next year and ..."

"Okay, okay," Slocum said throwing his hands up in surrender. "I'm not an idiot. I get the picture. What about his lawyer?"

"That's why I had Mr. Mills conduct a very discreet investigation. Possibly find a vulnerability there. Seems he has money problems and...." Dahlstrom said.

"A bribe? You think we can offer him a bribe? If that ever got out..." Slocum said incredulously.

"Certainly not," Dahlstrom responded. "Relax Craig. We're not idiots either. Just leave Mr. Kadella's incentive to me. I'll think of a way to make this attractive to him."

"And if he doesn't persuade his client to take the deal," Prentiss added, "I'm sure it will somehow leak to the press. That won't help at jury selection."

"I'm skeptical," Slocum said. "I don't see this happening."

"You just make the offer. If the defendant doesn't take it, well then, he takes his chances at trial," Prentiss said.

"Have you set a trial date?" Dahlstrom asked.

"We have a pretrial conference scheduled for next Tuesday. In my courtroom," Prentiss answered.

"What are you looking at for a trial date?" Dahlstrom asked.

"Well, the defendant refuses to waive his right to a speedy trial, so, it'll have to be soon," Prentiss said.

"Are you involved in the trial personally, Craig?" Dahlstrom asked Slocum.

"Oh, yes. I'm going to try this one myself," Slocum said sitting up straight and throwing his shoulders back. "Of course, one of my assistants will second chair but I'll be lead counsel."

"Are you ready for trial? How soon can you be ready?" Dahlstrom asked.

"Well, I, ah, I'd have to check with Steve Gondeck, but yes, I'm sure we can go soon," Slocum said hesitantly.

"Good," said Dahlstrom. "Judge, anything at all on a trial date."

"The defense has mentioned mid-August. But nothing's been decided," Prentiss answered.

"Move it up. Two weeks from now. First of August. Tell Kadella whatever you want but make him face an earlier date than what he expected. Cut his preparation time in half. Let's see if we can't bring a little pressure on him."

"Good idea, Governor," Prentiss agreed as Slocum silently shifted in his seat.

"Well, gentlemen," Dahlstrom said as he stood up from the sofa. "That should about do it for now. I'll have Daniel show you out. If anything develops, let me know." The last statement obviously not a request.

FIFTY-TWO

The following Tuesday morning Marc was at his desk working on one of the few cases, other than the State vs. Fornich, that he still had left. A pretty straightforward divorce case that was on the verge of settling and Marc wanted to go over the details of the agreement before presenting it to his client. Grateful for at least a brief respite from the all-consuming State vs. Fornich, he was carefully reading every word and double-checking every detail when the intercom buzzer broke his concentration.

"Yeah?" he softly inquired into the phone.

"Marc," he heard Sandra say, "there's a lawyer from Washington on the phone. An Andrea Elliott. She's on line two."

"Okay," Marc said. "I'll take it." He punched the button next to the blinking red light on his phone console and said, "Marc Kadella."

"Mr. Kadella," he heard the voice reply "this is Andrea Elliott. I'm an attorney in the Tax Division at the Justice Department and I've been assigned to handle the appeal of Karen Kadella's tax case."

"Okay," Marc replied. "What can I do for you?"

"Well, Mr. Kadella ..."

"Please," he interrupted, "call me Marc."

"Okay, Marc. Like I said, I've been assigned to handle the appeal and I was hoping you could give me some background on it. I don't know anything about it and I just have a few questions."

"You're kidding, right? You've been assigned a case on appeal and you have been told nothing about it and now you're calling me to get that information. I'm not surprised," Marc said pleasantly. "What would you like to know?"

"Well, briefly, just a little bit about what the case is about," Elliott said.

While opening his desk drawer and removing one of the case files to make notes and a record of the conversation, Marc began telling her the background of the case. He told her that his wife had been assessed unpaid payroll taxes for a restaurant she had worked for several years ago. That the IRS had hounded her and basically made their lives a living hell trying to collect the taxes. That they were told by the IRS and a number of self-proclaimed tax lawyers that because she signed checks for the business she was responsible for the taxes. Finally, after years of harassment, Marc had become fed up and sued the federal government. After several months of wasting the taxpayers' money defending the case the government admitted that check signing is not enough for tax liability and had basically surrendered.

"We settled the issue of Karen's liability but went to court over attorney fees. The judge was furious with the government's conduct and awarded every penny of fees I requested. That's pretty much it.

That's where we stand, and I guess, you people are now appealing that decision even though you don't have a snowball's chance in hell of winning," he concluded, doing his best to keep his annoyance and aggravation with the government out of his voice.

"Oh, I see," she meekly replied. "Um, ah, I was wondering if you could do me a little favor."

"What's that?" he asked.

"Well, could you fax me copies of the court's order and any memos that might be pertinent?"

"Excuse me?" he asked, incredulously, "You don't have them?"

"Well, um, uh, I'm sure they're around here somewhere, but ah, no I haven't seen them," she said.

Still holding the phone to his ear with his left-hand Marc placed his right elbow on the desktop, covered his eyes with his right hand and heavily sighed into the phone.

After a moment of silence, Marc continued by saying, "Let me see if I got this straight. You people are appealing an order that you can't possibly win. You've been assigned to handle the appeal and know nothing about the case. You don't have the file, haven't seen the orders and now you're asking me to send you copies. Why doesn't any of this surprise me?"

"Well, of course, you don't have to send them to me, but it would be quicker than waiting for the file to turn up and I could make a determination on whether or not to recommend an appeal to the solicitor general's office," she said sounding defensive.

"Excuse me?" Marc asked sitting upright in his chair. "Make a recommendation to whom?"

"The solicitor general," she said.

"I was told the SG's office had the recommendation for no appeal weeks ago."

"Oh, no," she said. "It's just now coming out of the trial division. You see, first the trial lawyer and the IRS make a recommendation. Then it goes to her boss at the trial division. That person then reviews the case and makes a recommendation. Then, it comes here to the appeals division and one of us reviews it and makes a recommendation. Then it goes to the head of the appeals division, my boss, and he reviews it and makes a recommendation and then it goes to the solicitor general's office and they review it and make a final decision on whether or not to appeal the case."

By this time Marc was again leaning on his elbow covering his eyes with his hand and shaking his head in disbelief. "So, it's been sitting on someone's desk at the trial division all this time," he said, a statement not a question.

"It probably still is," she softly replied.

"Okay, Andrea," he said, again sighing heavily into the phone. "I'll pull the file and fax you the stuff I think you'll want to see. But

I'm warning you right now, I've received orders about scheduling and things like that from the Eighth Circuit that I can't ignore. The clock is ticking here, and I can't just sit here hoping that someday soon you people get your act together and drop this thing. If I have to so much as get out of my chair to do any more work on this case, you people are going to pay me to do it. Okay?"

"I can't make that decision," she said.

"I know a judge in St. Paul who will be happy to make that decision for you. I'm just warning you. Someday soon somebody had better get it together or it's going to cost the taxpayers more money. I'll fax the stuff to you in a few minutes. I know where my file is," he added very sarcastically. "What's your fax number?" he asked. He wrote down both her fax and phone numbers and then said, "As soon as you review the papers, give me a call and let me know what you think. Thank you," he concluded and hung up the phone without waiting for her reply.

Leaning back in his chair, Marc tilted his head back to stare up at the ceiling and said aloud, "Ah yes. The glamour of practicing law. And the incredibly bright and interesting people you get to deal with."

A short while later, he was back at his desk listening to Madeline's latest report. "I checked with all of the bartenders at Chardelle's, that joint where Carl says he picked up the Gavin woman. Two of them, a Julie Graf and Jerry Douglas," she said, referring to her notes, "definitely remember seeing her in there on several occasions. Mostly weekends. Both the bartenders are college kids so, they work the weekend nights.

"Graf remembers her leaving a couple times with men. Very obviously much to Ms. Graf's disapproval. She says that's why she remembers her."

"Why's that?" Marc asked.

"Because she wore a wedding ring. Didn't hide it at all. Women don't really approve of that behavior the way men do. And they tend to notice it a little more."

"Bullshit," Marc said with a laugh.

"No, I think that's generally true," Maddy said staring back at him. "Anyway," she continued, "they both remember seeing Carl in there, which, I had gotten from them before. But neither of them ever saw Carl leave with anyone."

"What kind of place is it?"

"That's kind of the funny thing. It's a pretty nice place but basically a meat market. Carl seems to be more of a shot and a beer guy at the local saloon. Not a place he would hang out."

"How often did he go there?"

"Not much. Couple times a month or so. Usually sat at the bar. Stayed to himself, according to the bartenders."

"Did either of them ever see him talking to Gavin? Or any other women?"

"Julie Graf said she thinks he may have struck up a conversation with Gavin once or twice, but she wasn't sure."

"What about the other bartender, what's his name?"

"Jerry Douglas. He never saw them together that he can recall," Maddy answered, without referring to her notes.

"Carl swears he picked her up there once," Marc said. "Recognized her picture as soon as I showed it to him. Says it was the night before she was murdered. A Saturday."

"How can he be so sure?" she asked.

"You kidding? You've met Carl. He scores with a woman, any woman, even if he pays her, he probably marks it on his calendar. I can see that being something Carl would remember."

"I suppose," she said laughing.

"We'll need to subpoena both bartenders," Marc said.

"I asked them if they'd testify and both said they would," she answered.

"Still, I want to make sure. Drop subpoenas on both of them. I don't know if they'll do us any good or not, but at the very least the girl's testimony will show that the Gavin woman wasn't exactly a saint. And there were other men involved. Maybe one of them could've done it. Or, better yet, could be the killer of all these women. What about identification? Could Graf identify either of the men she saw leave with her?"

"No," Maddy answered. "She didn't think they were regulars. It can be a busy place on weekends, though. I have a few names to run down. Guys who the bartenders know who are in there regularly. I'll start with them and see if any can tell us anything."

"Good. Now, what about this eyewitness of theirs? This Hobbs guy."

"Martin Dale Hobbs," she began after flipping through a few pages in her notebook. "Not a lot on him. Seems to be a bit of street person. You know, kind of hanging around the fringes of the criminal types. No record, though. Which strikes me as a little odd, actually."

"Why's that?"

"Well, you know the type. Never really seriously involved in anything real bad, but always kind of around it. Tony did some quiet checking for me, especially with the drug crowd, found out a few of them kind of knew him. Or, at least know the name."

"Hmmm," Marc said, lightly tapping an index finger on his chin while he listened.

"And I mean, no record. Nothing. No convictions. No arrests. Not even a speeding ticket on his driving record. Nothing."

"That is odd," Marc softly replied. "Did you set up a time for an interview with him?"

"Tomorrow evening," she said. "Do you still want to be there?"

"Yeah, I do," he answered.

"The one thing I keep wondering about this Hobbs guy is: What was he doing there in that neighborhood at that time of night? It's nowhere near where he lives or his usual hangouts and it's not exactly the best place for a white guy to be wandering around. What was he doing there?"

"Good question," Marc said. "Drugs?"

"Maybe. But he can find drugs in other places," she answered.

"A hooker?"

"Same answer," she said shrugging.

"That could be a good possibility for us at trial," Marc mused aloud.

"Very carefully," she said. "Remember, he could have a perfectly sensible answer to that question."

"So, you don't ask the question. Ask it in a way that lets the jury answer the question. Or, at least try to cast a little doubt on his credibility," Marc answered. "What about Waschke? Have you started on him?"

"Just a little. Mostly stuff Tony gave me," she answered, again referring to her notes. "Exemplary cop, actually. Couple of shootings. Both justified. Citations for bravery, dedication etcetera. Regular promotions and a good history of closing cases with arrests and convictions. Also, his brother is the governor's Chief of Staff."

"Yeah, I know. Good political connections. Anything in his background? Anything useful?"

"Don't know yet. I'll start on that next. This won't be easy checking out people like this," she said.

"Be careful. Discretion."

"I know," she said. "Have you got a trial date yet?"

"We'll set it this afternoon. I have a pretrial with the judge today," Marc answered.

"Um, Marc," she said with hesitation, "I'm, uh, gonna need..."

"More money," he said without letting her finish. "I know. I'm working on it. How much?"

"Well, I figure, minimum, another grand right now and ..."

"I can give you half that now. Will that be okay for a few days? Joe's supposed to be coming in with more early next week."

"That'll be fine," she said flashing her dazzling smile. "How about you? How are you doing?"

"Hanging in there," he said with a shrug.

Fifteen minutes after Madeline left, Marc placed two manila file folders, each about two inches thick with papers, in his briefcase. He draped his suit coat over his left arm, grabbed the briefcase and headed for the door. Just before he reached the door leading to the exterior hallway, he heard Carolyn say, "Are you coming back today?"

"Yeah, probably later. Around four," he answered.

"Why are you leaving so soon?" she asked. "You don't have court 'til two."

"I'm going to go to the library and start working on Karen's appeal. I have to start working on it anyway and need to think of something besides Carl Fornich for a while," Marc answered.

"Starting to wear you down?" Sandy asked.

"Oh, I don't know," he said with a heavy sigh. "I guess it is a bit. It's just that, well, every time I turn around there's more bad news with that damn case. Some day I'm going to learn to listen to myself and go with my first reaction. I knew I shouldn't get involved with it, but now I'm up to my ass in it and there's no turning back. How's that old saying go? 'When you're up to your ass in alligators it's difficult to remember that your initial objective was to drain the swamp'. I'm starting to see exactly what that means. I'll see you later. I have to get out of here for a while," he said as he opened the door and stepped into the hallway.

FIFTY-THREE

Marc went down the backstairs and into the parking lot, his eyes blinking rapidly in the blazing midday sunlight. He went to his car, opened the driver's door, casually tossed the briefcase and coat onto the passenger seat and got into the steaming car. Marc tried to insert the key in the ignition, but they slipped from his hand and fell on the floor. He reached down to retrieve them and noticed his right hand was shaking. He picked up the keys and stared at them, transfixed by the increasing trembling of his hand. Marc held up his left hand and saw that it, too, was shaking rapidly as he stared, almost as though the hands weren't his, uncertainty and confusion clouding his thoughts.

Marc again attempted to stick the key in the ignition but now his hand was shaking so badly he had to grip his right hand with his left and carefully guide the key into the slot. Before starting the engine, he sat back in the seat, head back, eyes staring at the ceiling, his breath coming in short gulps, gasps and swallows. He could feel his heart beating rapidly as he tried to control his breathing. Attempting to normalize his functions, confusion and fear washing over him like a wave.

Slowly holding his hands up, now shaking so badly they looked blurred. His mind was acting as though he was outside of his body, watching himself as somebody else, his breathing still fast and shallow. Marc watched his hands, almost involuntarily, slowly move toward the steering wheel, still violently trembling as his eyes darted back and forth between them. When his hands came within an inch of the wheel he felt his arms quickly spring forward and his hands tightly grasp the wheel. At the same instant that his fingers made contact with the plastic surface, all of the air in his lungs rushed out and he slumped forward on the seat, his forehead lightly thumping against the top of the steering wheel.

Marc stayed like this, gripping the steering wheel, head and shoulders slumped over, eyes wide open and mouth agape, for almost four minutes. Slowly, while the sweat streamed down his face, back and underarms, his breathing began to normalize. Finally, he gently pushed himself from the steering wheel and sat back in the seat.

Releasing his grip, he noted that his breathing was normal again and he could no longer feel his heart pounding. He held his hands up in front of his face and clenched and unclenched his fingers several times, finally holding them both out, fingers extended, and saw that the trembling was gone. Marc placed his left hand on his chest, took several deep breaths to assure himself that he had normalized and then, sheepishly looked around the parking lot to see if anyone else had witnessed this spectacle.

Satisfied that the anxiety attack had passed, Marc started the car and slowly drove out of the parking lot. As he headed for Park Avenue and the quick trip into downtown Minneapolis, his mind kept replaying the scene in the parking lot his body and mind had just taken him through. He was still having trouble with his concentration and he gripped the steering wheel so tightly the knuckles of both hands were white. He continued to breathe in long, deep breaths as his body attempted to calm him and bring him back in control.

Arriving downtown Marc turned west on Seventh toward the government center, now relaxed but wishing he still smoked and had a cigarette. He parked his car in the underground ramp of the government center, gathered up his coat and briefcase and headed for the top floor law library.

He spent the next two hours in the library, poring over federal appeals court jurisdiction and procedures. Reviewing cases on the issue of a judge's discretion in awarding attorney fees against the U.S. Government and quickly learned that it is a relatively rare occurrence. While the government is involved in thousands of lawsuits annually, they usually win and almost never have to pay, even when they lose.

He began outlining his brief for the appeal, very confident that he would win and eventually get his money and even more because the government was wasting more of the court's time and resources, a source of great annoyance for all judge's.

After a while, an idea began to germinate in his mind. A way to possibly slap the government around a bit more and have some fun with their inefficiency and incompetence. He spent another hour researching that prospect before he had to put the large stack of books piled on the table away and head downstairs to his pretrial in Prentiss' courtroom.

On the elevator ride down to the fourteenth floor he stood silently staring at the console as the numbers for the floors ticked off as it descended. It stopped on 19 and two women got on, both lawyers whom he vaguely recognized as staff attorneys with the prosecutor's office. Marc's thoughts were still on the tax case and his idea for tweaking the government's nose.

He had a grin on his face and softly chuckled to himself as the car continued its journey. Both of his newly arrived companions gave him quizzical looks because of his odd behavior and as he stepped through the doors on fourteen they looked at each other and shrugged their shoulders while Marc walked off down the hallway to his destination.

FIFTY-FOUR

As he entered the courtroom he was immediately struck by two odd facts. First, he was mildly surprised to see both Steve Gondeck and the county attorney himself, Craig Slocum, seated at one of the lawyer's tables. Gondeck had to be there and Marc knew Slocum was going to try the case, but it was extremely unusual for Slocum to attend a pretrial. Marc had never seen it before since these things were a very routine matter and the county attorney's office could be represented by any of the staff lawyers.

As odd as their presence was what really struck him as extraordinary was the fact that both of them were actually on time. Early even. *One to mark down on the calendar,* he thought. As he stepped through the gate in the otherwise empty room, Gondeck rose to greet him while Slocum remained seated and after brief handshakes and greetings, Marc asked, "Is my client here yet?"

"He's on the way," Gondeck replied. "Should be here any minute."

"Okay," Marc said. "Should we go see the judge? I assume we're going to set a trial date today."

Slocum stood up, stepped over to Marc and gently took Marc's left elbow in his right hand. "Marc" he said, "you don't mind if I call you Marc, do you?"

"No, Craig, not at all," Marc said looking directly into Slocum's eyes with his best 'gosh, gee, shucks what a privilege that is' look on his face which drew a brief smile from Gondeck.

"Marc," Slocum continued, obviously unaware of what had just happened, "let's use the jury room for a conference first. Okay?"

"Sure," Marc replied a bit puzzled by the necessity of a conference.

The three of them went through a door next to the jury box and into the small room and took seats at the long table used by jurors during breaks and deliberations. Slocum took the chair at the head of the table, Gondeck to his immediate left and Marc to his right, a couple chairs down.

"Marc," Gondeck began, "we'd like to resolve this case."

"Good," Marc replied looking directly at Slocum. "Dismiss the charges. You've got the wrong guy."

"Well, we of course don't think so," Slocum said with an obviously patronizing smile. "In the interest of justice and economy, we are prepared to make your client an offer," he added as he leaned forward onto the table and folded his hands together.

Slocum maintained this pose, solemnly looking at Marc while a full minute's silence passed between the three men. Marc simply stared back, noting the poker-face expression Slocum maintained while

Gondeck leaned back in his chair, casually crossed his legs and unnecessarily smoothed his tie.

"I'm listening," Marc said to Slocum, breaking the silence while thinking, "This guy is trying to intimidate me. This might be amusing after all."

At that moment, a single rap on the door interrupted them, a deputy sheriff appeared and said, "Your client's here, Mr. Kadella. We'll have him in the conference room."

"Okay," Marc replied. "Tell him I'll see him in a little bit."

"Sure thing," the deputy replied as he quietly closed the door.

"Here's the offer, Marc," Gondeck said as he sat up while Slocum maintained his pose. "He pleads to two counts of second-degree murder. We drop everything else. We recommend thirty years. He's out in twenty. He's what, thirty-two? Thirty-three? Out in twenty, he still has a life."

"We believe that's extremely fair and reasonable," Slocum interjected.

"No doubt," Marc said looking back and forth between his two adversaries. "In fact, if Carl really is the serial killer, rapist-pervert monster you say he is, it's extremely generous. Which makes me wonder; if you're so convinced that he's guilty and your case is so solid, why are you offering this at all?"

"My personal conviction is," Slocum began somberly, "to give Mr. Fornich a chance at redemption. An opportunity to confess his guilt to God. Every soul is worth saving."

Marc stared wide-eyed at Slocum, his mouth partly open as another moment of silence went by. Without turning his head, he looked at Gondeck and said, "Is he serious?"

"That's not necessary!" Slocum thundered as he slapped an open palm on the table while Gondeck's shoulders hunched up slightly and a grimace creased his face as Gondeck reached over and lightly held Slocum's left arm just as Slocum began to rise from his chair.

"Craig, calm down," Gondeck said restraining his boss. "Marc, look. Okay, we'll lay it out. One of the counts he pleads to is Michelle Dahlstrom," he said quietly as Slocum slumped back in his chair inhaling deeply to regain his composure.

"Ah," Marc said nodding his head in comprehension. "The political pressure from across the river. I figured it might be getting kinda heavy since I haven't heard anything about any evidence on her case. This, at least, makes some sense," he added all the while avoiding Slocum. "The problem here is, my guy maintains his innocence. Says you have the wrong guy," he added.

"Come on, Marc," Gondeck said. "Let's look at the evidence. We have the murder weapon found at your client's apartment. We have an eyewitness that places him at the scene of the last murder. We have a semen sample found on one of the other victims. Blood samples on the knife from two of the victims. We have clothes that the eyewitness will testify look like the ones your guy was wearing when the witness saw him. Clothes that were found in a locker with a key that Fornich had on him when arrested. Hell, we even have a spontaneous on camera confession your guy made when he was being brought into the jail. And we have a history here of rape, assaulting women and assaults with a knife by Fornich on other inmates while in prison." All of these points were made by Gondeck in a soft, calm, professional tone while he ticked them off one-by-one on his fingertips.

"We will convict him, Mr. Kadella," Slocum said. "Maybe not for everything, but enough to put him away for longer than thirty years."

"Does Prentiss know about this?" Marc asked.

"No," Slocum lied. "Not yet. We wanted to put it to you first."

"Okay," Marc began, looking at Gondeck. "Now it's my turn to look at your evidence. You have a witness and we both know what can happen with them. You have a semen sample from a married woman with a history of picking up men in a bar. The bartenders will testify ..."

"We know about that, of course," Slocum interrupted.

"You have the so-called confession that was obviously blurted out by an angry and confused man in front of a howling mob of reporters. Meaningless. Prentiss shouldn't even allow it and it may be grounds for overturning on appeal.

"You found some clothes in a locker that you say were placed there by the defendant, but the clothes contain no physical evidence they were worn by anyone committing a crime. Which leaves us with the knife. No finger prints. No nothing. Nothing to tie it to Carl except a cop that claims he found it in Carl's apartment. A cop with a personal family tie to Dahlstrom, a father of one of the victims. Heavy duty political pressure on this cop to get an arrest on this case. A jury could very easily believe he might've planted it."

"Good luck proving that," Slocum said smugly.

"I don't have to prove it. All I have to do is point out the possibility and a jury could easily find reasonable doubt," Marc said, trying to keep the annoyance from showing.

Gondeck swiveled his chair to sit up straight at the table, held up both hands, palms out, one to each of the other two men like a referee separating boxers. "Look, Marc," he said moving his eyes from Slocum to Marc as he slowly lowered his hands to the table. "Let's not try the case now. You haven't told us anything we hadn't thought of ourselves. We believe, obviously, we're going to convict this guy. We also believe that we have the right man. You'll notice, the killings have stopped since we locked him up."

"Go ahead, bring that up at trial if you want a mistrial," Marc said, his brief flash of anger cooling.

"We know better than that. We'll be honest okay?" Gondeck continued. "Yes, we're under political pressure here. A plea saves everybody. We get a conviction. The governor and his family get closure and your guy gets a good deal. Not a great deal, but a good one. One he'll wish he'd taken when we convict him."

"Carl won't take it," Marc said flatly.

"Then it's up to you to convince him," said Slocum.

"No one's a virgin here, Marc. We all know that a good defense lawyer, and I consider you a good defense lawyer, can gently persuade a reluctant defendant to do what's right for himself," Gondeck said. "Take a few days to think about it yourself before you put it to him."

"What about sentencing?" Marc asked.

"We'll recommend the thirty years, but of course, that's up to Judge Prentiss," Slocum replied.

"What about Ramsey County? Have you talked to them? Will they allow the plea here?" Marc asked.

"Yes, we've talked to Ms. Rivera in Ramsey County," Slocum said referring to the Ramsey County Attorney. "She would take the plea on Michelle Dahlstrom and allow concurrent sentencing here."

Marc sat back in his chair, hands clasped together behind his head, lips pressed tightly while he silently contemplated the offer. "Well," he finally said as he sprang from his chair and picked up his briefcase. "Let me think about it. We'll go see the judge and see what he says about sentencing."

The two prosecutors went straight through the door leading from the courtroom to the judges' chambers area while Marc made a brief detour to let his client know he was there. He found Carl in the small conference room on the opposite side of the courtroom from where he had been with Slocum and Gondeck.

Carl was seated at a small round table, his wrists gripped by handcuffs, ankles shackled together, slumped over dressed in a one-piece orange jumpsuit. When Marc entered the room the two deputies rose to leave but Marc stopped them both. He briefly greeted Carl and told him nothing about the plea bargain but said he would be out to talk to him after seeing the judge. He left the room and went back to the judge's chambers to join the others already seated in front of Prentiss' desk patiently waiting for him.

"Hello, Marc," Prentiss cheerfully greeted him as the clerk closed the door behind Marc. "Come in and have a seat. Mr. Slocum here tells me there has been some discussion about a possible plea. Mr. Slocum ..." Prentiss said, turning back to the county attorney.

"Yes, your Honor, as I was saying, we've offered Mr. Kadella two counts of second-degree murder. His client pleads to the death of Alice Faye Darwin, the last victim, and Michelle Dahlstrom. We would recommend to the court a total of 360 months in prison. Thirty years."

"Hmmm, I see," Prentiss said quietly. "There is the jurisdictional problem, isn't there? Ms. Dahlstrom's death occurred in St. Paul, as I recall, didn't it?"

"Yes, your Honor," Slocum continued. "We've already squared that with the Ramsey County Attorney's office. Rosalie Rivera would appear in your court and take the plea personally and allow you to sentence."

"I see. Okay, Mr. Kadella, what do you think?" Prentiss said turning his head back to Marc.

"Well, your Honor," Marc said, "that's the offer, but I wanted to hear from you about sentencing before I put it to my client."

"Okay. Thirty years," Prentiss said musing out loud. "I guess that sounds reasonable, but I suppose I'd like a presentence investigation. I'm sure I'd go along with that in exchange for a plea, but we'd better do it by the book. Do you think your client will agree?"

"No, your Honor. I don't. He has maintained his innocence all along ..." Marc began.

"Well, I obviously can't accept a plea from someone who says he's innocent," Prentiss said.

"He could simply say he agrees there is sufficient evidence against him to make a conviction likely, your Honor. An *Alford* plea." Gondeck said. "He wouldn't really have to admit guilt."

"That's true, I suppose. Although in a case of this significance, better if he admits it," Slocum added.

"To save his soul?" Marc asked sarcastically.

"At any rate, we can work out the details if he agrees. To answer your question about sentencing, I am inclined to go along with the recommendation," Prentiss said. "Now, what about a trial date? I'm thinking this trial will last, with normal interruptions, five to six weeks. Would you agree, Mr. Slocum?"

"Yes, your Honor. That should be about right."

"Mr. Kadella?" Prentiss said to Marc.

"Probably longer, your Honor. That would be my guess. I'm figuring two to three weeks just for jury selection and ..."

"We're not going to screw around for three weeks selecting a jury," Prentiss said, immediately regretting the harshness of his tone. Careful, he thought to himself. Now is no time to alienate the defense and risk a motion for a new judge. "Marc," Prentiss continued softly. "I understand your concerns with the pretrial publicity and all. In fact, I've kind of kept my eye on the media and I've noticed that there really hasn't been much lately. It's my opinion that selecting a jury won't be that difficult. You'll see. Your client can have a fair and impartial jury in a few days."

"We'll see," Marc shrugged. "Six weeks will probably be enough."

"Good," Prentiss said, hiding his relief, "I need to be done by October first. So, I'm ordering a trial date for Monday, August eighth."

"Two weeks?" Marc said, almost coming out of his chair. "You're telling me I have only two weeks?"

"Will you be ready, Mr. Slocum?" Prentiss asked, ignoring Marc.

"Yes, your Honor," Slocum replied.

"Has discovery been completed?" Prentiss asked, turning back to Marc.

"I don't know, your Honor," Marc said. "I don't know if they've given me everything."

"Yes, your Honor," Gondeck said. "Except for our witness list," he added.

"Which you will provide to the defense no later than 5:00 P.M. next Monday. Understand?" Prentiss said, pointing an index finger at Slocum.

"Understood, your Honor," Slocum answered.

"How am I supposed to have time to interview all of their witnesses in less than two weeks?" Marc asked.

"And Mr. Kadella, I'll give you until 5:00 P.M. on Friday, August fifth to provide your witness list to the prosecution," Prentiss added, again ignoring Marc. "I don't want any last-minute surprise witnesses here gentlemen, is that clear? You'd better have a damn good reason for bringing anything up at the last minute. Any final pretrial motions will be heard that day. 9:00 A.M. August eighth. Good day, gentlemen," Prentiss said in dismissal.

The three lawyers left through Prentiss' courtroom, Slocum in the lead obviously in a hurry to get back to his office. Marc and Gondeck stood in the empty courtroom and watched as Slocum went through the exterior door and into the hallway. As the door closed behind him, Marc turned to Gondeck and said, "What is it with him?"

"He's an asshole," Gondeck replied. "It's that simple. But don't kid yourself Marc. I've seen him in front of a jury and he handles himself real well. Jurors seem to take to him for some reason. Don't know him I guess. So, don't underestimate him. I think defense lawyers tend to do that because he doesn't try many cases. Anyway," he said extending his right hand to Marc, "I'll get you our witness list. Let me know as soon as you can about the plea offer. What do you think, Marc? Will you recommend it?"

"I don't know, Steve," Marc said as the two of them released from the handshake. "I'll think about it. But I'm not going to talk to him about it today. I'll let you know but don't hold your breath. Are you guys open to a counter-proposal?"

"I'd have to say no," Gondeck answered after reflecting on the question for a moment. "If you think of one, run it by me and I'll listen."

"Well, like I said before, I don't think my client will take it no matter what anyway."

"I have to go, Marc. Give me a call," Gondeck said as he turned and passed through the bar.

Marc went into the conference room and spent a brief few minutes with his client after the deputies went into the courtroom. He told Carl about the trial date and gave him a quick progress report on the investigation. "You know Carl, if you could just give us one witness who could give you an alibi for one of these victims it could turn the whole case around."

"I know, Marc," he answered. "I've tried but the only night that I can think of is the Sunday for that one, the one I met in the bar. And that Sunday I just spent the night at home, watching TV."

"Well, keep working on it. Carl," he said quietly, "what about the clothes in the locker?"

"I told you before," he yelled, "they're not my damn clothes! Jesus Christ, man. How many times you gonna ask? It wasn't my knife. Those aren't my clothes."

"Okay, Carl," Marc said softly. "Well, keep thinking about the alibi. I'll see you again in a couple days. Do you need anything?"

"No," Carl said shaking his head. "Joe gets me the few things I need."

"Try to relax, Carl. I know this is a strain."

"I'm damn glad we've got a trial date. I can't wait to get this over with."

A half-hour after the lawyers had left his chambers, Gordon Prentiss stood at his window looking east toward the University of Minnesota and St. Paul. His mind was relaxed and he wasn't really thinking about anything in particular. More or less just watching the afternoon dwindle away when the private line on his telephone rang bringing him abruptly back to reality.

"Judge Prentiss," he said as he answered the phone.

"Gordon, it's Daniel Waschke. Will you hold for a moment please?"

"Certainly," Prentiss answered.

"Judge Prentiss?" he heard the governor's familiar voice ask.

"Yes, Governor," Prentiss answered.

"How'd it go today?"

"Well, we set an early trial date. August 8th. And Slocum made the offer for a plea to that defense lawyer, Kadella."

"Will he take it?"

"He might. I'm not sure. I think he might believe it's a good deal but how hard he'll sell it to his client is anybody's guess."

"That was basically Slocum's opinion, too. Well, thank you Judge. I just wanted your impression. I think it's time we gave Mr. Kadella a little personal incentive now. Keep in touch, Judge."

FIFTY-FIVE

The melodic thumping of the windshield wipers of Jake Waschke's pride and joy Corvette was the only sound to be heard in the car's interior as Jake cruised north on 35W toward downtown Minneapolis. He was in his personal car because he did not want to be recognized as a cop by any of the acquaintances of the man he was going to meet. Only a light rain was coming down now after night had fallen on the city but the spray from the freeway traffic still made the wipers a necessity. As he cruised through the moderately heavy evening traffic toward his destination, he allowed his mind to replay the scene he had lived the night before.

Daniel had finally talked him into a visit to his mother at her house in the northern St. Paul suburb where she lived. He didn't really care to see her, but he did want to talk to Daniel and it was becoming more and more obvious, or so it seemed to Jake, that Daniel was avoiding him. Jake believed he knew the reason why, so, he had made up his mind to let the matter lie until after the trial. As long as Daniel was in therapy and taking his medication, everything seemed to be under control. At least, there had been no more killings.

Jake arrived at his mother's shortly after 7:00 P.M. and saw that Daniel was already there. In fact, unknown to Jake, had been there for over an hour. As he pulled into the short driveway and parked next to Daniel's car, he couldn't help wonder at how easily Daniel could spend time with her. *Must have something to do with his therapy,* he thought. Confront your demons.

He spent the next hour with them, sitting by himself on the loveseat in her small living room, making small talk about their lives and catching up on family gossip about extended family members. Aunts, uncles and cousins Jake hardly knew and cared even less about. Daniel seemed quite interested but Jake had all he could do to not show his boredom. *At least,* he thought, *he no longer felt a desire to talk about the one subject they never discussed.* The family skeleton that was shoved deep into the closet. The time for his need to clear the air and come to grips with his and their past was years behind him. The only reason he kept even a minimal tie to his mother was to make Daniel happy. Jake believed it was somehow important and therapeutic for Daniel to maintain the charade of the happy family they had never been.

Jake interjected an occasional comment when he could and laughed at appropriate moments when his mother tossed out what she believed was an amusing comment. Mostly though, he sat in pained silence watching Louise down her scotch and water sedatives while she wheeled around in her motorized wheelchair, a result of the car accident that had left her partially paralyzed.

He found himself reminiscing about her when he was a child. A very attractive young woman back then, escaping the poverty and abuse of a lazy, drunken father by becoming pregnant with Jake and then marrying Jake's father. The only memories he had of the man were those provided by Louise. According to her he was a good provider and decent husband and father, ten years older than her when she delivered Jake shortly after her nineteenth birthday. He died in an accident working for the railroad when Jake was only two and Louise barely twenty-one.

Louise then spent the next thirty years going from one bad marriage to the next, one lousy relationship after another. Finally, husband number six had put her in the wheelchair and himself in a grave when another drunk driver swerved into their lane and hit them head on. The lawsuit held the other driver to be the cause of the accident, but because of her husband's blood alcohol content, Jake always had his doubts.

After an hour of forcing himself not to look at his watch, Jake muttered an excuse about meeting someone on police business, apologized and made for the door. Before leaving, he had done something he had not done for almost twenty years. He bent down, kissed his mother on the cheek and put an arm around her neck to give her a brief hug. Later, driving down the freeway, he could only wonder at the act with mild surprise. *Maybe,* he thought, *I did it because between the accident and the booze, she probably doesn't have long to live. Odd reaction, though. Been a long time since he cared about her or she about him.*

FIFTY-SIX

Jake left the freeway at the 31st Street exit, turned left to go under the overpass and continued north on the next one-way street. Reaching Franklin, he turned east and began looking for the man he wanted to find. Driving slowly, ignoring the horns of impatient drivers who got behind him on the well lit, wide avenue, he cruised along patiently surveying the street scene. The rain had stopped, and the city's flotsam began to surface. Block after block went by with no sighting of the man he sought and after almost three miles he ran out of the section of Franklin where he expected to find him.

He pulled into a Dairy Queen and reminded by the pressure of the belt around his waist, fought off the urge for a hot fudge sundae. Instead he kept going using the parking lot to turn the sleek car around and head back up Franklin to continue his search.

Three blocks past Chicago he stopped for a red light and pulled up next to a Hennepin County Medical Center ambulance parked along the curb, pointed in the wrong direction, its emergency lights flashing. While waiting for the light, he looked over at the sidewalk and saw the two EMS personnel attempting to help up a man leaning against a plexiglass bus stop shelter. There was obviously no sense of urgency about the scene, so Jake saw no reason to lend a hand. As he continued to watch it became clear that the man, in his mid-twenties but looking to be older than Jake, was too drunk to move.

The light turned green and as he turned his head to continue to drive, he caught a glimpse of movement of someone coming out of the shadows of the building on the corner. He quickly looked back and immediately recognized the movement as the man he sought. Jake jerked the steering wheel to the right, rounded the corner and pulled the sports car up to the curb directly in front of the shabbily dressed man.

Jake reached across the passenger seat, opened the door and yelled out, "Hey, dickhead, get in here."

The tall, skinny man dressed in tattered jeans, cheap sneakers and a sleeveless dirty sweatshirt, bent down to peer into the car, smiled and got into the passenger seat.

"Hey, Jake," Eddie Davis said. "How you doing? Haven't seen you for a while."

"I'm doing okay, Eddie. How about you? I was just cruising around when I saw you there on the corner. How goes things on the street?"

"To tell you the truth, Jake," Eddie said wearily, "I'm getting tired of it. Tired of living like this you know? Dirty all the time. Dressed like a bum and for what? To bust some junkie because he's too stupid to leave crack, heroin or whatever alone. It's bullshit, my man and a waste of time."

"So, put in for a transfer. You've earned it."

"Oh, I don't know," Davis said. "I'm just a little fed up. This kid, maybe sixteen, seventeen, I busted about a month ago. Got him into a rehab program. Looked like he might straighten out ..."

"Yeah?"

"Well, I found him yesterday in the basement of some shooting gallery off Lake and Pillsbury. Dead. OD'd."

"Don't get too close to these people, Eddie. They're all self-destructive as hell."

"Yeah, I know. It's not always so easy," Eddie replied as he reached over and pulled the cigarette pack from Jake's pocket. He lit one for himself and then one for Jake and said, "How's the big serial killer case going? You gonna convict this guy?"

"Who knows?" Jake answered as he pulled the car into the lot of a boarded-up gas station and parked. "The lawyers think so. At least believe there's enough evidence. But you never know."

"You know what you need, don't you? A confession."

"No shit, Sherlock," Jake answered. "No wonder you're a detective."

"Or, if you can't get that," he continued, ignoring Jake's sarcasm, "a jailhouse snitch. Somebody your boy confesses to. You know, that old statement against his own interest bullshit."

"Yeah," Jake said quietly as if contemplating what the undercover detective had told him. "That would be good. That would probably be the final nail in this guy's coffin. Probably wishful thinking. Who would he confess to?"

"Well, let me think about that," Eddie said as he tossed the cigarette through the open window. "In fact, I know just the guy. Small time wholesaler I got a line on. If he gets busted again, with his sheet, he'll get some serious time. Yeah, this loser should do just fine."

"I don't want to know the details and this conversation never took place."

"Absolutely, Lieutenant."

Marc stepped off the elevator on the twenty-fourth floor of the Walling Tower Building in downtown Minneapolis and found himself looking directly at the maitre'd of the Executive Inn. The tuxedo clad man looked at Marc, smiled indulgently and said, "May I help you, sir?"

"Yes," Marc answered, "I'm here to meet someone for lunch. A David Fitzpatrick."

"Oh, yes, of course. Right this way sir. He left word you would be coming," the man said as he led Marc into the plush dining room. As they approached the table where Marc's former classmate was seated with another man, Fitzpatrick rose from his seat to greet Marc with a cheerful smile and a warm handshake.

"Hey, Marc," Fitzpatrick said, "Good to see you. Thanks for coming. Marc, this is Darryl Haesly. Darryl, Marc Kadella."

"Well, Marc," Haesly said as they shook hands. "It's a pleasure to meet you. I've heard some very good things about you."

"Thank you. That's kind of you to say," Marc replied while wondering from whom he had heard these wonderful things.

The three of them all took seats at the table and for the next two minutes Marc and Fitzpatrick made small talk about friends, family and in general, a little catching up on their lives. All of which made Marc feel a little uneasy since he and Fitzpatrick had not been particularly close.

His classmate had made partner in the large corporate firm he had joined right out of law school and was obviously doing much better financially than Marc dared to dream about. Both the men wore expensive, tailored suits and the familiarity with the waiter led Marc to believe that an expensive lunch was a common occurrence. A treat Marc could rarely afford.

After the waiter had taken their order, Marc looked at Haesly and said, "So, Darryl, Dave said you wanted to talk to me about business. I'm a little uncertain about what business you and I could possibly have."

"Let me get right to the point, Marc," the small, older man said with a smile. "We have a desperate need for an experienced litigator."

"Darryl's chairman of the firm's hiring committee, Marc," Fitzpatrick added.

"Some things are coming together all at once that make adding an experienced lawyer to our litigation department not just a necessity, but absolutely imperative. And we don't have time to go through the usual hiring procedures. So, it's basically been put in my hands to bring someone on board. "

"I'm listening," Marc said after a long pause had passed between them.

"David tells me you would fit our needs quite nicely. And to be honest, I've done some discreet checking with some judges and lawyers I know who know you and you were highly recommended."

"I see," Marc replied, warming to the wine and flattery. "Are you offering me a job?"

"Well, yes, I am prepared to make you an offer today. "

"Which is?"

"I can offer you a position as a senior associate at a starting salary of $135,000 annually. Plus, of course, all of the usual benefits of health, disability and life insurance plus what we believe is a very generous 401(k) program. There is, one condition."

"Which is…" Marc asked.

"Well, it's like this, we need someone who can step right in and handle his own cases. As I said, the litigation department is quite overloaded right now. So, you'd be on a three-month probationary period. To demonstrate your ability to manage your own cases."

"Oh, I see," Marc said, clearly relieved. "Well, I've been handling my own cases for years. I really don't see that as a big problem," he added as he mentally calculated what the security of a $135,000.00 salary would be like and no overhead to pay for. "How soon do you need to know? What are you looking at as a time frame for hiring someone?"

"Good question," Haesly said. "Right now, you're the only candidate we're looking at. As I said, we've heard a lot of good things and I believe you'd fit right in. Remember, we are in a bit of a hurry. We want to hire someone no later than the end of next week. If you're not it, we need to know, very soon. Within a day or two."

After the waiter served their meal and departed, Marc asked, "What about my existing cases? I have a significant criminal trial scheduled to begin soon."

"Oh, that's right," Haesly said wiping the corners of his mouth with the linen napkin. "David did mention that you represented that man, what's-his-name, on that serial murder thing."

"Carl Fornich," Marc said, an uneasy feeling coming over him.

"Yes, I see," Haesly said quietly. "That does create a problem. We don't do criminal defense work and well frankly, we don't want to. Nor do we want any of our lawyers doing it at all."

"It is, ah, frowned upon," Fitzpatrick added.

"When is your trial scheduled?" Haesly asked.

"A week from next Monday," Marc answered.

"That's just ten days from now. How long is it scheduled to last?" Fitzpatrick asked.

"Five to six weeks," Marc answered quietly as he stared blankly past the two men, watching his opportunity for future security slip through his fingers. "But there might be a plea. I don't know yet. I don't suppose you could let me do this one trial first?"

"Well, no. I'm afraid not. You see, Marc. Not that we have anything against criminal work, of course. It's just, well, we have some very sensitive corporate and insurance clients with an image to think of and ..."

"What about the plea possibility?" Fitzpatrick asked.

"Well," Marc began to slowly explain. "It's a possibility. This is, of course, just between us," Marc added. "There's been an offer made. Fairly reasonable. I'm not sure if my client will go for it or not."

"What do you think?" Haesly asked quickly adding, "If you don't mind telling us."

"I'm beginning to think he should take it. The risks at trial are too great."

"I'm sure you'll convince your client to do the right thing," Fitzpatrick said giving Haesly a sly look as he placed a forkful of salmon steak in his mouth.

"Hello, your Honor," Marc heard Haesly say to someone behind him. He turned his head around just in time to see Margaret Tennant and another woman reach his table. All three men stood to face her with Marc feeling a brief flash of emptiness as she held out her hand to him.

"Hello, gentlemen," she said smiling at Haesly and Fitzpatrick. "Hello, Marc. How've you been?"

Marc took her hand and felt a small folded piece of paper pressed against his palm as they shook. "I'm fine, Judge. And yourself?" he asked as their hands released. Without the others seeing him, he palmed the paper and slipped into his pants' pocket while the others watched Margaret.

"I'm good," she said, still smiling. "Well, I just wanted to say hello. I'll let you get back to your lunch. Nice seeing you again. Gentlemen," she added to the other two, both of whom were oblivious to what had just occurred. Tennant turned and walked off with her luncheon companion as Marc continued to stare at her back. Haesly and Fitzpatrick sat down and after Tennant had passed through the entryway, Marc excused himself and headed to the men's room. He went into one of the stalls, locked the door and removed the paper from his pocket. He unfolded it and read the note.

Marc, I feel like I'm back in junior high again writing this note to you, but I did not want to say anything in front of the others. How've you been? I miss you and hope you miss me. Give me a call if you can find some time.
Margaret
P.S. Is that damn case going to end soon?

He stood in the stall of the empty restroom and read the note over three more times. Margaret had been in his thoughts a lot lately. Especially late at night when he crawled into his empty bed trying to clear his mind so sleep would come. He would see her face and hear her laugh and the loneliness the images brought on would only make sleep more difficult to achieve. He carefully folded the precious paper and lightly touched it to his lips before placing it into his shirt pocket. He exited the men's room and returned to the table where Haesly and Fitzpatrick were finishing their meals.

The three of them spent the next half-hour discussing the firm of Olson, Bennett, Rogers, Thompson, Costello and Haesly. Marc was given a brief history of the firm founded by Phillip Olson more than half a century ago, who died within the last year without ever retiring at the ripe old age of eighty-seven. They talked about the firm's core clients, well known corporations and insurance companies. Billable hours and bonuses which, Marc was told, could easily double his income if he was willing to put in the hours. And of course, possible partnership in the sixty-eight-lawyer firm in a few years. "Well, Marc," Haesly said as the three of them stood waiting for the elevator. "What do you think?"

"It sounds very good," Marc answered. "I have to let it sink in. I'll let you know by Monday. How's that?"

"Good," Haesly said as he pulled a small, shiny, brass flat container from his inside coat pocket. He flipped open the lid, removed a business card from it and wrote some numbers on the back. "Let me know as soon as you can, one way or the other. I wrote my home and cell numbers on the back. Feel free to call either one to let me know."

The instant Darryl Haesly closed the door of his office after returning from lunch, he hurried to his phone and quickly dialed. It was answered before the first ring finished and Haesly said, "It's Darryl Haesly, Governor. I just got back from meeting Kadella."

"How'd it go? Did he bite?"

"I think so, sir," Haesly answered. "We'll see if it does any good. I definitely got the impression he'd like to take the offer."

"We'll have to see if he can convince his client now," Dahlstrom said.

"Yes. We'll see. Sir," Haesly said, "I'm not sure he's an Olson, Bennett lawyer. You know the type. He's just a little too independent. Probably not much of a team player and a little, well, you understand not really our kind of lawyer."

"You mean he probably would balk at kissing your ass twice a day."

"That's not what I meant," Haesly said defensively.

"Yes it is," Dahlstrom said firmly. "That firm of yours owes the Party big time and besides, if you don't like him, dump him after ninety days. By then it's too late and who cares? I'd be forever grateful, Darryl. Remember that. Goodbye, Darryl. Keep me informed."

"Yes, sir," Haesly said as the phone went dead.

FIFTY-SEVEN

When Marc arrived back at his office he found Maddy Rivers impatiently flipping through an old PEOPLE magazine. She was dressed in jeans and a loose cotton blouse, her hair pinned up against the late July heat.

He stood in the reception area and looked her over as she dropped the magazine onto the coffee table and stood up. *She'd stop traffic if she was dressed in a tent,* he thought. She just can't hide it, even when she tries, which she doesn't very much. He turned to Sandy, who sat smirking at him, obviously reading his mind and lecherous thoughts. Sandy handed him his mail and one pink message slip which he saw was from his daughter. A pang of guilt swept over him as he read her name and moved toward his office door with Maddy on his heels.

"Thanks for coming," Marc said as he dropped the mail on his desk and placed the message slip next to his phone.

"I finally caught up with that Olson guy this morning," she said.

"What Olson guy?" Marc asked.

"The deputy. You remember. The one that stood guard while the two guys worked over Carl in the jail."

"Oh yeah, him," Marc said. "Did you serve the subpoena on him?"

"Sure, but I don't think it'll do any good. It's his word against Carl's and he says Carl's lying. Says he wasn't there. Didn't see anything, doesn't know anything," she added.

"Where are you with Waschke?"

"I'm going to do him, for sure, the next couple days," she said.

"I thought you already had," he said, obviously irritated.

"Hey, I have other clients. I can hardly live on what you've been paying me," she snapped.

"I'm sorry. You're right," Marc said holding up his hands as if to ward off an attack. "Still friends?"

"I suppose," she said, flashing that beautiful smile. "Just don't let it happen again."

"We have a trial date. August eighth," he said. "So, we need to get going."

"August eighth? I thought we'd have another week, at least."

"Prentiss moved it up. Wants to get started. I'll be ready. The first three or four weeks will be used up by jury selection and the prosecution's case, anyway. We won't have anything until at least September."

"I asked you here because something's come up," Marc continued. "There's been a plea offer made and I wanted to kick it around with someone before I put it to Carl."

"You're not seriously thinking about taking it?" she asked incredulously.

"Yes, I am. Look, hear me out before you jump to any conclusions. That's why I wanted to talk to you. I'm hoping you can be objective and play devil's advocate for me."

"Okay," she said flattered by the rare compliment about her intelligence rather than her physical assets.

He told her what the prosecution had offered and the judge agreeing to the sentence. They spent the next two hours going over the case and the evidence against Carl. The witnesses, the scientific reports and the likely testimony. They looked at all of it from as many sides, angles and perspectives as they could possibly think of. Discussed the various ideas they each had for putting it all in the best light possible to a jury. Trying to find ways to cast reasonable doubt on the totality of the prosecution's case.

"I think it'll come down to a couple of things," Marc finally said. "The eyewitness. That Hobbs character can be shaken at trial. It's not that tough. But the knife. That's another matter. That cop that was in the bedroom when the knife was found by Waschke, what's his name?"

"Mike Carlson," she said.

"He's sure he hadn't looked in the closet before Waschke?"

"Absolutely," she sighed.

"So, it may very well come down to the jury believing Waschke. A decorated, veteran police officer with impeccable credentials. A spotless record."

"You put it that way and Carl's hosed."

"What other way would you like me to put it?"

She crossed her legs, placed an elbow on her knee and holding her chin in the palm of that hand said, "So, we have to find a way to convince the jury that Waschke planted the knife. Simple."

"Yeah, no problem," he said sarcastically. "And of course, figure out how he got the knife in the first place."

"What about the locker key?" she asked ignoring Marc's comment. "Have you asked Carl about it?"

"Sure. Says he found it lying on the street. Has no idea who it belongs to."

"What are you going to do?"

"I think I'm going to gently try to convince Carl to take the deal."

"He won't."

"I know he won't want to, but the downside is horrendous. If he's convicted of one, just one count of first-degree murder it's a mandatory life sentence and a minimum thirty years. And with a case like this I can see this judge, hell any judge, giving him consecutive sentences for more than one conviction and he never gets out. He dies in prison."

"When're you going to talk to him?"

"No time like the present," Marc said looking at his watch. "Want to ride along?"

"Sure," she said quietly. "But I won't help you. I still think you have a case to put on."

"Yeah, I know I have a case to put on. Although winning it, that's another matter. Let me put it this way: Do I believe there's enough evidence to convict? That's the question."

"Do you?"

"Don't you?"

FIFTY-EIGHT

They waited silently in the jailhouse interview room while the deputies were retrieving Carl. Neither spoke for several minutes, Marc occasionally looking at his watch while Maddy stared straight ahead from her chair alongside the table.

"Have you changed your mind yet?" she broke the silence by asking.

"I don't know. A lot of ambivalence," he answered.

"Don't even tell him."

"I have an ethical obligation to at least put it to him. It's his decision to make. Not mine," Marc said as he heard the key turning in the door.

Carl entered the room followed by the looming presence of Big Train Johnson who nodded a brief greeting at Marc and Maddy and said, "Let me know when you're done, counselor."

"Sure thing, Deputy," Marc replied as Big Train turned and left the room. "Hey Carl, how are you doing?"

"Okay, Marc. Miss Rivers," he said. "What's up?"

"Sit down, Carl. I want to go over your case with you. The evidence and everything."

"Shit, Marc," Carl said as he slumped into the chair opposite his lawyer. "We been over this shit 'til I'm sick of it."

"We can't go over it too many times. You never know when we might think of something new. Besides, you got something better to do today?"

"Good point," Carl said smiling. "Say, uh, Miss Rivers, you got a smoke?"

"Sure Carl," Maddy answered reaching for her purse. "Please, call me Maddy. Miss Rivers makes me feel like an old maid."

"This is Hennepin County, Carl." Marc said. "There's no smoking in Hennepin County. You want to get arrested for smoking?"

"Yeah, no shit," Carl laughed as he lit the cigarette. "Getting busted for murder is one thing in this state, but you better be careful not to let them catch you smoking or the cigarette Nazis will nail your ass."

"Really," Maddy said smiling.

"Okay. Let's get down to business," Marc said as he slid his chair up to the table and placed a legal pad in front of himself with a neatly penned list on the first sheet. "The evidence, so far at least..."

"You mean there might be more?" Carl asked.

"Who knows?" Marc shrugged. "They're supposed to tell us everything, but you never know what they'll come up with at trial and claim it came up at the last minute."

"First off," Marc began, "the victims. All sexually assaulted. At least that's what the medical examiner will testify. Except for the one

225

semen sample there's no physical evidence found on or around any of them linking them to you or anybody else. No hair, fibers, blood samples, nothing. The M.E. will testify that they were vaginally penetrated with an object of some kind."

"How does he know that?" Carl asked.

"Because he's a doctor. A pathologist. An examination of the women's pubic area, vaginal walls would show this. Look, Carl, trust me on this. He can tell and he'll explain it at trial. What he can't tell is who did it or with what.

"All the victims," Marc continued, "killed with a single stab wound by a long-serrated knife, like the one the police have, under the chin upward into the brain. The rarity of that fact is enough to link all six of the Hennepin County victims together."

"Then there's the physical evidence. The semen sample found on the Gavin woman. Our own DNA analysis matches it to you and ..."

"I told you about that," Carl said crushing out the cigarette under his shoe and angrily kicking it across the room.

"Relax Carl. I'm just going over it," Marc said, rubbing his palm on his forehead before continuing. "Look, Carl. Let's get this straight. This is all going to come out at trial and you're going to have to sit there and quietly take it. Get angry, show your frustration and annoyance in front of that jury and we may as well pack it in now. Do you understand?"

"Yeah," he answered softly.

"Do you really?"

"Yeah, I do."

"Every time we talk about this you get all pissed off. Let me tell you something. It's not only going to come out, but it will be a helluva lot worse. The prosecutors are gonna make you look like some woman-hating, mad dog. And I have to tell you, I'm very concerned about how you'll react. I don't see you sitting there and calmly taking it."

Maddy shifted slightly in her chair moving her eyes back and forth between the two men. Marc calmly looked at his client while Carl stared at the floor.

"Where am I?" Marc asked looking at his list. "Oh yeah, the physical evidence. The blood samples from the knife. Two of them. Donna Sharon Anderson found by Lake Calhoun by an old guy walking his dog. Says he saw the guy who did it run off. Can't positively identify him but says he matches your size, height, weight and build.

"And the last one. Alice Faye Darwin. Murdered and assaulted in Powderhorn Park. One witness, an elderly woman, will testify she saw the victim being forced into the park by a man matching your description. But she was too far away to identify him. She told the cops that the clothes found in the locker could be the ones the guy was wearing."

"Can't we keep any of this out?" Maddy asked.

"Nope. Prentiss has already ruled. It's coming in. He'll give the jury the usual bullshit limiting instructions about not making too much of it. Who knows if that ever does any good?

"The locker key found in your possession when arrested. Locker Number 119. The bad news is, that links you to the clothes found in it," Marc continued. "The good news is, they found no physical evidence on anything in that locker to tie the clothes to any of the victims. Except, the clothes, and the bag, were washed, probably more than once, in a very strong detergent."

"I found the damn key," Carl said. "I wish to God I'd left it laying there. And so, what if the stuff was washed?"

"It looks like whoever did it was trying to hide something," Madeline answered.

"Carl," Marc said softly as he folded his hands together and placed them on the legal pad. "There's something I haven't had a chance to tell you, yet. I just found out myself a couple days ago. They found three quarters in that locker, in the change box, with your fingerprints on them."

"What!?" Carl exploded. "That's bullshit, man. That can't be."

"It's true, Carl," Marc said without reacting to Carl's outburst. "At least, I know the prints are a match. I had them checked myself. How they got there, I don't know but a jury can believe whatever it wants."

"I don't know. I mean, shit man. I don't know what to say," Carl said as he raised his hands and looked around the room. "I mean, shit. This is bullshit. I don't know what to say. Wait a minute, wait a minute," he said as he snapped his fingers several times. "You said, what was it? There's no physical evidence on the clothes. Nothing tying the clothes to the victims. Right?"

"That's right, Carl. By itself, the clothes in the locker mean nothing. I don't know, you tell me, what will a jury think?"

"I don't know," Carl said quietly. "I, ah, don't know what to tell you. I don't know how they could've got them coins with my prints. Probably planted them. Like the knife. I know," he said snapping his fingers again, "I had some change on me when they arrested me and ..."

"I already checked that," Marc said nodding his head. "You didn't have three quarters when you were booked. And all the change in your pocket at that time is accounted for."

Maddy quietly stood up and went to a corner of the room behind Marc, lit a cigarette and silently smoked it while watching the two men. Observing the scene with the realization that Marc was gently leading Carl to accepting the plea bargain. She had been initially shocked that Marc would, even for a moment, entertain such a notion. But now, listening to the mounting tide of evidence against Carl, she was

227

beginning to come around to the realization that maybe Marc was right. Maybe Carl's best chance was to take the deal.

A sadness came over her with the thought that a truly innocent man, and she still believed that Carl was innocent, could go to prison. Even admit to a crime he didn't do just because the prospect of losing at trial was so much worse. But here, in front of her eyes sat two men, two men whom she had grown fond of and cared about, were in the process of doing just that. *And* she thought, *an hour ago she would have been appalled at the prospect and argue against it with every fiber of her being.* Now, not only was she not going to utter a peep in protest but found herself agreeing with it.

Maddy found herself watching Carl, the obvious agony, stress and turmoil he was going through. She found herself reflecting for a brief moment on her first meeting with him. She remembered shaking his hand and during the entire interview had consciously held her right hand away from herself. The thought of having physical contact with him, actually touching a convicted rapist in a friendly manner, had literally made her skin crawl. The instant the door opened afterward she had gone straight to the women's restroom, holding her right hand in the air, where she had scrubbed as if preparing for heart surgery. She smiled to herself at the memory, wondering how this same man could have made her feel so dirty.

Carl sat silently, his face buried in his hands as Marc stood, walked around the table and gently placed a hand on his client's shoulder. "Carl," he quietly said, "let's forget that for now. I don't think we can come up with an answer about how those quarters got in that locker box. By itself, it's not that important."

Marc began to slowly pace around the small room while Carl straightened in his chair and motioned to Maddy, asking if it was okay to take another cigarette from the pack on the table.

"They also have the so-called confession that you made at the media when you were being arrested. Again, by itself, it's meaningless. An obviously angry, frightened man screaming at the horde like that shouldn't even be admitted into evidence. I can't say Prentiss is wrong in letting it in. I'm not even sure it'll hurt us. It won't help us, though. And they're going to bring in everyone they can from that hallway to testify. The judge will even let them show a tape of it."

"We need a new judge," Carl said.

"Too late. Besides, we wouldn't do any better at this point. He's no different than most of them. Most of them would allow this stuff in. There isn't enough reason to keep it out. The cops testified they read you your Miranda rights. Told you to keep quiet. They don't have to gag you.

"Then, there's your past convictions," Marc continued, still slowly pacing. "A rape conviction and an old assault on a girlfriend when you were a kid. I think Prentiss is wrong to allow the assault in.

Is he wrong enough to overturn a conviction on appeal? Probably not given everything else.

"There's the eyewitness. This Hobbs guy. He positively identifies you a block from the scene of the last murder running down the street."

"He's lying," Carl said as he exhaled a long stream of smoke.

"Obviously," Marc said. "But the question is: Why? Why is he lying and who put him up to it?"

"That big cop. What's his name? Waschke".

"Yeah," Marc said nodding in agreement. "That would be my guess too. The problem we're having is tying the two of them together. So far, no luck."

"Which brings us to the last piece of bad news," Marc said as he sat down and again folded his hands together on the legal pad. "The knife itself. They have blood samples from two of the victims taken from a knife found hidden in your apartment. Found by a veteran police lieutenant with an impeccable record."

"He's the asshole that's doing this to me," Carl said stabbing the tabletop with his right index finger.

"Yeah, yeah, Carl," Marc said softly as he reached over the table and gently covered Carl's hand with his own to calm him. "That would seem to be the case. Except," he continued as he let go of Carl's hand and leaned back, "I keep asking myself why? Why is he framing you? To get a conviction and close a politically hot case? Maybe. But how can he be sure arresting you will stop the killings? I mean, think about it. What does he look like if there's another murder while you're in jail? And how can he be sure it won't happen again? Does he know who the killer is and is protecting someone? Does he know the killer's gone? I don't know and unless we can come up with something solid there, this isn't Los Angeles. Simply making those claims to a jury here, probably won't get us far. I know this cop and he'll make a damn good witness for them. He won't be easy to rattle."

"So, counselor," Carl asked crushing out his cigarette. "What do you think?"

"Boil it all down and I think it'll come down to a couple of things. I mean, take each piece of evidence, by themselves, the witnesses and the physical stuff, and they don't add up to much. Except, the eyewitness who says he saw you running away. And the knife and the cop.

"This witness, this Hobbs guy. We may be able to cast some doubt on him. Who knows? Eyewitnesses aren't always the best evidence. It would actually be better for us if there was more than one. Then we might be able to get contradictory testimony. But if this guy is believable and sticks to his story, well, who knows?

"Then there's the cop and the knife. He's going to testify that he found that knife while conducting a legal search, hidden in a closet of your apartment. Taken along with everything else, do I think it's enough to convict you? I have to be honest, Carl. Yeah, I do."

These last words hung in the air of the small room while the three of them remained silently frozen in place. Maddy leaning against the back wall with an impassive look on her face. Feeling detached and uninvolved in the drama being played out before her. Marc leaning on an elbow on the table, softly staring at Carl with unblinking eyes while he allowed the words to work through Carl's thoughts sink in and let their full impact hit home. Carl blankly staring down at his hands as they rested on the formica of the tabletop, silently allowing the severity of what his lawyer had just told him to come to the surface of his conscious mind. A reality that he had known all along but had stubbornly suppressed.

After almost two full minutes of this frozen in place scene, Carl looked up at Marc, let out his breath in a heavy sigh and said, "Shit, man. I'm in deep trouble here ain't I? They could really nail my ass for this."

"Yes, Carl," Marc answered, almost in a whisper that Maddy could barely hear. "I'm sorry to have to be the one to tell you this, but somebody's got to and it's part of my job. Sorry."

"So, you made a deal with them," Carl said, a statement not a question.

"No," Marc replied shaking his head and leaning back. "No, I haven't made a deal with them ..."

"Good," Carl interrupted. "No deals. I'm not gonna take that bullshit again. I'll take my chances at trial."

"I haven't made a deal, but they have made an offer," he continued as he held up his hands to cut off Carl's protest. "Listen to me. Just relax and hear what I have to say. Nothing's been decided, but I have an ethical obligation to tell you what it is so, I just want you to hear me out. Okay?"

"All right. I'll listen but I won't take it."

"Carl, just relax," Marc said desperately controlling his frustration. "Just listen to the offer."

"Okay, tell me."

So he did, quickly and with as little inflection in his voice as he could. Consciously not wanting to slant the plea offer one way or another. Simply putting it out on the table for Carl to hear.

"Thirty goddamn years! Are you shitting me ..."?

"Twenty with good time, Carl."

"Oh, great. Fine. Twenty years. I do twenty years for something I didn't do. Do they really think I'll go for that? That's bullshit. They're crazy."

"No, Carl. I don't think they believe you'll take it," Marc said quietly.

"And what's this bullshit with the one in St. Paul? I ain't even charged with that. What kinda shit is that? The governor's daughter."

"That's why they made the offer at all, Carl. To tell you the truth, I don't think Slocum and Gondeck are happy about it. Slocum must think he's got a slam dunk case, or he wouldn't be trying it himself. He's up for reelection next year and a case like this will get him plenty of press. If he wins it'll probably get him reelected. If he loses, the whole thing could blow up in his face."

Carl stood up and began to pace. Rapidly at first. Then slowly and again more quickly. He crossed his arms and hugged himself several times. Stopped, paced, hugged, inhaled and exhaled heavily. Facing the wall, he leaned against it with the top of his head pressed against the concrete blocks and stared at the floor with his arms wrapped about himself. Stood this way for a minute then raised his head, rolled his eyes at the ceiling and heavily sighed. Looked down at the wall and lightly thumped his forehead against the cool, unpainted cinderblock.

Maddy had rejoined Marc at the table and they silently sat watching Carl trying to come to grips with the enormity of the decision he faced, Maddy believing Carl was about to face it and accept the deal. Marc waiting for the explosion. It came.

"Nooooo! No damnit, no," Carl bellowed. He remained in place, facing the wall, lightly pounding it with his fists as he repeated several more times his initial response. He turned his head to face the table and calmly said, "No, Marc. No. I just can't do it. I mean shit. Twenty years. Jesus Christ," he continued as he walked back to his chair, "I don't want to do no twenty years. It ain't even that. I took a deal before, ya' know, with the rape. Now, Christ, they want me to admit to something I didn't even do. What do you think?" he asked looking back and forth between Marc and Maddy, his eyes pleading for help. Some guidance. Some confirmation that these two people he trusted would agree with him.

"I don't know, Carl," Maddy said. "It's a tough choice and I'm not the one to say what your chances are at trial."

"Marc?" Carl asked, looking to his lawyer for help.

Marc paused for a long moment, folded his hands together and leaned up against the table to look straight into his client's eyes. "I have to look at the downside, Carl. If we lose, and don't kid yourself, the way it looks right now, we probably will, you never get out of prison. You die in there. If you take the deal, well, you still have a life someday. I know it's a tough decision to face, but I just don't know. I don't have a magic answer for you. Look" he continued as he straightened and waved a hand between them to cut off the conversation, "you don't have to decide anything right this minute. I just wanted to come down and put it to you. Let it all sink in. Let's give it a couple days and I'll talk to you again. I'll come down on Sunday and we'll kick it around some more, okay?"

"I ain't gonna change my mind," Carl said.

"Then you don't," Marc said. "We'll see. You think about it and we'll talk some more."

After the two of them had walked about a block toward the ramp where Marc had parked his car, Maddy looked at him and said, "Well, I guess that's that. We better get our ducks lined up for trial."

"What do you mean? I think he'll go for it," Marc replied

"Are you serious? Did you hear him?" she asked incredulously.

"I knew that would be his initial reaction. It always is. Give it a couple days and the thought of dying in prison won't sound like such a hot idea. We'll see," he shrugged.

Two days later Marc made the trip downtown to see Carl and again discuss the plea bargain with him. This time he was intentionally alone. He had spent the past two days trying to convince himself that he was being objective. Simply doing his job as Carl's lawyer; spell out the pros and cons of accepting or rejecting the offer and remaining professionally indifferent.

Fifteen minutes before leaving his apartment, while standing in front of the mirror knotting the tie he had decided to put on to look the part, he looked at his face in the mirror and finally admitted it to himself. He wanted Carl to take the deal. In fact, he wanted it badly. He felt guilty about it but the reality of what a quick end to this case would do for his own life was simply too great to deny. A real job with a decent salary. Patch things up with Margaret and have a nice relationship with a damn fine woman. And best of all, put an end to the stress of the case itself. The doubts had never gone away, never been too far beneath the surface. Was he really up to handling a case of this significance? A plea would put a stop to all of it.

"Well, Carl, what do you think?"

Carl sat facing him in the same chair in the same room they had met in two days before. He had entered the room with a smile on his face, a slight bounce in his step and had cheerfully greeted Marc. Now, as Marc's heart sank deeper and deeper, Carl sat silently shaking his head several times in response to Marc's question.

"No, man. I ain't gonna do it," he quietly said. "Not now. Not ever. I won't say I did something that I didn't do. Look," he continued as Marc silently listened, "I done time. I didn't like it and I don't want to go back. But I ain't afraid of prison either. I mean, I hate the thought, but I just can't bring myself to say I did something I didn't do. I'll take my chances at trial. You're a smart guy. I know you'll do your best and if they convict my ass, well, then they do. I ain't gonna admit to this and that's final."

"Okay, Carl. It's your call. Just so you understand what can happen," Marc said impassively as he saw his own future melt away.

FIFTY-NINE

On the morning of the first day of the trial, Marc stepped off the crowded elevator from the subterranean parking garage onto the second-floor courtyard of the government center. He headed for the bank of elevators on the court side of the building to make the trip up to Prentiss' courtroom when, half-way there, he was spotted by one of the local TV reporters hanging around the building. He was quickly surrounded by microphones and minicams but before a single question was asked, he said, "You all know there's a gag order on this case so I'm not going to hold a press conference here this morning."

Ignoring the statement, a female reporter from the Minneapolis daily paper asked, "Is it true your client turned down a plea bargain offer?"

"What?" Marc asked, looking at the woman. "Where'd you get that?"

"Have you seen this morning's paper?" she asked.

"No, no I haven't," Marc answered looking at the faces of the media mob surrounding him. "What's in it?"

"There's a story that your client turned down a very good plea offer from the prosecution," said a reporter from one of the local TV stations.

Inwardly furious that Slocum's office would leak plea discussions, Marc managed to maintain enough self control to seize the opportunity by saying, "My client is an innocent man so of course he would turn down any plea bargain."

"The prosecution claims...," the reporter began to say.

"The prosecution can claim whatever they want. My client maintains his innocence," Marc said, cutting her off. "That's all I'm going to say."

He began to move on toward the elevators when one of the reporters asked,

"Don't you want us to use your side of the story?"

Marc turned, surveyed the faces and cameras, and curtly said, "You people can use whatever you want. You will anyway. You always do. Whether it's accurate or not doesn't seem to matter much. Watch the trial. Pay attention and try to get it right. Other than that, I have no comment."

Later that morning, having had the chance to read the story in the paper, Marc waited patiently while Carl read the paper in an attorney conference room attached to Prentiss' courtroom. He was seated across from Marc, his hair neatly cut by Marc's barber, who made a special trip to the jail at Marc's request and a hundred dollars. Carl wore a conservative dark gray suit, white shirt and tie, courtesy of his brother, and looked like he could pass for an up and coming executive at any bank or corporation.

He finished the article, folded the paper and as he handed it back to his lawyer, said, "It makes me sound guilty as hell and makes them look like they're trying to be decent about the whole thing. Spare the public the expense of a trial and the families all the pain and everything. It's pure bullshit."

"We could probably get a continuance," Marc calmly said.

"No. No more delays," Carl said emphatically, "I'm ready. I want to get at this. Get it over with. Besides, in a few days, this'll blow over."

"Yeah, but we have to pick a jury today. Or, at least start. This story won't help."

"How many of them you think will have seen this?"

"Who knows," Marc said with a shrug.

"What about the jury? What are you looking for?" Carl asked.

"Twelve people who have done time for crimes they didn't do," Marc said. "I don't think we'll get that. Other than that, who knows for sure? Every lawyer has his own theory about juries. None of them are right and none of them are wrong. The simple truth is, we could probably take the first twelve people through the door and do just as well for either side.

"I guess I'm looking for younger, better educated types. Maybe a little more liberal. A little less inclined to believe a cop just because he's a cop.

"I have to go see the judge. At least raise a little hell about this leak to the media about the plea bargain. You have a seat at the table out front and we'll start jury selection in a little while. One last thing, Carl," Marc continued as he looked at his client. "I know we've been over this before, but I can't stress it too much. You have to stay cool. No matter what happens or what gets said. From this point on, out in that courtroom, you have to look like everything is going exactly as we expected. Okay?"

"Yeah, Marc. I know. I will. I promise."

"It's not for me, Carl. It's not my ass that's on the line here."

A half hour or so later, Marc was seated to Carl's left at the table on the right-hand side of the courtroom. The one closer to the jury box. Seated behind them, in the front row directly behind the rail separating the spectator area, sat Joe, Carl's sister and her husband. Behind them, every other chair was taken by the members of the media. On the other side of the aisle, the seats were almost all taken up by family members of the six victims. No one would be allowed to stand.

The jury selection would be done according to the rules of court procedure. Each juror would be questioned individually. First by Prentiss then by Marc and finally by the prosecution. Both sides had been given, the previous Thursday, the list of one hundred people from whom it was expected that twelve jurors and two alternates would be selected. Prentiss had made it clear that jury selection was going to be done no later than Wednesday at noon. Two days. Wednesday afternoon was a weekly golf time for the judge and this trial wasn't going to interfere with that. The trial was going to get underway with opening statements at 9:00 A.M. Thursday morning.

Maddy had spent Friday with a computer geek she knew gathering up as much biographical data on each of them as she possibly could. A process which Marc didn't want to know the details about. Marc had taken that information and gone over every member of the jury pool, trying to decide which ones to accept and which ones to remove.

Saturday had been spent at the office with all of the lawyers and staff in attendance, poring over the list. Arguing and cajoling. Everyone got in an opinion about every name on the list. Finally, by 4:00 P.M. Sunday, Marc had prioritized the one hundred names into a list that he believed would be to Carl's best advantage. At the top, number one on Marc's wish list of potential jurors, was a twenty-eight-year-old single man. A graduate student at the U of M majoring in medieval philosophy. At the bottom of the list, a sixty-two-year-old, retired Marine Corps Colonel with two tours of duty in Vietnam and was also a veteran of the first Gulf War. Marc was certain he would be at the top of Slocum's list and there was no way this man was going to be on the jury.

The first prospective juror was brought in, sworn and took her place on the witness stand. Prentiss took a minute to explain the selection process. Then Prentiss asked her several easy questions looking for obvious biases and hardships.

The idea behind jury selection is supposed to be to find twelve impartial people who will listen to the evidence and make their decision based strictly on the facts presented and the law as instructed by the judge. The reality is exactly the opposite. Both sides are trying to find people who are as biased as they possibly can be and hopefully, hear only what those biases permit and have their minds made up before the trial even begins. Their minds made up in a way favorable to your case. Since both sides of a trial are attempting to do that, the logic is that you will end up with a jury somewhere in between the two extremes. Which is exactly where they are supposed to be.

After Prentiss finished, Marc's turn came. Since the general information had been pretty well gleaned by Prentiss, he went right to specific questions for each of the panelists. Could you, Mr. or Ms. So and So keep an open mind, and wait until both sides had presented their case before making a decision? Do you understand that the accused, my client, Mr. Carl Fornich, is presumed innocent? Do you understand that the accused doesn't have to prove anything? That it is entirely up to the prosecution to prove the accused guilty beyond a reasonable doubt? This is a means of indoctrinating the juror. Elicit a promise from each and every one of them that they will keep an open mind, decide the case strictly on the evidence presented and an understanding that if the prosecution fails to meet its burden of proof, then they must come back with a not guilty verdict. Does it work? No one really knows. It's the rare person who will honestly admit he or she can't do these things and that person won't make the cut.

Slocum, while remaining seated, began by pleasantly introducing himself and gently tossing some soft questions to each of them. Things like: Have you ever been on jury duty before? Have you ever been arrested? Have you or any close family members been the victims of a violent crime? If a venireman answered any of these positively, he would then seek out more specific information about the particular question.

As a good trial lawyer can, he began the process of indoctrinating the jurors to the facts of the case. Asking questions designed specifically to inform the prospective jurors what the case is about in a way to slant the facts toward his side. This is improper and is not supposed to be allowed. A couple of times he went just a little too far and both times, as Marc began to rise to object, Prentiss would very mildly admonish Slocum to save it for presenting his case.

By five o'clock they had gone through more than twenty of them leaving the days work complete with the selection of five jurors. Prentiss, realizing that the pace would likely result in meeting his Wednesday tee time deadline, seemed more relaxed. Having already denied Marc's request to sequester the jury during the trial, he instructed the five not to discuss the case with anyone or watch any news programs or read any news articles about the case. With that, the first day of the State of Minnesota vs. Carl Milton Fornich, was complete.

SIXTY

"How do you think it went today, how'd we do with the selection?" Joe Fornich asked Marc when they had exited the building into the muggy August air.

"Not too bad, I think," Marc replied. "I got number fourteen on my list. The others don't seem too bad. Lost a couple I would've liked to have. Remember Joe, all we need is one. One juror willing to hold out."

"And Carl walks?" Joe asked.

"No, not necessarily. We get a hung jury and then the prosecution has to decide if they want to try it again. Usually they don't, but with this case, well, we'll see. I have to tell you Joe, with the evidence against Carl, hoping for an out and out acquittal, convincing all twelve that he's not guilty. That's probably a pipe dream."

"I have some more money for you," Joe said as he pulled a folded check from his shirt pocket. He handed it to Marc who unfolded it, looked at the amount folded it back the way it was and slipped it into his coat pocket. "I know it's not enough, but I've got more coming.

"Who're those two people sitting behind the prosecutors? You know, the ones they keep talking to?" Joe asked.

"Jury selection experts," Marc answered. "They're people who hire themselves out to do profiles on potential jurors. Try to come up with a psychological profile on the people you want on your jury. Help to select a jury that will lean your way."

"They work in the county attorney's office?"

"No, Joe. They're a private firm hired just for this trial."

"Why didn't we hire some?"

"Why do you think?" Marc asked, smiling. "Money. Those people don't come cheap. A case like this, with the taxpayers picking up the bill, the prosecution can spend whatever they want. Whatever they have to."

"The whole thing kinda seems a little unfair. A little one-sided. "

"What the hell does 'fair' have to do with anything? Life is unfair, Joe. No one ever said it isn't. Listen, I have to grab a bite to eat and get back to work on my jury list. I'll see you tomorrow."

"No, you won't. I can't make it tomorrow. I have to work. I'll be here as much as I can, but I can't take two months off, either. So far, the boss has been really good and I don't want to press it just yet."

The two men parted company, Joe toward the parking ramp where he had left his car, Marc back inside the building to do the same.

On his way back to the office he stopped at a fast food burger place on Lake Street for some supper. He spent the evening going over the remaining names on the list, knowing the prosecution's jury selection team would not be resting. All three of the other lawyers in

Marc's office stayed for a couple hours to offer their opinions on each of the remaining names. Maddy stopped by with a little more information that she was able to come up with on the panelists and to give Marc a preliminary report on her investigation of Jake Waschke.

"Jacob Albert Waschke," she began. "Two divorces, two kids from the first marriage. Father, Albert Stephen Waschke. Married his mother, the former Louise Marie Gingrich, November 8, 1964. Jake's father died two years later in a train accident. Worked for the railroad, the old Northern Pacific.

"He grew up in St. Paul. Graduated from Central High in '83. Joined the Army right after graduation. Got his military record, don't ask me how. A favor from a friend. Served as an M.P. Nothing remarkable but nothing to raise any eyebrows, either. Worked for the CID, Criminal Investigation Division, at Ft. Bragg until his discharge in '87. Normal promotions. Good reports all around. In fact, very good to excellent on all of his fitness reports."

"So, nothing in his early background to give us a hint what he's up to," Marc said.

"Well, I'm not so sure," Maddy said hesitantly. "Let me finish. Got out of the Army in '87, came back here and went to school at a local Community College. After two years, joined the Minneapolis Police Department in '89 and went to night school at the U. Earned a bachelor's degree in criminology in '91."

"So, he's got some education. I'm not surprised. He's obviously a pretty bright guy."

"Has a master's degree, Marc," she continued. "Sociology. A people studier."

"Interesting," Marc said.

"We've been over his record with the department," Maddy continued. "Very solid. A damn good cop, actually. Looking at just his life, nothing really there to indicate any kind of problem."

"What do you mean, 'just his life'?" Marc asked as he straightened in his chair and then leaned on the desktop.

"Well, you know, he's got a brother, Daniel. Almost four years younger than Jake. Born two years after Jake's father died."

"So, the mother remarried. So what?"

"That's right," Maddy said, nodding her head in agreement. "The mother remarried. A guy named Rodney Peterson. He'd be Daniel's father."

"Yeah, so, what's the problem?" Marc asked, genuinely confused and unsure of where Maddy was heading. "So, they're half-brothers. So what?"

"Seems Rodney died in some kind of accident in '76, when Daniel was eight and Jake eleven. An accident in the home was all I could find out, so far. Talked to an old neighbor of theirs who remembered it, sort of. Couldn't remember exactly what happened, just that it was some kind of accident."

"Maddy, where you going with this?" Marc asked, a puzzled look on his face.

"I'm not sure, Marc. When I first learned about all this, something kept working at my head. I couldn't quite put my finger on it, but something didn't quite make sense. Then, it occurred to me. Why, if the two boys had different fathers, why do they have the same last name? The name of Jake's dad?"

"That is a little odd," Marc quietly agreed.

"So," Maddy continued. "I did a little digging. Got a peek at their school records."

"Those are supposed to be confidential, aren't they? How'd you get at them?"

"Marc," she sighed. "I'll tell you this just once more. Men are basically superficial little boys. I know what I have and it's not too tough to get most men, to, shall we say, cooperate with me."

"You can probably get them to sit up and bark like seals," Marc said, both of them laughing heartily.

"Anyway, checking the school records, Daniel was Daniel Peterson up through the third grade. Rodney dies in June '76 right after school gets out for the summer. Daniel is Daniel Waschke when he starts the fourth grade less than three months later. His mother waits just long enough to put the kid's father in the ground then changes Daniel's name."

The silence hung in the air between them as Marc pondered the information. He leaned his elbows on the desk, rubbed his hands together, his brow furrowed as he thought over the significance or insignificance of Daniel's name change. They stayed like this for a couple of minutes. Finally, Marc broke the silence by saying, "I don't know. I'm not sure it means anything. I mean, is it really that unusual for a mother to want both boys to have the same last name? It's just, I don't know..."

"Change the kid's name that soon. That quickly. The woman just buried her husband and she can't wait 'til the body's cold to change the kid's name?"

"It does seem a little odd," Marc quietly agreed. "Well, check it out. Start with Rodney's death. What happened there? How'd he die? See if you can find some people that knew the family back then. Things like that. What's the neighbor's name? The one you talked to?"

"Mildred McDonald," Maddy answered without referring to her notes. "Those old records aren't so easy to dig up. Mildred gave me a couple more names, but I haven't had a chance to look yet. I thought I'd see what I could find out about Rodney's untimely demise. See what I can come up with as far as his relationship with the boys and their mother."

"Where's the mother? Is she still alive?"

"Don't know. I haven't been able to find her yet. I did come up with a social security number for her. It was in the school records. I'll check it out."

"I figure they'll put Waschke on the stand early. Probably first. Have him explain the killings and the investigation. What led them to Carl? If there is something there, it'd be nice to have it during cross-exam. But we can always recall him later. Do your best."

SIXTY-ONE

The next one and a half days of the trial were spent in the same way as the first. The prospective jurors would be led in by a deputy then briefed by the judge about the selection process. They would then introduce themselves and be questioned by the lawyers. Marc was becoming increasingly displeased with, what he began to suspect, Prentiss' bias. To have a juror stricken for bias Slocum barely had to give the judge a reason and that venireman would be politely excused. On the other hand, Marc found himself arguing strenuously to the bench about everyone he wanted dismissed and rarely did Prentiss rule in his favor. Usually, Marc would be forced to use one of his precious peremptory challenges until he was left with just one on Wednesday morning. Among the last ones called on Wednesday and living up to Marc's worst fears, was the retired Marine colonel. Not surprisingly, the man was quickly accepted by Slocum and Marc's objections overruled by Prentiss. With no other way to keep him off the jury, Marc was forced to use his last challenge to strike the man.

At last, just minutes before Prentiss' noon deadline, the final fourteen were seated in the box. Twelve jurors and two alternates. Seven women and five men among the first twelve and one of each for the alternates. As Prentiss went over his preliminary instructions, both Marc and the prosecution team went over their final list to see how each did. On the whole, Marc didn't feel he had fared too badly. Only two, including the male alternate, on the bottom third of his list. On the other hand, only one in the top ten. The vast majority, he believed, were listed in the middle portion of his rather unscientific, subjective rankings.

A few minutes past the noon hour, Prentiss finished his talk to the jury and looking back and forth between the lawyers, said, "We'll begin with opening statements at 9:00 A.M. tomorrow morning. I'll see counsel in chambers now. Court is recessed until 9:00 A.M. tomorrow."

After Prentiss left the bench and while the jury was led out, Marc shook hands with Carl and turned to walk back to the judge's chambers. An uneasy feeling swept over him as he watched the prosecution team practically celebrate a winning touchdown over the perceived quality of the jury selection. *Well,* he thought, *we'll see.*

Opening statements, gentlemen," Prentiss began after the lawyers had gathered in his chambers. "Mr. Slocum, how long?"

"Three to four hours, your Honor," Slocum exaggerated.

"Not a chance," Prentiss answered. "You'll keep it to two hours. Understood?"

"Yes, sir," Slocum answered, two hours being what he wanted anyway. "I'll try my best."

"Mr. Slocum," Prentiss continued, "that wasn't a request or a suggestion. Two hours, maximum. Mr. Kadella, how about it? Have you decided to do your open tomorrow? I know," he continued as he held up a hand when he sensed Marc was going to protest. "I know you don't have to tell me and you can wait until they're done presenting their case. I'm just asking. If you do decide to do it, how long will you need?"

"An hour, judge," Marc answered. "Maybe a little more, maybe a little less."

"That'll be fine. Gentlemen, we have a long trial ahead of us. We'll start taking testimony from the first witness tomorrow afternoon. Anything else? Good. See you in the morning."

The next day the crowd from the first day was back in place. There wasn't an empty seat to be found and in fact, a mob had been turned away because they couldn't get a seat.

While they waited for Prentiss to appear, Marc took the time to look around and study the faces in the room for the very first time. All wore the same serious, somber mask. A few made a little small talk with their immediate neighbors in hushed, whispered tones which accounted for the muted buzz that emanated from the crowd. He looked at Slocum, who was going over his prepared statement one last time. He noticed Slocum wore a nice, not expensive, not cheap, dark gray business suit, laundered white shirt and plain, unimaginative tie. Nothing that would distract a juror during his opening. Marc was silently pleased with himself that he had dressed the same, basic way. Only, in his case, he had saved his best, most expensive suit specifically for this day. He wouldn't wear it again until closing arguments.

At 9:05 the bailiff intoned the traditional "All rise" as Prentiss entered the courtroom and took his chair on the bench. After everyone had resumed their seats, Prentiss took a few minutes to question the jury about news reports or articles which, of course, none of the fourteen admitted seeing or reading. Satisfied, Prentiss looked over the room, settled his gaze upon Slocum and asked, "Is the State ready to proceed?"

"Yes, your Honor," Slocum replied after very slowly, deliberately rising from his chair.

"And the defense?" Prentiss asked, looking at Marc.

"Yes, your Honor," Marc answered after taking a fraction of a second longer than Slocum had to stand and face the bench.

"Mr. Slocum, you may proceed," Prentiss said.

Opening statements by the lawyers are intended to be an opportunity to give the jury an overview of the case. It is their opportunity to present the facts and evidence that the jury will hear and see during the course of what is known as each side's case-in-chief.

The lawyers are not supposed to present their arguments and opinions but simply state the factual evidence that each side will present and leave the argument until the end. That is what the final summation or closing argument is for.

Of course, that is the theory. There is a great deal of gray area here, depending upon the individual judge, as to what will be allowed. Slocum believed he didn't have far to go with all of the evidence he had at his disposal, so he played it straight and stuck to the case.

He started off by introducing himself and Steve Gondeck and by thanking the jury for taking the time out of their lives to perform this valued civic duty. Using an overhead projector, he placed in front of the jury a list of each of the victim's names with a small amount of biographical data listed for each. Names, birth dates, marital status, children, date of death for each of them.

Slocum went over the list one name at a time giving the factual evidence to be presented for each and every one. Trying to bring them to life. Make them the human beings they recently were, in the minds of the jury. An occasional sob or sniffle could be heard from the otherwise silent audience as Slocum went down the list.

During all of this, Marc began making notes. Not because he didn't know what was coming but because it was his job to keep Slocum honest. If the prosecution told the jury they were going to present a certain piece of evidence or hear a witness testify about something or other, and then if the prosecution failed to deliver or forgot about it, Marc would beat them over the head with it during his closing argument. It rarely happens, but when it does, it can be decisive.

After Slocum had finished with the victims he moved on to his witnesses and the evidence. Starting with Jake Waschke he led them through his upcoming case. One witness at a time. One piece of evidence at a time. Explaining what their testimony would be and the evidence to be presented all with a single thread to tie the entire case together. Leading the jury down a single path. A path that led to no other possibility, as presented by Slocum, than right to the lap of the man seated next to his lawyer. The man seated closest in the courtroom to the jurors, Carl Milton Fornich.

"The burden of proof in the American judicial system is on me, ladies and gentlemen. A burden that I agree with and gladly accept. And that burden of proof is that the state must prove, and the evidence that we present will prove, beyond a reasonable doubt, that the man who committed these terrible, heinous crimes is here today. Beyond a reasonable doubt, not beyond all doubt, but beyond a reasonable doubt, the evidence will show that Carl Milton Fornich is guilty of all counts of the indictments before you today. Thank you ladies and gentlemen."

Slocum had spoken for two hours and twenty minutes without looking at a single note. Two hours and twenty minutes that had seemed to be no more than thirty minutes, total. Marc grudgingly admitted to himself, Steve Gondeck was right. He did appear damn effective in front of a jury and as far as Marc could tell, hadn't missed a thing.

"Do you wish to give an opening statement, Mr. Kadella?" he heard Prentiss ask.

"Yes, your Honor," Marc answered after rising.

"We'll take a short recess, fifteen minutes, and then you can begin," Prentiss said.

Marc began his opening statement pretty much as Slocum had. He introduced himself and Carl, thanked the jurors for their service and began the process of poking holes in the prosecution's case. The process of creating a reasonable doubt in their minds.

Since there is no point in denying the evidence to be presented by the State, he acknowledged, in a vague, ambiguous and general way, the evidence that Slocum did not have. What he started doing was the process of pulling out the thread that Slocum had weaved through the evidence to Carl. Pointing out to the jury what was missing. Things such as: How could it be that in a county with a population of well over a million people, the State had only one witness? They had, of course, other witnesses. But none of them could identify Carl. And the one witness who does claim to identify Carl did not see him at the scene, but almost two blocks away on a dark, public street.

He pointed out the problems with the physical evidence as well. Six victims and almost no physical evidence that could link any of these crimes to his client. He was presenting argument of course. Supposedly impermissible during opening statements but by the time he drew an objection from Slocum and a mild admonishment from Prentiss, he had made his point.

"Keep an open mind," he said as he very gently, in a nonthreatening way, stepped up to within three feet of the jury box and stood before them. He paused for several seconds, quietly looked at each one of them as he stood before them with his hands folded in front of him. "Remember your promise. Each of you told me you would wait until all of the evidence had been presented. Until both sides had presented their case and then make your decision based on all of the facts and the law. The law, ladies and gentlemen, as Judge Prentiss will give and explain to you. The State must prove, beyond a reasonable doubt that my client, Carl Fornich, is guilty.

"Right now, and up until you decide otherwise," he continued as he slowly moved to his table to stand in front of Carl, "this man is innocent. It doesn't matter what the police believe or the prosecution believes. You are the one's that make the final decision. Until then, you must, not can, not should, but must, must presume he is innocent. And they have to prove," he said pointing at Slocum and Gondeck, "that he is guilty beyond a reasonable doubt. Meaning, if you have a reasonable doubt, then you must, not can, not should, *must* find the accused, not guilty.

"Remember your promise to me, ladies and gentlemen, and to yourselves and each other. Thank you, your Honor," he concluded looking up at Prentiss and returning to his seat.

Prentiss nodded at Marc, then turned his attention to the jury. He reminded them not to discuss the case with each other and certainly not anyone else throughout the course of the trial. Informed them they would be lunching together, a small victory for Marc, in the company of deputies and then turned back to the lawyers. "Since it's almost noon, we'll recess for lunch now. Mr. Slocum, we'll begin taking testimony promptly at one o'clock. Court's in recess," he concluded as he rose to go while the bailiff said, "All rise."

Marc spent the lunch recess grabbing a quick sandwich at an open-air sidewalk cafe and going over his cross-exam of Jake Waschke. He still didn't know with certainty that Waschke would be called first, but he figured it was a pretty safe bet. Besides, he had thought while anticipating Slocum's case, the whole thing would probably come down to Waschke and the witness, Hobbs. And Waschke was certainly the logical choice to kickoff the state's case and Hobbs to conclude it.

He took his seat at the defense table at 12:45 and continued going over his notes as the courtroom slowly filled up. A few minutes later, his client was brought in and took the seat next to him. Marc set aside his notes and made some small talk with Carl while they waited for the judge, jury and prosecution team to arrive.

"You may call your first witness, Mr. Slocum," Prentiss said after all of the principals had arrived and returned to their respective places.

"Thank you, your Honor," Slocum replied as he rose from his chair. "The State calls Lieutenant Jacob Waschke."

Direct examination of a witness is intended to be the witness telling the story and the lawyer remaining in the background. The attorney's role is to guide the witness through his or her story and remain as unobtrusive as possible. It's the witness and what he has to say, what he saw or did, that is supposed to be the focal point of the jury's attention. The attorney should serve as a guide and not the one doing the testifying. Of course, both the witness and the lawyer should know long before the witness takes the stand exactly what the testimony is going to be. Coaching, at least in theory, is not allowed. But preparation certainly is. You're not allowed to coach a witness by putting words in his mouth, but you better go over the exact story each of your witnesses has to tell, how they're going to tell it and how they will present themselves to the jury before you get there.

Jake, as a veteran of many years on the police force, had testified scores of times over the years. Most cops, including Jake, don't like it too much. They also realize it's a necessary part of the job. And having testified as many times as he had, Waschke knew exactly how to present himself to a jury. As Marc figured he would.

Jake had spent several hours with Slocum and Gondeck, going over his testimony from start to finish. Being the first witness up, and the one with the most knowledge about the crimes, investigation and evidence that led to the arrest, it would be critical to the State's case that Jake's testimony come off without a hitch.

The good direct examiner, which most veteran prosecutors are, will move the story along with soft, open-ended questions. What happened next? What did you do then? What did you see yourself? Keep the witness from straying and pay close attention to be sure he doesn't miss anything. One missed piece of evidence or an element of the crime overlooked and your whole case can go down the drain.

"Lieutenant Waschke," Slocum began from his seat after Jake had introduced himself to the jury. "How long have you been a police officer?"

Slocum deliberately started slowly with Jake's record on the force, years of service and any additional information about Jake's background and credentials. Building Jake's credibility in the minds of the jurors. Telling them that this was a witness worth listening to. Besides, the first witness up in any trial is probably the most important. The one that gets to testify while the jury is still fresh and alert. Any trial, but especially a long one, is going to become pretty boring after a while. It isn't television. A real trial moves at a snail's pace most of the time and it's the exceptional person who can maintain any good level of concentration during the entire time and through all of the testimony.

Slocum spent the entire first afternoon with Jake going over the preliminary stages of the investigation and reintroducing the victims to the jury. As each new murder came up, as soon as the victim's name was mentioned, Slocum would rise from his seat and approach the bench and witness stand carrying two photos of the woman about to be discussed.

The photos themselves had been the subject of a very thorough and heated debate between Marc and the prosecution at a pretrial hearing. Gondeck had represented the state without Slocum, as he had at all of the pretrial motions, and had argued for the introduction of many more and several very inflammatory photos to be shown to the jury. Photos at the crime scene. Gory and blown up shots of bound and naked women lying cold and lifeless.

Marc, of course, had argued that these shots would be too prejudicial and offer little, if any, evidentiary proof of his client's guilt. The only point to the photos, he had argued with some success, would be to play on the jury's emotions and should be totally excluded. Prentiss had ordered a compromise between the two positions. He would allow two photos of each victim. One taken before her murder and one after. And it was Prentiss himself who had gone over the photos and decided which ones would be allowed.

Slocum had decided to introduce them through Jake's testimony. Technically he should have used the person who took the photos to testify as to their accuracy. But he wanted them seen by the jury as soon as possible. Marc could have objected since Jake personally had not taken any of the photos himself and had no personal knowledge about the accuracy of the precrime photos. Marc had decided against it since he knew, one way or another, those photos were coming into evidence and he didn't want to risk alienating the jury with pointless objections.

Slocum moved slowly, deliberately around the courtroom with the photos. First showing them to Prentiss, then to Marc for any possible objection which Marc did with each of them. He would rise from his seat, identify the photo by exhibit number and for the record and to make sure the jury understood why he objected, would point out that the photos themselves offered no proof of any kind as to who committed these murders. Prentiss would politely overrule him, and Slocum would walk Jake through a series of questions to get the photos into evidence. Slocum would then carefully tack each photo into place on a large poster board placed on an easel in front of the jury box before moving Jake's testimony along.

The whole process was so time consuming that, by the end of the first day, Jake's testimony had only covered the crimes and investigation of the first two victims, Mary Margaret Briggs and Victoria Landry. It was effective though, Marc had to admit to himself. By the time Slocum tacked those pictures up, there wasn't a dry eye in the jury box.

After Slocum had finished with the Landry woman and Jake's involvement with her investigation, Prentiss interrupted him and called a halt for the day.

"We can pick up here in the morning at 9:00," Prentiss said. He then took a couple more minutes to remind the jury to stay away from newspapers and TV news and recessed for the day.

SIXTY-TWO

The next morning Jake and Slocum picked up the testimony where they had left off the day before. The poster board with the photos was back in place and the two men spent the entire morning session discussing and displaying victims number three and four, Kimberly Mason and Constance Ann Gavin.

"At what point did you first begin to believe these women were all the victims of the same man?" Slocum asked, an objectionable question that Marc let pass.

"The second victim," Jake answered, "Victoria Landry."

"Why?"

"Because of the obvious similarity between the method of the assaults and killings."

"What about Ms. Gavin?" Slocum asked.

"That one was a bit different," Jake said, looking directly at the jury.

"How so, Lieutenant?"

"Well, the first three were all similar in appearance. All tall, very attractive, slender brunettes. All killed, on a Wednesday or Thursday. Constance Gavin was different from them. More average in height and weight. Sandy colored hair. More blonde and more average looking. The others could be described as beautiful, even. She wasn't. Plus, she was killed on a Sunday evening. Not the same as the three before her or the ones later."

"What made you believe she was a victim of the same killer?"

"The method," Jake answered. "A single stab wound under the chin through the mouth and into the brain."

"Is this unusual?"

"Well, sir, in all my years on the force I'd never seen it before and I've yet to talk to another police officer here or anywhere else who has."

"Was there anything else about Ms. Gavin?"

"Yes. We finally obtained a solid piece of physical evidence. A semen sample was taken from the body."

"Was it tested?" Slocum asked as Marc tensed in his chair anticipating the objection he would make.

"Yes it was," Jake replied.

"And whose semen was it?" Slocum asked.

"Objection," Marc said as he rose from his chair before Jake could answer. "Lack of foundation."

"Approach, gentlemen," Prentiss said to the two lawyers. The judge flipped a switch on his bench area and the room was filled with a white noise that would block their discussion. "Mr. Kadella?" Prentiss asked looking down at Marc.

"Your Honor, this witness has no qualifications to testify about this evidence at all."

"Mr. Slocum," the judge whispered.

"Your Honor, even the defense analysis came back with a positive match. The jury has the right to hear this and hear it now. We're prepared to bring in all of the qualified experts to verify the testimony you want."

"You'd better be, Mr. Slocum, or Mr. Kadella gets a mistrial. Is that clear?"

"Yes, sir," Slocum said, smiling slightly at his victory.

"Your Honor ..." Marc said, beginning his protest but stopped when Prentiss raised a hand.

"I'm going to let him say it, Marc," Prentiss said mildly. "You'll have your shot at cross and I'll instruct the jury before he answers the question. Return to your seats."

"I'm going to overrule the defense's objection and allow the witness to answer," Prentiss said after the lawyers had sat back down. "However," he continued, facing the jury, "I must caution you first. This witness has not been qualified as an expert in this area and his answer is technically hearsay. Mr. Slocum assures me that an expert will be called and qualified to corroborate his answer. The witness may answer the question."

"What was the question?" Jake asked knowing full well what it was but not wanting to miss the opportunity to have it repeated for effect.

Marc remained seated at the table, an impassive look on his face while all of this was said. All the while thinking that Prentiss and Waschke had just made the whole thing worse. "Whose semen was it?" the court reporter said, reading from the record she was making.

"The defendant's, Carl Milton Fornich," Jake answered flatly.

"Are you sure?" Slocum asked.

"Don't press your luck, counselor," Prentiss said as Marc began to rise from his seat while a murmuring sound passed through the spectators. "Move it along."

"Yes, your Honor," Slocum said softly.

Jake testified for another half hour as several of the local TV news reporters slipped out of the courtroom to phone in the news about the semen match for the benefit of the noon broadcasts. Shortly after the noon hour and just before Slocum started on the next victim, Prentiss called a halt for lunch.

After the lunch break the lawyers met with Prentiss in the judge's chambers. Slocum had asked for the meeting to take one more stab at allowing Jake to testify about Michelle Dahlstrom. Prentiss, having already ruled on the subject, would have none of it. Since Carl was not charged with her death and believing that the court of appeals would overrule him anyway, Prentiss had ruled that no discussion of Michelle's death would be allowed. Try as he might to change Prentiss' mind, Slocum took the defeat good naturedly and they all went back to the courtroom to wait while Prentiss attended to some other business.

Shortly after two, Prentiss came out on the bench to begin the afternoon session. While Jake was making his way back to the witness stand Daniel Waschke quietly slipped unnoticed into the room. Daniel took the only empty seat available in the last row behind the defense table among the media members.

Jake spent the rest of the afternoon testifying about victim number five, not counting Michelle Dahlstrom. Donna Anderson, the woman found among the bushes along Lake Calhoun. He went over in great detail all of the events of his day leading up to the report of the sighting he had received over the police radio. He testified about his actions and the radio communications he had with the patrolman who had called it in. The report by the civilian walking his dog, the chase that followed and the crash of his car when he had spotted the man running down the street. He left out no detail of the event. The rain, the speed and the crash, except one.

"Did you get a good look at the man running down the street, Lieutenant Waschke?" Slocum asked.

Before he answered, Jake's eyes flicked over the crowd and for the first time he noticed his brother seated in the back. The two men's eyes locked and without looking back at Slocum, Jake said, "No. No I didn't. I must've passed out. The next thing I remember was waking up in the hospital with a bad headache the next morning."

At that point, Prentiss called a halt and recessed for the weekend. He again reminded the jury not to discuss the case with anyone or read or watch any news stories or reports about the case. With that, the trial's first week came to an end.

The sleek Corvette had barely come to a full stop when the man Jake was meeting was in the passenger seat with the door closed. Without bothering to greet his guest, Jake spun the car's steering wheel completely around, did a 180 in the middle of Hennepin Avenue and headed south toward Lake Street. Eddie Davis rolled down the window, lit a cigarette and silently smoked, waiting for Jake to speak. They cruised a couple of blocks through the light, late-evening traffic until Jake had to stop for a red light a block from Lake.

"Gimme one," Jake finally said. "So, what've you got for me?" he asked as Eddie handed him the cigarette.

"The guy I want, you know, the one for your trial, he's out of town right now. He'll be back in a couple of days."

"How do you know that? Where is he?"

"Texas. He's making his supply run. Goes down to Texas about once every couple of months. Picks up his weed and comes back. Don't worry. He's perfect for us and this way, I can bust his ass as soon as he gets back."

The light turned green and Jake pulled ahead, continuing his short journey while silently reflecting on the news. He made the turn onto Lake Street and headed toward Lake Calhoun before finally saying, "That's good. Yeah. That should work fine. You sure about this guy?"

"It'll be fine, Jake. Trust me. You'll love this guy. Make a great witness. Looks like a banker. Which is why he's so good at selling dope. He sticks strictly with marijuana. Nothing else. Quietly makes his run south with his girlfriend in a minivan. They must look like average Joe Couple on vacation. Anyway, he's got a record and if we nail him again, he's looking at serious time. He'll cooperate."

"Okay. Well, we'll see."

"Jake, there is one other thing. I think you should know. There's some broad poking around town asking a lot of questions. A real babe. I've seen her myself."

"Yeah, so?"

"She's poking around asking questions about you, personally. Here in Minneapolis and across the river."

"Really?" Jake said quietly as he continued to drive.

"Yeah. Real personal shit, ya know. And from what friends in St. Paul tell me, she's going way back. To like, when you were a kid."

"Hmmm. Interesting," Jake said. "You know who she is?"

"Yeah, I think so. You know Tony Carvelli?"

"Sure, I know Tony. He's a straight guy. What of it?

"She's a friend of his. A P.I. working for the lawyer, Kadella. Drop me off at the next corner," Davis said. "I just thought I'd let you know about your surprise witness and what I've heard about the babe."

"Thanks, Eddie. I appreciate it."

252

SIXTY-THREE

Marc was in the office early Saturday morning. He stood at his desk going through two weeks' worth of neglected mail, the only sound in the otherwise empty and silent suite coming from the coffee maker he had started when he first arrived. He had some catching up to do on what little remained of his practice and he needed a respite from the State vs. Fornich. He came upon a letter with a single page document stapled to it with the U.S. Department of Justice, Tax Division letterhead on the letter. Marc dropped all of the remaining mail on the pile on his desk and took a minute to read the letter and the document. He pulled up his chair and unable to suppress a smile, went to his rolodex and found Carolyn's number.

"Hi, it's Marc," he said when he heard her voice. "Can you come in for a couple of hours today?"

"You must've found the letter from the Justice Department," she said.

"Yeah, I did. They actually dismissed the appeal before I thought they would. Anyway, I want to get going on that thing we worked on, right away. I want to have it signed and served Monday morning."

"Okay, I'll be there in about a half hour. I figured you'd call this morning. I have to be out of there by noon, though. No later."

"That should be fine. We just need to finish it up. Most of the stuff is ready to go. I just need to finish up my affidavit."

Two hours later they were making minor corrections to the documents they had prepared when the front door opened and Chris Grafton came in. Even though it was a Saturday, Grafton was wearing a suit and tie and was mildly surprised to see Carolyn at her computer screen while Marc stood over her.

"What're you two up to?" Grafton asked.

"Us? Look at you on a Saturday morning," Carolyn answered.

"Have to meet a client. He's bringing money in, hopefully," Grafton said.

"Here," Marc said, handing a document to Grafton. "Take a look. This is what we're up to."

Grafton took the several pages held by his friend and began to read. He got through the first paragraph when his eyebrows shot up and he looked at Marc and said, "You're taking the United States of America to court on a Contempt Motion?"

"Yep," Marc answered, smiling.

"You're taking the government of the United States into federal court to ask a judge to find the government in contempt. Is that what I'm reading here?"

"Yes it is," Marc said, still smiling.

"Contempt of what?"

"Contempt of court for ignoring a valid court order and not paying me my money fast enough. And for jerking me around and wasting the court's time with this appeal bullshit. It's all here in my affidavit. Got it all spelled out nice and neat to show the judge how they screwed around, ignored his order and wasted more of the taxpayer's money and time with this appeal nonsense. This appeal that several people have admitted they just did to buy themselves more time and cover-up their incompetence."

"I like it," Grafton said, laughing. "I've never heard of such a thing, but I love it. Pretty ballsy. I hope you nail their ass. What're you asking for?"

"I tried to find some grounds to have someone put in jail, but I can't do that. So, I'm asking for twelve thousand dollars plus an additional five hundred per day until they comply and of course, more attorney fees."

"Well, good luck. Go get 'em. I think it's great. What about service?" Grafton asked.

"I'll have Maddy do it. She'll have to get the original judge in St. Paul to have him sign an Order to Show Cause ordering them to show up and then serve it on the U.S. Attorney's office in Minneapolis. "

"Why don't you just mail it to Washington?" Grafton asked.

"That's the best part," Marc said. "The rules say I have to serve it on the local office of the U.S. Attorney. They're not handling this, Washington is. So, I'll strictly follow the rules and serve it on the office downtown. They have nothing to do with this and they won't know what to do with it. I have to give them thirty days' notice so, I figure it will take three weeks, at least, for them to figure out what it is. All the while the clock is running and by the time I do hear from someone, the time will be about up. We'll see, but I'm dead serious about this. I'm tired of being jerked around by these people and from what I saw when we were in court the first time, this judge is going to be furious."

"Well, good luck. Let me know when the hearing is. I'll come down and watch this time."

Marc spent the rest of the day working on the few remaining cases he had, doing anything he could to clear his mind, if even briefly, of Carl's case. With the most recent check he had received from Joe Fornich, he caught up on both his personal and business expenses and paid Maddy another five hundred. When he had finished, he stared at the one hundred sixty-seven-dollar balance in his checkbook and wondered how long he could stay in business at this rate.

Just before he left to go home, he picked up the phone and for the third time that day, almost dialed Margaret Tennant's number. Remembering his bank balance, he decided against it and simply went home for another quiet Saturday night in front of the TV.

SIXTY-FOUR

"We left off on Friday, Lieutenant," Slocum said, beginning Monday morning's testimony, "with you in the hospital following the murder of Donna Anderson. Do you recall that?"

"Yes, sure," Jake answered.

"What did you do after that, as far as your investigation goes?"

"Pretty much what we'd been doing after each of the other murders. We investigated the life of the victim. Found out anything and everything we could about her. Jobs, friends. What she did in her free time and with who. Where she went and who she saw. Basically, her entire life."

"Why?"

"We did that with all of the victims. Then we would feed all of the information, especially the names of people she knew or had some connection to, however remote, into the computer. Try to come up with some common connection between her and any of the others."

"Did you find any such connection, Lieutenant?"

"No, we didn't."

"Any at all between any of the victims?"

"Except for the similarities in physical appearance, date, time and how they died, no. None at all."

"Did you draw any conclusions from that lack of any connection, Lieutenant?"

"Objection," Marc said rising from his seat. "Lack of foundation and calls for speculation."

"I'm going to allow the witness to answer," Prentiss said, overruling Marc's objection. "He's qualified to speculate a little here and give an opinion. He's a veteran police investigator, Mr. Kadella."

Thanks for reminding the jury, Marc thought as he sat back down, regretting that he had objected in the first place.

"It looked like he was after a certain type of woman. Physically, I mean. Tall, slender, brunettes. Very attractive. Other than that, they appeared to be random. No common connection."

Jake spent the rest of the day testifying about the final victim, Alice Fay Darwin. Describing how close he had come to catching the man at Powderhorn Park at the time it happened. Testifying about the efforts by the police in searching the neighborhood that night and then, finally, the lucky break that had led them to Carl. Jake told the jury about the witness who had seen someone fleeing the scene. Slocum and Jake slowly, carefully, and methodically went through the phone call from Hobbs, the identification and arrest of Carl and of course, the most crucial testimony, Jake's discovery of the knife.

Slocum knew the knife was easily the most important piece of evidence against Carl. It was the only piece of physical evidence that the jury would have, could see, touch and examine to their hearts content, which would tie Carl Fornich to at least two of the victims. Slocum was going to make certain that this witness, probably his most credible one, was going to definitely tie that evidence to the defendant. The lab technician who had matched the traces of blood found on the knife of two of the victims would come later. Jake's job was to simply explain to the jury how the knife turned up and to use that testimony to get the murder weapon into evidence and in front of the jury.

"After you found the knife hidden in the defendant's closet, what did you do next?"

"I put it in this plastic bag," Jake said, holding up the knife, still in the same plastic bag. "I sealed it, marked it for evidence and had it sent to the lab for a check of fingerprints or anything else."

"Was anything found?"

"Objection, your Honor," Marc said, not bothering to stand.

"Lieutenant," Prentiss said to Jake. "Did you personally conduct any lab tests or check it for fingerprints."

"No, your Honor. I did not," Jake answered, looking up at the judge.

"Then, Mr. Slocum, the objection is sustained. Move along."

Marc smiled imperceptibly at his small victory. Even though he knew that a more qualified expert witness would be brought in to do the blood analysis of the knife samples. Hopefully, one not as easy for the jury to follow and possibly, the blood samples wouldn't have quite the impact later in the trial that they would now.

Jake concluded his testimony by recounting for the jury the events leading up to the discovery of the clothing seemingly hidden by the defendant in a public locker. That he had played a policeman's hunch about the key Carl had in his possession when arrested and put one of his detectives back on the street to track down the locker and what was found inside.

Slocum methodically took him through the process of identifying each article found in the locker, including the bag. Jake identified each one by matching the identification tags with his own evidence notes and positively identifying the article as one taken from the locker. Jake also made a mental note to be sure to go over the clothes with Marty Hobbs before he testified to be sure to say they looked like the clothes Carl was wearing when Hobbs saw him on the street.

With the introduction of the clothing found in the locker, Jake's direct examination was complete. It was almost 6:00 P.M. at that point so Prentiss recessed for the day. Marc's first shot at examining a witness in front of this jury would wait until the next day. A brief reprieve that he was silently grateful to receive.

SIXTY-FIVE

"Thanks for coming Tony," Marc said to Carvelli as the two men entered Marc's office. Marc took his seat behind the desk while Tony closed the door.

"Hi, sweetheart," Tony said as he bent down and lightly kissed Maddy on the cheek, while she remained seated in one of the chairs in front of Marc's desk.

"Hello, Tony," she smiled looking at Marc's eyebrows, raised in mock surprise.

"If you two are through slobbering on each other, can we get down to business?" Marc said. "Have either of you come up with anything, anything at all tying Waschke to this witness, Hobbs?"

"Nothing so far, counselor," Carvelli said from the chair next to Maddy. "This is a touchy business, though. Jake's a popular cop. Got a lotta friends in the department. I'm finding it to be a real touchy subject."

"How about you?" Marc asked looking at Maddy. "Anything?"

"Nothing," she answered, shaking her head. "Are you sure there is one?"

"Has to be," Marc sighed. "Look," he continued, "if you believe Carl is innocent then there's only one logical explanation for the evidence. Especially the knife. Waschke planted it. How he came up with it, I don't know ..."

"Could've found it at the crime scene," Tony interjected. "The last one. Wasn't he the first one on the scene? He could've found it there. I don't believe it though. I've known Jake too long."

"Maybe you don't want to believe it," Maddy said.

"And if you believe Waschke planted the knife, how else do you explain the witness, Hobbs?"

"Maybe Hobbs saw someone who looks like Carl running down that street that night," Maddy offered.

"Yeah, yeah that could be," Marc said nodding in agreement. "I still don't quite buy that. I still don't believe it. Too much of a coincidence. There's gotta be a connection somewhere."

"Could be Jake's been using him as a snitch. Any good detective will have confidential informants that only they know about. That would explain Hobbs' clean record. Jake got it wiped for him," said Carvelli. "If that's the case, you won't find it. Jake's too good to make that kinda mistake."

"Well," Marc said, "keep looking. It's there. And if we find it, we win."

They ordered Chinese, which Tony paid for, and spent the rest of the evening going over Marc's upcoming cross examination of Jake Waschke. Tony played Jake's role and Maddy the judge and jury while

Marc went through his questions. They practiced the examination, sharpening each question to be asked, each area to be probed. All three of them going over each piece of evidence including the police reports and Jake's testimony looking for weaknesses to exploit, holes to widen.

The cross examination of a witness during a trial is, in theory, the mirror image of the direct examination of the same witness. During the direct examination the jury's attention should be focused on the witness and what he is telling them. The good cross examiner will have the jury's attention focused on the lawyer. It is the lawyer who is, in effect, doing the testifying in question form. This is done by asking short, simple, precise questions. Very narrow, very focused questions worded in a way to elicit only yes and no answers. The witness had his chance to tell his story during the direct examination. Now it's the other side's chance to take that witness' story and turn it around to benefit his client's case. The purpose is to get all of the facts before the jury so that they can make an informed decision within the confines of the law. The reality is, of course, each side wants the jury to hear only the facts and truth that they want them to hear and in a way that they want the jury to hear it, all in the search for justice.

On the morning of the day when Marc would get his first shot at the prosecution's case, his cross examination of Jake Waschke, he awoke at six, a half hour before his alarm was set to go off. He rolled onto his side, pulled the blanket to his chin and tried to go back to sleep. He laid like this for several more minutes, his eyes wide open and his mind already going over his upcoming exam. Finally, realizing sleep would not return, Marc tossed the blankets aside and headed for the bathroom.

Two hours and a pot of caffeine later, as he was putting the finishing touches to the knot of his tie, he began to feel a slight tightening of his chest and trembling in his fingers. Marc stood in front of his bathroom mirror, held his hands out in front of his face and watched the fingers lightly shaking as his breath began to quicken. He took a half dozen deep breaths, clenched and unclenched his fists several times then toweled off the small beads of perspiration from his brow. "Relax," he said to the man in the mirror. "You've done this many times. You'll be all right once you get started. You know that."

"Yeah," he answered himself still staring at the image looking back from the glass. "But never this important. Never with an innocent man facing such a horrible fate.

"Just be careful with this cop," he continued. "He's nobody's fool and if he gets a chance he'll bury you with a mistake. Just stick to the script. Don't go wandering around. You'll do fine. Besides, it's not your ass on the line.

"Good point," he concluded as he reached for the light switch and headed for the door.

SIXTY-SIX

"Good morning, Lieutenant Waschke," Marc began from his seat next to Carl. "I have a few questions for you, but before I start, I noticed during your examination by Mr. Slocum that you were very cooperative with him. I would appreciate it if you would be as cooperative with me. Will you do that, Lieutenant?" Marc asked, pleasantly smiling at Jake. This question is basically a rookie lawyer's tactic, but it works. And it's effective. Show the jury that you're really a pretty reasonable fellow with a job to do. At the same time elicit a promise of cooperation from a potentially dangerous, adverse witness. How can he possibly answer this question with anything but a yes? No, I won't be cooperative with you? Of course, the witness can't say that, even if it is true.

Like jury selection, every trial lawyer has a theory about cross examination. A few, only the very best, are confident enough with their own experience and ability to go fishing in front of a jury. To risk probing into unknown areas looking for things they are not fully prepared to deal with. Marc was not among those elite few. He always kept in mind what a wise old professor, a judge with many years of experience, once told him in law school. Make your point, say what you have to say then shut up and sit down.

"Certainly," Jake answered.

"Thank you, Lieutenant," Marc said.

"Now then, Lieutenant Waschke, you've been a police officer for twenty-three years, as I recall, is that correct?"

"Yes, almost twenty-four."

"You've been assigned to homicide for over ten years now?"

"That's correct."

"And during those almost twenty-four years as a policeman have you ever been involved in a case of this significance?"

"Certainly. They're all significant," Jake answered, taking the opportunity that Marc gave him with the loosely worded question.

"Have you ever investigated a so-called serial killer case before?" Marc asked, ignoring Waschke's response.

"No. Just this one."

"Ever been involved in a case where the press scrutiny was this intense?" Marc asked waving his right arm toward the press section of the courtroom.

"No," Jake mildly replied. "I can't say that I have."

"Ever been involved with one that the mayor gave weekly press briefings about?"

"Not that I can recall, no."

"Ever been involved with a case where this many detectives devoted their full and exclusive attention to making an arrest?"

"No, I don't believe so."

"So, Lieutenant, I'll ask you again, have you ever been involved in a case with this much significance?"

"No, I guess not."

"This much media and political pressure?"

"Well," Jake began, squirming slightly, almost imperceptibly for the first time. "No, I guess not but..."

"Thank you Lieutenant," Marc said cutting off the forthcoming explanation.

"Did you attend the weekly press conferences held by the mayor?"

"Pretty much all of them, yeah."

"Did you have to answer questions by the press yourself?"

"Yes, a few times."

Marc continued his questioning about the public, political and media scrutiny of the investigation for a few more minutes. It was a fairly safe area to probe. One that Waschke could hardly deny but it served a couple of purposes.

First, it made the point with the jury that the police were under a lot of pressure to solve this case. The media had been screaming headlines for months, terrifying the citizens and causing the mayor's office no end of grief. All of this would, of course, eventually be heaped on the shoulders of the man on the witness stand. By itself, hardly enough to cast doubt on Carl's arrest. Especially since it could be easily refuted by Slocum on redirect examination by going through the lengthy list of people who had been investigated, questioned and released. Possibly, Marc hoped, it would be a small building block on the way toward creating a reasonable doubt.

Second and more importantly, it was a fairly safe area for Marc to start his case. An area of questioning, a factor in the investigation, that Waschke could hardly credibly deny. And it gave Marc a chance to get things moving and calm himself down.

"When was the first time you met Martin Hobbs?" Marc asked abruptly, changing subjects.

"It was the morning after the last murder," Jake answered, the muscles in his neck tightening as a warning bell went off in his head. He had anticipated the question. Had prepared himself and Hobbs for it, all the while hoping the subject wouldn't come up.

"He called the police?"

"Yes, that's right."

"Asked to speak to you, personally?"

"Um, I don't recall," Jake said after considering the question for a moment. "He may have. Other people had during the investigation."

"Thank you, Lieutenant," Marc said, cutting him off before he could get going without Marc to guide him.

"The night of the Powderhorn Park attack, did the police canvas the neighborhood? Go door-to-door to try to find someone who may have seen anything?"

"Yeah, sure. We checked everybody within a mile."

"Did you find any other witnesses?"

"Well, we had another one, a woman named Mildred..."

"Was she able to identify anyone?"

"No, she wasn't."

"Anyone else?"

"No."

"Anyone living along Chicago Avenue between Lake and 35th?"

"No."

"Chicago's a pretty busy street, isn't it Lieutenant?"

"I guess."

"And isn't it true that Chicago and Lake is one of the busiest intersections in Minneapolis?"

"I suppose, yeah."

"And in the entire city of Minneapolis, you were unable to find anyone else who claims to have seen the accused running down the street that night. Do you find that a little strange?"

"Objection, argumentative," Slocum said from his chair.

"Sustained," Prentiss ruled. "Move along counselor."

Marc had been getting a little carried away with this line of questioning and was actually thankful for the interruption. He needed to get back on track and besides, he had made his point. Believing that Waschke and Hobbs had concocted Hobbs' identification, he had scored the point he wanted to make. Waschke, in open court, under oath and in front of the jury had testified he had not met Martin Hobbs before. Now, all he had to do was come up with proof of a connection between them. And he had pointed out to the jury that on a busy street in a large city only one person claims to have seen Carl.

"The night the accused, Carl Fornich, was arrested," Marc began the next question intentionally referring to Carl as the accused and not the defendant, a subtle reminder to the jury, and used his name to make sure the jury would see Carl as a human and not just the defendant. "You had his apartment staked out for several hours, is that correct?"

"Yes, as I recall."

"Mr. Fornich arrived home around eight o'clock, is that correct?"

"About that time, yes."

"And you and your officers moved in to make the arrest immediately, is that correct?"

"Yes."

"Carl didn't try to run, did he?"

"No."

"Didn't struggle at all, did he?"

"No, he didn't."

"In fact, he offered no resistance whatsoever, did he?"

"Objection, irrelevant," Slocum said as he rose from his seat.

"Sustained," Prentiss replied. "The jury will disregard."

"Now, Lieutenant," Marc continued, "after the arrest, you entered Mr. Fornich's apartment to search for evidence, is that correct?"

"We had a search warrant," Jake answered somewhat defensively.

"I'm sure you did, Lieutenant. But that wasn't my question," Marc said holding his hands up as if to reassure the witness of the innocent nature of the question.

"Yes," Waschke said. "We went in to search."

"You, personally, Lieutenant. Did you search in the living room?"

"No, I didn't."

"The bathroom?"

"No."

"The kitchen?"

"No."

"Isn't it true you were the first one in the apartment?"

"Um, yeah. I believe I was."

"So, Lieutenant, you went into the apartment, walked into the bedroom and began searching the closet, is that correct?"

"Well, um, yes, I guess so," Jake answered, fidgeting slightly.

"And found the knife?"

"After a minute or so, yes I found the knife," Jake answered.

"Was anyone else searching through the closet with you?"

"There was another officer in the bedroom," Jake answered.

"He was searching through the bedroom, was he not?"

"Well, yeah, he was."

"Did anyone else see you find the knife in the closet?" Marc asked, very slowly, very deliberately.

"No. I was the only one searching the closet," Jake answered as slowly and deliberately as Marc had asked to show the jury he didn't care for Marc's attempt to impugn his integrity.

At that moment, for the briefest instant, unnoticed and unseen by anyone else in the packed judicial theatre, the two men's eyes met and locked together. For the first time since the arrest, the unstated passed between them, unheard by anyone else. As resounding and clear as if the lawyer had arisen from his seat and loudly proclaimed: "I know what you did". And Waschke heard it just as clearly but it was the lawyer who blinked first and decided to simply let the moment pass.

Marc, realizing he had no proof that Waschke had planted the knife, decided he was on dangerous ground with the jury. To accuse a policeman with Jake's record, a record that had been spelled out clearly to the jury by Slocum during direct exam, of planting evidence is a risky business. A jury could easily take offense with such a tactic in a city where the police are, in general, respected. Besides, he had made his point. Time to shut up and move along.

"Lieutenant, does the name Thomas Hardee mean anything to you?" Marc asked knowing even if he received a negative response he could easily refresh Jake's memory.

"Yes, it does," Jake answered, nodding his head, relieved that this lawyer was done with the knife questions.

"How about James Lindgren?"

"Yes."

"And Bryan Sorenson?"

"Yes."

"Isn't it true, that all three of these men were questioned about the death of Constance Ann Gavin?"

"Yes, they were."

"Isn't it also true they were all investigated about her death because at one time or another all three of these men had sexual relations with her?"

"Yes, it's true," Jake answered as a slight stirring occurred in the courtroom. "They all had alibis," he quickly added,

"Your Honor," Marc said to Prentiss, "nonresponsive and I ask that the witness's response be stricken and the jury instructed to disregard."

"The witness's answer shall be stricken and the jury will disregard the answer," Prentiss said half-heartedly knowing full well the jury couldn't disregard the last part of Waschke's answer.

"Did your investigation turn up any other men who may have been involved with Ms. Gavin?"

"No. "

"No other names?"

"Right. No other names."

"But you did hear of the possibility of other men, didn't you Lieutenant?"

"Yeah," Jake answered, shifting slightly in his chair. "We heard some rumors."

Marc was tempted to continue along this line, but he forced himself to stop. He had obtained the admission he wanted: there were other men besides Carl sexually involved with this victim. Marc strained at this self-imposed leash, sorely tempted to go down this path but realized he would probably do his client more harm than good. Besides, if there were any more names of men known to the police, they would have checked them and Marc would have the names. And even if the three had alibis, which Marc knew ahead of time, he could still use it in closing to try to cast doubt on the physical evidence presented. The DNA matched.

At this point Prentiss interrupted him asking Marc if this was a good time to break for lunch and called the recess. Marc found himself staring at the clock, amazed that the morning had gone by already.

Marc spent a few minutes in the adjoining conference room with Carl. His client had asked to talk to him as the courtroom was emptying for the lunch break. They went into the small room and Marc took a seat at the table while Carl paced around, obviously unhappy.

"Why didn't you go after that lying sonofabitch more about the knife?" Carl asked after taking the seat opposite Marc. "You know he planted the thing."

"Oh, shit," Marc said lightly slapping his palm against his forehead. "I forgot to ask him that. By the way, Lieutenant," he continued in mock seriousness, "isn't it true you planted the knife in the closet?

"Why, yes I did. Did I forget to mention that?" Marc said, lowering his voice pretending to be Waschke. "Come on Carl, get serious. This isn't TV. He's not going to break down on the witness stand and admit it. We have to get some proof."

"All right. I get it," Carl said smiling.

"It's a long trial. A lot of witnesses still to come. We take them one at a time. With each one we try to score a point or two to support our theory of the case. I got what I wanted out of this cop. He admitted he didn't know Hobbs before this. He admitted no one else saw him find the knife and he admitted there were other men screwing the Gavin woman. We're building our case to use at closing argument. That's when I tie it all together and try to convince the jury that there's reasonable doubt. Convince them that the evidence isn't as good as it seems to be."

"Okay. I see what you mean. What do you think? You think the jury will believe he planted it?"

"Would you? We'll see. But without that tie between Waschke and Hobbs, well," Marc continued as he rose to leave. "I just don't know. I'll see you in a while."

SIXTY-SEVEN

He met Maddy for lunch and the two of them went over the morning's testimony. She had been in the courtroom and confirmed Marc's opinion that it had gone pretty well. No major gaffes or surprises. She had watched the jury's reaction and the only noticeable stir she had observed was when Marc had gone over the sexual history of Constance Gavin. Bill Gavin, the husband had been present during this testimony and Maddy reported that he had maintained a stoical expression throughout and had not drawn any attention to himself, a possibility that Marc had been concerned about.

"How much longer do you think Waschke will be on the stand?" Maddy asked between bites of her deli sandwich.

"Probably finish today. I don't have that much more to get from him. I'm sure Slocum will have some redirect. Maybe a few questions on re-cross. Why?" Marc asked.

"Just curious. They're probably going over his redirect now, don't you think?"

"I'm sure. After today, you need to get back on finding Waschke's mother. We need to know why he's doing this. Try to find her through Daniel. Or, maybe one of the kids."

"I'm going to the social security office. I've got her number and I'll get some unsuspecting man to track her with that. Don't worry, you'll see. We'll find her, but I'm not sure you're going to get anything there."

The afternoon session was late getting started because Prentiss had other judicial duties to take care of concerning other cases. Phone calls to return, a pair of opposing attorneys to meet with. Finally, shortly after two, Prentiss came out on the bench.

"Lieutenant Waschke, after you arrested my client, Carl Fornich, the police conducted a thorough search of his apartment, is that correct?" Marc began his continuation of the cross examination of Waschke.

"Yes, that's correct," Waschke replied feeling much more relaxed after his lunchtime meeting with Slocum and Gondeck.

"Did you bring in a crime lab team?"

"Yes, we did," Waschke replied.

"The police searched the bathroom?"

"Yes."

"The living room?"

"Yes."

"The kitchen?"

"Yes."

"Were Mr. Fornich's possessions impounded for analysis, including the furniture?" Marc continued.

"Yes."

"His clothing?"

"Yes."

"The kitchen and bathroom items?"

"Yes."

"In fact, isn't it true that every item of every kind was taken by the police and analyzed in the police lab?"

"Yes, I believe that's true."

"Was the apartment carpeted?"

"Yes, it was. At least the living room and bedroom were."

"Was the carpeting thoroughly vacuumed and the debris analyzed?"

"Yes, it was."

"Now, Lieutenant, on any of the clothes taken from the apartment, was any blood found?"

"No."

"Any hair samples, other than Mr. Fornich?"

"No."

"Any fibers that could be tied to any of the victims?"

"Yes."

"Really," Marc said trying to hide his shock at this revelation.

"Some denim fibers were found on the first victim, Mary Briggs. These matched some found in the defendant's apartment," Waschke explained.

"Denim fibers. You mean blue jeans, don't you Lieutenant?"

"Yes. Levi's 505 jeans."

"Levi's 505. How many hundreds of pairs of Levi's 505 jeans are sold in the Twin Cities every day?"

"Um, several, I guess. We couldn't nail it down specifically."

"I see," Marc continued, relaxing again. "Suffice it to say, Lieutenant, that's a fairly popular brand don't you think?"

"Objection," Slocum said, dramatically rising slowly from his seat.

"Sustained," Prentiss said.

"All right. Let me ask you this. Do you own a pair of Levi's 505 jeans?"

"Yes," Jake answered hesitantly. "I believe I do," he added as Slocum sheepishly sat down amid the mild laughter in the courtroom.

"What do you think, Lieutenant? You think Mr. Slocum does?"

"Mr. Kadella..." Prentiss started to say as the laughter became louder.

"Withdrawn. Sorry your honor."

Marc took a moment to look at his notes, having forgotten where he had left off. He found his spot and continued by repeating his original question about fiber samples on the items taken from Carl's apartment. For the next half hour, he went over the list of impounded items. Slowly, carefully, methodically eliciting a negative response from Waschke about the evidence, or lack of it, found at Carl's apartment.

He went through the same procedure with Carl's car. Having been impounded, it too had been gone over with a microscope in an effort to find something, anything that could tie any of the victims to Carl. Marc went much further than he had originally intended. His purpose, of course, was to show the lack of evidence against his client. A process he could have done with a carefully chosen ten or twelve questions. But he was rolling and feeling a bit cocky and decided to show the jury what a thorough job the police had done and how little they had actually come up with.

"May I approach the witness, your honor? "Marc asked Prentiss as he stood up.

Unlike on TV, in Minnesota the lawyers are to remain seated while questioning a witness. Most people under those circumstances are nervous enough without a lawyer hovering over them. The lawyer needs permission from the judge to approach a witness, which is routinely granted.

"Certainly," Prentiss replied.

Marc went to the table of the prosecution exhibits, picked up the plastic bag containing the knife and walked slowly, deliberately to the witness. He stood next to an impassive looking Waschke as he held up the knife and continued his questioning.

"Lieutenant Waschke, I'm holding in my hand the knife you testified you found in the defendant's apartment the day after Alice Darwin was murdered in Powderhorn Park, is that correct?" he asked setting the knife on the ledge of the witness stand.

"That's the knife, yes."

"You discovered this knife in the defendant's closet, correct?"

"That's correct."

"On a shelf in the closet behind some empty boxes and clothes?"

"Yes."

"Was the shelf examined?"

"I believe so," Waschke answered narrowing his eyes slightly while looking at Marc.

"Were any blood samples found on the shelf?"

"No, I don't believe so."

"Any hair or fiber samples that could be tied to the any of the victims?"

"No."

"Any water spots?"

"What? What do you mean by water spots?"

"Any spots on the shelf that would have been caused by water dripping onto the surface?"

"Um, no. There weren't," Waschke answered.

"Now, Lieutenant, the knife must have been washed, is that correct?"

Slocum began to stand to object to the question as calling for a conclusion, thought better of it and silently dropped back into his seat. Obviously, if the knife had only minute traces of the blood of two victims on it, it must have been rinsed off at some point before it went on the shelf.

"Yes, I suppose it was," the big cop answered with a slight shrug.

"The sinks in the apartment were taken apart and examined, weren't they Lieutenant?"

"Yes, they were."

"Was any blood found?"

"No."

"Any samples of any kind?"

"No."

Marc picked up the knife, placed it back on the table with the other exhibits and slowly, almost casually, walked back to his seat at the defense table. He took his seat and picked up the legal pad with his notes on it and went over the list while the courtroom silently waited for him. He wasn't looking for anything in particular. In fact, he knew he had covered all of the ground he could and had scored the points he wanted. Enough, at least, to argue during closing that the knife had been planted. He looked over his notes simply as a way to buy himself a little time and decide if he wanted to press just one more issue.

"Do you have any more questions of this witness, Mr. Kadella?" Prentiss finally asked after waiting patiently for almost two minutes.

"Um, I'm sorry, your Honor," Marc replied. "Yes, just a few more."

"Please get on with it then, Mr. Kadella."

"Yes, sir. I'll be brief," Marc answered the judge.

"Lieutenant Waschke," he continued turning his attention back to Jake. "Isn't it true that among the kitchen utensils taken from Mr. Fornich's apartment, there were two carving knives, other than the one from the closet?"

"Yes, that's correct."

"Isn't it true that both of those knives were analyzed?"

"Yes, they were."

"And nothing was found on either one, was there?"

"No, there wasn't."

Marc stared silently at Jake, while Jake stared back at him. Both men maintaining a calm, relaxed expression yet neither man blinking. They stayed this way for ten or twelve seconds, Marc with his hands folded together on the tabletop, Jake with his arms casually crossed in his lap. Marc broke the silence by quietly, softly and still without breaking his trancelike expression or shifting his eyes, saying, "I have no further questions for this witness, at this time, your Honor."

The rest of the day was used up by Slocum conducting a redirect exam of Jake. The redirect is the opportunity the lawyer gets to rehabilitate his witness' testimony. If anything is brought out during cross examination that requires a more thorough explanation, this is the time. It is also intended to be restricted to only those things covered in the cross exam. The theory is that you had your chance during the direct exam to bring out testimony and new areas are not supposed to be allowed during redirect. Slocum played it pretty straight and the only testimony he wanted to explain were the alibis of the three men who had been investigated for the death of Constance Gavin. The other three men they knew of who had sex with her. Again, without the use of notes, Jake testified that all three men had been thoroughly checked out and their alibis held up.

SIXTY-EIGHT

A few hours after Jake was completing his testimony in a Minneapolis courtroom, fifteen hundred miles almost due south, a man backed his Plymouth minivan into a garage in McAllen, Texas. As he turned the key to shut off the engine, his friend pushed the button of the garage door opener activating the electric motor to close the double door of the attached garage. Wally Bingham exited the vehicle, walked around to the passenger side, slid back the side panel door and the two men began working on the van's interior. They quickly removed the two passenger chairs, setting them on the floor of the garage, while a woman leaned against the wall patiently watching. After removing the chairs, Wally got inside the van, peeled back the carpeting and the two men removed the screws holding in place three feet by six feet section of the floor and removed it from the van as well. Hidden under this panel was an eight-inch-deep compartment large enough for Wally to transport the one hundred kilos of marijuana he had driven to Texas to purchase.

After removing the floor panel covering the hidden storage space, the two men went into the house through the garage doorway and began carrying the contraband out to the van. The woman, Wally's girlfriend Marlys Fletcher, got into the van and started placing the tightly bound, cellophane wrapped one kilo bricks into the hidden space. After all, one hundred bricks had been stored, the two men quickly, expertly replaced the floor panel, carpeting and chairs. The van now weighed two hundred twenty pounds more than it had a little while ago, but except for that, its appearance was no different than any of tens of thousands of suburban vehicles throughout America. Which was, of course, precisely the point.

The next morning, Wally and Marlys loaded their luggage into the back of the van, gave Wally's long-time friend and co-conspirator, Dante Gregore, a hug and a kiss from Marlys and headed north for the trip back to Minnesota. Several hours later they were cruising up I-35. Just another anonymous, middle class white couple in an anonymous minivan passing through America's heartland.

While Marlys snoozed in the passenger seat next to him, Wally allowed his mind to wander, to relieve the boredom in this extremely unscenic part of the country **and** began day-dreaming about his life and where he was.

He thought about Dante, the friend he had just left behind in McAllen. *Now there was a story,* he thought with a smile. A father who, three days after receiving the news of his widowed mother's death in the late 50's, laid down his Soviet army assault rifle and literally, with no one watching him, put hands in the air and walked to the West

German checkpoint to begin his journey to America. Another Soviet army border guard defecting to the West.

Then, ten, no, Wally thought, *almost thirteen years ago now, Wally and the defector's son met while serving in the Army, forming a life long friendship and criminal enterprise.* Dante was a conduit. A weigh station in the pipeline moving marijuana, and marijuana only, from points in the South to feed the great American dope appetite. The smugglers brought in the supply to Dante five or six times a year and Dante would distribute it to the wholesalers, of which Wally was one. It was Wally who had set Dante up a few years ago and Wally who had given Dante access to other wholesalers. On the grand scale of the mountains of grass coming in, their's was a tiny ant hill. But Wally had it all figured pretty well. Keep it small, low-key and don't attract attention. Stay away from the hard stuff, cocaine and heroin. And as Wally had explained to Dante, retire with a couple million in the bank by the time they were thirty-five. Best of all, they were right on schedule and living a pretty comfortable life in the meantime. Beats the hell out of working for a living, he reminded himself.

Wally had been busted twice, the second time getting him eighteen months in prison. In the beginning, the thought of any time in a serious prison had terrified him. He was initially sent to a medium security place that, except for the loss of freedom, hadn't been too bad to deal with.

After he had been there a few months, an asshole biker idiot decided to have a little sport with Wally, who was by no means a fighter but a good-sized man in pretty fair shape. Before things really got going, Wally had landed one extremely lucky punch. He had drilled his antagonist squarely on the nose, smashing it flat causing an eruption of blood and sending the fool to the floor flat on his back. Before he could get up the guards were there, and the next thing Wally knew he was in a cell in the maximum-security prison in Stillwater, surrounded by real criminals which Wally definitely did not consider himself to be. In fact, now that it was over, the whole experience had not been nearly as bad as his imagination had led him to believe.

Wally and Marlys took three days to make the trip back, a trip that could have been done in one. They paid cash for everything along the way. Gas, meals and the inexpensive motels they stayed in. No credit cards, no checks. Wally had several sets of false IDs to use for check-ins at the motels. No trail that anyone could follow between himself and Dante. Timing the trip he had made many times, just after sunset on Friday evening, the minivan came over the hill on 35W in Burnsville to see the Cities lit up and spread out before them.

He got into Minneapolis and dropped Marlys off at her apartment. The two of them mostly lived together but Wally insisted on maintaining a separate residence. A place where they could go when he needed a break from the business. He kissed her goodbye, assuring her as he always did that he could unload the merchandise by himself, got in the van and drove home. He pulled the van into the garage, hit the remote to lower the door, got out and began the process of dismantling the back of the van to unload the weed.

A half hour later, when he was about half done storing the bricks of grass in the hole below the wood-burning stove, the otherwise silent garage interior was shattered as the small door leading to the backyard of his little house came crashing down. Within seconds, a half dozen heavily armed men and women came pouring through the door, flicked on the lights and leveled shotguns at Wally who was already spread-eagled against the wall.

"Hi Wally," one of them said putting his face next to Wally's ear while another patted him for weapons. "How you doing, Wally?"

"Not too bad, officer," Wally said quietly as his hands were roughly removed from the wall, jerked behind him and handcuffed. "It is officer, isn't it?"

"Yes indeed," Eddie Davis said showing Wally the badge of a Minneapolis detective. "And I guess you know you're under arrest, don't you Wally?" he continued with mild sarcasm.

"Do you have a warrant, officer?" Wally politely asked.

"Yes, we do, Wally," he said waving the paper in his face. "And I have a copy for you, too. Here," he continued as he folded one of the carbons and neatly tucked it in Wally's shirt pocket. "You can read it at your leisure. You'll have plenty of time later. Since this is now what, Wally, your third time? Enjoy asshole."

A couple of hours later, during the booking process, while he was emptying his pockets for the inventory clerk, he removed the folded copy of the search warrant and took a minute to read it over. He didn't have to go very far when a slight, involuntary smile turned up the corners of his mouth. He started to say something to the guard, caught himself and silently folded the single sheet up again. As the inventory guard was placing Wally's possessions in a manila envelope he quickly thought about what to do with the paper. It occurred to him what to do with it while watching the guard begin wrap the string around the two catches to seal it.

"Here," he said to the clerk while handing him the paper through the slot on the counter through the plexiglass. "Put this in there too. My lawyer will want it and," he shrugged, "that's as good a place as any to keep it."

The sheriff's clerk took the paper and without looking at it, placed it in the envelope with the other items and finished sealing it.

While Wally was being led to his cell he couldn't help smiling at the thought that the police were storing his get out of jail free card for him. For, what Wally had seen that had made him smile, was a mistake on the search warrant. The address was wrong. The address on the warrant was for 4348 Pallantine Avenue and Wally's address was 4343

Pallantine. What really had Wally smiling was his own cleverness. Instead of blurting out the mistake to his jailers, he had enough savvy to keep his mouth shut, save it for his lawyer and not give the cops the opportunity to correct the mistake. *Good thinking, Wally old boy*, he thought to himself over and over as he was led upstairs.

He was feeling pretty good, pretty confident about how it would all turn out and then, as he was shoved into his cell and the door slammed behind him, he remembered his merchandise. A quarter of a million dollars worth of good Mexican grass about to go up in smoke and not the way it was intended. *Oh well*, he thought as he sat down on the edge of a bed in the otherwise unoccupied cell, *the price of doing business*. He stared at his feet for a moment, silently removed his Nikes and as he was about to lay back on the bunk, looked up and saw his neighbor in the cell across from him, staring back at him through the bars.

"Well, hello friend," he jovially said to Carl Fornich.

SIXTY-NINE

For the next three weeks the trial settled into an almost monotonous routine. The prosecution, which meant Steve Gondeck since Slocum didn't want to bother with 'B' witnesses, plodded along presenting mostly the insignificant witnesses and evidence, what little there was of it. Some family members of the victims testified as to what a kind, decent wonderful person she had been. Friends and co-workers relating to the jury the last day of the victims' lives, none of which, of course, contributed to the question of guilty or not guilty. All of this was designed and presented solely for the purpose of tugging at the jurors' heartstrings and playing on the emotions of the men and women selected to decide Carl's fate. Try to paint the picture of the victims as people you would like to have as friends or neighbors and the accused some monstrous, psychopathic pervert that, at best, needs to be locked up and kept apart from all of us good, decent, upstanding citizens and should actually be castrated, shot and then hanged.

There were minor, routine and necessary delays as well. Judge Prentiss had cases pending before him that could not be kept completely on hold. Several times during this period he would hear motions on other cases. Always early morning, between eight and nine. He would have the oral arguments by the opposing attorneys in the courtroom. Invariably these hearings would go beyond the allotted time, lawyers being the verbose creatures that they are. Prentiss would, naturally, need further time to dictate an order, answer phone calls and almost daily, have an in chambers meeting with Marc, Gondeck and Slocum for last minute arguments about upcoming testimony.

It was Marc who usually requested these meetings. The parade of witnesses during this time had little to offer and Marc was continuously objecting to the prosecution's tactics. Always to no avail. Long before the case had reached this point, Marc had come to realize that Prentiss was going to give the prosecution all of the room they needed to present their case. At the very least, Marc kept reminding himself, he would continue to object and build a record for a possible appeal. A thought that brought a black cloud of depression over him. The prospect of handling an appeal of a guilty verdict in this case was not something he looked forward to and in fact, was something he was determined he simply would not do. If Carl lost and wanted an appeal, he was going to have to find another lawyer to do it.

On the Wednesday of the third week following Jake Waschke's testimony, an afternoon break necessitated by Prentiss' golf game, Marc was seated at his desk going over the prosecution's witness list. The trial itself was into its fifth week and Marc was beginning to feel the strain. Getting by on five or six hours of sleep each night and a diet of deli sandwiches and fast food was starting to take its toll. He consoled himself with the fact that Slocum's list was starting to dwindle and they were entering the homestretch of the prosecution's case.

There had been some tense, uncomfortable moments when Marc had sensed, more than seen, Carl fidget slightly in his chair. Without being noticed by the jury, Marc would reach over and lightly place a hand on Carl's arm to reassure and calm his client. When Detective Jefferson testified about the locker key and the clothes obviously hidden in the mall locker. When family members of the victims had testified and the worst, the climax to this morning's testimony, the introduction of Carl's criminal record. Up until that point the jury's boredom was starting to show and in fact, several had even nodded off during some of the more mundane moments. Carl's criminal history, especially the rape conviction, had sent a palpable jolt of energy through the courtroom and an obvious shot of adrenaline through the jury. Marc, of course, had known it was coming and had slyly studied the jury's reaction. Several of the jurors were unable to resist casting a distasteful glance at Carl and Marc had caught himself unconsciously leaning slightly to his left, away from Carl so as not to be held guilty by association in the minds of the jurors. He had stopped himself but smiled now at the recollection. A smile that quickly collapsed with the realization that the jury would have all day to think about Carl's past and get it firmly imprinted into their collective memories.

Marc laid the list he had been perusing on the desk, lifted his arms over his head and sat for a minute, rolling his head from side to side while stretching. He got up from his chair, went to the window, opened it and stood staring at the traffic under his office along Lake Street. It was a beautiful, warm, sunny September day in Minnesota. The kind the citizenry really appreciated now with summer going, the kids back in school and the leaves starting to turn. Indications that winter's ugly head would soon be rearing which, by January, would cause all of the saner inhabitants of the nation's icebox to wonder just why the hell they lived there. *It's days like this one,* Marc silently thought, *that keep us here.* He stood at the window staring at the people on the street, the traffic moving along and one particularly attractive young woman, not much older than his daughter, all the while fighting a battle with his conscience. The imaginary angel on one shoulder kept whispering in his ear to get back to work and the imaginary devil on the other telling him he deserved a half day off.

Leaving the window open to allow in the fresh air and the noise from the street, a noise he found oddly soothing, he returned to his chair. Just as he was about to let the little devil win the argument, the buzz on his intercom went off. He stared at his phone with the little blinking light for several seconds in between buzzes. Finally, reluctantly, he picked up the receiver.

"Marc," he heard Sandy say, "there's a woman on line one, a lawyer from Washington."

"Thanks, Sandy. I'll get it," he replied as he punched the button for the call. "Marc Kadella," he said.

"Mr. Kadella, my name is Sharon Marzell. I work for the Tax Division of the U.S. Justice Department," he heard a frosty voice say. *Great,* he thought. *One with an attitude. This could be interesting.*

"What can I do for you, Ms. Marzell," he answered in a flat, professional tone.

"I've just been assigned to handle this contempt motion of yours," she said with obvious distaste. "Frankly, Mr. Kadella, no one here is amused by this, so I thought I'd call and see what you are going to do to settle it."

"Excuse me," Marc said feeling his neck muscles tighten and the warmth spread through his face. "What I'm going to do to settle it?"

"Yes. Are you interested in settling this case or are you simply trying to embarrass the United States Government?" Marzell said, her attitude becoming even more hostile and condescending.

Weeks of stress, tension and sleepless nights came boiling up in Marc and the last comment was the pin prick that released the pressure. "Am I willing to settle it?" he exploded. "Let me tell you something. I have done nothing but try to settle this thing for ten years! All I've gotten out of the U.S. Government, the IRS and the Justice Department is indifference, inefficiency and incompetence! And I have to tell you, Ms. Marzell," he continued bellowing into the phone as Sandy quietly closed his door, "I'm getting a little tired of it. Embarrass the United States government? You people should be embarrassed. But I'll tell you something, no, I'm not trying to embarrass the government. I'm trying to get you people to do your job, take court orders seriously and stop jerking people around like this. And I'll drag your asses into every court in this country if I have to to get you to do it!"

"Um, ah, I'm, ah sorry, Mr. Kadella," she meekly replied. "I didn't mean ..., I guess, um, I didn't know you were having problems. It's just, well I was just handed this so, whatever happened before really isn't my fault and ..."

"And that's another thing!" Marc let loose with another blast. "Every time I turn around I've got another government employee telling me 'It's not my fault. Sorry, I'm not to blame, I'm not responsible.' Is that line of bullshit part of your training? Something you're all taught your first day on the job? Well, I don't give a damn anymore. It's time somebody in Washington took responsibility and time for you people to decide what you're going to do to settle this thing. Don't lay it on me!"

"Well, um, I'll ah, certainly look into it right away and get back to you," Marzell softly said, obviously wanting to end this phone call as quickly as possible.

"Please do," Marc replied, going from blistering anger to icy calm in the space of a heart beat. "I'd appreciate that. Goodbye," he concluded, gently hanging up the phone without waiting for a response.

SEVENTY

Later that night, Jake Waschke parked his department issued sedan in the back of the strip mall and restaurant where he had met Marty Hobbs and where his irrevocable journey had begun. He went into the restaurant through the same back door and seated himself in the same booth facing the front to await the arrival of his late evening companion.

Jake ordered a glass of beer and after the waitress delivered it, silently sipped at the glass while he waited. The strain of the trial was starting to show on Jake. His original belief that a witness and weapon would be enough for a conviction had begun to fade. Replaced by uncertainty and doubt. He kept reminding himself that an acquittal wouldn't be the worst thing that could happen. If this guy Fornich were to walk it wouldn't be Jake's fault. At least the killings have stopped, his brother was getting help and maybe the tugging he constantly felt at his conscience would cease. A pressure that he contained with the certainty that putting this scumball Fornich away was likely crime prevention. The guy had a history, Jake reminded himself, and sooner or later would attack another woman. "So, how come you're not sleeping so well?" Waschke quietly said to himself.

He looked up at the sound of the door opening in the sparsely populated restaurant and saw the man he was waiting for come in. Jake slid over on the booth's bench seat as far as he could while Eddie Davis dropped heavily onto the seat across from him. Jake ordered two more beers and they silently waited until the waitress had served them and left.

"It's getting a little cool around here at night to be dressed like that isn't it?" Jake asked, referring to the sleeveless black sweatshirt Eddie was wearing "Why don't you get a couple more tats? I think you've missed a spot or two," Jake continued, referring to Eddie's arms.

"It's street shit, man. Helps me blend in. Besides, I kinda like it. It's artsy."

"So, where are we with this snitch? What's his name, Wally…"?

"Bingham. Wally Bingham," Eddie said. "Oh, Wally's coming along just fine. In fact, I had a little chat with him today. At his request without his lawyer. He's all set. No problem."

"You're sure?"

"Oh yeah," Eddie said as he rolled back his head and laughed. "We got all his assets frozen. Everything. A good bust and his ass is going down. He can't even make bail. Two hundred grand. Cash. No bond. We got the judge convinced Wally's a flight risk."

"How about you? You okay with this?"

"Look, Jake," Eddie whispered as he leaned forward on the table. "There ain't a cop in this town doesn't owe you. Or, at least, respect you. If you say this guy Fornich is guilty, that's good enough for me. I got no problem here. I'll trade a grass dealer for a serial killer any day. You just tell me when you want him. No problem."

"All right Eddie. I appreciate that," Jake replied as he took a drink of his beer.

The trial picked up the next day with the testimony of Mildred Jackson and Marvin Henderson. Mildred testified about seeing what would turn out to be the last victim, Alice Darwin, being led into Powderhorn Park. She told the jury of her call to the police and the difficulty she was having dealing with her own guilt. How she couldn't shake the feeling that maybe if she had acted a little more quickly or done something right away, Alice would still be alive.

Marvin told the story of his late evening stroll along the walkway surrounding Lake Calhoun, an event he was no longer able to enjoy because of what happened that night. The night he interrupted the mad killer and discovered Donna Anderson. Marvin choked back tears as he relived the horror in vivid detail. Describing for the jury the sight of the naked, muddy, bloody corpse and how he had been unable to sleep through a single night since. Awakened every night, usually several times, by the image of the body and the eerie, cold laughter of the man who had ran from the bushes.

Of course, neither of these witnesses could identify Carl, or anyone else. They could add nothing to the real question before the jury. The sole purpose of their testimony, as far as Marc could tell, was to inflame the jury's passions. Show the jurors, like the family members of the victims, that these murders touched people. Affected the lives of more than just the victims themselves. Marc's cross exam of both witnesses was very brief and mild. Two or three soft and easy questions to point out to the jury that neither could identify Carl except in a very general way. Approximate height and weight that could be Carl but could also be any one of thousands of others.

The rest of that day was taken up by the head of the police crime lab, Paul Jacobson. Slocum started slowly, showing Jacobson's credentials and building his credibility in the minds of the jurors. Rather than gloss over the scarcity of physical evidence, Slocum met it head on. Laid it out in the open and have his expert now on the stand explain it away. There were three good reasons for him to do this: First, take away the defense's thunder. Don't give the defense attorney the opportunity to use this fact the way he wanted. Second, bring it out. There is no point denying that there wasn't much physical evidence found to tie the defendant to the crimes. Let the jury learn in a way that your expert can rationally explain. Finally, give the jury an explanation for the lack of evidence.

"Now then, Mr. Jacobson, would you say it's unusual to not find hair samples, fibers, blood stains from crimes like these?"

"Unusual?" Jacobson began his answer. "I suppose you could call it that. But it's not surprising to me."

"Why is that?"

"We searched his apartment and car and analyzed all of the clothing and items found. None of the victims, as far as we know, were ever in his apartment or his car. So, it's hardly surprising there were no samples from any of the victims found there. And if the clothing that was worn by whoever committed these crimes was not kept there, he wouldn't have brought any samples home. Any hair, blood or fibers."

"What about the car?"

"Same answer. If he didn't use the car immediately after the crimes, if he got rid of the clothes he was wearing and washed himself off before getting in the car, again, no samples."

"Objection, speculation," Marc said as he rose from his seat.

"Overruled," Prentiss said. "This witness is an expert and I'll allow some rational explanation here."

"Mr. Jacobson, the knife, the murder weapon, was found in the defendant's apartment with traces of blood on it. Were the sink pipes in the apartment examined?"

"Certainly."

"Anything found?"

"No, they were completely clean."

"Is that unusual?"

"Not really. The pipes were pretty new. Completely clean of any residue at all. No hair, blood or even soap scum. Hot water would've easily rinsed anything away."

After asking for and receiving permission to approach the witness, Slocum picked up the clothing found in the locker and held them up in front of the witness.

"Now then, Mr. Jacobson, I'm showing you the clothing found in the locker, opened by the key the defendant had in his possession when arrested. Do you recognize these items?"

"Yes, I do."

"Were these items analyzed?"

"Certainly."

"What, if anything, did you find?"

"Well," he began, "we found no blood or hair or other samples on the clothes. We did find the clothes and the bag had been thoroughly washed in a very strong industrial strength detergent. In fact, they had been recently washed several times. At least three or four times."

"How do you know that?" Slocum asked while he slowly turned and stepped toward the jury box while holding up the clothes.

"Because there was substantial evidence, chemical residue, from the detergent. It was layered on the clothes. Especially the blue jeans. A simple rinsing from a normal wash cycle will not remove all of the chemical compounds from the clothes. Not a detergent this strong."

"Would a detergent as strong as the one used on these clothes," Slocum said as he draped the jeans and windbreaker on the jury box rail and placed the tennis shoes on it as well, "remove blood stains?"

"Objection..." Marc said as he began to rise.

"Overruled," Prentiss ordered before Marc could finish.

"Absolutely. In fact, quite easily with just one washing," the witness answered.

"Were the clothes washers in the defendant's apartment building analyzed?"

"Yes, both of them."

"Did you find any evidence of the detergent used to wash these clothes in either washer?"

"No, none at all."

"Did you find evidence of other detergents?"

"Sure. Quite a bit. There's always some residue. The machine itself will not completely rinse away the detergent. There's always some left over. Especially under the lid."

"What, if anything did that tell you?"

"Objection, speculation," Marc tried again

"Overruled, Mr. Kadella," Prentiss said having difficulty containing his obvious annoyance.

"The clothes were not washed at his apartment."

"Do you know where they were washed?"

"There are a lot of laundromats in this city. No, we never did find it, but we can't possibly check them all."

Slocum turned, faced the jury and stood silently, expressionless, and looked over each one of the jurors. He took a minute and looked into the eyes of each of them to satisfy himself that they all got the point. The point, of course, being that the reason there was so little physical evidence was because Carl Fornich was a very clever man. Smart enough to know to keep the clothes thoroughly cleaned and away from his apartment and car. Smart enough to hide the evidence.

Slocum slowly, carefully, picked up the clothes, walked back to the evidence table and put them back in place. He returned to his seat, faced Prentiss and said, "I have no further questions, your Honor."

Prentiss turned the witness over to Marc who spent the next half hour questioning him about the lack of evidence. But it was weak and almost pointless. Slocum had done a great job of explaining it away to the jury and Marc's questions were lame and half-hearted and he knew it. As he was about to give up, the light came on in his head.

"Mr. Jacobson, is it your position that the jury should believe that the defendant went to considerable lengths to keep the clothes out of his apartment?"

"The jury can believe whatever they want. I'm just here to testify about the facts."

"Okay. Fair enough. You testified the clothes were washed three or four times, is that correct?"

"Yes."

"And it's your opinion they were not washed at his apartment and not washed with the detergent you found in his apartment?"

"Yes, that's right."

"And the clothes were not found in the apartment, is that true?"

"Correct."

"In fact, based on your scientific analysis, as far as you can tell, they were never in the apartment, true?"

"Yes, as far as we can tell," Jacobson said shifting slightly in his seat and shrugging his shoulders.

"So, Mr. Jacobson, would you say that, if those articles of clothing are the defendant's, he was being careful with them? Washing out the evidence and hiding them? Keeping them away from his apartment?"

Jacobson shifted again and glanced quickly at Slocum who was considering an objection. An objection he decided would be ill advised. He had just spent considerable time and effort getting the jury to believe exactly what Marc was going over and an objection would make him look foolish. Worse, it would make him look like he was now trying to hide something.

"Yes, I would say that," Jacobson finally answered. Marc leaned forward, placed his elbows on the table, locked his fingers together and held his head up with his chin resting on the back of his hands. He sat this way, without expression, staring at the witness for a long fifteen seconds while everyone in the courtroom waited for him. Wondering where he was going with this questioning that seemed to support the state's case.

Finally, without moving, he quietly asked, "He supposedly went to all this trouble to hide the clothes, yet, the knife, the murder weapon itself, was found in his apartment. Can you explain that, Mr. Jacobson?"

"I don't know," Jacobson answered. "Got careless, I guess."

"Pretty dumb, wouldn't you say?"

"Objection. Argumentative," Slocum said as he began to rise.

"Withdrawn," Marc said, "I have nothing further, your Honor."

Slocum finished the day by calling a fingerprint expert from the State's Bureau of Criminal Apprehension, commonly referred to as the BCA. He went through his normal routine of carefully establishing her credentials. Detailing for the jury her education, background and experience to convince the jury of her credibility and expertise. Amanda Evans looked anything but the part of a bookish, technically-oriented, criminal evidence analyst. Petite, pretty blond in her late forties she had turned down job offers from all over the country, including the FBI, in order to stay close to home and family. She had been with the BCA for almost twenty years and when Amanda said a set of fingerprints matched a particular person, her reputation was such that few argued with her and none did so successfully.

She and Slocum, mostly Amanda, spent about an hour and a half going over the fingerprints taken from the quarters found in the locker's change box. Using an overhead projector with blowups of the prints and a telescoping pointer, Amanda gave the jury a concise, easily understood and authoritative rendition of the science of fingerprint analysis and carefully and convincingly made the case that the prints on all three coins belonged to Carl Fornich. And if that wasn't enough, the state introduced a two-foot-high stack of computer printouts Amanda obtained by running the prints from the coins through the FBI's data base. The result of that search came up with only one match; Carl Fornich.

Marc sat quietly throughout her testimony. Admiring her as a witness and a professional. Of course, none of her testimony surprised him since all of this had been gleefully made known to him by Slocum weeks ago. Marc hired his own fingerprint expert to do a comparison, just to be sure, who had come to the same conclusion. Marc's expert had found a few minor discrepancies as there always are, which Marc was prepared to bring out when Marc called him during the defense's case.

"Ms. Evans," Marc said, beginning his cross examination, "were there other coins found in the locker box?"

"Yes, ten in all," she pleasantly answered.

"And did you run a fingerprint analysis on all of them?"

"Yes, I did."

"Did you find anything?"

"Well," she began, "there were usable prints on three others, but the four remaining coins were too smudged."

"Of the three coins, were you able to match them to anyone?"

"No, I wasn't."

"Specifically, did any other coins match the defendant's fingerprints?"

"No, they didn't."

"Would it be safe to say that ..." he began to ask, then stopped himself. He was tempted to ask her if someone besides Carl had deposited the other coins but knew that she couldn't answer the question for sure. In fact, he realized, it was altogether possible that Carl could deposit other coins in the locker without leaving good prints or even smudging those prints already on the coins and he didn't want the State's fingerprint expert pointing out that fact to the jury.

"Withdrawn, your Honor," he said. Marc continued to stare at the witness, fighting the urge to continue along this line. He had already scored the only point he was going to; the fact that someone else had used the locker. To push further could invite disaster.

"I have no further questions, your Honor," Marc finally said with a friendly smile at Amanda.

SEVENTY-ONE

The next day, Friday, the medical examiner, Dr. Howard Palen, was first up for Slocum. Another opportunity for Slocum to put on a show. The media, having had the good doctor's testimony leaked to it ahead of time, was back in full attendance. The courtroom was packed with them again giving Slocum the audience he craved. And the media, mostly the locals since the nationals had long since departed, couldn't resist the ghoulish voyeurism of reporting the details the M.E. would spell out about the deaths of each of the women.

While Marc and Carl sat passively maintaining an indifferent, even semi-bored composure, Slocum put on his show for the voters. He started slowly, as was his style with a well-prepared expert witness, going over the doctor's schooling, professional qualifications and years of experience. Palen, for his part, did an excellent job. Having testified at trials too numerous to recall, he was so good at it he hardly needed Slocum's help. The two of them went over the medical details and cause of death, one by one, of each of the victims. The single stab wound beginning under the chin and thrust upward, through the mouth and into the brain.

"So, doctor," Slocum asked, "would you say that all of the victims died from a similar wound?"

"No, not similar, Mr. Slocum," Palen began his answer. "I would say, it is my medical opinion, that they were all identical."

"Identical?" Slocum repeated making the single word response a question.

"Yes, identical. Each one was exactly the same and I would say each one made by the same knife."

With that Slocum rose from his seat and strolled to the evidence table, picked up the plastic bag containing the knife and without asking for Prentiss' permission, walked over to the witness stand. He handed the knife to Palen and took two steps back, a move designed to allow the jury to watch both men as Palen's testimony reached its conclusion.

"Now then, Doctor Palen," Slocum said, slowly drawing out what everyone knew was coming. "I've just handed you State's Exhibit 8. Do you recognize it?"

"Yes," Palen answered as he turned the knife over in his hands.

"And how do you recognize it, doctor?" Slocum asked quietly, patiently standing still in his two thousand-dollar, charcoal, double-breasted suit, hands folded solemnly in front of himself.

"I was given this knife and two others taken from the defendant's apartment and asked to compare them to the victims' wounds."

"Did you do the comparison?"

"Yes, I did."

"And," Slocum said after making a ninety degree turn to his right to face the jury, "what, if any, conclusions did you draw?"

"This knife, and only this knife, was a perfect match. An exact fit, if you will, of the wounds that caused the deaths of all six victims."

Then, while standing absolutely still and continuing his surveillance of the jurors, Slocum carefully, deliberately went through the lists of the victims. Asking Palen as he ticked off each name if the knife he held matched the entry and death wounds of each one of them. And of course, as each victim was named, Palen affirmatively answered that the knife, State's Exhibit 8, was an exact match for each one of them. At that point, having scored probably the most dramatic and damning testimony so far, and without returning the knife to the table, Slocum returned to his seat and turned the witness over to Marc.

Marc asked for and obtained permission to approach the witness. For no apparent reason, he quickly walked up to the witness stand and gently took the bag with the knife in it away from the doctor. He rolled up the plastic bag around the knife while beginning his questions and as unobtrusively as possible, held it in his hand the blade pointing upward, along the inside of his arm to get the damn thing out of the sight of the jurors.

He confined his cross to a few very carefully chosen questions about entry points and the angle of the wounds as he slowly moved away from the witness. Standing about ten feet in front of the defense table, he stopped his backward movement and asked, "So, Doctor Palen, could you tell whether the victims were stabbed by a right hand or a left?"

"A right hand. Very clearly," Palen replied.

"It would be your testimony then that whoever stabbed each of these victims is right handed?"

"Yes, that would be my medical opinion," Palen answered as he shifted slightly in his chair, a curious look on his face. With that, Marc turned to the table and with one quick motion tossed the knife in the bag at Carl. Carl, with a well rehearsed, startled look on his face, reached up and snatched the knife and bag out of the air just before it would have hit him in the face. There was a slight gasp from several of the spectators and the eyes of each of the jurors remained transfixed on Carl as he held the bag up in his hand for two or three seconds, allowing all of them a clear opportunity to see that he had caught it with his left hand and then tossed it onto the table top.

Before a startled Slocum and Gondeck could respond, Marc turned back to the witness and said, "Thank you, Doctor." Then, turning his eyes to the bench, said to Prentiss, "I have no further questions, your Honor."

"Your Honor," Slocum indignantly bellowed, "I must object."

Prentiss slammed down his gavel to silence the buzz in the courtroom, looked at the jury and forcefully said, "The jury will disregard the defense counsel's theatrics and as for you, Mr. Kadella," he continued turning a withering gaze at Marc who remained standing in place, an innocent look on his face, "any more stunts like that and I'll hold you in contempt. Is that clear?"

"Yes, your Honor," Marc meekly replied.

"May we approach, your Honor?" Slocum angrily asked. Prentiss turned his look back at Marc, angrily narrowed his eyes and stabbed a finger toward him while saying, "I want counsel in chambers now. We'll take a brief recess."

Back in the judge's chambers, an obviously calmer Prentiss said to Marc, "I oughta slap you with a fine for that little stunt."

"I want his client on the stand now. To testify whether or not he is right handed or left," Slocum seethed.

"Not a chance," Marc said. "You even bring up the subject of him testifying and I ask for a mistrial."

"And I have to give it to him," Prentiss replied.

"If and when my client testifies, you can ask him then," Marc calmly said to Slocum.

"Relax Craig," Prentiss said. "The jurors aren't fools. They'll see that for the staged stunt that it was. But," he continued sternly looking at Marc, "I'll tolerate no more of it. Any more and I throw your ass in a cell. Clear?"

"Yes sir," Marc replied.

As they filed out of the judge's chambers to go back into the courtroom, Steve Gondeck, who had quietly watched it all with an amused look on his face, gently pulled at Marc's elbow as Slocum passed through the back-courtroom door. Standing in the back hall, Gondeck whispered to Marc, "How'd you know?"

"How'd I know what?" Marc quietly asked.

"How'd you know which hand?"

Casting a quick glance around to be sure he wouldn't be overheard, Marc whispered back, "It wouldn't have made any difference." He smiled slyly, winked at Gondeck and went through the door back to his seat.

The remainder of the day was taken up by the State's DNA expert. What could have been an excruciatingly painful two days of mind-numbingly boring testimony had been reduced, by prior agreement, to a couple of hours. To move the trial along Prentiss had obtained an agreement from both sides about this witness and the DNA testimony. Marc agreed to basically allow it in, the match between Carl's DNA and the semen sample found in Constance Gavin's vagina, without contesting its accuracy.

Slocum agreed to forego the charts, graphs and long-winded explanation in exchange for Marc's stipulation. Also, Marc's DNA expert and findings would not be put before the jury. A brief explanation of the witnesses' credentials, a summary of scientific DNA analysis techniques, a straight forward statement about the match with Carl and the witness was off the stand and the trial recessed for the weekend.

As the courtroom emptied Carl turned to Marc and said, "I still don't understand why we didn't put up more of a fight with the DNA stuff."

"Carl," Marc said patiently, "we've been over this. Prentiss made it clear that the evidence was coming in. He was determined that this guy was going to tell the jury it was a match. There was no point in fighting it. This way, the jury hears it without making a big deal out of it. All it really proves is you had sex with the woman and you heard him, it could've been as much as 48 hours before she died. Besides, this way the jury doesn't know we had the sample tested and our expert came up with the same conclusion. It wasn't worth fighting. We wouldn't have won."

"All right. I guess," Carl shrugged. "Was the judge really pissed about the knife trick?"

"He wasn't pleased," Marc said chuckling as he finished packing to go. "I'll see you tomorrow."

The two men rose together, shook hands and as Carl was being led away, Marc turned to leave and saw Maddy waiting for him at the back of the now empty courtroom.

"Where the hell have you been?" he asked, trying to be angry but finding it too difficult just by seeing her.

"Whatever happened to: Hi, Maddy. It's nice to see you again?" she said.

"Hi, Maddy. It's nice to see you again. Where the hell have you been?" he repeated as he stepped through the door, holding it open for her.

"Chicago. Didn't you get my message?" she asked as they headed toward the elevators.

"No. Wait. Maybe. Yeah, I do remember. That was at least two weeks ago. I thought it was just gonna be a few days. You're just now getting back?"

"Sorry," she said. "My dad was sick. He's okay now but I stayed longer because of it," she shrugged as they continued walking. "And I settled my suit with the city."

"Your harassment case? That's great. How'd you make out?"

"All right. We structured it over a period of years, so I guess I won't have to worry about money for a while. Marc," she continued while he pressed the down button to summon an elevator car, "I found her."

"Found who?" he asked.

"Waschke's mother," she whispered.

"You did? Where? Let's go see ..."

"Hold it. She's not home. I was there today. Relax. I'll go back. I'll get her."

"Do I dare ask how you found her?"

"It's not important," she answered coyly. "Besides, I didn't do anything illegal or that I'd be ashamed of."

They rode in silence in the crowded elevator car down to the second-floor courtyard. After leaving the building, they found an empty park bench on which to continue their conversation.

"How's the trial going?" she asked.

"I don't know," he said after a long pause. "I think we're behind on points. Before today I thought we were holding our own, but Slocum scored pretty good with the knife today. I know damn well Waschke planted the knife. But unless we can find a solid motive for it, I don't think the jury's will buy it. They'll want somebody to pay for all these murders and right now, Carl's looking like a pretty good candidate."

"Don't worry. We'll see what the mother has to say. I have a feeling it's there. Somewhere. Something in his past. Something having to do with his brother's name change," she said.

"I hope so," he sighed. "If not, then it'll come down to shaking this Hobbs guy ..." he said quietly, without conviction as he stared blankly at the pedestrian traffic moving in and out of the big building.

"How about you?" she asked, gently placing a hand on his shoulder. "How are you holding up?"

"Me? Oh, I'm okay," he said, weakly smiling at her. "When this is all done, one way or another, I'm going to take a few days off just to sleep and eat normally again. Listen," he continued looking at his watch, "I have to go. I have to get back to the office. I'm expecting a call from Washington. See if you can find the mother this weekend."

SEVENTY-TWO

Marc arrived back at his office a few minutes past 5:00 P.M. to find it almost deserted. Sandy Compton was the only one left and she was getting ready to leave when Marc came in through the entryway door.

"Well, there you are," Sandy said. "That lawyer from Washington, Sharon Marzell, has called three times this afternoon," she continued handing Marc three pink message slips. "She said she'd wait all night for your call."

"Really," Marc said grinning as he took the slips from Sandy's outstretched hand. "They must be getting worried. We go back to court next Wednesday afternoon and I'm betting this judge will nail their ass."

"Well, give her a call so she stops bugging me," Sandy said as she slung the strap of her purse over a shoulder and came around her desk toward the door. "How's Carl's case going? The papers make it sound like he's pretty much convicted."

"Do they really?" Marc asked, a look of concern on his face and in his voice.

"That's the impression we all get," she answered sweeping an arm around the office space.

"Great," he said glumly.

"Don't go by us," she said softly. "We've all become too jaded with too many years in this business."

"True enough," he said arching his eyebrows. Then, with a shrug of his shoulders, he added, "If he gets convicted, he gets convicted. I gave it my best shot. My conscience will be clear. Have a good weekend, Sandy. I better go make this call. It's after six in D.C."

"You have a good weekend too, Marc," Sandy said as she opened the door to leave.

Marc went into his office, took his seat at the desk and made his call. Marzell answered it before the first ring had finished and Marc smiled to himself with the thought of how much her attitude had toned down since their first conversation.

"Thanks for calling, Marc," she began. "I wanted to let you know we've made a lot of progress on resolving your wife's case."

"That's good," Marc said casually. "Like what?"

"Well, we've released the tax lien on your house, I have it right here and I'll fax it to you now if you want."

"It needs to be filed with the county," Marc answered. "You guys didn't have this much trouble filing the original lien. I want you to file the release too. Fax it to me, but make sure it gets filed."

"No problem," she said. "Don't worry, I'll take care of it. I also have the check for your fees. If you'd like, I'll Fed Ex it overnight to you."

"Federal Express?" he asked dryly. "The U.S. Government doesn't use the U.S. Postal Service? They use Federal Express? Why doesn't that surprise me?" he added.

"Well, um," she began. "I don't know about all of the government, but yeah, we use Fed Ex here at Justice. Anyway…"

"Send it here to the office to be delivered on Monday," Marc interrupted. "No one's around on weekends. Besides, I've waited this long, a couple more days won't matter."

"You sure? Okay. That's fine," she answered. "As to the refund, I've been assured by the Service they're doing their best to get it figured but it'll take some time because …"

"They better hurry. We're going to court on Wednesday," Marc said, silently smiling at the thought of her twisting in the wind a bit. "They've had months, Sharon."

"I know, I know," she wearily replied.

"Listen, Sharon. I don't care that much about the refund. You'll grab it to offset our taxes anyway. I got no problem with that. I do want it done but it's not that big a deal."

"Good. That's great, Marc," she said with obvious relief. "We'll get it done. I promise. I'll see to it personally. Now," she continued, "about your contempt motion. I've been authorized to offer you the two thousand in additional fees plus another five hundred as a, sort of, fine or payment for your troubles."

"We'd already agreed to the two grand for fees, Sharon," Marc reminded her.

"I know we did. Then there's the extra five hundred. I don't think you appreciate how extraordinary that is. No one around here has ever heard of anything like it. That offer comes down from the division head. Second only to the U.S. Attorney General," she added in an obvious attempt to impress him.

"Well, if five hundred's the best you can do, I'll drive downtown St. Paul on Wednesday," Marc calmly said rejecting the offer.

"Marc, look," she answered with an audible sigh, "I'm trying to get this thing done and save the taxpayers some money."

"Now you're trying to save the taxpayers some money? After all of this? After the years of bullshit from the IRS, the lawsuit and the aftermath of the case, now you're trying to save the taxpayers some money? At this point, Sharon, I don't think there are too many taxpayers that would be sympathetic. Look, I know you're personally working hard and doing your best. If five hundred bucks is the best they can come up with, I'll see you in court. Have a nice weekend, Sharon," he concluded with a smile knowing a nice weekend was the last thing she would have. And smiling, too, at the thought of a nine-thousand-dollar check on the way to solve at least some of his short-term financial problems.

SEVENTY-THREE

After leaving Marc at the government center downtown, Maddy went back to her apartment and made a light dinner for herself. She relaxed for about a half hour, grabbed her gym bag and headed for the health club. Trying not to be too rude, she brushed off several would-be suitors as she went through her two-hour routine. Ignoring the envious looks she invariably received from the other women, she went through first, the machines, then the free weights and as always, capped it all off with four miles on the track. She drew more stares from the semi-crowded women's locker room as she quickly showered, dressed and left.

Now, she was sitting in her three-year-old black Audi coupe parked a half block from the small, stuccoed house of Louise Curtin. She had been on station for over two hours watching the obviously empty, darkened home becoming more pessimistic about her chances of seeing Jake Waschke's mother tonight. She glanced around the quiet, tree-lined street, looked at her watch again, decided she'd give it another hour and turned back to the romance novel she was reading by the light beaming down from the small dome light.

The romance novels were her one secret, frivolous indulgence. The shrinks would probably explain it as an escape. The search for the hole in her life she would like to fill with one truly meaningful love interest with a decent man that wanted her for all of her and not just lusting after her physical attributes. She had had her share of boyfriends over the years. With the emphasis, she would remind herself, on the word boy. With one exception, mostly immature, insecure children in a man's body. The exception turned out to be the worst of the bunch. A charming, handsome doctor in Chicago that was not only married and cheating on the woman that put him through medical school but cheating on Maddy as well. It was after she found out about the wife and other girlfriend that she had finally had enough of Chicago, packed her bags and headed to Minneapolis and a fresh start. Many hours of counseling later had convinced her to be patient and sooner or later, the right one would walk into her life. *Someone like Marc*, she thought to herself reflecting on it. A little younger would be good. One that doesn't already have children and would want one or two. But definitely one with a little substance to him.

She looked up at the still darkened house, sighed deeply, as she always did after reflecting on her loneliness and went back to her book. Ten minutes later the Audi's interior suddenly filled with the light coming from the headlights of a car that had pulled up directly behind her. She set the book face down on the passenger seat, removed the small .32 caliber semi-automatic handgun from her purse and holding the gun in the palm of her right hand out of sight alongside her right leg, waited for the cop to tap on her window.

A moment later he did just that. She pushed the window's button causing it to hum downward and opened it halfway. Her eyes were stung by a flashlight's beam and she reflexively held her left hand up to avoid the glare and try to see the face behind it. Neither spoke for a long ten seconds and Maddy felt, more than saw, the second cop approach the car.

"Is there something I can help you with?" Maddy asked finally breaking the silence.

"Out of the car," she heard the voice say from behind the light.

"Let's see some identification," she said.

"I said out of the car, now," the voice angrily replied.

Scared now, but maintaining her calm, she pushed the button on the window and it quickly hummed upward. By the time it had completely closed, the second man had slapped his gold shield up against the window as she heard the same voice yell, "Open the damn door, now."

She opened the window another inch and said, "You boys lost? That looks like a Minneapolis badge to me."

The voice came again, this time quieter and directly from the small opening in the window, "You get out of the car now or I bust the window open. Am I being clear to you?"

"Okay, officer," she replied as she unlocked the door and let the small pistol slip from her hand between the seat and the console.

The two men stepped back from the door as she exited, the silent one that had flashed the badge kept a hand under his cheap sport coat obviously holding the handle of a gun. The one with the flashlight still directed into her face slammed the car door closed as she stepped away from it. "What are you doing here?" he asked abruptly.

"I might ask you two boys the same question," she replied looking them both directly in the eyes. With her height and the two-inch heels of her boots she was as tall as the one with the light and taller than the second one. "Minding my own business. Which, by the way, is none of yours."

"That's it," the second one said as he stepped toward her removing his hand from beneath his coat. He grabbed her left bicep, twirled her around and roughly slammed her up against the car. He kicked her feet apart and began running his hands over her, starting with her arms and back but giving her breasts, buttocks and legs extra attention.

"Having a good time, Bill?" the one with the flashlight asked with a quiet laugh.

"Yeah, having a good time Billy?" Maddy sarcastically mocked him.

He shoved her completely up against the car and with both hands gripping her butt, put his mouth to her ear and said, "I've had better, bitch."

"I doubt it you dickless wonder," she said doing her best to keep the fear from her voice.

"Hey," she heard the other say as she felt Bill being pulled off of her. "Hold the light. I think you may have missed a spot. I better check her again," the other one said as Bill took a half step backwards and began reaching for the flashlight.

More angry than scared now, Maddy quietly said, "I don't think so, asshole." With that, she rifled her right elbow directly into the face of the lecherous cop and drilled him squarely on the nose almost smashing it flat as the blood exploded from it. The man let out a loud yell, dropped the flashlight and grabbed his face with both hands.

In the same instant, Maddy made a quick half-step toward Bill by crossing her left foot over her right, pulled her right leg up and with all of the power and force she could summon, drove her right heel directly down on the instep of Bill's left foot, breaking several bones and disabling the man with one blow. He screamed from the sudden excruciating pain, bent forward to grab his foot just as Maddy stepped into him and drove her left knee directly into his face sending him flat on his back onto the asphalt.

She then turned her attention back to the first one, wheeling on her right foot she spun around and drilled him with a kick from her left foot squarely onto the left side of his head and face. The force of it drove the top of his head banging into the door of her car with a sickening thud and his now unconscious body slumped heavily to the ground.

Maddy quickly stepped over to the moaning Bill, reached inside his coat and yanked his semi-automatic service gun from the shoulder holster. Holding the gun in her right hand she ran her left hand over both of his ankles checking for a second gun. Finding none and satisfied he didn't have one, she stood up and casually tossed the pistol across the trunk of her car and onto the boulevard grass. She quickly repeated this process with the bigger cop and threw his gun in the general direction of where she had thrown the first one.

Leaning against her car, Maddy surveyed the carnage she had caused while Bill lay moaning and the bigger one came out of his stupor. She stood like this, her arms casually crossed over her breasts while Bill struggled to sit up.

"You know Billy," she finally said, "I'll bet you're right. I'll bet you have had better than this."

"Harry," Bill weakly said to his partner. "You okay?"

Harry, almost unconscious, finally managed to sit up on one elbow while the blood still flowed from the pulp that was recently his nose. "No, I ain't okay. She broke my damn nose," he said.

"On that face, Harry," Maddy said, "it's not gonna matter much."

"You'll pay for this, bitch," Bill said.

"Why do I doubt that?" Maddy asked. "Let's see you two idiots explain this. Explain what you were doing here in the first place and how you two big strong men managed to get your butts kicked by a woman. That should be interesting. I'm looking forward to it."

"Where's my gun?" Bill weakly asked.

"Over on the grass along with dickhead's here," Maddy said jerking a thumb toward the still groggy Harry. "Now, Harry, be a good boy and roll your fat ass out of the way. I'm leaving now, boys. Have a good evening." With that, she got back in the car, started the engine and drove off leaving the two men in the street.

"And you wonder why you can't find a good man?" she quietly asked herself as she headed off steering the sleek car with her left hand while retrieving the small handgun with her right. She replaced the gun in her purse, picked up her cell phone and flipped it open. She punched in the phone number she wanted, turned the corner and headed back toward St. Paul. The phone was answered by a familiar voice on the second ring and Maddy said, "We've got a problem."

"What?" Marc asked.

As she drove she told him about what had just occurred.

"Great. So Waschke knows we're looking for his mother. Which, if he's obviously this worried about it, makes me believe there's something there. Something he doesn't want us to find out."

"What do you want me to do?"

"Get out of there for now. Cool it with her for a couple days and we'll see. Let me think about it. We have to find her though."

"Agreed," she said as she cut off the call.

SEVENTY-FOUR

Monday's testimony was taken up by media witnesses. A sampling of the people who had been part of the mob at the jail when Carl had been arrested and brought in. Slocum had presented a list of over thirty people who had been there at the time, all of whom had personally witnessed Carl's outburst when, Slocum alleged, Carl "confessed" for the cameras. It was a ridiculous claim Marc had pointed out, since, at that point, Carl hadn't been charged with anything, was obviously distraught, without the benefit of counsel and the whole thing was technically hearsay though clearly admissible by the myriad exceptions to the hearsay rule. Slocum's list had been the subject of much argument and Prentiss had finally ruled that the prosecution could present three of these people to testify and let the jury view one of the videotapes.

Through the jury selection process, it had come out that virtually every one of the prospective jurors had seen the tape anyway, so Prentiss ruled that seeing it again wouldn't make much difference. Marc made his objection for the record to preserve the issue for an appeal and quietly accepted yet another adverse ruling from the bench.

Slocum took each witness through the process and had each one testify as to exactly where he or she was and exactly what he or she heard Carl say. With each one, Marc limited his cross exam to a few brief questions about the situation. He asked them simple, yes or no questions about the lights flashing from the still cameras, the ones blazing away for the minicams and the cacophony of voices yelling questions at a man surrounded by the police. Questions designed to show the jury that Carl had been scared and confused by a pack of braying jackals in that hallway. By the time he finished with each of them, he had them all but apologizing for their own behavior as he finished up with contempt laden questions. Each of them fumbling with the same lame excuse, "We're just doing our job," as the jury looked on with obvious distaste.

During the lunch recess Marc made a call to the office to check for messages and find out if his check from the government had arrived. Carolyn told him it had, which flooded him with considerable relief, and told him that a federal magistrate's clerk had called. He quickly dialed her number and the woman told him that the judge handling the contempt motion he was bringing against the U.S. Government had requested a settlement conference first. It was Marc's motion and he didn't have to agree to it, but the judge was asking that the hearing be pushed back a couple of hours and the parties meet with a magistrate to see if a settlement could be reached. Marc wasn't too crazy about the idea. He wanted to go back before the original judge and listen to the government's lawyer try to explain why they had not abided by his order. Since it was the same judge requesting the settlement conference, Marc didn't want to be the one appearing unreasonable.

He spent a few minutes on the phone with the magistrate's clerk and waited while she called Washington to set up the time with Sharon Marzell. He then called his soon-to-be ex-wife, Karen, and told her what was going on and that the magistrate wanted Karen to be there too.

He grabbed a quick bite to eat and went back to the trial to spend the afternoon finishing the media witnesses.

The next day Marc arrived early and was surprised to see both Slocum and Gondeck already there patiently waiting for him. After yesterday's testimony Marc believed that the prosecution was down to their last witness, Martin Hobbs. Marc had awakened that morning feeling better than he had for weeks. The result of a combination of getting the money he had won from the government and the realization that the prosecution's case against Carl was about to be concluded. The sight of both prosecutors actually a half hour early caused the warning bells to ring in his head.

"Marc, something's come up," Steve Gondeck said to him as Marc passed through the gate in the bar of the otherwise empty courtroom.

"What?" Marc asked warily as he dropped his briefcase onto the defense table and looked first at Gondeck, who was seated on the edge of the table facing Marc, then down at Slocum. Slocum was seated at one of the table's chairs with his legs crossed and hands folded in his lap wearing, what seemed to Marc at least, another in a seemingly endless supply of expensive suits, silk ties and heavily starched, immaculate white shirts, the gold cuff links gleaming as they peeked out from under the coat sleeve.

"Well, um," Gondeck began, "We have some witnesses to add..."

"I don't think so," Marc said staring at Slocum, cutting off Gondeck in midsentence.

"I told you Steve," Slocum said with a weary sigh. "I told you he wouldn't be reasonable. We'll just have to go see the judge."

"Reasonable?" Marc asked glaring at the county attorney. "You guys try to come up with some last-minute surprise witnesses, plural," the last words said to Gondeck who slightly nodded then sheepishly looked away. "I object to it and I'm not being reasonable? A tactic for which you are well known among the defense bar ..."

"A criminal's lobby," Slocum interjected derisively as he straightened in his chair to glare back at Marc.

"Oh, that's right," Marc responded rolling his eyes heavenward while clasping his hands in mock prayer. "I keep forgetting. God personally sent you here to smite the wicked and protect the oppressed. Forgive me, your Eminence."

"This is pointless," Slocum fumed as he got out of his chair and stomped toward the door leading to the chamber's area. "We'll see the judge."

Marc and Gondeck maintained their positions as the county attorney went through the door, still visibly steaming. After the door had finished closing behind him, Gondeck looked at Marc and said, "Why did you have to do that?"

"Because he's a pompous, self-righteous asshole and it felt good."

"I know he's a pompous, self-righteous asshole," Gondeck replied, his shoulders sagging as if in weariness. "But he's also my boss and I have to live with the prick."

"So, what's this about surprise witnesses?" Marc asked as he eased himself onto the defense table directly across from Gondeck.

"You're not gonna like it," Gondeck began. "Late yesterday, two of them came forward, separately. As far as we've been able to figure, neither knows the other nor even knows about the other."

"And?" Marc asked when Gondeck paused.

"And," he continued, "one of them is a guy named Edward Hill. You ready for this? Hill will testify that he was one of the guys who kicked the shit out of your client in jail and it was Fornich's idea."

"What?" Marc said. "That's bullshit, and you know it...."

"I don't think so, Marc," Gondeck replied shaking his head and holding up his hands to cut Marc off. "We were as skeptical as you at first. Questioned the hell out of him. Did a thorough background check on him. He's very believable. Says he and another guy, both biker types, second guy's name is Steve Frechette ..."

"What's the witness' name?" Marc asked wondering what else could land on him in this trial.

"Edward Hill," Gondeck answered. "Anyway, Hill swears Fornich put them up to it."

"Why?"

"Sympathy, police brutality. That kinda bullshit," Gondeck said with a shrug. "And we want to bring in the sheriff's deputy, Olson. The one Fornich claims witnessed the whole thing."

"He's on your list. You don't need my permission for him."

"I know," Gondeck said nodding. "I just thought I'd warn you."

Just then the door Slocum had gone through a few moments before opened and Slocum reappeared. "The judge is waiting," he said, obviously annoyed.

"We're coming," Gondeck replied as he stood up. "I was just filling him in a bit."

"Fine," Slocum steamed and went back through the door. Again, it closed behind him as the two men headed toward it. While they walked across the carpeted floor along the front of the empty jury box,

Marc whispered to Gondeck, "How many tickets you figure we could sell to his ass kicking?"

"Everybody in the C.A.'s office, at least," Gondeck replied with a grin.

As Marc grasped the door handle and was about to open it, Gondeck gently placed his left palm against the door to stop him. "Marc," he quietly continued turning serious again, "that's not the worst of it. You didn't let me finish. We got another guy yesterday. Been in jail for a few days on a drug bust. Marijuana wholesaler."

"So?"

"Says your client confessed to him about the killings. All of them."

"What is this shit, Steve?"

"I swear, it's true," Gondeck said holding up his right hand as if taking an oath.

The in-chambers discussion about the surprise witnesses, a stunt that Marc reminded Prentiss he had specifically warned them about when the trial began, was predictably acrimonious and for Marc, futile. Prentiss wasted little time in ruling in favor of the prosecution. For Marc's benefit he made a show of sternly lecturing Slocum and Gondeck, but Marc had the uneasy feeling that it was insincere. Prentiss did agree, reluctantly, to grant Marc an hour to consult with his client before testimony would begin.

"It's bullshit," Carl seethed at Marc in the small room. "I had them kick my ass? That's bullshit."

"Keep your voice down," Marc quietly replied. "There's a courtroom full of people out there," he continued gesturing toward the door.

"And I confessed to this other guy? This Bingham guy?" Carl whispered, leaning on the table to get as close to Marc as he could. "Confessed to what? I ain't done nothing to confess to," he said while staring angrily, his eyes unblinking, directly into Marc's face. "Do you believe it?"

"What? No. What do you mean, do I believe it?"

"Do you believe I had those two assholes kick my ass and do you believe I confessed to this other guy, this asshole Bingham?" Carl asked, a pleading look on his face and in his voice.

"No, Carl," Marc softly said returning Carl's look. "Do you know him?"

"Know who? Bingham? Yeah, I know who he is. He's in the cell across from me. Been there, I don't know, four or five days now."

"What about the other guy, this Ed Hill?"

"No, I didn't know their names. They jumped me in the can, worked me over real quick and left me lying there while the guard, what's-his-name, Olson, watched it," Carl said as he leaned back in his chair, folded his arms across his chest and stared up at the ceiling.

"This is just great. I might as well go plead guilty right now and get it over with," he said dejectedly.

Marc sat quietly, his hands folded together on the tabletop, his eyes shifting about the room, uncertain as to what to say. The two of them sat this way for a couple of minutes, neither of them speaking, both lost in their own thoughts. Marc, momentarily mentally reviewing the possibility of making a plea agreement and then quickly dismissing it. Carl, sneaking a glance at his lawyer, trying to read Marc's thoughts. Marc's reaction.

"Look, you're not changing your plea," Marc said, breaking the awkward silence. "What they have here are a couple of jailbirds trying to save their own asses. I'm sure they've both made some kinda deal with the cops and prosecutors. That doesn't make them the most credible witnesses."

"Yeah," Carl said, nodding in agreement. "Yeah, you're right. The jury should be able to see that don't you think?"

"Yes, I do," Marc answered as he reached across the table and gently patted Carl's left forearm. "Let's go hear what they have to say."

When they left the judge's chambers, Gondeck went into the courtroom and seeing Jake Waschke in his usual seat, gestured for him to follow Gondeck into a meeting room at the side of the courtroom. The two of them went in and found Wally Bingham seated at the table and after they had seated themselves opposite their witness, Gondeck said, "Okay, the judge has ruled that you will be allowed to testify. We went over your testimony last night and you did great. Just remember to take your time and don't rush it. If we need more information from you, Slocum can always ask a follow-up question."

"Hey," Wally began to answer. "I'm not an idiot. Didn't I do okay last night?"

"You did great," Gondeck said acknowledging how well he had done while being prepared for today's testimony.

"I'm not some dipshit street hustler," Wally continued looking directly at Jake. "I know what's what and I can testify just fine. You'll get your guy. He told me all about everything," he said all the while thinking, "Since I have my get out of jail free card because you screwed up the search warrant, I am going to mess this up and shove it right up your ass."

"Did somebody put you up to this?" Gondeck asked for at least the tenth time.

"No one put him up to it," Jake said.

"How many times you gonna ask me that?" Bingham answered.

"All right. You wait here and we'll bring you in when we call you," Gondeck said not really believing a word this guy had to say.

300

SEVENTY-FIVE

After a brief greeting to Carl's brother, the two men took their seats at the counsel table and waited patiently for the morning session to begin. A few minutes later, the jury was led in, Prentiss took his seat on the bench and Slocum solemnly rose to call his witness. Marc stole a glance around the spectator's section and not the least bit surprised, noticed that the press was back in full attendance. *Funny,* he thought, *how they always seemed to know when Slocum was about to give them something.*

Edward Hill was brought in through a side door opposite the jury box. A door Marc knew led to the in-custody area. Hill was a tall, well built man and though Gondeck described him as a biker type, today he looked like Joe Citizen come to court to help see justice done. Unknown to Marc, but not to Carl, his hair was freshly cut. The long, dirty-blonde, scraggily mess replaced by a neat, well-groomed look. Hill still sported a moustache, neatly trimmed, but the goatee and four-day stubble were gone. A light blue, button down pressed shirt, dark slacks and black loafers had replaced the leather vest, dirty jeans and biker boots he normally wore. Marc glanced down at the small slip of paper Carl slid to him with the note Carl had scribbled on it: *'Doesn't even look like the same guy'* the note read.

Hill was sworn in, took his seat on the stand and with Slocum's guidance, told his story. He had been arrested on a car theft charge, along with another man, a casual friend named Steve Frechette. They had been in the Hennepin County jail for two or three days while awaiting arraignment and a chance to make bail.

He continued to testify, over Marc's hearsay objection, that Frechette came to him late one afternoon and told him a guy Frechette knew from prison wanted them to do him a favor. This guy, Frechette told him, was awaiting trial for the serial killer murders that Hill had heard about and wanted to pull a stunt on the cops. He wanted Hill and Frechette to knock him around a bit. Nothing serious but just enough to cause some cuts and bruises.

"Why did he want that?" Slocum prompted.

Frechette told Hill it was to get some sympathy in the press. Maybe even make a police brutality claim against the cops. So that night, a Saturday night when the jail was very busy and the guards didn't have time to keep an eye on everybody, he and Frechette met the guy in one of the johns and worked him over a bit. Hill testified it was one of the strangest things he had ever done; beat somebody up while he just stood there and took it. In fact, Carl actually helped them do it. He had pointed out places he wanted them to hit that would cause cuts and bruises but not hurt him too much.

It only took a few minutes and afterward they simply left him lying on the floor in one of the stalls. The next day, Sunday, they heard he'd been taken to the hospital. On Monday, Frechette and Hill were brought to court, made bail and walked away from the whole thing.

"Was there a guard at the door of the restroom watching the assault?" Slocum asked.

"No, there was no guard watching," Hill answered. "Just me, Frechette and him," he continued pointing at Carl. "I heard about that later. That he claimed a guard was watching and saw it all. I laughed when I heard it. That's a total lie."

Slocum then tackled the issue of Hill's credibility head-on. Instead of leaving it for Marc to explore and possibly shred his witness, Slocum did the smart thing and brought it out himself.

After making bail, Hill and Frechette split up. The last Hill heard from Frechette was that he was going to either Texas or Florida. He wasn't sure which. Some place down South. Hill went to Wisconsin for a couple of weeks but came back to Minnesota about three weeks ago.

"Where are you currently residing?" Slocum asked.

"In the Hennepin County jail. I got picked up on the bench warrant that was out 'cause of when I skipped bail."

"Why did you decide to testify?"

"I'm hoping to get some deal for the charges against me on the car theft. The cops wanted me to rat out some guys I know on a stolen car chop shop, but I won't do it. Too dangerous. Those are some bad dudes. But this guy," he continued again pointing at Carl, "well, you know, a car theft is one thing but a serial killer, that's a whole different deal."

After being asked by Slocum, Hill calmly testified that no promises had been made to him. He had come forward entirely on his own and in fact, the cops were extremely surprised at his story. He had spent the entire day, yesterday, being questioned by the police and prosecutors. Obviously they were very skeptical about him and his story. A couple of them even flat out told him they thought he was lying. They checked him out, checked out Frechette and found out Frechette had been in prison with Carl and had been in the same cell block with him for several months. It wasn't until after that that the cops began to believe him. All in all, Marc glumly realized, a very credible, very believable performance.

At that point Slocum turned the witness over to Marc who stood up and made the obligatory objection. Pointing out for the record, and the jury, that this witness' testimony was totally irrelevant since it added nothing to the question of guilt to the charges brought against Carl. Prentiss politely overruled Marc and the cross examination began.

"Mr. Hill," Marc began looking directly at the witness with barely disguised contempt, "how many times have you been arrested?" By tossing out an open-ended question, he was breaking the cardinal rule of cross examination: Never ask a question if you don't know the answer. He was fishing a bit but figured this was safe enough water to toss out a line or two.

"Um, I'm not sure. A few times, I guess," Hill calmly answered.

"Well, Mr. Hill, let's try to narrow it down. More than ten?"

"Yeah, I guess."

"More than twenty?"

"No, not that many."

"So, you've been arrested for a variety of crimes somewhere between ten and twenty times is that correct?"

"Yeah, I guess so."

"How many felony convictions do you have?"

"Three," Hill answered, still looking calmly at Marc.

"Have you done time in prison?"

"Yes, once in prison. A couple times at the county workhouse. I got nothing to hide here, counselor. Does your guy?"

"Your Honor," Marc angrily said as he rose from his seat.

"Mr. Hill," Prentiss sternly said to Hill jabbing his right index finger toward him. "You will restrict your answers to the questions asked. Is that clear?"

"Yes, your Honor. Sorry," Hill fumbled trying to sound apologetic.

"The jury will disregard that last remark," Prentiss admonished the jurors knowing full well they couldn't. "You may continue, Mr. Kadella."

"Thank you, your Honor," Marc said as he sat back down.

"Mr. Hill, the reason you're presently in jail is because you were arrested for grand theft and then skipped bail, is that correct?"

"Yes," Hill said, now leaning forward slightly to speak directly into the microphone.

"If you are convicted of the present charge, do you believe you'll get another prison sentence?"

"Yes, I believe I will. That's why I'm here. I told you that before. I'm trying to cut a deal. Get some leniency but that don't mean I ain't telling the truth."

Marc continued along this line of questioning for a few more minutes, but it was pointless. Hill made a very convincing, very credible witness. Marc could, and would, make the argument during his summation that Hill was a career criminal trying to win favor from the prosecutors and even if Hill was to be believed, he offered nothing as far as Carl's guilt or innocence was concerned. It was weak though, and he knew it. No promises had been made to Hill and at the very least, it looked like Carl was up to something with the assault allegations. Trying to hide something. Besides, Marc had a greater concern on his mind after this morning's revelations.

Marc finished up his questioning of Hill by going over Hill's attire and freshly groomed appearance. The questions were designed to point out to the jury the lengths the police and prosecution would go to present Hill as a model citizen. Hill readily admitted to all of these claims; that his clothing, haircut and freshly shaved appearance were provided by his jailers. His manner was calm, cool and dignified and Marc finally began to realize that it was himself and not Hill who was coming across badly to the jury. He wrapped it up, unable to shake Hill, and turned him back to Slocum.

On redirect examination Slocum limited himself to one question. "Mr. Hill," he asked, "why should this jury believe you?"

Hill sat back and waited for a long moment, presenting the appearance of someone thinking the question over before answering even though Marc knew it had been thoroughly prepared by Slocum and Hill the night before.

"Because I've been honest," Hill answered. "I've been completely above board here today. I've told them everything. No promises have been made to me and I've honestly told them my motive for coming here today. That don't mean I'm not telling the truth. I am."

Before the lunch recess, Prentiss decided to have Slocum put Sheriff's Deputy Thomas Olson on the stand. He brought out Olson's service record for the jury. Eight years as Deputy Sheriff. He brought in his fitness reports and supervisory evaluations all of which were in the range of good to excellent. No complaints about him and no previous problems with inmates. He had been on duty the night Carl was assaulted but could not absolutely account for his specific whereabouts at the time especially since the exact time had never been established. Only an approximate time. He emphatically testified that he was not there when it happened. He did not witness it and certainly did not stand guard during the assault.

Marc, realizing he could get absolutely nothing favorable from this witness, passed on a cross examination of Olson completely.

"I'm glad you're here," Marc said to Maddy as he gently took her by the elbow to lead her through the hallway doors as the crowd dispersed for the lunch recess. "Did you get my message?" he asked referring to his call to her earlier that morning after he had been informed about Slocum's surprise witnesses.

"Yeah," she answered quietly as they followed the crowd toward the elevators. "I got their arrest records, but I haven't had time to do any real digging yet. What was that all about? Why did Prentiss allow that business about the assault?"

"Because he wants to make sure Carl is convicted," Marc whispered as he looked over the arrest records Maddy had given him. "Looks like our Mr. Hill was pretty straight in there. What about Bingham?" Marc asked rhetorically as he turned to the other report.

"A marijuana dealer," Maddy answered. "Nothing about coke, crack, heroin. None of that kinda stuff. I don't get it, though. The cops are holding a big sentence over his head. Seems pretty harsh for dealing grass."

"They set him up," Marc flatly answered. "They put him next to Carl and then phonied up this confession business. It's an old trick. Carl swears he never confessed anything to the guy. Hardly said a thing to him. Which is why they wanted Hill to testify. Now, if I put Carl on the stand and he denies it, denies that he confessed but put Hill up to assaulting him himself, Slocum can use it to go after Carl's credibility. Pretty smart tactic by Slocum."

"Yeah, I see what you mean. Hill made a great witness, at least what I saw. I missed the direct exam."

"Oh, he was good. Come on let's get some lunch," Marc said leading her over to the bank of elevators now that the crowd was gone.

"There's something bothering me though," Marc continued as they waited for a car.

"What's that?"

"Did you see the size of Hill? He must have a good fifty pounds on Carl. And the other guy, this Frechette. He's another biker type. The two of them could stomp Carl into dog food. And yet, when you look at Carl's injuries, he really wasn't hurt that bad."

With that, they both looked at each other, a puzzled expression on their faces as one of the elevator indicators bonged and the doors began to open to take them down.

SEVENTY-SIX

A sheriff's deputy led Wally Bingham through the same side door that Ed Hill had come from earlier that day. Wally was dressed much like Hill had been except that Wally wore a white shirt and tie and unknown to Marc, his appearance was essentially unchanged from what it normally would is. Wally was no social rebel. No gang member flipping off society. Wally was a low-key businessman. Complete with P&L statements, employees whom he hired and fired and his own personalized retirement plan. A plan that had just received a major bump on the road to a Caribbean beach house.

Wally was sworn in and took his seat on the witness stand. Slocum started right in with the issue of Wally's credibility by bringing out for the jury Wally's arrest record and reason for being in the courtroom. He readily admitted to his arrest and conviction record and told the jury that he was testifying because he had made a deal with the police and prosecutors.

"And what exactly is the deal you made?" Slocum asked.

"Well," Wally began. He shifted in his chair, stretched his neck and let his eyes flicker back and forth several times from the jurors to Slocum before slowly continuing. "Um, well, ah, I was told I was looking at fifteen years in prison. You know," he added, wiping a hand across his forehead, "for this, ah, latest arrest. Which, um, I would've had to do like, ten, I guess, with good time. So," he shrugged his shoulders slightly, "I, ah, cut a deal for three years."

"You were promised that?" Slocum asked in a slightly incredulous voice.

"Huh? Oh, no. No, I mean, that's right. What they told me was, um, they'd, you know, recommend it to the, ah, judge. Yeah, that's right," Wally continued quietly, snapping his fingers as if in recollection, "They said they'd recommend it but couldn't promise it."

"So, the only promise made was that my office would recommend leniency in exchange for your cooperation and if you agreed to plead guilty, is that correct?"

"Objection," Marc said rising from his chair. "He's leading the witness, your Honor."

"Overruled," Prentiss answered after a short pause. "You may answer."

"Yes, that's correct," Wally answered as he leaned forward to the microphone, his hands folded so tightly together in his lap the knuckles were turning white.

They spent the rest of that afternoon going over Bingham's story. How he became friendly with Carl while in jail. How Carl began by dropping hints to him about the case against him. That maybe the cops had the right guy after all. Then, finally, in small doses at first, Carl began to admit to the crimes. That Wally, acting as sort of a big brother figure for Carl, would comfort Carl to get him to open up and get these things, that were obviously eating him up inside, out into the open.

There was a problem with Wally's testimony though, and everyone in the courtroom could see it. While Ed Hill had been comfortable, composed and confident, Bingham's story was stilted, jerky and unsettled. Slocum was having difficulty drawing it out of him eliciting several objections from Marc for asking leading questions. Questions that were asked in a way that practically put words into Bingham's mouth. Each objection was overruled by Prentiss, but the jury was getting the message, Marc hoped.

It took most of the afternoon just to get Bingham to the point where he could begin to give the details of Carl's "confession" and before that line of questioning began, he looked up at Prentiss and said, "Could I get a glass of water, your Honor? Would that be okay? I mean, it's kinda warm in here."

"Certainly," Prentiss answered as he motioned to one of the deputies to get Wally some water. Prentiss looked up at the clock on the wall and asked the lawyers to come up to the bench. He knew, of course, what was coming and decided it was time to give Slocum a break. Give him the evening to get his witness more composed and his testimony smoothed over.

"Any objection to calling a halt for the day at this point?" Prentiss asked as his eyes drifted over the three lawyers arrayed beneath him.

"No, your Honor," Slocum whispered back with poorly disguised relief.

"Yes, your Honor," Marc said. "I'd like to finish with this witness today."

"How much longer?" Prentiss said looking directly at Slocum.

"Probably a couple of hours, at least," Slocum answered with a shrug.

Prentiss paused for a moment, lightly tapping a finger against his pursed lips as if thinking it over even though his mind was made up. "No, that would be too late. As I recall, Mr. Kadella, you have a hearing in federal court tomorrow afternoon, is that right? If we start with a new witness tomorrow, a witness I understand is central to the State's case, I may not be inclined to cut off that witness at noon," he said staring down at Marc, his eyebrows arched, and a stern look on his face. "No, we'll break now and finish with this witness in the morning," Prentiss concluded.

"What do you think?" Carl asked Marc after the jury had been led out, Slocum and Gondeck had packed and left and the spectator's section had almost emptied.

"I think this Bingham guy is the worst witness of the trial," Marc answered shaking his head and smiling. "Maybe the worst witness I've ever seen."

"I thought so too," Joe Fornich piped in from behind the rail. "I mean, it looks like he's obviously lying. Like he's real nervous up there."

"How do you think the jury's taking it?" Carl asked Marc.

"I'm not sure," Marc answered solemnly. "They're hard to read. I've been watching them and," he paused, "I just don't know. They're all paying close attention. They all look serious," he shrugged. "Whether or not they believe him, I can't tell. I have to believe a couple of them will see this for what it is. The cops setting the whole thing up. We'll see."

When Slocum exited the courtroom and entered the exterior hall overlooking the courtyard on the second floor, his demeanor was calm, cool and collected. He stood in the hallway basking in the lights blazing for the TV minicams and politely deflected the reporters' questions with a politician's smile and friendly "no comments". All the while acting as though all was in order and everything was going as planned even though inwardly he was seething and about to explode. Steve Gondeck deferentially stood to one side, patiently waiting for his boss to finish the impromptu press conference knowing he was in for a monumental ass-chewing as soon as they got back to their office. It was Gondeck's job to prepare each witness for Slocum's questions. Make sure that all was in order so that Slocum could put on a smooth performance for the voters through the very media people who were now questioning him about Wally Bingham.

As Slocum and Gondeck rode up in the crowded elevator to the county attorney's office, Slocum silently stared straight ahead, his hands held together in front of him. Gondeck stood next to him, his arms at his sides holding in each hand a small suitcase-size briefcase filled with the case documents and papers they used during the trial. Gondeck, too, was seething and also mentally calculating how long he and his wife and kids could last while he looked for employment. Steve was a damn fine trial lawyer in his own right and the man standing next to him was getting to be too much to take. Gondeck truly liked his job and by the time they stepped off of the elevator he had resigned himself to endure it one more time.

As Gondeck closed Slocum's office door, his boss shocked him by calmly saying, after seating himself on the edge of his desk, "Okay, that didn't go well. It didn't go well at all. But Prentiss gave us a break. We have tonight to get this Bingham guy straightened out and smoothed over. We'll order some food brought in, have him brought up here and spend the evening with him."

"Okay. Sounds all right," Gondeck said while standing with his hands placed on the back of a chair in front of the desk. Slocum, still leaning against the desk, staring at the wall behind Gondeck, quietly asked, "What do you think, Steve? You think the cops put him up to this?"

After pausing for a moment, thinking over the question, Gondeck said, "I don't know. I honestly don't know and at this point, we don't dare ask. We have no choice now but to play it out."

"True," Slocum said. "Anyway, have Doris order in some Chinese from that place I like, she knows which one, and you and I will get to work and see if we can't salvage this guy. And Steve," he continued just as Gondeck started to turn the knob on the door, "let's make damn sure we don't have the same problem with Hobbs."

"I didn't think we'd have it with Bingham," Gondeck replied.

"See to it," Slocum said, his lips pursed together and his eyes angrily narrowed.

"Yes, sir," Gondeck politely answered.

It didn't help. They both spent the entire evening going over Wally's upcoming testimony. They went over it several times and included Gondeck playing the part of the defense lawyer and drilling Wally much more harshly than Prentiss would allow Marc to do. Wally was poised, calm and seemed as ready as a witness could be by the time they finished just before midnight. He had his facts down cold as they went through the details of each murder as they had been supposedly told to him by Carl. Finally, satisfied that Wally would make a completely different impression the next day, Slocum called a halt and Wally was taken back to his cell, no longer the one near Carl.

But the next day he was the same stumbling, fumbling, nervous Wally that he had been the day before. And the testimony that had been rehearsed to last less than two hours the previous evening, took more than three hours in front of the jury. With the usual midmorning break mixed in, Slocum finished just before 12:30 and Prentiss, mercifully for the prosecution, called a halt for the day so that Marc could get to his settlement conference in federal court and Prentiss could make his tee time. Wally had not been a total disaster for Slocum, but no one could read from the jurors' expressions if he had done any good, either. Marc's shot at Wally would come the next day.

As Wally was leaving the witness stand unnoticed by anyone in the courtroom, he looked directly at Jake Waschke who glared back at him and was not amused when Wally scratched the side of his face with his middle finger and while smiling slyly at the police lieutenant.

SEVENTY-SEVEN

Marc held the door open for his wife, Karen, and the two of them entered the tiny courtroom in the Federal Building in downtown Minneapolis. Only two people, a woman and a man, were there when they arrived. Marc, assuming the woman was the lawyer from Washington, Sharon Marzell, quickly walked over to her, put a smile on his face and stuck out his hand "Sharon?" he asked her.

"You must be Marc," she said in return as she rose to greet him.

Introductions were quickly made and Marc found out the man with Marzell was a lawyer from the U.S. Attorney's office in Minneapolis, Donald Felton. When Marzell introduced him to Marc he couldn't help sarcastically thinking, *At least the taxpayers didn't have to pay to fly him in and put him in a hotel. He got here on an elevator.* A minute or so of awkward small talk followed during which Marc got the definite impression from Felton that the local U.S. Attorney's office was quite impressed with the audacity of Marc putting the U.S. Government's feet to the fire with this contempt of court motion.

A clerk came out and ushered the four of them into the magistrate's chambers. The U.S. Magistrate, Carmen Espinoza, was a woman Marc had met before when she served as a state district court judge in Hennepin County. He had appeared before her a couple of times on minor matters and although he doubted she would remember him, he remembered her as being a decent, reasonable and very competent jurist. The local legal grapevine had her rumored as getting the next federal district judgeship available in Minnesota. She stood up from behind her desk and pleasantly shook hands and greeted all of them. When all four had taken a seat in front of her, she began what was basically an informal conference.

"I understand," she began, "the only issue to resolve is additional attorney fees for the appeal and contempt motion. Is that correct?"

"Well, um, no your Honor," Marc cautiously said. "In fact, we've settled attorney fees. They've agreed to an additional $2,000 in fees. I think the government should have to pay some penalty for the way this matter was handled. Not abiding by the court's order in a timely fashion, wasting more of the court's time with this so-called appeal they knew they couldn't win and brought for the sole purpose of buying more time and stalling and for dragging everyone through all of this." The last part of his statement was said very slowly and deliberately as he ticked off each point by tapping the fingers on his left hand with the index finger of his right. Out of the corner of his eye he could see Marzell squirm in her seat and Felton look away from the magistrate to avoid eye contact. Marc suppressed a smile at their discomfort all the while silently pleased with himself for having the good sense to emphasize the waste of the court's time and resources.

"Okay. Let's see what we can do today then," Espinoza pleasantly replied with a slight smile at Marc. "Just so everyone knows," she continued while turning to look at Marzell and Felton, the smile having disappeared, "Judge Townsend sent this file over to me with explicit instructions that he wants this case settled today. Ms. Marzell?"

"Well, ah, obviously, your Honor, the government doesn't believe it has done anything wrong that should warrant sanctions and..."

"Ms. Marzell," the magistrate said interrupting her, "just so you know, I've read through the file on this case," she continued as she placed her right hand on the inch-thick manila folder that was lying on the desktop. "I have a pretty good idea what's gone on here. I tell you what," she said as she straightened in her chair still looking sternly at Marzell. "Why don't I talk to the parties separately and we'll see what we can do. Would that be okay?" The last part she said as a question looking at Marc and Karen, her pleasant smile having returned.

"That's fine, your Honor," Marc replied.

"Why don't you two wait in the courtroom and I'll talk to the Kadella's first?" she said to Marzell and Felton who were both out of their seats before she finished.

"Sure thing, judge," Marzell answered as Felton opened the door.

When the door closed behind the two government lawyers, Espinoza turned back to Marc and Karen and said, "This has been quite an ordeal for you two, hasn't it. Especially you," she said looking at Karen.

"You have no idea," Karen said. "It hasn't been pleasant."

"I'm sure," Espinoza said with obvious sympathy. Turning to Marc she asked, "Have you gotten everything you're supposed to from them?"

"We still haven't received any word on the refund yet, which isn't a big deal. We owe close to ten thousand dollars in taxes anyway and they'll use the refund to offset against that."

"How much do you think the refund will be?" Espinoza asked.

"Probably around three grand would be my guess."

"Okay," Espinoza nodded while making notes on a legal pad. "Have you been paid?"

"Yes, your Honor. I got the check a couple days ago."

"Okay," she said making more notes. "Let me ask you this: Give me a figure. What do you realistically think they should pay here today?"

"To get the U.S. Government to stop acting like this? To stop doing this to people and obey court orders? To slap them for having done it? I don't know," Marc wearily said holding his hands out palms up. "What really fries me about this is, as a lawyer in private practice, if I had handled a case this poorly, not only would I be facing judicial sanctions, I'd be facing a malpractice suit from my client and I'd have to explain myself to the Office of Professional Responsibility. And all of it would be deserved. Because it's the government, no one's to blame, no one's responsible and no one is ever held accountable for their conduct. It's time somebody slapped them for it."

"I can't argue with any of that," Espinoza agreed. "How about this, how about an additional five thousand that they have to pay to offset taxes that you owe?"

"What do you think?" Marc said turning to Karen.

"I want an apology," Karen said. "In fact, I want them to take an ad out in the paper apologizing."

"Well," Espinoza said laughing, "I don't think they'll agree to taking out an ad in the paper, but I think we can get an apology for you. I don't blame you, either. They owe you one. How about if we do it in the courtroom and make it part of the record? Would that be enough?"

"And I'll get a copy of it from the court reporter for you. Okay?" Marc said.

"What about the five thousand?" Espinoza asked, turning serious again.

"That's fine," Karen answered, pleased with the thought that the government, after all the years of aggravation she had been put through, was finally going to have to admit they were wrong and apologize to her for it.

"Done deal," Marc said as he stole a quick glance at the clock behind Espinoza and noted they had been in there alone with her for only five minutes.

"Good. Why don't you send them in now and I'll see what we can do," Espinoza said as Marc and Karen rose to leave.

They waited in the empty courtroom, Karen seated while Marc paced, for about fifteen minutes. They could hear the voices coming from the magistrate's chambers, loud and obviously acrimonious, though they couldn't make out what was being said. Finally, Karen looked at Marc and said, "Is there a place we can get a cup of coffee around here. Sounds like they may be a while."

"Yeah," he answered. "There's a cafeteria down in the basement. Let me just stick my head in and let them know," he said as he walked over and lightly knocked on the door.

Espinoza told them she would send her clerk for them when they were needed, and Marc and Karen went down to the cafeteria.

"What do think? "Karen asked as they sipped their coffee. "Do you think they'll take it?"

"I'm praying they don't."

"Are you serious? I'm scared they won't."

"If they don't take the deal we go back in front of the original judge and he'll know we accepted the deal proposed by the magistrate and they turned it down. Oh, yeah, I hope like hell they turn it down because this judge will nail their ass good."

A half an hour after they had gone downstairs they re-entered the still empty courtroom. The loud voices were no longer to be heard coming from the chambers and Marc looked at Karen and shrugged his shoulder to indicate he didn't know what it meant. They resumed their previous places and a few minutes later Espinoza came out smiling brightly to announce they had a deal.

A short while later Espinoza, having donned her black robe and taken her seat on the bench, presided over the formality of reading the agreement into the record. Marzell, with obvious distaste, apologized to Karen into the record on behalf of the federal government. Thus ending the case of Karen Kadella vs. The United States of America.

"Let me see if I have this straight?" Karen asked Marc as they stepped through the building's glass and chrome doors to exit into the afternoon's warmth and bright sunshine. "When we brought the lawsuit against the government we owed them, either together or just me, over forty-five thousand dollars in taxes. Is that about what it was?"

"Yeah, sounds about right," Marc answered as he turned to go toward the lot where they had parked.

"And now," she continued walking alongside her estranged husband "we owe maybe two thousand total."

"Maybe a little less. Two grand at most," Marc answered grinning at the thought.

"And on top of that, you get over eleven thousand in attorney fees for doing it?"

"Amazing isn't it," he said looking down at the shorter woman.

"What happened up there, anyway? While we were in the cafeteria," Karen asked.

"I'm not sure," Marc replied. "Lot of yelling. I think Espinoza chewed their asses and let them know they better settle, or the judge was going to nail them good if they didn't. Several phone calls back to Washington. I guess they weren't too crazy about being fined like that."

"Tough shit," Karen said. "Is this it? Is this thing finally over?"

"Yeah," Marc sighed. "I think it is. They don't want to hear from me again, that's for sure. Marzell told me," he continued with a soft laugh, "they have my picture up on a dart board at the Justice Department. I think she was kidding but I wouldn't swear to it."

"So, how does it feel to kick the ass of the United States Government?" she asked.

"Not bad," he said grinning from ear-to-ear. "Not bad at all. Actually, I'm just glad it's finally over."

They arrived at the street corner and while they waited for the traffic light, she said, "How's your trial going? I haven't been following it real close, but the way the papers make it sound, your guy's guilty and is going to get nailed."

"Really?" he said with a quizzical look as they stepped off the curb. "I think we're doing okay. You never know though," he continued with a shrug. "I think we're scoring our points. I guess we'll just have to see what the jury says."

"How's business?"

"You'd think with all of this publicity and free advertising I've been getting I'd have a line at the door. But it's not happening. Maybe if I win. Who knows?"

They arrived at her car and as she was opening the door, she said, "Try to see the kids. They're wondering if they still have a father."

"Don't start, Karen. I don't need this from you right now, okay?" he answered with more anger and bitterness than he wanted. Without another word between them, she slammed the car door as Marc turned and walked off.

SEVENTY-EIGHT

Jake Waschke stared back at the face of the old man in the mirror, the hands pushing and pulling on the sallow skin around the tired looking eyes. The face had aged several years over the last few months and he found himself wondering if he would ever sleep through the night again. He bent over the bathroom sink and splashed cold water on his face three or four times and rubbed his hands vigorously across it in an attempt at a quick revival. While the water dripped off of his chin, he leaned on the cheap vanity top and moved slowly toward the mirror until his nose almost touched the glass, staring intently into his eyes.

"A vacation," he said quietly. "When this thing is over, a vacation. Maybe that'll do it."

He sighed heavily, toweled off his face, looked at his watch and headed for the bedroom to change his clothes. He had a late evening meeting to attend and he wanted to be early.

The waitress, a different one than the one who had waited on him the first time he met Marty Hobbs in this small restaurant, placed the glass of beer on the napkin and walked away happy with the two-dollar tip.

The trial had dragged on at a snail's pace and now, he glumly thought, *yet another delay.* This one brought on by some kind of personal problem that the judge had, he had been told. Jake had anticipated the prosecution presenting its final witness. Hopefully, the one that would nail down a conviction and undo the damage done by Wally Bingham.

Wally had not been a total disaster. At least that was Steve Gondeck's read on the jury's reaction to his testimony. But Jake wasn't so sure. He thought Wally came across as obviously lying. And worse, put up to it by the police. He had held up pretty well during Kadella's cross-examination during the morning session. At least Kadella had not been able to get him to admit he was lying because the cops had cut a deal with him. Kadella had scored the point though and would no doubt hammer it to death during his closing argument. They needed Marty Hobbs. Needed him bad. An eyewitness who would put the defendant at the scene without anyone else to refute it should be enough, Slocum and Gondeck both believed.

He thought about Marc Kadella for a while. Jake wasn't like most cops. He didn't hate or even dislike defense attorneys. He understood their role and even approved of it. The thought of the police running loose without some checks and balances was not a place Jake would choose to live. He also knew it was always the cops who hated lawyers the most who ran the fastest to the best, most expensive ones when it was their ass accused of something. And Kadella was starting to earn his respect. What looked to be a slam dunk case had turned into a close thing because of him.

While he sat in the booth waiting for Hobbs, a couple of thoughts that had been scratching the back of his mind came to the surface. John Lucas had shown up in court today. Jake had seen to it that John was kept informed of the trial's progress and Lucas had only attended a couple of times and only for a short while each time. *Why today*, he wondered.

He pushed this thought aside as another, more significant one came into focus. What had Kadella's investigator, that Rivers woman, been doing parked on his mother's street? Why was she digging into his past?

He knew the answer of course. They must have guessed that it was him that had set up their client. They may have figured out who, but they didn't know why. And the why was the most important piece of the puzzle. Without it, the lawyer could harp all he wanted trying to convince the jury his client was framed. *But without the reason why, well,* he thought, *this isn't L. A. and it likely wouldn't stick.* Knowing it and proving it were two very different things.

He had tried to subtly convince Louise to get the hell out of town for a while. Even offering to pay for a trip to California to visit her sister. A sister she hadn't spoken to for fifteen years. Louise wouldn't go for it though and Jake didn't want to press too hard. He had tried to keep Rivers under surveillance but that had become too impractical. Especially after those two idiots had confronted her. He softly chuckled to himself at the thought of what she had done to them. Grudgingly respecting her for it. He was concerned about what Kadella might find but not too worried. The only way he could get to the truth was through Louise and Jake couldn't imagine she would possibly open up to him.

Jake finished his beer and looked around the almost empty dining room, searching for the waitress. The front door opened and Marty Hobbs walked in just as he caught the waitress' attention. He wiggled his empty glass at her and held up two fingers of his other hand. She smiled, nodded and headed for the bar as Marty slumped onto the booth's seat opposite Jake.

"Hey, Jake," Marty said as he slid across the bench seat to the far corner. "What's up?"

"Nothing, Marty. I just wanted to get together with you one more time before you testified. Just to make sure everything's cool."

"Yeah, I'm cool," Marty whispered. "Fact is, I was pissed today. I thought I'd get up there. Like, I'm really wired."

"You're what?" Jake asked, wondering if Marty was on something.

"No, no. Easy, dude. No, I'm wired to, you know, testify. Man, it's a rush, you know. Me getting to help put this psycho away."

"I thought you didn't want to testify," Jake said.

"No, no. We gotta get this dude, Jake. Me and you. You say he did this shit, that's good enough for me. We gotta nail his ass."

"Okay. That's fine," Jake nodded soberly as the waitress approached with their drinks. After she left, Jake said, "I want to go over your statements and your testimony again. One last time before tomorrow."

"Oh, man," Hobbs said as he set his glass back on the table. "I been over this so many times the last couple days…"

"We'll go over it again," Jake said holding up his left hand to silence Marty. "It's important that your testimony comes off smooth and believable."

"You're right. Okay. I'm cool," Marty said.

"You looked good today. The shirt and tie and the haircut. That shit helps," Jake said as he pulled a small sheaf of papers from the inside pocket of his sport coat and for the first time realizing that when this trial was over, Marty Hobbs was going to have to depart this life. "Let's go over your statement here so there's no glitches in your testimony tomorrow."

SEVENTY-NINE

Earlier that same evening, after everyone else in the office had left for the day, Marc sat at his desk going over the same statement. The one made by Hobbs to the police. He went over Maddy's investigative report on Hobbs for probably, he thought, the twentieth time. Looking for something, anything that he might be able to use to rattle him and cast doubt on his credibility. Frustrated after, once again, failing to find anything, he was about to pack it in when he heard the phone ring.

"Marc Kadella," he said as he answered it.

"Marc," he heard a familiar female voice respond, "it's Carolyn. I just got home and I remembered I forgot to drop off the mail at the post office today and that McCarthy letter you wanted sent is still there. Sorry," she began to apologize.

"Oh, that's okay, hon," he replied. "If it goes tomorrow, that's soon enough."

"Oh, that's a relief," she said. "With the pressure you've been under lately I thought I screwed up and was in for a butt chewing."

"No," he laughed. "Don't worry about it. Is the mail on your desk?"

"Yeah, it is."

"I'll get it and drop it off at the post office myself. I was just about to leave anyway."

"Good. Get out of there. Go home and relax. You need a night off. Will you be in tomorrow?"

"We'll see how the trial goes. I'll check in a couple of times for sure."

"Okay, Marc. Bye now," she said.

Carolyn hung up the phone and walked back to the front entryway. She had been in such a hurry to call Marc that, when she had arrived home and came in the front door, she had forgotten to drop her purse on the small table at the bottom of the stairs. Instead, she had gone straight into the kitchen and made the call to Marc, hoping to catch him before he left the office. Carolyn, her husband and the two kids still at home, lived in an old style two-story built in the twenties with the stairs coming down right at the front door. A big old cozy four bedroom they had bought after three years of marriage, one child and a second on the way.

She went up the stairs and instead of going into her bedroom, she turned right and knocked softly on the first door on her left and opened it a crack. She paused for a very brief moment, looking at the boy, a young man now she mused, seated on the end of the bed. He was in the last stages of dressing himself in his hockey equipment, attaching the Velcro strips that secured the massive shoulder pads. A brief smile flickered across her lips and she could literally feel her eyes sparkle while she looked at him. Jimmy was her middle child, an older brother in college at the U of M and a daughter she could hear across the hall. She loved them all, of course, but Jimmy was her secret favorite. An admission that always caused a twinge of guilt. He had been, at least in her eyes, the most beautiful little boy she had ever seen with his perfect blonde hair and bright blue eyes. Now this strapping six-footer, the mischievous one of her three children, was turning into a handsome young man right before her eyes.

"What's up, Mom?" he asked without turning his head.

"Are you about ready? Your dad'll be home soon and we have to go if we're going to be on time," she said.

"I could drive myself. You don't have to be there," he said even though he would be secretly disappointed if at least one of his parents didn't come to watch him play.

"Did you eat something?" she asked, ignoring his statement.

"Yeah, I did. Heated up some spaghetti. Pasta's good. Lots of protein."

"Good. Well, I'll get changed," she said as she quietly pulled the door closed. The door opposite opened and Sarah, the thirteen-year-old, stuck her head out. "Are you ready to go?" Carolyn asked.

"I'm not going. I hate hockey."

"I know, sweetheart," Carolyn answered as she turned to go to her bedroom. "You've told us many times before and yes, you are going so get ready."

"God, I hate hockey!" Sarah practically screamed at her mother's back and slammed her bedroom door while Carolyn quietly laughed.

A few minutes later the three of them were walking down the front porch steps, Sarah glumly, reluctantly bringing up the rear when a car turned into the driveway. Instead of continuing to her car, Carolyn and the two kids hurried to the one pulling up. Her husband popped the Buick's trunk lid to allow Jimmy to stow his equipment bag while Carolyn got in the front passenger side and Sarah the backseat behind her.

"Do I have time to change?" he asked as Carolyn reached across to kiss him.

"Nope. Sorry. Should've gotten here sooner," Carolyn answered.

"Hi, baby. What's wrong?" he said to Sarah who sat with her arms crossed against her developing breasts, her chin down, obviously displeased.

"Hi, Daddy," she softly, pleasantly answered. "I hate hockey."

"Really? I don't remember you ever mentioning that before," he mockingly said to her, which brought a smile to both her and Carolyn as Jimmy took the seat behind his dad.

"Hey, Dad," Jimmy said as he lightly patted his father on the shoulder. "How you doing?"

"You know," he began to answer as he turned in his seat to look down the driveway while backing up the car. "I'm beginning to see Sarah's point of view. I mean, spring hockey, summer hockey and now, fall hockey. Whatever happened to just winter hockey?" he asked Carolyn.

"One word: scholarship," Carolyn answered, a reminder that their older son, Matt, was about to begin his second season on the Gopher's varsity team and Jimmy was a better player than his brother.

"Oh, yeah," he said as he turned to go down the street. "Now I remember."

The hour long, unofficial, practice session for the Donner High School hockey team was almost half over when Jimmy scored his first goal. A ripping thirty-foot slap shot that blew past the goalie so fast the puck was in the back of the net before he could lift a glove. Carolyn, a hockey mom with well over a decade of experience, was on her feet leading the cheers as if Jimmy had just won the Stanley Cup.

She resumed her seat on the bleacher board, gently poked her husband in the ribs with an elbow and said, "Your son just scored."

"Yeah, I noticed," he answered softly.

"Well," she said arching her eyebrows at him, "try to control yourself."

"It's a practice game, Carolyn."

"Are you all right?" she asked, concern in her voice. "You seem a little preoccupied. Everything okay at work?"

"I'm sorry, babe," he said as he looped an arm around her shoulders and gave her an affectionate kiss. "Yeah, I'm okay." He turned to the man seated behind him, said something to him that Carolyn couldn't hear and a moment later Carolyn saw the man hand him a cigarette. He stood up and headed toward the end of the bleachers while Carolyn watched him go, now genuinely concerned. He rarely smoked anymore and when he did, she knew him well enough to know, there was something bothering him. She sneaked an occasional glance at him through the glass doors as he smoked and paced in front of the arena.

Later, at dinner, he was more quiet than usual and the rest of the evening he was preoccupied and distant.

"Okay, buster," she said to him as she pulled back the blankets on their bed, got in and moved over to her side. "Let's have it. What's wrong?" She laid on the bed propped up on her left elbow watching him prepare to join her.

He unclipped the holstered pistol from his belt and placed it and his detective's shield on the dresser while she silently watched him, waiting for a response. He began to undress, and she continued to wait, a look of concern on her face.

"Can you talk about it?" she softly asked.

"I need to see your boss," he finally answered.

"Which one?" she asked although she was fairly certain she knew the answer.

"Marc," he answered as he slipped off his trousers. He placed them neatly on the chair next to the closet door and removed his socks letting them drop to the floor. He leaned against the dresser, his butt on the edge clad only in his shorts, looked down at her and said, "I think I better see him. We need to talk."

"You want to talk about it?" she asked.

"No, hon," he said smiling weakly at her. "I think I better see Marc first."

"Okay," she nodded. "I'll talk to him tomorrow. You guys can set something up. Now, John Lucas," she said patting the bed next to her, "get your butt in here. You look like you could use a little lovin' and I know I sure could."

The next morning, after Sarah and Jimmy had left for school and the two of them were about to leave for work, he handed her a sealed, plain, white envelope. "Here," he said as he placed it in her hand. "Just give this to Marc. Don't open it. Don't show it to anybody else. The less you know right now, the better for both of us. Okay?"

"Okay," she answered placing the envelope in her purse.

"I'll tell you all about it later. For now, just trust me. Okay?"

"Of course I trust you," she said her eyes narrowed with concern.

"Relax," he said as he put both arms around her and gave a hard squeeze. "I'm not in any trouble," he continued as he kissed her.

EIGHTY

Marc tried waiting patiently for the deputy to bring Carl up from the jail, so they could confer before the court session began. He smoothed his tie for the third or fourth time, looked at his watch less than a minute after he last checked it then, finally, crossed his legs, leaned back in the chair and began lightly drumming his fingers on the tabletop. After a minute or two like this he heard the doorknob click open and Carl came into the small conference room. While the deputy held the door open for him, Marc caught a glimpse at the spectator area and noted it was rapidly filling up. *Full crowd again today*, he thought as Carl slumped heavily into the chair across the small round table.

"Is this lying sonofabitch actually gonna testify today?" Carl asked without a greeting or an attempt to hide his bitterness.

"Yeah, it looks like it," Marc quietly replied as he sat up, folded his hands on the table and leaned forward. "We talked to Prentiss and he said the problem that came up yesterday is over now so, we'll wrap up the prosecution's case."

"Any more surprise witnesses gonna show up? Any more bullshit I gotta listen to besides this asshole what's-his-name?"

"Not that I know of," Marc said shaking his head two or three times. "You going to be okay? You seem a little stressed today?"

"I don't know," Carl said, his eyes darting about the small room. "I'm just sick of sitting there listening to this shit."

"We're doing just fine, Carl. Hang in there. After today, the worst will be over then we get our shot."

A short while later everyone in the crowded courtroom was sitting back down after Prentiss had taken his seat on the bench. Prentiss looked down at Slocum and gave him permission to call his next witness, which he promptly did. Marc and Carl both turned in their seats to watch Marty Hobbs come in from the hallway through the room's double doors. He calmly passed through the gate in the bar, went quickly to the witness stand was sworn in and took the seat behind the microphone. Marc had personally spoken to Hobbs on two occasions and not surprisingly, the man seated in front of him, held little resemblance to the scruffy street hustler he remembered. He leaned forward into the microphone as he spoke and gave his name and address for the record and remembered to turn his head slightly to the left to look at and speak to the jury.

Slocum started slowly by tossing softball questions to him. Background things to relax a potentially nervous witness, develop his credibility and build rapport with the jury. Tell the jury that this witness was basically an ordinary, everyday kind of guy. Someone, essentially, just like themselves. He spent the best part of an hour with these things:

school, work, family, friends. He touched on Hobbs' criminal history which, of course, there was none. Any dealings with the police? Ever been a witness in a trial before? Any personal gain in being here? All answered firmly in the negative. Slocum was smooth and very much in control. Easy to listen to and he had a natural sense for when to move things along, before the inanities became boring and the jury's attention would begin to wane.

Marc allowed himself the luxury of a slight, unnoticed smile or two during the performance. Hobbs had been thoroughly and at least to Marc's trained eye, obviously well prepared. He hoped the jury would see it that way as Hobbs went through his routine of sitting up straight while the question was asked, leaning toward the microphone to answer and then shifting his gaze to the jury while speaking. Unfortunately for the defense, Slocum noticed it too and eased the effect by having the witness admit to a bout of nervousness.

Slocum made a smooth transition into the case at hand and Marc could sense, more than see, his client tense up. Carl's composure had been a source of concern for Marc from the very beginning. He could only wonder what it must be like, how difficult it must be for an innocent man to sit in jail for months and calmly take in weeks of damning testimony and evidence, all directed at you. Designed, manufactured really, for the sole purpose of painting you as a crazed, mass murderer. This morning's brief meeting had clearly shown Marc that the strain was starting to take its toll.

Hobbs was sitting back in the chair, becoming more relaxed, more comfortable. Marc could only guess but he figured the initial questioning may have made Hobbs a bit uncomfortable. Talking about himself and his seemingly empty life was not something Marty Hobbs liked to do, Marc believed. He testified about his knowledge of the case before he became personally involved. The news reports in the paper and on TV. The conversations he had with friends and coworkers.

Slocum moved him on to the events of the night of the last murder, the death of Alice Darwin, in Powderhorn Park. Hobbs testified he was walking down Chicago Avenue, heading towards a friend's house when, all of a sudden, he looked up and saw a man running down the sidewalk right at him.

At this point Marc unobtrusively reached down between his and Carl's chairs and silently opened his briefcase. He had laid it on the floor under the table between them when they had first sat down leaving the clasps undone. He slipped his right hand inside and while continuing to watch the witness, immediately felt his cell phone, placed strategically where he would find it quickly. With a practiced touch, he ran his index finger over the buttons until he found the correct speed dial, pressed the button to send and returned his hand to his lap. Exactly thirty seconds later, he again reached into the briefcase and hung up the phone.

"And then what happened?" Slocum asked.

"Well, like I said, I was walking down the street and I see this guy turn the corner up ahead and come running right at me. So, I keep walking, I mean, I didn't think nothing of it at first, so I kept walking then, I was about three or four houses from the corner of 35th and Chicago, and right as I was going past a streetlight, the guy comes up on me."

"You were walking past a streetlight?"

"Yeah, right when he got to me. And he kinda spooked me, too."

"Why was that, Mr. Hobbs?" Slocum asked. "Why did he spook you? Do you mean frighten you?"

"Well, yeah he did a little. 'Cause when he got to me, he slowed down. Stopped running and looked right at me. And his face, well, he looked wild. It was a cool night. Not hot at all and his face was all sweaty and his eyes ... well, his eyes were kinda wild looking, wide open and staring right at me and he had this kinda smile on his lips. But not really a smile. More like a, I don't know, a sneer I guess."

"Is it fair to say you got a good look at him?"

"Oh yeah," Hobbs answered, nodding his head several times for emphasis. "Yeah, I gotta real good look at him. The light from the streetlight shined right on his face. I'll never forget it."

At that precise moment the courtroom door leading into the hallway opened and Maddy Rivers strolled in. She stood inside the doorway, looking over the crowded gallery, ostensibly trying to spot an open seat. There was a slight, almost imperceptible stir arising from the spectators as she stood in the aisle. Of the players, it was Steve Gondeck who noticed her first. He had glanced back over his shoulder after sensing the commotion and almost wrenched his neck when his head swiveled at the sight of her. Maddy had done up her hair and spent a half hour with makeup that morning. She was wearing four-inch heels and a low-cut black dress whose hemline stopped just above her knees. All very tasteful that would not have looked out of place at a symphony, an opera or a Broadway play. On a scale of one to ten, she looked like a twelve and in a matter of moments every eye in the courtroom, with the exception of Marc, Carl and Slocum, was no longer fixed on the witness.

"And is that man in the courtroom this morning?" Slocum asked as Maddy slowly moved toward a seat she knew would be waiting for her. Reserved by Joe Fornich in the front row directly behind Carl.

"Um, oh yeah," Hobbs stammered his answer trying to avoid the distraction that even Prentiss could not resist. "Yeah, that's him there," he said pointing at Carl, remembering to look at the jury, none of whom were paying the slightest bit of attention to the witness.

Slocum, still oblivious to the distraction, said, "Let the record reflect that the witness has identified the defendant, Carl Milton Fornich, your Honor."

There was a pause in the proceedings as Prentiss, and everyone else, continued to watch Maddy as she slipped past the three people between herself and the open chair. Finally, snapping back to his surroundings, Prentiss said, "Yes, of course, the record will so state. You may proceed um, Mr., um, Slocum..."

"Thank you, your Honor," Slocum answered, puzzled at why the effect of the identification had not been more dramatic. "What did you do then?"

"Well," Hobbs began with a visible gulp. He then went on with his story and for the next hour he and Slocum told the jury how he had called the police the next day and the entire sequence of events that he had gone through that led him up to today.

About halfway through Hobbs' testimony, the part that came after Maddy's entrance, Marc could again sense Carl tensing up. At one point he patted him lightly on the arm, but Carl quickly jerked it away. After Hobbs had talked about spotting his photo and picking him out of a lineup, Carl clenched his hands together on the table and would no longer look up at the witness. Then, just as he was about to finish his direct exam, it happened. The explosion Marc had feared, counseled and repeatedly warned Carl about from the beginning.

"Sonofabitch!" Carl roared as he slammed a fist down on the table and came out of his chair.

"Carl...," Marc quickly said, a look of panic in his eyes as he reached for his client.

"No, damnit," he snarled at Marc. "I'm sick to death of this shit," he bellowed. "You're a goddamn liar," he yelled, now pointing an accusing finger at Hobbs as he began to climb up on the table while Marc stood up and grabbed at his shoulders to try to force him back in his chair. Carl turned his head to Marc, a wild, angry look in his eyes, roughly shoved him back with a push to the chest as the deputies began to move.

"You weren't there! You didn't see me there you lying sonofabitch," he screamed while kneeling on the tabletop. Except for the three deputies, no one moved. No one else said a word. The jurors all stared, wide-eyed, transfixed on the accused whose demeanor, until this point, had been exemplary. Slocum and Gondeck both sat quietly, Gondeck a hand lightly over his mouth. Slocum a sly smile coming to his lips. Prentiss too, was momentarily frozen. Uncertain, for the few seconds this scene played out, what to do.

But the deputies definitely knew what to do. Years of training and experience came immediately into play for the two men and one woman. They were on him like cats. All three pouncing at the exact same instant and while Carl continued to yell and struggle, they had him face down on the table in seconds and while the woman and one of the men held him, the third wrenched his arms behind his back and none too gently, snapped the handcuffs into place.

"Remove him from the courtroom," Prentiss bellowed from the bench after finally snapping to. "Now! I want him out of here immediately."

Without waiting for the judge's order, the three deputies jerked Carl over the table and quickly half walked, half carried him toward the door to the holding area. As they dragged him across the courtroom, Carl continued to yell the same phrase, repeating it over and over. "You weren't there. You didn't see me..." while Marc stood frozen in place watching several months of extremely hard work being led away.

EIGHTY-ONE

Marc reached down with his left hand and scooped up another handful of pebbles. He leaned forward on the park bench, elbows on his knees, and one-by-one, idly tossed the tiny stones into the water, the scene from the courtroom being replayed in his mind. It was like a videotape that he couldn't shut off. In a continuous loop, the morning's events kept going round and round in his head as if he had been a spectator, watching the show but not involved. Carl kneeling on the table, screaming and pointing at Hobbs. The deputies surrounding him, slamming him down on the table, snapping the handcuffs on then dragging him across the room and through the door. All the while Carl struggling and yelling that same hideous, ear-piercing phrase. "You weren't there. You didn't see me there."

Without being aware of it, Marc must have looked at the jury to see their reaction because that image too kept replaying itself as part of the overall scene. Each of them staring at Carl, their eyes wide open, unblinking. Several of them with their mouths open in disbelief. Shock registering on all of their faces. How could they possibly not wonder how Carl would know whether Hobbs was there or not and did not see him there if Carl wasn't there? One of them coming to this conclusion is all it would take. If one of them made that point in deliberations, just one, the rest of them would jump on it like a pack of ravenous wolves and Carl would be gone. Case closed.

The mental videotape continued to roll replaying the discussion, the argument, in chambers following Carl's removal. Slocum and Gondeck arguing vehemently that there had been enough delays in the trial, that they were almost finished with Hobbs and Carl should be brought back in chains if necessary and forced to participate today. Marc arguing that the defendant had a right to be in court during all proceedings, that to have him seated in the courtroom manacled would be highly prejudicial and that a delay over the weekend would not cause any harm.

Much to Marc's surprise, Prentiss agreed with him. But he admonished Marc strenuously that there had better not be any more disruptions like this morning's and again, he denied Marc's request to sequester the jury, even just for the weekend.

After court recessed, Marc had gone to his car and driven aimlessly around the streets of Minneapolis, barely aware of his surroundings with no conscious thought of where he was going or why. The videotape in his head going round and round until he found himself seated where he was now. A park bench on the edge of Powderhorn Lake, flicking pebbles with his thumb into the water, his tie dangling loose, his suit coat carelessly tossed next to him and his shirt beginning to stick to his back from the unusually warm, September day.

Marc straightened up against the back of the bench, looked up at the bright blue sky and heavily sighed. His head swiveled to his left to look at the spot he had consciously, deliberately avoided. The stand of tall conifers where it all began. The place in the park where the body of the last victim had been found. He tossed the remaining small stones still in his hand into the water, wearily stood up and turned to look around at his surroundings as if seeing them for the first time and found himself wondering what had brought him here today.

He bent down and picked up his coat, idly tossing it over his left shoulder. He stepped around the end of the bench and started walking down the asphalt pathway that circled the small lake, a pond really, past the pines and up the hill leading out onto the city streets. He had been over this ground himself a couple of times before, looking for any inconsistency he could find in the police reports or the testimony of the eyewitnesses. He had been unable to find one before and could come up with no good reason to be here now except it was as good a place as any to be at this moment. Away from crowds, reporters and telephones.

Marc continued his stroll, the mental images still playing in his head, and after a few minutes, he found himself on Chicago Avenue idly looking around, up and down the sidewalk where Hobbs claimed to have seen Carl. He stood on the sidewalk, his coat still over his shoulder, staring vacantly up at the streetlight, the exact light that Hobbs claimed illuminated Carl so clearly, in the exact spot where Hobbs testified the light pole stood. He stared up at it for almost a minute with no conscious thought whatsoever as to why he was doing it. *Perhaps,* he thought, *he was hoping it would speak and illuminate him with the truth as clearly as it did the sidewalk that night.*

"Get a grip," he softly said to himself as he turned to go back in the direction of the park to retrieve his car.

"Are you from the City?" he heard a voice say from the front of the house closest to him.

It didn't immediately register that the question was directed at him and when there was no response from him, the voice repeated the inquiry, "Excuse me, sir, but are you from the City?"

This time the voice caught his attention and he turned his head and shoulders toward the sound and said, "I'm sorry. Were you talking to me?"

"Yes, sir. I was just wondering if you were from the City."

"No, ma'am," he said as he turned to face her, his coat slipping from his hand at his side. The voice came from a middle age black woman who stood about fifteen feet from him on the small, neat lawn of the third house from the corner. She stood staring at him, her hands fisted and planted on her hips, a displeased look on her otherwise pleasant face.

"Oh," she said with obvious disappointment. "I thought maybe somebody finally decided to get off their ass and come out here from the City. They're really starting to piss me off, excuse my language."

"It's okay," he smiled. "At one time or another they piss off just about everybody. Well, have a nice day," he said as he tossed the coat back on his shoulder and turned to go.

"All I want is for them to get out here and fix that damn light," she said a touch angrily.

With that Marc stopped dead in his tracks, swiveled to face her and said, "What? What did you just say? What light?"

"That one right there," she said pointing to the street light that had been the focus of Marc's attention. "It's been out for months and I'm tired of calling 'em to get out here and fix it. If this was Kenwood you can bet they'd been out here the same day," she said, now with both anger and disgust.

Marc, his heart starting to pound, his mouth going dry and palms wet, took a couple of short steps toward her and said, "When did it go out, ma'am? Can you remember about when it was?"

"I don't have to remember 'about' when it was. I know it was April 14th when I first called 'em cuz April 13th is my grandson's birthday and the kids was here playing in front of the house and I noticed that light was out. It's a damn busy street sometimes and I keep an eye on the kids. So, I called the City the next day. And I've called them at least ten times since and they still ain't got out here to fix it."

"You're positive? I mean, I'm sorry, I don't doubt you," he stammered when he saw the look of annoyance on her face. "It's just that, I'm a lawyer and a man's life may depend on it."

"Oh," she said softly. "Yes, sir. I'm sure of it. April 14th."

"Did you make the calls from this house? From your home phone?"

"Yes. All of them," she answered. "Would you mind telling me why it's so important?"

"We can get the phone records," he said quietly to himself. "We'll get a subpoena for the phone records. I'm sorry ma'am. It's about, well," he continued with a big grin as he stepped up to her, placed his free right hand lightly on her shoulder, looked her straight in the eyes and said, "I think I might love you. Hi, my name's Marc Kadella and I'd like to talk to you if you have a few minutes."

EIGHTY-TWO

Marc took the building's back stairs two at a time as he headed toward his office. He went through the doorway and as he stepped into the reception room all movement and sound came to an abrupt halt when the occupants saw him standing there. Carolyn had been conferring with Barry Cline and Sandy was working at her computer. All three looked at Marc, all motion and speech suspended as the three of them stared at him while he looked back at them. Concern on their faces, puzzlement on his. It was Connie Mickelson, after appearing in her office doorway, who broke the silence first.

"We heard the news on the radio, Marc. About your client this morning. How bad was it?"

"Oh, Carl's little outburst, you mean," Marc said after thinking for a moment. "Well, not good. I've been moping around for a couple of hours now wondering what to do about it. But hey," he said as he tossed his coat onto one of the reception area chairs and clapped his hands together, "we're not out of this thing yet. I got a witness. I found a witness who can and will testify that that little bastard Hobbs is lying. I've known it all along and now I think I can prove it. Has Maddy called in?"

"Not yet," Sandy answered. "How'd she do this morning?"

"Oh, wonderful," he exclaimed. "It was better than I hoped for. You should've seen her. Even Prentiss couldn't take his eyes off her," he laughed, the first good, genuine laugh he had in weeks.

"What did you do?" Barry asked cautiously, suspiciously. So he told them.

How he and Maddy had set it up for her to make her entrance at the exact moment she did. How Marc had waited until just before Hobbs' identification of Carl, he had slipped a hand into his briefcase and pressed the speed dial button of his cell to call Maddy and signal her to make her entrance. Her phone buzzed, she waited another thirty seconds and then came into the courtroom, dolled up and dressed to kill. The two of them had thought it through, set it up and timed it for, hopefully, maximum effect. An attempt to distract at least some of the male jurors so that Hobbs' identification would lose some of its impact. Steal some of the show away from Slocum.

"It couldn't have been better," he said amid the laughter of his office mates. "I didn't dare look at her for fear I'd start laughing. Every one of the jurors was staring at her. Even the women. Prentiss, too. I glanced over at the prosecutors and Slocum, what an ass he is, he was oblivious to the whole thing. But Gondeck, I thought he was gonna step on his tongue. And Hobbs had trouble getting the words out to answer the question. It was just about perfect. And then," he added turning serious, "Carl throws it all away."

"How much damage do you think Carl did?" Connie asked.

"I don't know. A lot, that's for sure. It was about as bad as it could be. Anyway..."

"Oh, Marc," Carolyn interrupted him. "I almost forgot," she continued as she stepped to her desk and pulled her purse from a drawer. "John gave me this to give you. I don't know what's in it, but he says it's important," and she handed him the plain white envelope she had been given that morning.

Marc pulled his car into the space next to the dark blue Chevy sedan, the only one that looked like a police car among the dozen or so cars parked in the lot. After Carolyn Lucas had given him the envelope from her husband Marc had placed the call to John's cell, left a message, waited for the return call and the two of them had set up this meeting. The note and the brief phone conversation had been vague. Lucas had merely said he had some information for him about his trial and he wanted to meet with him secretly and as soon as possible.

Marc exited his car and began quickly walking up the asphalt toward the zoo at Como Park. The lot was on the south side of the park, about two hundred yards from the zoo. John had told him where to park and said he would meet him somewhere between it and the zoo grounds.

He hurried along the walkway, glancing around through the trees half expecting Lucas to leap down from one of them. As he came around a slight bend he saw him seated on a park bench about fifty feet away. When he approached the bench, Carolyn's husband stood and the two men shook hands and exchange a brief greeting.

"Hi, John," Marc said. "Nice to see you again. How've you been?"

"All right, Marc. And you?" John answered as the two men took their places on the bench and half turned to face each other.

"So, what's this all about, John?" Marc said cutting right to the point as men are prone to do when faced with a serious issue.

Lucas sighed heavily, placed his left hand over his mouth while continuing to look directly at Marc who was staring back with a questioning expression. They stayed this way for a moment, then Lucas removed his hand from over his mouth and quietly, almost in a whisper, said, "I have some information for you, but before I tell you, I want your word about something. I want your word that you won't call me as a witness. Will you do that? Give me your word?"

Marc sat quietly for a few seconds, as if thinking it over, nodded his head a couple of times and said, "Okay, John. You got it. I won't call you as a witness."

"Good. Okay," Lucas said with obvious relief. "I'll tell you what I know," he began. "This guy Hobbs, that witness who testified today, he and Jake Waschke know each other. In fact, they've known each other for a long time. Hobbs is Jake's personal snitch."

"I knew it," Marc hissed between clenched teeth. "I knew it had to be a setup."

Lucas turned in his seat, leaned forward, placed his forearms on his knees, lightly held his hands together and looked away from Marc before continuing. "The first time I saw Hobbs was at the jail when they arrested your client, Fornich. I knew I'd seen him somewhere before. He had a familiar look, but I couldn't place it, you know what I mean?"

"Sure," Marc said wanting him to go on.

"Anyway, it kinda buzzed around in my head from time-to-time. Kept nagging at me, just beneath the surface. So, about a week ago, almost out of the blue, I wasn't even thinking about it, the light went on and I remembered when I first saw him."

"When?" Marc asked quietly.

"It was about four years ago. A gang shooting here in St. Paul. A drive-by by some gangbangers from Minneapolis. So, of course, the St. Paul guys go to Minneapolis to get even. Now we had overlapping homicides between the two cities. Three guys get killed. A couple of others shot up. That's when I first met Jake. We worked the case together," he said as he sat up, leaned back against the bench and turned to again face Marc.

"Jake said he had a good snitch who might know something about the shooters and all so, we went to see him. Jake told me his name was Marty and Jake had him in his pocket. I remember because when Jake went to this pool hall to talk to him I stayed in the car and made some notes.

"Anyway, since he was Jake's snitch, I didn't want to interfere, so I didn't talk to him, but I did see him. He came to the door with Jake and I got a good look at him. It was Hobbs. No doubt in my mind. Just to be sure, I dug out my case notes and sure enough, there it was. He gave us some good information, too. Right on the money. We were able to use it to get a confession from one of the bangers and then he turned on his buddies. Wrapped up the whole thing."

Marc leaned back and draped his right arm across the back of the bench and sat this way, silence between the two men for over a minute while Marc thought over what he had just been told. He quickly replayed Hobbs's testimony, the part where he had specifically denied knowing any police officers or having any inducement to testify.

Finally, after the uncomfortable minute had passed, he turned his head back toward Lucas and said. "So, let me get this straight. You've known for a week now that Hobbs was lying and you're just now coming forward? It took you a week to decide to do the right thing?"

"It's not that simple..." Lucas began to protest.

"Yes it is, John. Don't give me this cop bullshit about protecting a brother officer the 'thin-blue-line' crap," Marc interrupted fighting to remain calm and keep the anger out of his voice.

"Wait a minute," Lucas said staring angrily at Marc. "That's not bullshit. You don't understand ..."

"You're damn right I don't understand. I don't understand what the big decision could be. Let me think: 'Do I come forward and rat out a corrupt cop or do I let an innocent man go to prison for the rest of his life?' That's a tough one all right, John," he added sarcastically. "That's a no-brainer, John. You don't let an innocent man go to jail," he said as he dropped his right foot to the ground and angrily stabbed the index finger of his right hand into Lucas's chest. "Period. You don't do it. I don't get it. I don't get you guys at all. That whole thing about cops covering each other's asses no matter what. It's so morally corrupt. So morally bankrupt it's unfathomable to the rest of us. I just don't..."

"I'm here aren't I?" Lucas quietly said stopping Marc cold.

Marc leaned back again, the anger receding and placed his hands in his lap. He nodded his head several times while looking down at his hands before softly continuing. "Yeah, you're here. Okay. You're doing the right thing and it's not too late. But I'll tell you right now, all bets are off as far as calling you as a witness. If I have to, I will."

"You sonofabitch," Lucas snarled. "You gave me your word..."

"I lied," Marc said simply. "I knew it when I said it, it was probably a lie. I don't like myself for it, but I did it."

"Damnit, Marc," Lucas seethed, "you don't know what you're doing to me."

"Yeah I do. It would probably kill your career, which I don't understand either. You should be a hero for coming forward, but the department would crucify you."

"Exactly. I'll be finished. No one will ever want to work with me again."

"Grow up, John," Marc said, turning angry again. "I have a higher responsibility here and so do you. I'm an officer of the court and so are you. Look, I'll do everything I can to avoid it. I'll only call you if I have absolutely no choice but I'm not going to lose this thing to save your ass. I can't. I have no choice. But," he continued, "I came up with some new information that may be enough. We'll see. I can't promise you, though."

"Okay. Fair enough. I guess I knew that going in," Lucas glumly replied.

Marc paused at the bottom of the stairway, his left hand holding the hand rail that ran up the wall, his right hand holding his coat that was draped over his shoulder. He stared up at the light at the top of the stairs, his mouth partially opened in weariness as he continued to mentally work his way through his emotional turmoil. John and Carolyn Lucas were good, dear friends. He had known them both for years. He loved Carolyn like a sister. Of all the people whom he knew, it was Carolyn who had helped him through the rough times when his marriage had broken up. Been there for him when he needed a friendly voice, a word of encouragement or a pat on the back. He had been to their home many times. Had watched their kids grow up.

Now he was faced with the very real possibility of ruining their lives to uphold his professional responsibility and the prospect of it made him feel, literally, sick to his stomach. He was beginning to believe he would save Carl now and what should be a joyous feeling instead brought him close to the edge of vomiting.

Marc trudged wearily up the stairs, one heavy foot after the other as he used his hand on the rail to pull himself along. He finally reached the top and plodded the few steps down the hall to the office door. He silently stood in the hall, his hand on the door knob, listening for sounds coming from inside and praying that everyone was gone so he wouldn't have to face any of them. Fearing that John had called Carolyn to tell her what had happened.

Hearing no sounds coming from within, he slowly turned the knob, quietly opened the door, eased his head through it and looked around, relieved to see everyone gone on this Friday evening.

He went into his office, tossed his coat on a chair, slumped into his seat and stared across his desk at the Monet print his wife had given him that hung on the wall behind the client chairs. The phone in the outer office rang and he turned his head to watch the blinking light on his phone. He let it ring two more times before he lifted the receiver from its cradle, punched the button on the blinking line and wearily said, "Yeah, Marc Kadella."

"Marc, hi, it's me," he heard Maddy's excited voice say. "I'll be there in about fifteen minutes to pick you up."

"Why? Where we going?" he quietly asked.

"I've got someone you need to talk to," she answered. "I've just spent the last two hours with her and she's agreed to see us tonight. You have to hear this for yourself. You won't believe it."

"Who?" he asked, straightening in his chair.

"Louise Curtin," Maddy said. "Jake Waschke's mother."

EIGHTY-THREE

When Maddy left the courtroom following Carl's tirade, she walked around on the bridge between the two sections of the government center, ignoring the gawkers, impatiently waiting for Marc. After a half-hour or so, she spotted him exiting the courtroom, his head down, shoulders slumped, practically dragging his briefcase as he wearily plodded toward the elevators. They rode down together, not speaking, except to exchange a brief greeting when she first intercepted him. Maddy didn't know what to say and Marc was obviously not interested in discussing the spectacle they had just witnessed. They separated in the underground parking garage, Maddy to head home, Marc to wander around the city until he stopped on the park bench in Powderhorn Park.

She made the short trip to her high-rise building on the edge of downtown and took the elevator to her eighth-floor apartment above LaSalle. She quickly exchanged the dress and heels for sweats and sneakers, spent several minutes washing her face and brushing out her hair then took the elevator back down to the street and headed out for a brisk three-mile run.

Maddy made a conscious effort to work her mind while she ran. Tried to think about anything else except the outburst by Carl, but it proved to be too difficult. She didn't feel the same sense of personal loss, personal betrayal, that Marc was going through. Hers was a more detached, objective analysis of the damage done. She still believed in Carl's innocence, part of the team that was standing up for what she believed was right. Justice? She wondered. Maybe. But it was even more basic, simpler than that. It was the difference between right and wrong and she couldn't help wondering if Carl had thrown it all away.

She stood in the shower letting the hot water stream over her. Rinsing her body and clearing her head and giving her a chance to get back in focus on what she had to do. After a light lunch, she laid down for a nap and awoke two hours later, surprised at how easily she had fallen asleep and how well she had slept once she did.

Maddy drove to the address for Waschke's mother and waited in her car, parked two doors down the street. She sat for about fifteen minutes in the midafternoon sun, watching the house looking for signs of activity, before deciding to give the doorbell a try. She moved the car to the front of the house, marched up the sidewalk and rang the bell. Just as she was reaching for it to ring it a second time, she heard the deadbolt snap back, the doorknob turn and found herself looking down at a woman in a motorized wheelchair.

After spending two hours with Louise, she had driven back into the city, placing her call to Marc from inside the car while heading down 35W. She picked him up at his office a short while later and listened with rising optimism as he explained to her the events of his afternoon. He told her about his chance encounter with Antoinette Hardy, the burned-out streetlight and the revelations by John Lucas at Como Park. Despite repeated inquiries from Marc about what she had learned from Louise Curtin, she managed to keep the information to herself, merely repeating several times that he should be patient and hear it from Curtin herself.

She made a quick stop at a liquor store a few blocks from Louise's home. Maddy was in and out in a few minutes and they arrived at the house just a few minutes later.

They exited the car and Marc followed her up the front walk, impatiently waiting while she rang the bell, holding her purchase by the neck still in its brown paper bag. Maddy looked down at Marc standing on the handicap access ramp just below her while they waited for the door to open. She smiled at him, patted him on the shoulder then turned her head back to the door at the sound of the deadbolt being opened.

After introductions were made, Marc followed behind the whirring wheelchair as Louise led him into her living room while Maddy went into the kitchen. He glanced around taking in the small, neatly kept home, noticed several well tended plants and the large, beautiful Himalayan Siamese lying in front of the TV, licking his paws and with an indifferent expression, surveying the intruders. Marc took a seat on a small sofa, noting with mild surprise the absence of cat hair from the beast in front of the tube. The two of them made a little awkward small talk while they waited for Maddy to return. Marc studied her face and realized that, at one time, this was a woman that could have given Maddy competition. Age and alcohol had taken their inevitable toll, but in better days Louise Curtin had been quite pleasing to the eye.

Maddy entered the room carrying three small glasses, the fingers of her right hand inside of them clamping them together, and a bottle of Johnny Walker Red, now bagless, in her left. Without comment, she placed the tumblers on the table, unscrewed the cap from the bottle and began pouring. She half filled one, handed it to Louise, and splashed a small amount into each of the other two, sliding one in front of Marc as she sat on the sofa next to him and took a small sip from her glass.

"Hi, Bubba," Maddy said looking at the feline who stared back, his pale blue eyes unblinking. "Isn't he the most beautiful cat you've ever seen?" she asked Marc, giving his ribs a light poke with her elbow while they waited for Louise to finish her drink.

"Don't mind Bubba," Louise said to Marc as she pushed the chairs control stick forward to move closer to the coffee table. She stopped at the table directly opposite Marc and held the empty glass up for Maddy. "Thank you, dear, you're very sweet. And so beautiful," she sighed as Maddy poured two fingers for her.

"He won't attack, will he?" Marc asked, half-seriously, nodding toward the cat.

"Oh no," Louise said with a throaty laugh from a voice that had endured too much scotch over the years. "He's really quite nice. A very calm cat. Besides, I'll let him out in a bit and he'll go out and find something to kill. He only eats things smaller than himself."

"Wonderful," Marc dryly replied.

"Louise," Maddy softly began. "You need to tell Marc what you told me this afternoon."

"Yes, I know," she sighed. "You know, dear, I feel a lot better than I have in years. Talking to you today, telling you about it and all. Getting it off my chest. Well, I feel like a weight has been lifted. I feel sad, too."

"Marc needs to hear it, Louise. A man's life depends on it."

"Yes, I know," she whispered. "It's just, well, it will be difficult for the boys. Especially Daniel. But it's time. Time it came out. It's just that, well, it was so long ago and," she paused to sip from her glass. "I guess I had hoped it wouldn't matter anymore."

She turned her head to look at Marc and lowered her eyes to avoid the intense look on his face. She began in a soft, quiet voice that was difficult for Marc to hear. He leaned forward, his elbows on his knees, his hands folded together, and his head directly above the untouched glass Maddy had placed before him. Having already heard the story, Maddy dropped her purse on the floor by her feet, leaned back and crossed her right leg over her left, moving only to splash more scotch into Louise's glass a few times while she Marc the story.

When she finished, Marc stood up and casually paced about the room. Thinking it over and contemplating how best to use what he had been told to help his client. After a couple of minutes, he took his place back on the couch, picked up the still untouched glass and tossed the small shot down his throat before beginning.

The three of them discussed the trial and Louise, reluctantly, agreed to testify. They made arrangements for Maddy to pick her up Monday morning and escort her to court. Finally, just before they were preparing to leave, Marc noticed Louise's hair. The years had caused it to noticeably fade and it was streaked with ample amounts of gray, but he could clearly see that she had once been a very attractive, striking, brunette.

"How tall are you?" he abruptly asked Louise.

"What?" she asked, uncertainty in her voice. "Five-ten, why?" she answered looking at him with a puzzled expression.

"Oh, um, nothing. I was just, um, curious," he stammered as Maddy looked at him, her eyes wide and her mouth slightly open.

It was dark when they left her and as they walked toward the car Maddy reached over and gripped his arm, a little too tightly, her nails digging in. Marc was too stunned to notice, his mind almost numb, as she asked, "You thinking what I'm thinking? That Daniel's symbolically killing his mother?"

"I don't know," Marc replied, weariness in his voice. "It's a theory. You didn't think of it before?"

"No, I guess not. I guess I didn't notice she was a tall brunette. You know, like the victims..."

"Listen," he said as they reached the curb in front of her car. "We've got some things to do. It's a little late tonight, but I'll see you at the office in the morning. We have to plan our strategy and get some subpoenas served this weekend. This thing isn't over."

EIGHTY-FOUR

The court deputy unlocked the hallway door and as soon as Marc heard the bolt click open he pushed the door back and led the crowd into the empty room. He went through the thigh high gate and as the spectator section began to fill, emptied his briefcase onto the defense table. He removed everything from his briefcase and placed the contents on the table in an orderly arrangement, preparing for the upcoming testimony.

After completing his task, he casually strolled the few steps to the table where the deputy had arranged all of the exhibits entered, so far, into evidence. He stood at the table gazing down at the assortment of items used by the prosecution as evidence against his client, his hands in his pants' pockets, trying to appear casual so as not to be noticed by the crowd finding seats behind him. With his left hand he picked up the sealed, plastic bag containing the locker key and as he lifted it close to his face, he took his right hand out of his pocket bringing with it a small, metal object. With his back to the spectators, he held the bag and without anyone else able to observe him, compared the key in the bag with the one he had removed from his pocket. Finding what he believed he would, he quickly placed the bag back on the table, calmly looked over three or four more items strictly for appearances and turned back to the defense table slipping the key in his hand back into his pocket.

A short while later a contrite and chastened Carl was led in and took his seat next to Marc. They made some idle small talk, Carl fully aware by now of everything Marc and Maddy had discovered over the weekend and waited for the other players to appear.

A few minutes later Slocum and Steve Gondeck appeared, took their seats at the prosecution table as the jury was being ushered into the box seconds before the bailiff intoned the "All rise" for Prentiss' entry. After allowing everyone to retake their seats, Prentiss spent two or three minutes sternly rebuking Carl for his behavior on Friday, just in case any of the jury members had forgotten about it, as if they possibly could. Marty Hobbs was recalled to the witness stand and the show was underway.

Slocum solemnly, slowly rose from his seat, his hands grasping the lapels of his suit coat, and informed the court that he had no more questions of the witness. Prentiss looked down at Marc, politely nodded and gave Marc permission to begin his cross examination.

Before his stroll through Powderhorn Park and his chance encounter with Antoinette Hardy, Marc had prepared a cross exam of Hobbs that could easily last all day. Maddy had investigated Hobbs all the way back to the cradle and Marc had decided to attack this witness. Show the jury that maybe he wasn't the upstanding citizen that Hobbs and Slocum had claimed. He was going to put the life of Martin Dale

Hobbs under a microscope and refocus the entire trial away from Carl and onto the credibility of the State's eyewitness and hope the veneer would crack away. At least enough to create some reasonable doubt. In the process of the preparation, he had almost completely filled two legal pads with questions and Saturday had tossed both of them into the trash. He had new ammunition and decided, the less said, the better.

His initial strategy with Hobbs had been to treat him with contempt. The same way he had treated Ed Hill and Wally Bingham. Career criminals who would say and do anything to save their ass from a prison sentence. Despite Hobbs' clean criminal record, Maddy had dug up enough dirt and found a couple of witnesses willing to testify that Hobbs wasn't quite so pure after all. Marc needed to cast enough doubt on his credibility to give Carl a chance. He had to reveal the names of those witnesses to Slocum and Slocum had effectively dealt with it during Hobbs' direct exam. Now Marc had the element of surprise and had decided to go easy with Hobbs to avoid setting off any alarms that might give Hobbs the chance to explain things.

Marc started in with a few preliminary questions. He had used Maddy to play Hobbs role on Saturday, practicing the questioning for a couple of hours until he had pared it down to less than a half hour. Using a few very short questions, all of which seemed innocuous and clearly called for a yes answer, he went right to the scene of Hobbs walking down Chicago Avenue the night of the last murder.

"And then, Mr. Hobbs, you were walking down the street on the east side of Chicago, heading south, away from Lake Street, correct?"

"Yes, that's correct."

"And you looked ahead to the next corner?"

"Right," Hobbs answered after a pause, uncertain if the question was complete.

"And you saw a man turn the corner and come toward you?"

"Yes, that's right."

"And he was running toward you on the same side of Chicago as you were on, is that right?"

"Yes, that's right."

"He was running north and you were walking south?"

"Yes," again after a brief pause.

"Was he running hard or jogging?" Marc asked slightly breaking the rule about not asking a question unless he was certain of the answer.

"He was running, not jogging," Hobbs answered without hesitation.

"And you testified that as he came up to you he stopped running and looked right at you, is that correct?"

"Yes," Hobbs answered, looking at the jury and nodding his head for emphasis.

Careful now, Marc thought to himself. *Don't make a big deal of this. Don't give him a chance to correct himself. You just want him to say it again.*

"And you testified you were about three or four houses from the corner of 35th and Chicago, passing under a streetlight, when he looked at you, is that correct?"

"Yes."

"And you saw his face from the light of the streetlight, correct?"

"Yes," he answered with another nod.

"You kept walking south after this man passed you, is that right?"

"Yes."

"To continue your trip to your friend's?" Marc asked pleased with how relaxed and unwary Hobbs looked on the stand.

"Yes."

"Did the man who passed you start running again?"

"Um, I think so," Hobbs answered. "I can't say for sure. I mean, I don't remember if I turned around to look at him or not."

"What is your relationship with police Lieutenant Jacob Waschke?" Marc asked, abruptly changing directions to see if Hobbs would look startled, which he did not.

"My relationship?" Hobbs answered with a puzzled expression. "I'm not sure what you mean."

"Did you know Lieutenant Waschke before that night?"

"No."

"Had you ever met him?" Marc asked, becoming almost imperceptibly less casual.

"No. Before that night, I had never met him," Hobbs answered, outwardly appearing calm and truthful, inwardly reeling at the shock.

"You had never served as an informant for him?"

"A what? I'm not sure what that is."

"You know, someone who gives the police information about crimes in exchange for favors. Had you ever done this for Lieutenant Waschke?" Marc asked as he made a half turn in his chair to look at Jake seated in the aisle seat directly behind Slocum. Jake appeared calm and relaxed, inwardly pleased at how well Hobbs was handling this and with his own foresight for having prepared him for it.

"No," came the calm reply. "I have never been a police informant for Lieutenant Waschke or anyone else."

"Really? You had never met Lieutenant Waschke before yet, the next day you called the police and specifically asked for him, is that correct?"

"Yes."

"And you want the jury to believe you asked for him personally just because you had seen him on TV?"

"That's what happened," Hobbs answered with a shrug. "I want the jury to believe it because it's true."

341

Marc leaned forward placing his forearms on the table, his hands held together as he leaned forward and rested his chest against them. He stared, unblinking, at the witness silently sending an unmistakable message to Hobbs who looked back in Marc's direction but avoided eye contact with him. The unmistakable message that Marc conveyed to the snitch was that he was lying and Marc knew it. The problem he had, or so Hobbs believed, was proving it.

"I have no further questions of this witness at this time, your Honor," Marc softly said without turning his head away from Hobbs. "However, the defense reserves the right to recall him," he finished, narrowing his eyes in an ominous gesture that only the witness saw.

"Any redirect, Mr. Slocum?" Prentiss said.

"No, your Honor," Slocum replied after quickly regaining his composure, slightly rattled with Marc's very brief cross examination. Despite Steve Gondeck's assurance that Marc was a capable defense lawyer, Slocum's opinion of him from the start of the case had not been very high. In fact, Slocum was originally disappointed that one of the local heavyweights had not been retained to represent Fornich. The media play and of course, the conviction, would have been that much better. Now, an alarm bell went off in his head. Marc's cross of the state's main witness left him with an uneasy feeling, something about it was not quite right. No one could be so incompetent as to barely cross examine the only eyewitness. Kadella had something up his sleeve that had not been revealed.

"You may call your next witness, Mr. Slocum," Prentiss announced.

Slocum stood up, paused for effect as he surveyed the room, clasped his hands together behind his back, thrust out his chin and in his best baritone solemnly said, "The State rests, your Honor."

"Mr. Kadella?" Prentiss asked turning his head to Marc. Marc rose to address the bench and as he half turned to push his chair back, he noticed the entryway door behind him open and a man walked in. Daniel Waschke stood in front of the double doors looking over the spectator area. Seeing the only available seat in the back row just to his left he quickly moved to it, nodding an acknowledgement to his brother who had turned and saw him come in when he had heard the door pushed open.

"The defense moves the court to dismiss all charges on the grounds that the State has failed to present adequate evidence to support the indictment, your Honor," Marc said, going through the formality of requesting dismissal to preserve the record.

"Denied," Prentiss ruled. "Are you prepared to call your first witness?"

"In a moment, your Honor. May I approach the bench?"

"Certainly," Prentiss answered.

Marc picked up three sheets of paper from the table and handed one each to Slocum and Gondeck as the three of them walked toward the bench. Slocum and Gondeck quickly read them over before they reached Prentiss, Slocum's face reddening with anger, Steve Gondeck remaining calm and impassive as Marc handed the third sheet to the judge.

"What is this?" Prentiss snarled.

"An amended witness list, your Honor," Marc calmly whispered back while thinking, *Go ahead asshole. Deny me the right to do it after you let Slocum do the same thing. I dare you.* A thought which Prentiss could clearly read in Marc's eyes.

"Your Honor..." Slocum began to protest but was abruptly cut off when Prentiss held up his right hand.

"Court will take a brief recess. Fifteen minutes," Prentiss announced, "and I'll see you gentlemen in chambers."

"I'm going to want this on the record your Honor," Marc said as Prentiss rose to leave.

"That's fine," Prentiss answered hiding his disappointment. He had hoped to get out of there and have the upcoming discussion off-the-record, realizing that was the only possible way he could rule against the defense.

"Who are these two people?" Prentiss asked Marc after they had all taken seats in the judge's chambers and the court reporter had set up her equipment. "This, Antoinette Hardy and Louise Curtin? I know who Daniel Waschke is and you better have a good reason for putting him on the witness stand."

"Witnesses that came to my attention over this past weekend, your Honor," Marc politely replied.

"Your Honor, this is just extremely..." Slocum began to bluster a protest.

"Is what, Mr. Slocum?" Prentiss said, sternly glaring at Slocum. "You have a reasonable argument to make for why I should deny the defense the right to do something I already allowed you do to? If so, let's hear it."

"No, your Honor," Slocum meekly replied remembering the stenographer.

"I will give you the right to recall them for cross examination at a later time after you've had time to interview them and prepare. In the interest of fairness, I have little choice but to allow it. However," Prentiss continued looking sternly at all three lawyers, "this had better be the end of it. Am I understood?"

"Yes, your Honor," Slocum and Gondeck replied in unison.

"Mr. Kadella?"

"We'll see, your Honor," Marc calmly, defiantly said. "We'll cross that bridge if we come to it."

Prentiss continued staring directly at Marc. Silently seething at the impertinence of a criminal defense lawyer showing the temerity to defy him. Without taking his eyes from Marc's face, who was staring right back at him with a relaxed but definite 'fuck you' look in his eyes, Prentiss said, "Back out to the courtroom, all of you."

EIGHTY-FIVE

While the discussion about Marc's witnesses was taking place, Jake found his brother in the hallway among the crowd milling about, stretching their legs before the trial resumed. Daniel was standing at the glass wall, staring blankly at the opposite side of the building watching the county employees going about their business.

Jake walked over to the younger man, stopped behind him, leaned his head down over Daniel's right shoulder and whispered directly into his ear, "What're you doing here?"

Without turning around or even moving his head, Daniel quietly, casually replied, "I don't know. I was served with a subpoena late last night ordering me to be here today. So," he shrugged, "here I am."

Daniel continued to stare while Jake nervously paced around the semi-crowded hallway. Daniel not thinking about anything in particular. Jake trying to figure out a good excuse for why Daniel should leave and get the hell out of there. Before he could come up with a plausible reason, a deputy appeared through the doorway to let everyone know court was resuming.

Upon hearing her name called, Antoinette Hardy rose from her seat toward the back of the room on the side behind the defense table. She politely stepped past three spectators and reached the aisle between the two sections. She was dressed in her best dress. The navy blue one with white trim, black flats and a small hat that matched her dress only partially covering her short curly hair with the touches of gray starting to appear. She stood up straight, threw back her shoulders and with more dignity than she felt, nervously clutching the small hand bag, walked toward the front.

Marc had stepped to the gate and politely held it open for her and they nodded to each other as she passed, Antoinette nervously smiling at him as he reassuringly, lightly squeezed her right arm as she walked by. She walked up to the witness stand was sworn in by the clerk, took her seat and the defense's case was underway.

Having spent two hours at her home the day before, Marc was able to conduct her questioning without even bothering to use his notes. He sat at the table while he led her over the preliminary questions about name and address and how they had met but saving the details of their meeting.

"On which side of Chicago is your house located, Mrs. Hardy?"

"It's on the east side, between 34th and 35th," she politely answered.

"How far from 34th?"

"We're the third house from the corner."

"Mrs. Hardy, were you in the courtroom this morning while I questioned the State's last witness, Martin Hobbs?"

"Yes, I was," she answered.

"Did you hear all of the questions and answers, ma'am?"

"Yes, I did."

"What were your impressions, if any, about Mr. Hobbs's testimony?"

"He was lying," she answered emphatically which immediately brought about a minor explosion in the courtroom as some spectators audibly gasped, several yelled and media people began noisily pulling out notepads to write down what they had just heard. The jurors, the only ones that mattered, all noticeably sat up to stare wide eyed as if they had not heard her correctly. "He's not telling the truth," she added.

At this exact moment, while everyone else stared in awe at the witness, Marc stole a quick glance at Jake Waschke, the only one in the courtroom who noticed that the expression on his face had remained totally impassive and unchanged when the witness verbally crucified his snitch with her accusation.

Prentiss slammed down his gavel and forcefully yelled, "There will be order in this courtroom or I will have the deputies clear it."

At the exact same moment, Slocum and Gondeck both came out of their chairs and Slocum vehemently said, "Objection, your Honor this outrageous..."

"Both of you sit down," Prentiss told them regaining his control. "Mr. Kadella," he continued looking at Marc, "you'd better have the goods to back that up."

"I do, your Honor," Marc replied while watching the juries' reaction and noticing neither Slocum nor Gondeck dared look at them. "Bear with me and we'll get there."

"All right then, objection overruled, for now, but you'd better be careful here."

"Yes, your Honor."

"Why do you say that, ma'am?" Marc continued.

"Because, Mr. Kadella, the way he told it, he must've been right in front of my house. You know, when he said he saw the man go by him."

"Go on, ma'am, tell the jury what you told me," Marc prodded after she paused.

"He said he got a good look at the man's face because of the light from the streetlight in front o' my house. Well, sir, that light's been out since April 13th, my grandson's birthday. And I still can't get the City to get off their butts, sorry your Honor," she added sheepishly glancing up at Prentiss. "They still ain't got out there to fix it."

As Marc rose to address Prentiss, he stole another glance at Slocum and Gondeck, both of whom sat staring impassively at the witness. Both trying to look as if this was the most natural testimony they had heard and was exactly what they expected. Marc looked at Prentiss and said, "May we approach, you Honor?"

After Prentiss had granted permission, the three lawyers went up to him and Marc whispered, "Judge, we have her phone records detailing all of her calls to the city engineer's office to report the light. We are prepared to bring in the record keeper from the phone company to authenticate it unless Mr. Slocum will stipulate to it and allow it in now."

"Mr. Slocum?" Prentiss asked, masking his displeasure with the recent turn of events, while Marc handed Slocum, Gondeck and the judge copies of the phone records.

Slocum took a minute to glance over them, his mind racing so furiously he wasn't even seeing the document in his hand let alone reading it. "Um, yes, I guess that will be okay, your Honor. Save the court's time. We'll so stipulate," he finally muttered.

"Very well, Mr. Kadella. Admit it through this witness," Prentiss told Marc.

They went back to their seats, Marc delighted with his minor victory. The phone records weren't essential. Probably weren't even necessary judging by the looks the jurors were giving Slocum and Gondeck. But he wanted the document into evidence. He wanted it back in the jury room to be passed around the table to serve as a constant reminder that the State's only eyewitness had lied about a key piece of testimony.

Marc spent a few minutes with Antoinette, going over the phone record detailing the calls she had made to the City. He moved about the courtroom now, his turn to play the actor, having the document marked, questioning the witness about all of the calls and after it had been formally entered into evidence, he walked over to the jury box, handed it to the juror closest to the witness, turned to Prentiss and concluded his questioning.

Prentiss turned her over to Slocum who impressed Marc with his ability to compose himself after his case had taken a shot to the groin, rose and politely passed, for now, on cross examination of the witness.

As she passed by the defense table, Marc stood up and briefly shook her hand in both of his. She peeked around Marc and smiled at Carl who looked back at her, a grateful look in his eyes as he silently mouthed the words "thank you" to her. She silently said "you're welcome" back to him, smiled at Marc then quickly left the still buzzing courtroom as Prentiss told Marc to call his next witness.

Marc, still standing, nervously looked at his watch, turned to the back of the room and just as Antoinette was leaving, saw Tony Carvelli guiding a wheelchair bound woman through the door. Marc, with obvious relief, turned back to Prentiss and said, "The defense calls Louise Curtin, your Honor." Before the words had completely left his lips, he turned his head to look directly at Jake Waschke who couldn't prevent himself from jerking upright in his seat, his eyes wide as he watched his mother rolling toward the gate. He looked over at Daniel who returned Jake's stare with a wide-eyed, puzzled expression on his face and a shrug of his shoulders

Slocum, seeing Jake's reaction, stood and said to Prentiss, "Your Honor, we demand to know who this witness is and the nature of her testimony before she's allowed to take the stand."

Jake bolted out of his seat, turned back to see his brother also standing as their mother whirred past them toward the gate leading to the well of the court.

Louise looked up at Jake as she passed him, said "I'm sorry," to him when she saw Jake glaring at Tony as Jake said, just loud enough for only Tony to hear above the rising commotion from the crowd, "What the hell is this, Carvelli?"

Tony released his guiding grip on the wheelchair handles, turned to Jake, stared back at his old friend and said, quietly, "It's over Jake. It's all done. Shut up and sit down."

Prentiss, hardly able to conceal his anger with the disruption, rapped his gavel twice, and yelled, "That's it. Recess. I want everyone, all of the lawyers and," he continued pointing the gavel at Jake, "you too Lieutenant, in my chambers now. I'm gonna find out what the hell is going on here."

Marc had remained standing impassively the entire time and was the first one through the door with Slocum and Gondeck right behind him. When all three men had entered Prentiss' office, Prentiss standing behind his desk still in his robe, looked at Marc and angrily said. "All right Mr. Kadella, who is that woman and what is she doing here?"

"I think we should wait for the Lieutenant before I tell you, Judge," Marc answered. He turned to look through the door and two or three seconds later, Jake appeared.

"Come in, Lieutenant," Prentiss said with a beckoning wave of his hand. "Now then, who is she?"

"She's Lieutenant Waschke's mother, your Honor," Marc answered. "And she's going to tell us why the Lieutenant planted evidence to frame my client," he continued after turning to look directly at Waschke.

"What!? That's ridiculous," Jake answered.

"Is it?" Marc calmly said. "Do you really want me to put her on the stand? Air the family history. Tell the courtroom, all those reporters, why and what lengths you'll go to protect your brother," he continued as he took a couple of short steps toward Jake as he thrust his hands into his suit pockets.

"I heard the story, all of it, Friday evening. I knew all along it was you. Had to be. But I couldn't figure out who you were protecting and why. If you were protecting someone, that is. Or, did you just want a conviction? But that didn't make sense unless you were sure the killings would stop."

"This is bullshit. I don't have to listen to this," Jake said looking first at Marc who had stopped when he reached the small table between himself and Waschke, then at the silent stares of the other three men.

"It was you, Jake," Marc quietly said as he pulled his right hand from his pocket. He held up an object he had taken from his pocket, a small shiny brass key with a square handle. He held it up and slowly moved his hand so the four men could all get a look at it then tossed it on the table where it rattled a bit before himself and the police lieutenant.

"What do you say, Lieutenant?" Marc continued. "Should we get the key off the exhibit table? Go down to the locker where you planted the clothes for your detective to find. Check it out and see if that key, the one out there now, fits the lock? It won't and we both know it.

"This key here," Marc said pointing to the one he had removed from his pocket, while Waschke silently stared at it, the blood drained from his face, "is the one for locker number 120. The one right next to where the police found the clothes that are in evidence. Looks like the same key as the one found on Carl and was inventoried when he was arrested. Identical in color and shape. Except this one's just a little bit smaller. Close enough so that a casual inspection wouldn't pick up the difference."

Marc reached down and picked up the metal key with the number 120 stamped into it, held it up between his right thumb and index finger, turned to Prentiss and said, "I got this yesterday and before court this morning, your Honor, I compared it to the one that's been placed in evidence. They're not the same size. That one out there, that's the one my client did have on him when he was arrested. Lieutenant Waschke here," he continued pointing the key at Jake, "according to the chain-of-custody slip, checked the key out of the inventory room and back in. He was also the one who gave it to Detective Jefferson to search for the locker. He couldn't be sure what Jefferson would find in the locker that fit Carl's key so, he planted the clothes, gave that key to Jefferson and when he put the key back, he put the right one, Carl's key, back into inventory. He also was the one who planted the knife. I don't know where he got it, but he did it."

"Well, Lieutenant?" Prentiss quietly asked.

"It's over, Jake," Marc softly said. "I don't want to put your mother on the stand, but I will. I also know about you and Hobbs. Don't ask me how but I know he's your snitch and if I have to I can prove it."

Jake looked at Marc, his lips tightly pursed together, a sadness in his eyes. He sighed heavily, turned and stepped past an obviously stunned Slocum and Steve Gondeck. As he approached Prentiss, still standing behind his desk, he reached into the inside pocket of his sport coat, removed the leather folder with his badge and police identification and placed it on the desktop. He then again reached under his coat, unclipped his holster and placed it and his handgun next to the wallet with his badge. He stood over the desk, the tips of the fingers of his right hand lightly brushing over the objects he had just placed there, staring at them in the silent room for several seconds.

Finally, he lifted his head, looked at the judge and quietly said, "I'll surrender these to you, your Honor and that's all I'll say until I talk to a lawyer."

"Shit," was the next word spoken by Slocum, as he collapsed heavily into the leather chair he had been standing in front of.

Marc looked at Gondeck and ignoring Slocum, said, "Steve, I want the charges dismissed, now. This thing needs to come to an end."

Gondeck looked down at Slocum seated in the chair, his right elbow on the armrest, the hand on his forehead as he stared down at the floor. "Craig?" Gondeck quietly asked the county attorney.

Slocum sat silently for a few more seconds, weighing his political future, then, finally, nodded his assent. "You do it," was all he said.

Prentiss picked up his phone and told his clerk to send in a deputy sheriff. Jake walked to the window and looked down at the construction site for the new stadium and across the river to the University campus. Marc returned the key to his pocket alternating his eyes between the back of the big cop and the slumped form of Slocum. He found it funny, in an ironic way, that he felt better looking at Slocum than he did Waschke. It occurred to him that Waschke maintained more dignity though his life was irreparably shattered than did the lawyer who had nothing more significant than political problems to clear up. After a few minutes the deputy came in, stood in the doorway surveying the scene, awaiting instructions.

Gondeck moved over to Jake, lightly placed a hand on one of his shoulders and softly said, "Jake, the deputy's here. We're going to have to place you under arrest. Will the cuffs be necessary?"

"No," Jake quietly replied as he turned back to the room's interior.

"Take the Lieutenant across the street and have him booked on a charge of obstructing justice. That will be enough for now. There will be more charges later. Get him a lawyer and I'll be over in a while," Gondeck said to the deputy who looked at Prentiss who nodded his assent.

As Jake was walking toward the door, he stopped, turned back to Marc and stuck out his right hand. After a brief hesitation, Marc grasped it in a firm grip and the two men shook. Waschke weakly smiled and half-seriously, said, "I'm looking for a good lawyer. Want a client?"

EIGHTY-SIX

Slocum slipped out the back way and took the elevator back to his office leaving Gondeck with the job of facing the courtroom and dismissing the case against Carl. When they had retaken their places after the discussion in chambers Marc had managed to contain himself and gave no indication to Carl what was coming. At first, no one seemed to notice that Slocum and Waschke were missing but as soon as Prentiss had resumed the proceedings Steve Gondeck stood and moved the court to dismiss all charges and Carl, though it took a while to sink in, was a free man.

Bedlam erupted in the courtroom and around the defense table with a good deal of hugging, back slapping and even a few tears. After a few minutes Prentiss ordered everybody out and Carl was taken away, this time without the handcuffs and leg irons, to go back to the jail to retrieve his possessions and be processed out of the jail and released.

After being proclaimed by Joe Fornich to be the world's greatest lawyer and assured that Joe would leave no stone unturned to get him paid, Marc finally had a moment with Tony Carvelli.

"Where's Maddy?" Marc asked, sorely disappointed she had missed the celebration.

"She went out to Stillwater this morning," Tony answered. "She called me early this morning and asked me to meet her at Jake's mother's place and bring her here today. Said she had to go out to the prison to check something out," he shrugged.

"Can you get Louise home?" Marc asked.

"Sure, no problem," Tony answered. "And hey, congratulations counselor," he growled. "You did a helluva job."

Marc stood in the almost empty courtroom staring at the back of Tony's leather coat as he helped guide Louise Curtin through the door. Tony paused in the doorway, looked back at Marc and the two men gave each other a casual wave as the door swung closed.

Marc made a half turn to look at Steve Gondeck, the only other person still in the courtroom. Gondeck had stepped up to Marc and after shifting his briefcase to his left hand held out his right to his friendly foe.

"Congratulations, Marc," he said. "So, tell me," he continued after the two of them had released their grip, "what was she going to testify to."

"You don't want to know," Marc said.

"Yes, I do," Gondeck replied. "In fact, now that I probably have to prosecute Jake, I have to know."

Marc looked at him for a moment then said, "Yeah, I suppose you're right."

"And it's not privileged. I could force you to testify," he added with a sly grin.

"Okay," Marc solemnly answered. "I guess so. When Jake and Daniel were kids, I mean real young maybe as early as when Daniel was four or five, his father, Jake's stepfather, abused the boys. Sexually. Bad stuff, I guess."

"I figured it was something like that," Gondeck said with clear distaste.

"Daniel, mostly. At least he got the worst of it. Jake too she told me. Anyway, it went on for a few years. He stopped entirely with Jake when he got to be about nine or ten. Big enough to fight back. Jake, the big brother," he continued as he held up his hands, palms upward, and shrugged, "finally put a stop to it."

"How? I mean, what did he do?"

Marc leaned forward and shifted his eyes about the room, checking to see if anyone else was listening, then whispered, "He killed the old man."

"What?" Gondeck said, his eyes wide.

"Relax. He didn't mean to. From what Louise said, the guy had it coming. A real asshole. Drunk a lot and beating her and the boys. Forcing Daniel to do things. Oral sex and what-have-you. One Friday night," Marc continued leaning back against the edge of his table while Gondeck continued to stare in disbelief, "the old man's sitting in the kitchen getting shitfaced drunk like usual. He gets up to go down in the basement for more booze and does a header off the second step onto the concrete and breaks his fool neck. Dead instantly, she told me."

"Sounds like an accident," Gondeck interjected.

"Yeah," Marc agreed. "That's what the coroner ruled. But it wasn't exactly an accident. Jake had plugged a burned-out lightbulb into the socket at the bottom of the stairs. Then, he rigged up a rope on the stairs and waited for the old drunk to come down. He starts down the stairs, flips on the light and nothing happens. He tries to go down the stairs in the dark except Jake is hiding down there waiting for him. When Jake hears him on the stairs, he pulls the rope tight, trips him and down he goes."

"Jesus Christ," Gondeck softly said. "How old was he?"

"Maybe eleven or twelve. Told Louise about it. Said he did it to protect Daniel. Said he didn't mean to kill him. Just scare him so he'd leave Daniel alone."

"I'll be damned. Quite a story. Pretty gutsy for a twelve-year-old kid."

"I'll say. Anyway, Daniel's been a little screwed up ever since. Both boys blamed their mother, especially Daniel. She told them she didn't know what was going on, but they never really believed her. You think Jake'll be prosecuted for it? For the killing?"

"No, not much chance of that at this point," Gondeck replied. "We can probably use it to get a plea out of him and leniency. What a mess," he sighed.

"What about Daniel Waschke?" Marc asked.

"We're going to have to look at him real hard. Since your guy didn't do it and considering what Jake was up to, that makes Daniel suspect number one."

"The politics are going to be interesting."

"That's putting it mildly," Gondeck said. "There's going to be a political shit storm over this. Why do you think Slocum is hiding under his desk? He isn't just in the eye of the hurricane over this clusterfuck, he is the eye of the hurricane."

"Nobody deserves it more," Marc replied. "Well, Steve, I have to run. See you around."

"Marc, congratulations again. You did a great job for your client."

EIGHTY-SEVEN

Maddy had been inside jails and prisons before, in fact, many times. Every time she left one though, she always did the same thing, the same thing she did now. The moment she stepped through the door leading to the public parking lot at the prison in Stillwater, she looked up at the sky and took in several deep breaths. Inhaling what she felt was the sweet air of freedom. It always amused her when she would hear some loud-mouthed politician pandering for votes conning people about how good convicts had it in prison. You could bet, she firmly believed, the idiots that whine like that had never been inside one of these places. As she walked toward her car she always had the same sensation, the same thought: *I'm getting in my car and going home and you're staying there. I get to do whatever I want, go wherever I want and you're staying there and go where you're told, when you're told and do what you're told. Have a nice night.*

The weather where she was, east of the Cities, across the St. Croix River from Wisconsin, was clear, sunny and beautiful. She had removed the light, tan, wool jacket that matched her slacks and had tossed it on the backseat. As she headed west on Highway 36 to go back to Minneapolis, she could see the dark, gray skies coming across the prairie. She pushed the car to seventy-**five,** reached in her purse to retrieve her phone, flipped it open, punched in the number, pressed the call button and put the phone to her ear. She had news she couldn't wait to share with Marc and wanted to try him at the office in case he was back from the trial. She had not heard a radio or seen a TV all day and the news of the trial had not yet reached her.

She held the phone to her ear and softly cursed when she realized the batteries were too weak. Maddy tossed the phone on the passenger seat, pushed the speedometer to eighty and turned the radio on. Within a few minutes the radio announcer came on with the day's big story, the sudden and unexpected dismissal of all charges in the serial murder trial that had captivated the media, the entire state and a good part of the nation, for the past several weeks. The announcer also told Maddy about, what appeared to be, the related arrest of Minneapolis homicide detective, Jacob Waschke.

"Holy shit," Maddy whispered, her eyes wide staring straight ahead as the news sank in. Instead of being elated though, a gloominess came over her as gray as the mass in the sky inexorably moving toward her, and she toward it.

Earlier that day, after practically floating out of the courtroom, Marc had spent almost two hours being interviewed by just about every newspaper, TV and radio station in the upper Midwest. He was patient, cheerful and cooperative with all of them. Publicity like this couldn't be bought he realized, and he figured he better play it for all it was worth. His practice was in a shambles and truth be told, he was practically on the verge of bankruptcy.

After a quick lunch at the burger joint down the street from his office, Marc parked in the lot behind the building, took the backstairs two at a time and entered the office acting like Caesar returning from Gaul. Everyone was there, waiting for him, including a couple of bottles of champagne, the good stuff Chris Grafton pointed out to him amid the congratulations and laughter.

"Where's the broad?" Connie Mickelson asked him shortly after his arrival.

"The what?" he asked giving her an admonitory look while shaking his head.

"Okay, okay, Mr. Politically Correct. Where's Madeline?"

"She went to Stillwater this morning," he answered. "I'm not sure where she is. I was hoping she'd called by now. Why?"

"Because I'm taking everybody out to dinner tonight. You know, to celebrate the big victory. And," she continued slyly, "I've got some news of my own."

"Don't tell me, husband number, what, fourteen lined up?" he said as the others laughed.

"Number five, smart ass," Connie laughed punching him playfully on the arm. "At least, I think it's five. Yeah, five. Anyway, bring Maddy along if you talk to her."

Marc spent the rest of the afternoon on the telephone. There had been a half inch stack of congratulatory phone messages waiting for him when he returned, and the calls poured in all day. Shortly after 4:30 P.M., with the phone still pressed to one ear, he heard a rap on his door and Carolyn stuck her head in. With his free hand he waved her in and motioned to a chair.

"That's interesting as hell, Paul," he said into the mouthpiece while Carolyn closed the door behind her. "I'm not sure what it means, but thanks for calling. It is kind of strange. Makes you wonder doesn't it?"

Carolyn stood patiently by the door while Marc listened to the caller for a few seconds. "Listen, I have to go but if anything comes up, I'll let you know." After another pause he said, "I'd appreciate it, Paul. Thanks. Bye now," he concluded and hung up the phone.

"What's up?" he asked Carolyn as he let his feet drop from the desk top.

"Maddy's here," she answered, "and I ..."

"Oh, good," he said interrupting her and standing at the same time. "What?" he asked seeing Carolyn still standing.

"I just want to thank you for not bringing John into it, the dumb ass."

"My pleasure, sweetheart," he said as he came around the desk, his arms extended to her. While they gave each other a warm, friendly hug he asked, "Any problems at home?"

"Well, we're okay," she said with a smile as they released each other. "I let him know I wasn't real happy that he didn't tell you sooner. And I have to admit, I was pretty worried about the consequences if he had to testify."

"Carolyn, I'm just delighted it wasn't necessary," he said softly. "Now, let's get Maddy in here."

After they had both taken their seats, Marc behind the desk, Maddy in a client chair, she added, "So, it's over?"

"Yeah, it's over," he answered grinning.

"There's something weird here, though," she continued. "I went out to the prison today ..."

"I heard," he said.

"And I got some strange information."

"What?"

"Seems our boy Carl was pretty good with a knife."

"We heard about that. So?"

"He had a neighbor, the guy in the cell next to him. I heard they were pretty good friends."

"How good?" Marc asked cocking his eyebrows.

"Not that good," she said seeing the look in his eyes. "The guy in the cell next to him was none other than a certain Walter Bingham. Remember him?"

"Excuse me? What? Are you serious?" Marc said obviously shocked.

"You don't suppose ..." Maddy began to say.

"Wait," he said holding up a hand to stop her. "Just before you came in. I was on the phone to a lawyer I know, Paul Eberhard. He represents good ol' Wally. Wally walked from all charges. Seems the cops screwed up the search warrant. Paul told me Wally pointed it out to him right away, as soon as Wally showed it to him. They had the wrong address on it and Paul said he got the feeling Wally knew it all along."

"You think Carl put him up to it? That he and Carl set up his testimony? Get on the stand and look like he's obviously lying to try to make the jury pissed at the prosecutors? You think Carl's that clever?" Maddy asked.

"I don't know," Marc said after reflecting on it for a moment. "Maybe. I don't know. It's a pretty good stunt if they did it. Pulled it off pretty good, too."

"You want more weird?"

"No. What?" Marc said.

"Guess what Carl's cell number was?"

"What?" he asked, puzzled. "His cell number? I don't know why?"

"Come on, think about it. Guess what his cell number was? And what we didn't notice before, what was his apartment number?"

Marc continued to look at her with a puzzled expression. Then, after three or four seconds, his face changed as the light went on. "Don't tell me: 119?"

"You got it. And good old Wally was in 120. And guess who was in 118?"

"Don't do this to me," he laughed.

"Steve Frechette. Remember him? He was the other guy that assaulted Carl. The one Ed Hill testified about. The one we couldn't find. I can't believe the cops overlooked all this."

"Why not, we did? What the hell does this mean?" Marc asked, clearly reflecting on the news. "That Carl's got a thing for the number 119 now? So what? And he was helping us out from inside the jail? Again, so what?"

"I'm not sure what it means but it strikes me our boy is a lot smarter than he let on."

"It's ...," Marc said staring at her and shrugging. "It's, I don't know. I'm not sure what it is. I guess it all worked out all right."

"I guess," she said nodding in agreement.

EIGHTY-EIGHT

Maddy turned the key to her apartment door, pushed it open, walked in and dropped her purse and keys on the small table by the door. The skies had opened up while they had been in Malloy's celebrating Marc's victory and Connie's most recent engagement with, arguably, the best steak dinner in the Cities. Everyone in the office, including spouses and Connie's betrothed, had wined and dined the evening away until just before midnight when the rain had finally let up and everyone made a hasty exit to their cars. Just before she had reached her building the rain had started again making her, once more, very grateful for underground parking.

She threw the wall switch illuminating the living room with the light from a table lamp in front of the picture window across the room and headed for the kitchen. She made the right-hand turn into the kitchen, turned on the light and found the cordless phone on the table where she had left it that morning. Concerned with the battery strength after it spent the entire day out of the recharger, she quickly dialed Marc's number. Holding the phone to her left ear, she wiggled out of her jacket while listening to it ring. After the fourth ring she was becoming disappointed with the expectation that his answering machine was about to pick up when she suddenly heard his voice.

"Hi, it's me," she said.

"What's up?" he replied.

"Well, there's been something kind of bugging me and I didn't get a chance to talk to you about it at dinner."

"What's that?" he asked.

"Well," she said with hesitation, "it's probably nothing and it's too late to care, but I can't help wondering about it."

"Spit it out, Madeline," he said with pleasant impatience.

"The quarters. You know, the ones the cops found in the locker with those clothes Waschke planted. How the hell did those quarters with Carl's prints on them get in that coin box?"

"Waschke must've planted them too," Marc replied.

"Where'd he get them? Carl didn't have three quarters on him when he was arrested and if he had found them in Carl's apartment there were other cops there. Someone would've noticed," she said as she paced over to the kitchen counter, her jacket held lightly in her right hand her back to the doorway.

After a long moment of silence between them, Marc finally said, "I don't know. I'm not sure where they came from, but you're right about one thing, it doesn't really matter anymore."

"I know," she sighed. "It's just one of those little loose end kinda things that's been bugging me. That and the things I found out at Stillwater today. Maybe we'll find out from Waschke's trial."

"Maybe. Look Maddy, it's been a long day. Get some sleep and I'll talk to you tomorrow. We'll see about getting paid. We earned it."

"Yeah," she laughed softly. "We sure did."

They said their goodbyes and she stood at the counter, staring blankly at the phone still in her hand chewing on her lower lip. She unconsciously shrugged her shoulders and as she was placing the phone in its receptacle, she felt more than saw or heard, a presence in the room an instant before her hair was jerked back and her head snapped upward.

"Hello, Madeline," she heard a familiar voice whisper directly into her right ear. She could feel the bumps of the serrated knife blade against her throat as her eyes stared with unblinking terror at the kitchen ceiling, her body frozen and her breathing suspended.

For the first three or four seconds her mind became an uncomprehending void, her senses having totally abandoned her as her subconscious prepared for death. When her consciousness began to reappear, she felt herself being pushed up against the counter by the force of the man as he leaned heavily against her. Her heart was pounding wildly in her chest and she felt herself starting to breathe again as she heard the voice whisper, "God, you don't know how long I've waited for this."

She could feel the tip of his nose touching the inside of her ear and heard him inhale, a hissing sound coming from his mouth as the air passed over clenched teeth while he continued to hold her head back, his fingers entwined in her hair, the knife pressed against her throat. She could feel his erection pressing against her right hip, but now her breathing was starting to normalize, her heart slowing and her eyes refocusing.

A wave of revulsion passed through her when she felt his tongue pass over the side of her face and across her ear. The grip on her hair loosened for an instant and her head moved slightly away as the pressure decreased. He jerked her head again and she let out a short yelp from the pain it caused.

"What do you want, Carl?" she was able to say in a whispered croak.

"The same thing you do," he whispered back into her ear. "The same thing you've wanted since we first met. The same thing you all want but most men are afraid to give it to you. A little rough and tough."

"No, Carl. That's not true," she replied, surprising herself with how calm she was as her mind began to work again. "Put the knife down and we'll do it nice. I'll show you. You're right. I've wanted you from the start, but not like this. You don't need the knife."

"This," he said holding the blade before her eyes, turning it over and over. "No. I can't put my friend away," he said softly in an eerie, almost childlike voice. He jerked her around to face him, the two of them staring into each other's eyes and he said in his normal voice, "Don't jerk me around, Maddy. This is the same knife I did that whore with. Our beloved governor's daughter. See the tip?" he asked, still using the same normal inflection as he held the point of the knife an inch from her left eye. "I bent the tip on the inside of her goddamn skull so don't try any bullshit here. Okay bitch? Play ball and maybe you live. Anymore bullshit and it's lights out. Understand?"

Maddy nodded her head slightly, less than half an inch to avoid poking herself in the eye. Carl moved the knife back under her chin and pressed the point against her skin hard enough to prick the surface and draw a drop of blood. Still firmly holding her head back with the grip on her hair, he leaned his head close enough to her to touch the tip of her nose with his and slowly and calmly said, "I said, do you understand?"

"Yes," she whispered flatly without any fear in her voice or her eyes. "I understand."

"Very good, Madeline," Carl said moving his head back, smiling at her. "Now, let's go out in the living room and have a little fun. At least, it'll be fun for me. You," he shrugged, "well, we'll see."

Carl took a half-step back and with the knife point still under her chin and his grip on her hair, began pushing her toward the open kitchen entry way. He forced her down the short hallway between the kitchen and bedroom out into the living room. He roughly began to guide her to the open space between the television against the wall to their left and the couch to their right. Just as his pace began to quicken Maddy abruptly stopped which caused Carl to run into her from behind and just as he did, the knife moved a couple of inches away from the underside of her chin.

In that instant, her right hand shot up and her fingers wrapped themselves around the wrist of his right hand the one holding the knife. She drove the sharpened, half-inch nail of her thumb into the soft flesh of the underside of his wrist, digging it in as deeply as she could, breaking the skin, drawing blood and pinching a nerve that made him cry out in pain.

Keeping her grip on the wrist of the hand with the knife now pointed right at her face, she immediately reached back and down between his legs, grabbed his testicles and squeezed with all of the strength her fear and anger could give. Carl began to scream and as she continued to dig her thumbnail into his wrist, she pulled down on his scrotum, let her legs buckle straight down and as her knees hit the floor she rolled her shoulders forward and flipped him over her back onto the floor.

Carl rolled two or three times across the carpeting, his right hand still clutching the knife, his left thrust into his groin to ease the wave of fire that washed up from his balls into his chest.

Maddy remained motionless, kneeling head down on the floor for two or three seconds while her mind began to grasp what her reflexes had just accomplished. Overcoming his pain, Carl managed to struggle to his knees, then to his feet, glaring at Maddy, his face a mask of rage and pain. As she sprang to her feet, he continued scowling at her, his right hand holding the knife, waving it slowly back and forth, his left hand still massaging his sore and swollen testicles.

"You whore! You bitch!" he snarled. "I'm gonna make you sorry you were ever born."

"Give it up, Carl," she heard herself calmly say. "It's over. You either put the knife down now, or I'll take it away from you and cut that teeny little dick of yours off and shove it down your throat."

Carl moved toward her, slowly, still moving the knife around in a small circle, his left hand now extended in front of him as if for balance as he slightly crouched. Maddy eyed him over as she cautiously moved backwards, watching the knife while looking for an opening. He backed her up toward the entryway door and then, when he got close enough, he lunged forward and swiped at her from right to left and upward with the knife. Dipping her right shoulder, Maddy dodged to her right to avoid the blade as it slashed by, pivoted on her right foot and snapped a sharp kick with her left leg, driving her left heel into his midsection.

Quicker than she believed he was, as Maddy's foot began to make contact with him, Carl's right hand flashed back just missing her throat but slashing her across the left shoulder. The blade sliced through her blouse and opened a jagged four-inch gash a half inch deep through her skin. Not enough to incapacitate her but enough to put her on her knees.

The power of her expertly planted foot drove Carl to the floor and almost knocked the wind out of him. Years of prison time and jail food, with little to do but exercise, had made him lean and a lot stronger than his slender frame showed. He was back on his feet with catlike quickness and furious now with the brazenness shown by this woman, he made a headlong charge at her, just as she was pulling herself up.

Maddy saw him coming just in time to grab his right wrist and avoid the knife thrust as he slammed into her. They crashed against the small table along the wall by the entryway door. Carl, with a crazed look in his eyes, tried desperately to turn the knife toward her. His left hand came up, grabbed her throat and slammed her head against the wall. She was powerless to prevent this; all of her strength being used with her two hands struggling to keep the knife from slicing into her beautiful face. She stared at the knifepoint, the wound in her shoulder ebbing her strength away as the point crept closer and closer to her eye.

Carl kept pushing and choking with his left hand literally lifting her off the floor, crushing her against the wall and choking off her air. He knew he was winning and it would soon be over, but in the back of his mind, he also knew that the darkness within him, the insatiable hole, would still be empty if it ended too quickly. Just as Maddy slipped up onto the table, his grasp on her throat eased and as it did, she released her right hand hammered it against the hand at her throat, knocked it aside and bobbed her head to the right as the knife flashed past her ear to stick into the wallboard behind her.

As Carl began to pull the knife from the wall, while still sitting on the table, Maddy raised her legs up and under him until her knees touched her chin, planted both feet on his chest and as his left fist smashed into the side of her face, shoved him back with all of the strength she had left.

Carl flew backward, his arms flailing, still clutching the knife as he sprawled across the living room floor. With the force of the push, Maddy and the table crashed to the floor, her purse spilling open inches from her face. She lay on her right side, stunned and gasping for air, her head pounding from being hammered against the wall, her eyes watered, blurry and unfocused from the pain. The gash across her shoulder was pouring blood and she could feel her strength rapidly expire. Maddy forced her mind to snap back and without lifting her head, she turned her eyes to see her attacker slowly rising from the floor. Carl staggered a bit and moved from in front of the lamp, the light causing a bright reflection that caught the attention of her eyes from an object peeking out from the opening of her purse.

Realizing what it was, she reached over to it with all of her remaining strength, grabbed the shiny bright metal object and in one quick motion, rolled onto her back, thumbed off the safety, pointed it toward the madman and squeezed off a shot. In the confines of the apartment, the gun roared like a cannon, the explosion ringing her ears. Maddy had expected to see Carl go down, but instead, the crash of the lamp and the sudden darkness made her realize she had missed him completely and had blown up her table lamp. She hesitated for just a moment, the room now only partially illuminated by the spill from the overhead kitchen light, aimed and fired again. This time the small bullet found its mark as Carl staggered back and went down on one knee, gripping his left side.

She struggled to her feet, still pointing the gun at Carl. They stayed this way, two wounded, desperate animals staring at each other, the only sound in the room their heavy breathing. Carl, his eyes glazed and unfocused, the blood oozing from between his fingers as he held the wound, snarled, "You bitch. You shot me, goddammnit."

"And I'll do it again if you don't put the knife down, now!" she roared.

He hesitated for a moment, the small caliber bullet causing less pain than he would have believed. Then, the monster within him reared up and as he started to rise, he howled like the wounded animal he was and came at her. Maddy calmly pointed the gun directly at his forehead, squeezed the trigger and heard nothing. The blast she expected didn't come because, as small caliber automatics are sometimes prone to do, it had failed to eject the last shell.

Carl came on howling his wounded animal scream, expecting, almost hoping, that the lights would go out forever. Instead, he felt a sharp pain on the top of his head as the gun bounced off it when Maddy, in blind desperation, threw it at him. The blow staggered and stopped him, causing a gash to open on his scalp and blood to come gushing from the wound. He stumbled backward, still holding the gunshot wound with his left hand and saw Maddy come charging toward him.

When the gun failed to fire her mind snapped completely. She rifled the useless weapon at him and with her eyes on fire with hate, her teeth flashing like an animal's fangs, her hands held out before her like claws, she threw herself at him. She saw the knife flash toward her and her mind, still coherent enough to send out reflexive messages, ordered her to turn slightly and avoid it, grabbed at the wrist with her left hand while she slammed her clawlike right hand into his face and eyes. Maddy managed to slow the knife thrust but not stop it completely and as the point entered her right side just above the hip, she felt her fingernails digging into the softness of his eyeballs.

Carl screamed from the pain as the fire erupted in his brain from the slicing of her fingernails into his eyes and face. Maddy, her hatred, anger and fear fed by the attack, jerked his hand backward extracting the bent tipped blade from her flesh. Carl released his grip on the knife and tried to grab his ravaged face with both hands, but she wouldn't release his wrist to allow it. Without realizing what she was doing, she twisted his arm down, spun him around and pinned the arm behind his back. She grabbed a handful of hair at the back of his head and with her last ounce of strength, screamed, "GET THE FUCK OUT OF HERE!" and drove him across the room head first through the bay window overlooking LaSalle Avenue.

As the glass exploded outward, a blast of cold, wet wind swept through the room, the rain hitting Maddy in the face. She stood at the open window, numbly staring down at the sight of Carl's body hurtling silently downward. She watched, her mind working in slow motion, his arms flapping as if attempting flight, the world frozen in place. Just Maddy staring out as the rain poured in while Carl slowly sailed the eight stories down to land on his face on the roof of a three-day old Lexus coupe, its owner, a wayward husband having parked it in a most inconvenient place and time.

The noise from the explosion as Carl hit the car reached her eight floors up, causing her eyes to blink and her mind to start working. Maddy blinked several more times before her consciousness took over again. She gasped at the sight of Carl, the blood from his splattered head seeping out and pooling in the rain on the car's crushed roof. She looked herself over, her right-hand clutching at the wound in her side, her left hand holding her shoulder. She turned away from the window and began to stagger toward the kitchen and the telephone. She took three or four difficult, shaky steps, the room began to spin, and she went down.

EIGHTY-NINE

Marc's sleeping mind heard the first three rings of the telephone, but it wasn't until the fourth ring started that his eyes snapped open.

"Yeah," he groggily said just before it would have gone off for a fifth time.

"Marc? It's Tony," he heard the gruff voice say. "I'm down at Hennepin County Medical Center. Get yer ass down here."

Less than thirty minutes later, Marc heard the soft bell sound as his elevator approached the floor with the room number Carvelli had given him. He stepped through the doors when they were just opened wide enough to permit it and saw his P.I. friend pacing in the hall a few doors down.

"How is she?" he asked.

"Like I told you, she'll be okay. She got cut up a bit and lost a lot of blood. She's gonna need some rest, but she'll be fine," Tony answered as a very young, white coated woman doctor emerged from her room.

It was then that Marc first noticed the police officers. A male and female plainclothes, obviously detectives, and two uniforms. Marc and Tony stepped over to the doctor and Marc asked, "How is she? Can we see her?"

"Are you the Marc she asked for?" the doctor asked.

"Yes I am. How is she?" he asked again, less patiently.

"She'll be fine. She's pretty beat up and she'll need rest, but she'll be fine in no time. You can see her but make it short. And this gentleman," she said pointing her pen at Tony, "can go in too."

The two of them went in past the looks of the obviously annoyed detectives and Marc inaudibly gasped at the sight of her. He went to the bedside, gently took her hand in his and smiled down at her as she weakly opened her eyes and looked up at him.

"Hi sweetheart," he whispered. "How are you feeling?"

"Just great," she groaned, clearing her throat from the discomfort of the tubes in her nose.

"Hi, Tony," she said weakly as she squeezed Marc's hand.

"You're going to be fine, baby," Marc said.

"Carl. Is he dead?" she rasped.

"Oh, yeah. Extremely," Tony answered.

She closed her eyes, softly sighed, opened them, looked directly at Marc and said, "Good, the sonofabitch."

She woke up a little bit then and they stayed in her room for a few more minutes. The three of them making awkward small talk, mostly reassuring themselves that she would, indeed, be all right. It didn't take long before she began to tire, and the two men decided it was time to go. As they were preparing to leave, Marc bent down and kissed her lightly on the cheek and knowing it would cheer her up a bit, said, "I never thought I'd live to say this, but you look like hell."

She smiled weakly at him and said, "So do you, asshole."

"Yeah, but I just got out of bed," he laughed. "I'll be back later today. Get some rest."

They stopped in the hall to talk to the police who agreed, reluctantly, to leave her alone for now. Marc made it clear that he was her lawyer and there was to be no questioning without him being present. The police left and one of the uniforms stayed behind to guard the door. Satisfied, Marc and Tony headed out themselves.

When they reached the sidewalk, Tony said, "That's something isn't it. All along they had the right guy and didn't know it."

"I feel like an idiot," Marc answered.

"Why? How would you know? Besides, you did your job. I feel bad for Jake though. Threw it all away because he thought he was protecting his brother and look at that now."

"What do you mean?" Marc asked.

"You haven't heard? Daniel Waschke was found in his car in the garage yesterday with the engine running. His wife found him when she came home. Rumor has it he wrote a note to Jake. Says he's innocent. The only thing bothering him was his wife was having an affair," Tony related to an obviously stunned Marc who was staring back at him, his eyes wide and his mouth open.

"Well, counselor, it's almost 7:00 A.M. and I been up most of the night. See you later."

"Wait a minute," Marc said. "How'd you find out about Maddy?"

"Cop friend called me from the hospital. Knew I knew her. I'm gonna take off. See you later," Carvelli said as he turned and walked off down the street.

Marc, still a bit shocked by the events of the past twenty-four hours, strolled over to a small retaining wall that circled the hospital's entryway. He sat down on it watching the light, early morning downtown traffic cruising past him on the wet street. He sat there contemplating those events with a sense of wonder and relief. After about fifteen minutes he heard a voice from beside him say, "Hey sailor, looking for a good time?"

He turned his head toward the voice, smiled at the sight of Margaret Tennant and as his heart picked up a couple of beats, said, "God, is it nice to see you."

"How is she?" Margaret asked as she sat down next to him and slipped an arm through his.

"She'll be fine," Marc answered. "With the scars she'll have, no more posing for PLAYBOY any time soon, but I don't think that's a problem," he said smiling at her as he lightly brushed his fingers across her cheek.

"How about you? How're you doing?" she asked.

"Me?" he asked. "I'm okay," he shrugged. "No. No, that's not really true," he continued as he turned away from her to look straight ahead. "I feel a little shitty, truth be told."

"Well, little wonder. The guy you believed was innocent ..." she began to say.

"No, that's not the problem. In fact, that doesn't bother me at all," he interrupted her. "You know what's bothering me?"

"What?"

"I'm beginning to believe every rotten thing you've ever heard about lawyers is absolutely true."

"Why?" she asked, laughing softly.

"This morning, on the way down here, after Tony called and told me what happened and I knew that Maddy would be all right, well, all I could think of was: After Carl went out that window, there isn't a snow-balls-chance-in-hell that Joe Fornich is going to pay me now."

Thank you for your patronage and I truly hope you enjoyed **The Key to Justice**, my very first attempt at writing a novel. It was a great experience and I am very gratified to know that so many readers liked it and that my efforts were not wasted.

Dennis Carstens
Email me at: dcarstens514@gmail.com

Desperate Justice

An excerpt:

Marc Kadella set his meal on his small dining room table. An unidentifiable mass of a frozen diet-food concoction, his feeble attempt to lose a few pounds. As he was pulling out the chair to sit down to his supper, he heard the ring of his cell phone go off on the coffee table in the living room.

"That was quick," he said aloud as he rose from his seat to retrieve the phone.

"Yeah, this is Marc," he said as he put it to his ear.

"Mr. Kadella, this is Judge Prentiss' clerk, Rhonda Petrie," he heard the female voice say.

"Will you please stop calling me that," Marc answered her pleasantly. "You say Mr. Kadella and I want to hand the phone to my Dad. Please, Marc will do just fine."

"I know," he heard her say laughing softly. "It's just that the judge was walking past my desk just then and he can be a stickler about protocol."

"I take it the jury's in," Marc said.

"Yes they are. We're calling everyone. Thirty minutes?" she replied.

"I'll be there," Marc responded. He folded the telephone closed, picked up his meal, dropped it in the garbage and joyfully said, "There's my excuse for grabbing a burger later," grabbed his suit coat off the couch and headed toward the door.

As he drove toward downtown Minneapolis, Marc let his mind wander to reflect back over the past few months and the events that brought him to where he was now. Marc had been a mostly anonymous lawyer, one of tens of thousands, eking out a living as a solo practitioner, struggling along the way, some good years, some not-so-good years, renting space from a successful woman lawyer, Connie Mickelson. They shared the space with two other lawyers in a building on Lake Street, a couple of miles from downtown Minneapolis. Marc mostly enjoyed what he did, practicing 'street law', criminal defense and divorce work being his bread and butter.

About six months ago, another lawyer whom Marc had barely known, Bruce Dolan, had contacted him. Dolan had called him about representing a friend of a good client of his. There were two co-defendants and Dolan could not represent both due to a potential conflict. He went on about how impressed he had been with Marc's handling of the *Fornich* case and because of the seriousness of the charges, his client wanted to be sure the man Dolan could not represent would receive good representation. Would Marc be interested and when could they meet?

Marc had been quite flattered that an attorney with a national reputation such as Bruce Dolan would think of him to co-counsel a case but at the same time, a little alarm bell in the back of his mind began to go off. Marc had been around long enough to heed these types of signals.

Dolan had represented the men at the bail hearing and assured the judge, a typical Hennepin County liberal woman, that the defendants were not a flight risk, the public was not at risk of harm from either man and reasonable bail should be set. In fact, by the time Dolan got done portraying the two accused as misunderstood Boy Scouts, the audience half-expected the judge to apologize to them for the inconvenience of their arrest. At the same time, the lawyer from the county attorney's office was practically jumping out of her own skin in an effort to be heard. She presented ample evidence that the two men were really career criminals and jail was precisely where they belonged.

In the end, almost starry-eyed at having the great Bruce Dolan in her courtroom, along with her normal empathy for all criminal defendants who were obviously driven to crime by being victims themselves, the judge bought Dolan's argument which surprised even Dolan. Bail was granted in the amount of half a million dollars each which was quickly provided by Cashman Bail Bonds, a silent subsidiary of Leo Balkus, and Ike and Butch were released that same day.

Two days after the bail hearing, Marc Kadella received the call from Dolan. He was in his office, the one he rented from one of his office mates, Connie Mickelson, his landlord and good friend, when one of the secretaries buzzed him to let him know Dolan was on the phone for him. After fifteen minutes on the phone listening to Dolan's explanation, Marc agreed to come to his St. Paul office and meet with him and the two defendants.

Marc grabbed his suit coat from the hook on the back of his office door, picked up a briefcase and went into the reception room area to find the entire office standing around waiting for him.

After a ten second silence during which they all stared at him and he looked them over with a puzzled expression, Connie broke the awkward silence and asked, "What's up with you and Dolan? You gonna get too famous for the rest of us?"

"Very funny," Marc replied.

"So, what did he want," asked another of the lawyers in the office, Chris Grafton.

"He's got a case with co-defendants and he's asked me to take one of them and co-counsel," Marc said. "Could be a good deal. Says I could get a decent check out of it and he'd do the heavy lifting. Besides, I could learn some things doing a trial with him."

"From what I've heard, he could learn a few things from you about ethics and honesty," Marc heard one of the secretaries, Carolyn Lucas, say.

"Now, now, Mrs. Cop's wife" Marc said to her in reply while waving an index finger at her and smiling. "Judge not, less ye be judged, or however that goes."

"Just the same," Connie interjected. "His reputation is well deserved. Don't turn your back on him and remember who you represent. You know who Leo Balkus is?"

"Yeah," Marc answered. "I know who he is. And I know Dolan is his lawyer, so?"

"Just be careful," Connie said.

"Yeah, why?" Marc answered.

"I hear those two jamokes that got arrested are Leo's guys," Connie said. "Just be careful. Remember who Dolan works for and it's not those two idiots. His first priority will be to protect Leo."

"How do you know that?" Barry Cline, another one of the lawyers that shared office space with Marc asked.

"I know people and hear things," Connie said.

"No, no," Marc said, holding up a hand to Barry. "She's got a point. I'll keep it in mind, Connie. And thanks. I better go," he continued as he headed toward the door.

Marc followed the shapely, young receptionist toward the back of the suite of offices until they came to what was obviously a conference room. She opened the door and stood aside for him and as he entered the room, she said, "Bruce will join you in just a few minutes. There's coffee and water for you and I'm sure it won't be long." She turned to leave, and the two men seated at the oval-shaped conference table both tilted their heads to watch her as she closed the door.

Marc introduced himself to the men, reaching across the table to shake hands. As he took one of the very comfortable, slightly over-stuffed leather chairs across from them, the larger of the two men said, "So, you must be the lawyer Bruce found to represent me."

"That's up to you, not Bruce," Marc replied to Butch Koll. "He asked me if I'd be interested and I said I'd come and meet you. Whether or not I represent you will be your call, and mine. Not his."

"Okay," Butch said. "Bruce says you're pretty good. You did that serial killer case last year."

"I remember that," Ike interjected snapping his fingers. "You got him off. You did good work on that case, counselor."

"Thanks," Marc replied with a slight shrug, silently pleased with the compliment, even if it came from a career criminal.

At that moment Dolan came in through the door and stepped right up to Marc, extended his hand to shake and said, "Sorry to keep you waiting. You've met our clients?" he asked nodding toward Ike and Butch as he walked to the head of the table and pulled out a chair.

As he did so, Marc looked him over and was again as impressed as the first time he had seen the man. Dolan stood six foot three and weighed a trim two hundred pounds. He had dark hair with just the right touch of gray at the temples and in his mid-fifties looked to be in great shape. About ten years ago, Marc sat in the gallery of a trial Bruce was conducting. Marc had spent several days watching him and the prosecutor of the case, who was also a terrific trial lawyer himself, dueling with each other. Marc could no longer remember much about the case, but he had learned a lot from both of them.

"Have we met?" Dolan asked him as he took his seat at the head of the table. "You look familiar."

"We had lunch at the same table at a CLE seminar a couple years ago."

"Sure," Dolan said snapping his fingers in recognition. "Now I remember. You were sitting next to Judge Tennant. Anyway, these are for you," he continued as he handed a stack of papers to Marc. "Police reports, witness statements that the cops got from the people in the bar. Prelim autopsy report."

"I need to talk to Mr. Koll alone, if you don't mind," Marc said.

"I knew you would," Dolan replied. "Tell you what, Ike and I will go to my office and you two can use this room. Take all the time you need. I'm down the hall in the corner. Just let me know when you're done."

After the two men left, Marc spent fifteen minutes quickly scanning the police report, giving a cursory look through the stack of witness statements not bothering with the preliminary autopsy report at all. If he took the case the final report would be more informative.

About an hour later, after Marc had received his retainer by a check drawn on Dolan's trust account and after Marc and Butch had left, Leo, Ike and Dolan listened to the recording of the conversation they had made from the bug in the conference room. After the third time, Leo asked Dolan, "What do you think?"

"I was right about Kadella. He's even quicker than I expected. This should work out just fine," the lawyer replied.

Catherine Prentiss checked the time on her watch, took one last drag of her cigarette before dropping it on the ground and crushing it with her shoe. She began walking slowly toward the building's entryway and as she got to the door, paused to look over her reflection in the glass. Even with everything that weighed her down mentally and emotionally, she still took pride in her appearance. Her dark blonde hair with the light blonde highlights was stylishly cut. Her navy-blue silk blouse and tan skirt accented her still trim figure. *For forty-seven,* she thought, *she still looked damn good.*

"How are you feeling?" her psychiatrist, Dr. Jeffrey Chase began after they had taken their seats and he turned on the recorder that would make an audio record of the session on his laptop.

"About the same," she replied.

"Do you think the medication is helping?"

"Mmmmm. Possibly. I guess I'm feeling a little more level. Not quite as much up and down."

"Are you still drinking?"

"No, at least very little," she lied.

"If you drink alcohol and take antidepressants, the alcohol can counteract the benefits of the medication. It can even make things worse."

"I know, Jeff," she replied obviously a little irritated.

"Okay, this is now, what, your fourth session?" he asked.

"Yes, that's right."

"Do you feel it's helping you?"

"Yes, definitely," she lied again.

"Really? That's interesting since I don't believe you're being completely forthcoming. We haven't even started to talk about what's really causing your problems."

"Oh, and just what do you think that is?" she said with obvious annoyance.

"I'm not sure," the therapist said ignoring her sarcasm. "I have some ideas, but it would be best to hear them from you. It's better if you search within yourself and be honest with yourself. It doesn't help you to lie to me."

"You think I'm lying?" she asked looking away from him to avoid eye contact.

"You need to answer that question. We can sit here for months avoiding the problem, but it won't do you any good."

She continued to silently stare out the window, not sure how she wanted to respond. Like any good therapist, Dr. Chase quietly, patiently waited for her reaction. They stayed this way for almost five minutes while Catherine contemplated her next step.

Catherine turned her head away from the window, looked back at Dr. Chase, heavily sighed and said, "You're right, I have to open up and talk to someone about this. I know you are bound by patient confidentiality, but I want your word, I want to hear you say it, that you will not tell anyone."

"Of course, you have my word, I won't tell anyone. Now Catherine, you need to tell me why you are so afraid of your husband that you can't even admit it."

"How did you know that?" she asked, genuinely surprised.

"I've been doing this over thirty years," the balding, slightly pudgy mid-fifties psychiatrist replied. "So, tell me."

"My husband the Honorable Judge Gordon Prentiss, is, pure and simple, a monster."

Made in the
USA
Columbia, SC